ANGELA HUNT

let darkness come

MIRA

ISBN-13: 978-0-7783-2653-3

Recycling programs
for this product may
not exist in your area.

LET DARKNESS COME

www.MIRABooks.com

Printed in U.S.A.

let darkness come

And we all go with them, into the silent funeral,
Nobody's funeral, for there is no one to bury.
I said to my soul, be still, and let the dark come upon you
Which shall be the darkness of God.

—T.S. Eliot, "East Coker"

Epigraph

And we all go with them, into the silent funeral,
Nobody's funeral, for there is no one to bury.
I said to my soul, be still, and let the dark come
   upon you
Which shall be the darkness of God.
                              —T.S. Eliot, *East Coker*

Chapter One

The night was made for murder.

She waits until his breaths are deep and even; waits until he snores in a regular rhythm. Then she slips out of bed and moves to the window, raising the blind until a wave of silver moonlight floods the room.

She won't risk waking him by turning on the lamp. Moonlight suits her purposes; it has always suited her nature.

She creeps into the bathroom and pulls the basket with his sharps and bottles from beneath the sink. These she transfers to the nightstand, then she lifts a syringe, unwraps it, and presses the thin needle into the neck of a bottle.

He took his insulin before bedtime, a dose guaranteed to stabilize his blood chemistry throughout the night. This second injection will stabilize him forever.

She measures out fifty units of regular insulin and drops the bottle back into its basket. The gentle chink of glass against glass does not rouse him. The man sleeps like a log, particularly on nights when he is so full of himself that he can't resist berating his wife.

Idiot. White trash. Slut.

Never again will those words pass his lips. Never again will she wear long sleeves on hot summer days.

Never again will his fist slam into her belly.

She lowers herself to the mattress, lifts the syringe in her left hand, and gently tugs on the covers with her right. His snoring halts, then erupts in an explosion of breath. His body has sensed the abrupt change in temperature, and his fingers fumble at his pajama top, searching for the comforter.

When he stops moving, she slides the thin needle into the pale flesh of his abdomen and presses the plunger. The instrument of death makes no sound, nor does its bite make him flinch. The needle has nipped at this flesh many times.

Like a loving mother tucking in a child, she covers him again and stands as he slumbers on, oblivious to his fate.

She returns the basket of supplies to the bathroom vanity and tosses the syringe into the trash. Her gaze falls on the mirror, where a ghostly image of her form is reflected in shadows. Then she crawls back into the warm bed and closes her eyes, willing herself to sleep.

Chapter Two

Kate Barnhill, the paralegal assigned to the second-floor associates, sticks her head into Briley Lester's office. "Did you get rid of the dragon lady?"

Briley holds up a handwritten memo and drops it into the Busch file. "Case dismissed," she says, sighing. "Now I can move on to the next innocent and misunderstood client." She stares at the stack of folders on her credenza. "Look at all those dog cases. Franklin is breathing down my neck about clearing at least five files a week, but it takes time to handle clients properly. And since most of these are civil cases, I'm a little out of my element."

Kate tucks a strand of blond hair behind her ear and steps into the room. "At my last firm, they'd just send the client a letter saying the case wasn't worth their time."

"And now I understand why you don't work there anymore." Briley picks up the next file and skims the case summary. "This concerns a real estate deal. Don't we have an associate in real estate law?"

"The red-haired guy back by the water cooler—he's handling real estate." Kate reaches for the file, jingling a loaded charm bracelet on her wrist. "I'll carry it over."

"I've never seen anybody in that office."

"That's because he's always out in the field, or so he says. But though he may not be around much, somehow he manages to bill two thousand hours per year."

"No wonder I'm getting nowhere in this firm—I'm breaking my neck to bill fifteen hundred. More and more

these days I can't remember why I ever became a lawyer."
Briley picks up the next file, skims the summary report, and
frowns. "Haven't I represented Clive Thomas before?"

Kate smiles as she moves toward the door. "Surely you
remember the dognapper. You pleaded him down to nine
months in Cook County Jail."

"You're right—the Chihuahua thief." Briley drops the
folder onto her desk. "Now he wants to sue the state over
the inmates' food. He says it's nutritionally lacking."

"You going down to the jail to brush him off?"

"No," Briley answers, settling into her creaky desk chair.
"Him, I'm writing a letter."

Chapter Three

In the windowless waiting room outside the morgue at the Cook County medical examiner's office, Erin Tomassi shivers beneath a thin blanket. Her brain buzzes with the faint rumblings of a headache while disjointed memories of the morning jostle in her mind. Impossible to believe that she's sitting in a public place in her robe, pajamas, and slippers. Impossible to believe that Jeffrey lies in the room beyond, lifeless and blue.

She stares at her hand and counts off five fingertips, one for each year of their marriage. Jeffrey is thirty-five years old; men of that age do not die in their sleep. But dead is what he is, or so the EMTs insist. They have to be mistaken, because Jeffrey is king of whatever hill he's climbing. When it comes, Death will have to wait for an appointment like everyone else.

An older man in a lab coat steps into the drab room and offers a sad smile. "Coffee?" He gestures toward a pot on the counter. "It's not very good, but it's hot."

She shakes her head. "I'm fine."

The man moves toward the counter and takes a foam cup from a slanted stack. As he pours, he glances in her direction. "Do you need to call someone to pick you up?"

"That— My father-in-law is on his way."

The man pours two sugar packets into his cup, then stirs the brew with a ballpoint from his pocket. "Never a spoon around when you need one," he says, a thread of apology in his voice as he taps his pen on the side of the cup. "Are you sure you wouldn't like a cup of coffee?"

"Never learned to like it." She catches her breath, horrified that the words have sprung so easily to her lips. If Jeffrey were here, he'd tell her to take the coffee, drink it, and act grateful for it, because one never offended voters by refusing offers of kindness.

She lowers her eyes, afraid the man might see a trace of the emotions warring in her breast. Jeffrey might be dead…and if he is, she will mourn him, but she will be free. Free to refuse cups of coffee, to sleep past seven, to stay in her house and ignore the clamoring world. If she can trust what the EMTs told her, she will finally be able to relax inside her own home. She'll be able to slip on her pajamas and go to bed without a sense of dread.

But Jeffrey *can't* be dead. Because the city is still running, the sun still shining, and the planet still turning. Most telling, she is still breathing…and Jeffrey always said she'd die before he did.

He'd make sure of it.

Chapter Four

A wintry wave of grief shivers the skin on Antonio Tomassi's arms as he stares at the body of his dead son. Beside him, Jason keeps murmuring, "How? How could this happen?" but Antonio cannot think or reason. Shock has engulfed him in its numbing wake, and he can barely maintain an upright posture.

He places his hand on Jeffrey's lifeless shoulder and feels a shudder move through his core. No parent should ever have to experience this kind of cold.

The baby-faced assistant in the lab coat hugs his clipboard. "The M.E. will want to do an autopsy. It's routine in matters like this."

When a perfectly healthy young man stops breathing for no apparent reason, he means.

"How could this happen?" Jason asks again. "How does a guy like Jeff die in his sleep? He was fit, he worked out—"

The youngster shrugs. "We can't say until we have the autopsy and toxicology results. It would help us to know if he had any preexisting medical conditions...."

"He was strong," Jason insists. "My brother was in perfect health."

"Diabetes." Antonio pries the word from his unwilling tongue. "Jeffrey had diabetes."

"But that was under control," Jason argues. "He hasn't had any health problems in years. Jeff knew how to manage his condition."

"If he was getting worse, his wife would have said something." Antonio focuses on his only surviving son. "Did you see Erin? Is she here?"

Jason jerks his chin toward the door. "She's curled up in a chair out there. In shock, if you ask me."

Antonio exhales softly. He can't blame his daughter-in-law for being stupefied by this unexpected turn of events. No one was more alive, more oursting with energy and potential, than Jeffrey Tomassi, Illinois state senator and potential U.S. congressman. No man in Chicago had a brighter future, but in the space of a heartbeat it had…vanished. Why?

The intrusive idiot in the white coat clears his throat. "We'll release the autopsy results as soon as we know something. Toxicology reports, however, can take up to six weeks—"

"I won't wait that long." Antonio fixes the youngster with a hot stare. "I want those results as soon as possible."

"But the reports usually take a couple of months. There's a backlog at the lab, and things are going to get worse, especially with the holidays approaching."

"I am Antonio Tomassi," Antonio says, buttoning the top button on his overcoat, "and you will have the medical examiner call me as soon as those reports come in. I will not rest until I know what killed my son."

Chapter Five

Kate steps through the doorway and deposits a grilled chicken salad on Briley's desk. "Fifteen bucks should cover it," she says, holding out her hand. "And yes, I tipped the delivery guy."

Briley pulls a five and a ten from her wallet and drops the money into Kate's palm. "Thanks, that looks good." She takes the lid off the salad and pops a crouton into her mouth. "Delicious. Just a hint of garlic."

"By the way—" Kate glances at Briley's computer "—are you keeping up with your e-mail?"

"Why?"

"Franklin just sent a memo to everyone working on the Bishop case. He's scheduled most of the witness interviews for Friday. I have to pull all the documents you'll need."

Briley winces. "This Friday?"

"At 8:00 a.m. in the conference room. And if you don't finish on Friday, he wants you to come in on Saturday."

Briley exhales an exasperated sigh and flips the pages on her desk calendar. "Another Saturday down the tubes. Bad enough that the associates here are expected to work twelve-hour days—"

"Pay those dues with a smile, honey. Put in your hours, write out a few hundred legal briefs, and bankroll your retirement. When you're a partner, you can play golf and put *your* underlings to work."

"I wish I had your confidence."

Kate slips away as Briley's cell phone rings. She glances

at the caller ID and smiles as she snaps the phone open. "Hey there. I was beginning to think this day was going to be a total bust."

Timothy Shackelford's warm voice draws her gaze to the photo on the corner of her desk. "Your boss giving you a hard time?"

"No harder than usual. But it looks like I'll be working Friday night. Either that, or I'll have to work Saturday."

"Bummer. Now I'll have to impress some other woman with my charm and good looks."

"That's what I like about you, Shackelford—your boundless optimism." She grins at his framed picture. "By the way, how's *your* client?"

"Sleeping like a baby. I'm beginning to think he's traded cocaine for Rozerem. Whenever he gets a little shaky, he pops a pill and goes to bed."

"I thought sober companions were supposed to keep their clients *away* from drugs."

"The nonprescription variety, sure. But I've already told Dax that after tomorrow, there'll be no more sleeping in daylight hours. But I didn't call to talk about him—I called to ask if you've heard the news."

Something in his voice sends a ripple of apprehension through her bloodstream. "What news?"

"Jeffrey Tomassi passed away. Turn on your TV—the reports are on every local channel."

Briley snatches a wincing breath. Last night she and Timothy attended a fundraiser for the charismatic state senator. The event appeared to be a huge success, and no man ever looked healthier or more like a winner than Jeffrey Tomassi.

She reaches for the remote in her desk drawer and powers on the small set on a shelf of her bookcase. "Do they suspect foul play?"

"They haven't said. But I'll bet that house is crawling with detectives right now."

Briley clicks until she sees a somber newscaster standing

outside a three-story brownstone. She lowers the remote, knowing that she's found the right station. "I'll call you later," she tells Timothy, distracted by the story unfolding before her eyes.

Chapter Six

The sun has begun to melt black patches into the frost-filigreed roof by the time the driver pulls up to the brownstone in Lincoln Park. Antonio Tomassi steps out and ducks beneath the yellow crime-scene tape, then holds it as his daughter-in-law follows. Erin hasn't spoken since leaving the medical examiner's office. Her blue eyes are glazed, her face pale, her long hair mussed. She is still wearing satin pajamas beneath her flannel robe, and she hasn't stopped shivering since they left the building.

A uniformed cop hurries toward them. "I'm sorry, sir, but we can't have you disturbing the area until we've finished our investigation."

Antonio gestures to the dazed woman at his side. "I'm Antonio Tomassi, and this is my daughter-in-law. I'm taking Erin to my house, but first she needs to get a few things."

The cop frowns and grips his belt. "Wait here and let me get the lead detective. They're almost finished dusting for prints."

Erin lifts her head. "Is someone inside? Jeffrey doesn't like strangers in the house."

Antonio grips her arm and leads her to the garden bench beneath a skeletal maple. "Let's get out of the way, my dear. We'll sit until the detective comes out."

"All right." She obeys as meekly as a lamb, keeping her hands in her pockets.

He sits beside her, grateful that she has finally decided to speak. Perhaps she can help him make sense of this madness.

"Erin," he begins, "what can you tell me about this morning? When you got up—" his voice breaks "—what happened?"

Her eyelids droop as a cold wind rattles the leafless branches overhead. "I woke up," she says, a quaver in her voice. "I woke up and Jeffrey was still asleep. I didn't want to bother him, because he didn't have any appointments until later. I went into the bathroom, splashed water on my face, and walked into the kitchen for some toast. After making breakfast, I put Jeffrey's on a tray and carried it into the bedroom. He was still sleeping, so I left the tray on the dresser. Later, when I heard the clock strike nine o'clock and realized Jeffrey was still asleep, I knew I should wake him up. He and Jason play racquetball, you know, every Wednesday morning."

Antonio nods as a lump swells in his throat. "Go on."

She closes her eyes again. "I went in and shook him, but the minute I touched him I knew something was wrong. His face was blue, and his skin…felt like rubber. I stepped back and picked up the phone to call 911. The woman asked if Jeff was breathing, and I said I didn't think so. She asked if I knew how to do CPR, and I said I thought I could, but she'd better send someone. I tried to pump his chest, but it didn't work. The next thing I knew, men were pounding on the door, so I let them in."

"Did he act sick last night? Did he complain of a headache, anything?"

Her eyes fly up at him like a pair of bluebirds flushed from a shrub, then she looks away. "He was fine last night. He was…strong enough."

Antonio drops his hand to her arm as an older man in a blue overcoat comes out of the house and walks toward them. He studies Antonio and thrusts his hand forward. "Mr. Tomassi? I'm Mark Malone, Homicide."

Antonio nods, pleased that the fellow knows his name. "Detective, do you know my daughter-in-law? Erin Tomassi."

The cop looks at Erin, his eyes crinkling in sympathy.

"I'm terribly sorry for your loss, ma'am. I'd be happy to let you inside, but first I was wondering if you had a moment to answer a few questions."

Erin blinks, then glances at Antonio. "Do I?"

He pats her arm. "You will always have time to cooperate with the police. I'll wait until you're finished, then we'll gather your things and get you settled at the house. We're going to take care of you."

Erin smiles her thanks as the detective pulls a small notebook from an inner coat pocket and flips it open. "Mrs. Tomassi, Dispatch has a record of your 911 call placed at 9:05. According to the EMTs first on the scene, your husband was unresponsive when they arrived. The medical examiner has tentatively put the time of death at around 2:00 a.m."

Erin shudders, as if she can't bear to know she spent most of the night sleeping beside a dead man.

The detective licks the tip of his pen, then props one foot on the end of the garden bench. "I hate to intrude at a time like this, but I need to know—had your husband been under any kind of professional care?"

Erin widens her eyes. "Like…a doctor?"

"A therapist, perhaps? A psychologist or counselor?"

Antonio opens his mouth to protest, but the detective cuts him off with a sidelong glance.

Erin shakes her head. "Jeffrey wasn't the sort to unburden himself in front of anyone."

"So he wasn't seeing a counselor?"

"No."

"Did he ever mention suicide?"

"No!"

"Has anyone in the family ever committed suicide?"

She glances at Antonio, then shakes her head. "Never."

"Was your husband a heavy drinker?"

"Not really. We were out last night at a fundraising event, but he had very little to drink. Maybe one glass of wine, early in the evening."

"Was he on any medication?"

"Only his insulin. He's a diabetic."

"To your knowledge, did he ever use recreational drugs?"

"No, he did not." Her voice is uninflected, pushed through the pale face she wears like a mask. "Jeffrey was a committed public servant. He would never want to set a bad example by using drugs."

"Any change in his routine lately? Any deviation in sleeping habits, eating routines, a lack of interest in his work?"

"No."

"Any loss of interest in his favorite activities or his family?"

She closes her eyes. "No. I doubt you could find a more attentive and involved man than Jeffrey."

"Involved in his work?"

"Involved in everything. He never did anything by half measures."

The detective scribbles something in his notebook, then looks up. "Anything unusual happen before you two went to bed last night? Did he say or do anything out of the ordinary?"

A one-sided smile tugs at the corner of Erin's mouth as she looks away. "We came home, we got dressed for bed, we reviewed the evening. After that, I wasn't feeling well, so I took a couple of pills and went to bed. Next thing I knew, it was morning."

"What kind of pill?" the cop asks.

"Oh…sleeping pills. Ambien. When I'm hurting, the pills help me sleep."

The detective makes another note and offers Antonio a grim smile. "Thank you for your cooperation. I'm sorry to ask a lot of questions at a time like this, but it's routine in situations of unattended death."

Unattended death… The words tighten a new knot in Antonio's throat. He wouldn't let one of his dogs die an unattended death, yet his beloved son had died without comfort, without hope. Had Jeffrey awakened in pain? Had he been able to speak? Had he called for help, for his father?

He looks at his daughter-in-law, whose pale cheeks have been reddened by the cold. Why didn't Erin hear anything? She's such an attentive wife, a good girl for Jeffrey. Surely she would have awakened if he'd struggled or called out—

But he can't think about those things now. If he does, he'll buckle like a marionette with cut strings and be no good to anyone. Erin needs him now; so do Jason and the girls.

He'll consider how and why Jeffrey died when he's prepared to do something about it.

But he *does* need to speak to this detective. He stands and steps toward the front gate, then motions for Malone to move closer. When the man approaches, he turns his back to Erin and lowers his voice. "Have you found any sign of an intruder? Do you suspect foul play?"

Malone tucks his notebook away. "I really can't say at this point."

"There are security cameras, you know. Jeffrey was quite vigilant about security."

"Yes, sir. We saw the cameras aimed at the front and back entrances, so we looked for the control center and found it in a closet. I've skimmed the tapes, but I saw nothing unusual."

"What about the alarm? They had a good system."

"They did, and the alarm wasn't tripped. We found no signs of an intruder at the doors or windows, so right now I'd say we're looking at a natural death. But the medical examiner won't be able to confirm that until after the autopsy."

Antonio digests this news in silence, watching as men and women in blue jackets stride in and out of the house, many of them carrying bins filled with plastic bags, all neatly labeled. Within those bags he sees syringes, insulin bottles, scraps of paper, a comb, and toothbrush. They're doing a lot of work for a so-called natural death, but then, Jeffrey was not an average citizen. He maintained a high profile, and people who rise above the crowd can't help but tempt others to take potshots at them.

As the wind blows the scent of wood smoke over the

street, he turns his attention back to the detective. "Those questions you asked Erin...do you think my son might have committed suicide?"

The cop lifts his chin. "Do you?"

"Not a chance. Jeffrey had everything to live for, and he loved life."

"I understand he was preparing to run for higher office?"

"He felt he'd grown stagnant as a state senator. We were certain he could win a seat in Congress, so we were testing the waters. Quite successfully, I might add."

"Enemies?"

Antonio frowns. "Jeff's opponents squared off against him in the courts of public opinion. He never mentioned anyone more threatening than those rabid radio talk show hosts."

The detective shrugs. "I don't see any reason to suspect foul play. But we'll know more once we review the medical examiner's report."

The man turns, as if to walk away, but Antonio catches his arm. "You and your team—you did a thorough search, right? Got everything you needed?"

"For a man who doesn't believe his son had enemies, you seem convinced that something's amiss."

"I'm not convinced," Antonio says. "But if the autopsy reveals that someone *did* harm my son, I don't want you to miss a thing. If someone murdered my boy, I want that person to pay."

Chapter Seven

Drawing a jagged breath, Antonio rubs the tense muscles at the back of his neck and approaches the morgue. For more than a week, he has been waiting for the autopsy results. As an exercise in courtesy he has refused to badger the chief medical examiner, but he has also spread the word that he would appreciate timely answers to the questions of how and why Jeffrey died. If the reason for Jeffrey's death lies in a genetic health problem, Jason might be affected, too. The boys, after all, are twins.

The baby-faced assistant who escorted Antonio into the morgue last week greets him in the waiting room and leads him to the medical examiner's unimpressive office. "Wow," the idiot says, lingering after Antonio takes a seat. "I've never seen toxicology results come back so fast. You must have friends in really high places."

Antonio swallows his irritation and crosses his legs at the ankle, waiting for the M.E. to arrive. Insensitive creatures like the man in the doorway have no business working with the public; they should be confined to interaction with computers and cadavers. Let them impress lab rats with their painfully obtuse observations, but keep them away from grieving fathers who can't understand why fools survive and the brilliant die young.

He looks up, distracted, when the door opens and a fresh wave of formaldehyde-scented air flows into the room. The chief medical examiner enters, followed by a man with a familiar face. "Detective," Antonio says, standing. "What an unexpected pleasure."

The cop shakes his hand. "I wish we were meeting under more pleasant circumstances."

"Does your presence mean I'm about to hear bad news?"

"Mr. Tomassi, I'm James Drew." The M.E. gestures toward the chair. "If you'll have a seat, I'd like to share my findings. I've asked Detective Malone to join us because he has news, as well."

Antonio draws a deep breath and sinks back into the proffered seat. The detective slides a stool from beneath a counter and perches on the edge, notebook in hand.

The M.E. pulls a folder to the center of his desk and laces his fingers. "First, Mr. Tomassi, let me say how sorry I am to be in this position. I was acquainted with your son, and knew him to be a man of great strength and moral courage."

Antonio struggles to swallow over a suddenly tight throat. "Thank you."

"That's why—" Dr. Drew opens the folder "—it's hard for me to share this report. Your son was in excellent physical condition, as you've assured us, but the toxicology report indicated elevated vitreous insulin."

"What—" Antonio pauses to steady his voice. "What does that mean, exactly?"

The M.E. folds his hands again. "The vitreous is the clear, jellylike substance found between the eye's lens and retina. Insulin overdose is almost impossible to prove, because insulin breaks down in the body postmortem. Even the vitreous fluids will not reveal an overdose of insulin unless the fatal dose was massive—an unfortunate exception which does apply to your son's case."

Antonio lifts his hand to his mouth, taking a moment to compose himself. "My son would not have made a mistake with his injection. He knew how to use a meter, he knew to be careful. He's been giving himself insulin injections for years."

Drew presses his lips together. "That's what I suspected.

Since the dosage that killed your son was probably more than fifty units, I must conclude that the injection and the overdose were intentional."

Antonio shakes his head. "Jeffrey wouldn't kill himself. Maybe he was drunk. Maybe he didn't realize what he was doing—"

"His blood-alcohol level was consistent with what his wife told Detective Malone. He had very little to drink that night. And we found no indication of other drugs in his system."

Unable to make sense of this news, Antonio presses his fingers to the bridge of his nose. "Did you double-check your results? Repeat the tests, or whatever you had to do?"

"We were extremely thorough." Dr. Drew softens his voice. "And that's why I've asked Detective Malone to meet with us. Because insulin overdose is so hard to prove, it's virtually impossible to establish whether a fatal dose was self-inflicted without a detailed scene investigation and careful police work. The detective has some information he'd like to share with you."

Feeling as though he has aged ten years in the past five minutes, Antonio turns his attention to the quiet policeman. Silence sifts down like a snowfall, a dense quiet broken only by the shush of cars moving on the street. The detective props his notebook on his bent knee, then looks squarely into Antonio's eyes. "Mr. Tomassi, it's my duty to inform you that our investigation has led us to believe your daughter-in-law may have had a hand in your son's death. In the bathroom trash can we found a syringe marked with finger-prints we assume to be hers. In a basket beneath the vanity we found your son's insulin supply. One half-empty bottle also bore this second set of fingerprints."

Antonio stares at the cop, his heart drumming in his rib cage. "You can't believe that Erin—"

"I'm sorry to have to tell you that we have officers on their way to your home. They're carrying a warrant for Erin Tomassi's arrest."

Chapter Eight

Erin looks up from her book when the housekeeper raps on the guest-room door. "Yes?"

"Visitors for you, Mrs. Tomassi. They're waiting downstairs."

"Thank you."

She pulls herself off the settee and moves to the mirror, staring at the wan face that seems to have nothing in common with the woman she once was. Jeffrey's been gone nine days; the funeral is a faded memory. Any day now, feeling should begin to creep back into her fingers and toes, energy should return to her step. How long has it been since she experienced an unexpected surge of happiness? How long since she felt alive?

She picks up the brush on the dresser and runs it though her hair. Her oval face is plain and unpainted, a look her husband would never have approved.

But Jeffrey is no longer here to express his opinions.

She runs her hands over the sweatpants she slept in and checks the T-shirt she found in a dresser drawer. She doesn't look much like a politician's wife, but that's okay. At this moment, she's nothing to anyone. A nobody.

Reporters surrounded her at the funeral, and for a few days they loitered outside the gates of this house, peering into cars and rummaging through garbage cans in search of anything that might qualify as news. But then Antonio called a press conference and said the family would wait for the results of the police investigation before making any further comments. Thankfully, the photographers disappeared and the phone stopped ringing.

Erin steps into the hallway and descends the stairs. Who could be calling? Who knew she was here? She has few friends of her own, and since the funeral, Jeff's friends have vanished.

At the bottom of the stairs, she turns into the great room. A man and woman are standing by the fireplace, both of them wearing overcoats and scarves. The woman is studying the photographs on the mantel, while the man seems more interested in the elk's head on the paneled wall.

They turn in her direction when a floorboard creaks under her sock-clad feet.

"Erin Tomassi?" the man asks in a voice that is all business.

"Yes."

"We're Detectives Hoff and Lorning from the Eighth Precinct. We're here with some follow-up questions about your husband's death."

Erin offers a tentative smile and gestures to the sofa. "Won't you have a seat?"

The woman—Erin isn't sure if she's Hoff or Lorning— perches on the edge of a wing chair. "Mrs. Tomassi," she says, glancing at a small tablet she's pulled from her coat, "you told another investigator that your husband was a diabetic."

"That's right."

"Did he use an insulin pump or syringes?"

"Syringes. He was used to them."

"He kept those in your master bathroom?"

"In a bin beneath the sink. I'm sure your investigators found them." She shifts her gaze to the man. "Why this sudden interest in Jeff's medication?"

As relentless as a bloodhound, the woman continues. "Did he store insulin in any other location?"

Erin blinks. "Why would he? I suppose he might keep a bottle in his car or at his office, but I don't know that for certain. At home he kept all his supplies in the bathroom."

"Did your husband administer his own injections?"

Erin glances from the woman to the man, whose features have hardened in a disapproving stare. "Yes. Needles make me queasy."

"Did he ever ask you to inject him?"

"No. He wouldn't."

"Why not?"

Erin spreads her hands, unable to explain. "I don't know. I don't think he trusted me to do it right."

The male detective reaches inside his coat pocket and pulls out a zippered storage bag. "Mrs. Tomassi, do you recognize this item?"

"I don't know— May I see it?" The cop stands and walks forward, dangling the clear bag in front of Erin's eyes. She reaches for it and feels a pang of panic when she realizes he is not going to let her hold it. Why doesn't he trust her?

The bag contains a drinking glass, the small size typically used for juice. She turns the plastic until she can see the *T* etched in the glass. "This looks like one of our juice glasses."

"This was taken from your bathroom," he says, indicating a frosted panel where someone has written *Master Bath* on the plastic. "Do you recall who last used this glass?"

"Me, I suppose. Jeffrey didn't use a glass in the bathroom, because he was always dropping things."

"So the fingerprints on this glass—they're yours?"

"Unless someone else touched it."

The two cops exchange looks, then the woman pulls a folded paper from her jacket and holds it aloft. "Erin Tomassi," she says, "we have a warrant for your arrest. You have the right to remain silent—"

Erin scrambles to her feet. "There's been some kind of mistake."

"Ma'am?" The housekeeper moves into the arched doorway, her eyes dark and narrow. "Why are the reporters outside again?"

"—and anything you say can and will be used against you in a court of law."

Erin steps toward the housekeeper. "Call Antonio," she says, horror snaking down her spine as the man pulls handcuffs from his belt. "Tell him everything that's happened. Tell him I did not kill Jeffrey."

"You have the right to an attorney during questioning—" the woman continues.

Erin winces as the man slaps the cuffs on her wrists. "I don't know why you're doing this. Didn't you hear me? I didn't kill my husband."

"—and if you cannot afford an attorney, one will be provided without cost."

When the male detective takes hold of Erin's arm, she leans in the opposite direction. "I'm not dressed to go out. I'm not even wearing shoes!"

"You won't need 'em," the woman answers, taking Erin's other elbow. "The jail issues footwear to all incoming prisoners."

Erin takes a deep, quivering breath to calm the panicked pulse beneath her ribs. "Hurry," she calls to the housekeeper as the cops lead her toward the front door. "Please have Antonio call someone. I need a lawyer."

Chapter Nine

Briley has just stepped out of the pink-marble ladies' room at Franklin, Watson, Smyth & Morton when another associate nearly runs her over in the hallway. Jim Myers is carrying a stack of files under one arm and focused on the paper clutched in his free hand.

"Hey!" After stepping out of Jim's way, she peers over his shoulder and spies the *Chicago Tribune*'s online masthead on a printout. "What's so interesting?"

He looks up, his eyes flashing when he recognizes her. "Did you hear the latest about the Tomassi case?"

"What?"

"They just arrested the wife."

"Wow." She crosses her arms and leans one shoulder against the wall. "Any word on the cause of death?"

"Nothing in this update, but we'll probably be among the first to hear."

"How's that?"

"Didn't you know? Tomassi keeps a couple of our real estate attorneys on retainer, and the firm represented the family in a civil suit back in '96. They won three-point-something million in damages."

Briley whistles. "What kind of case was it?"

"Libel, I think. Anyway, the Chicago papers learned not to publish rumors about the Tomassis."

She laughs. "You make them sound like the Mafia."

Jim glances right and left, then leans closer. "I wouldn't

say that too loudly, if you know what I mean. The family business is respectable, but I wouldn't want to dig into their books. What we don't know can't hurt us."

"Oh, come on."

"Watch what you say. And by the way, these files are for you."

Briley stares, dumbfounded, as he dumps his burden into her arms.

"The case involves three teenage girls charged with battering a classmate over tickets to an Oprah taping. Franklin thinks you should be first chair on this one."

"Why, because I have breasts?"

"Maybe because you used to be a teenage girl. All I know is, he wants you to look over the files and talk to the state's attorney. See if you can plead them out as a group."

She makes a moue. "What if I don't *want* to deal with an overblown catfight?"

He grins. "Come on, Counselor, remember your oath to help the defenseless and oppressed."

With that sorry jibe ringing in her ears, Briley carries the files to her office and dumps them on her desk. Three years of practicing law in a respected firm has brought her— what? A good income, sure. Steady work. Approving smiles from the woman next door. But what good has she actually accomplished?

She used to dream about making a difference in the world, but three years of dealing with criminal defendants has taught her that the practice of law would be far more enjoyable if she didn't have to deal with so many guilty people.

Her father dealt with people every day, and he loved his work until the day he died. She'd thought she could honor his altruistic example by practicing law, but the unending parade of remorseless clients has dulled her idealism.

Serving others is a noble goal, but a lawyer who hopes to make a real difference is doomed to eternal frustration.

* * *

Because Dax Lightner is having lunch with a producer, Timothy is free for a couple of hours. Delighted by this unexpected opportunity, Briley slips into a restaurant booth and smiles across the table. "It's so good to see you in daylight," she says, reaching out to catch Timothy's hands. "I can't believe I have you all to myself for an entire meal."

"Or at least until Dax and his producer have a falling-out," Timothy says, grinning. "My man's been a bit touchy the past few days."

"Is he really as bad as all that?" Briley struggles to keep any trace of annoyance from her voice. "I mean, he's been out of rehab for what, three weeks now?"

"Which only means the confidence rush is over." Timothy's eyes darken as they search her face. "And you know addicts. It only takes an instant for someone to slip."

"You've never slipped."

"I have a good support system. But even here in Chicago, Dax is surrounded by people who'd do anything he asks, including getting him another fix." Timothy shakes his head, sending a sheaf of dark blond hair into his eyes. "I seem to be the only person willing to tell him no."

"You're paid to tell him no. And I wish the man would develop a little backbone, because it's awful not being able to see you as much as I want to."

"Come on, give the guy a break." Timothy squeezes her fingers, then releases her hands. "You should meet him sometime. I think you'd like him."

Briley snorts. "Like I'd have anything to say to a British movie star. I don't hang out with people who grace the cover of…well, *People*."

"Not everyone in rehab is an A-lister. Most are just like me and you." His mouth twists in a crooked smile. "You know what they say — if you want to bake a cake, you have to crack a few eggs."

"Who on earth says *that?*"

"I do. I made it up. I'm trying to say that if you want to make a difference, sometimes you have to make a mess." When she doesn't respond, he smiles and spreads his hands. "You know—when you crack the egg, the runny part and the yolk splash all over the counter."

Briley shakes her head. "Remind me never to bake a cake with you."

Timothy picks up the menu and scans the front cover. As the waitress at the next table scrapes food from a plate, he lifts his gaze: "What's good at this place?"

Ignoring his obvious attempt to change the subject, Briley lowers her voice. "I know you want to help your client. I love that you're the kind of man who wants to help others. But honestly, Tim, how long are you going to take these gigs? When you're working, we can only see each other in bits and snatches."

He drops his menu. "I thought you'd understand. You work long hours."

"But they're dependable."

"Surely you have legal emergencies."

"A well-run case never results in dire situations. One thing I learned from my father's example is that you can't let people eat you alive. You have to set boundaries. You have to compartmentalize. Otherwise people will take and take until you have nothing else to give."

Compassion struggles with humor on his strong face as he studies her. "Do you remember the first time we met?"

"Of course."

"If I'd been mingling at that benefit on the *front* side of rehab, I don't think you'd have looked at me twice. I wasn't worth much when I was using, and I didn't believe in anything but my next fix. But once I got clean, I was able to find myself again. And then I found you…and you're one of the reasons I've been able to stay clean."

Briley blinks away a sudden rush of tears. Timothy is

always waylaying her with some sweet declaration when she has something important to discuss.

"You're not clean because of me," she insists. "You're clean because you're a strong person. You have character."

"So do you." He picks up his menu again. "So does Dax, though he doesn't realize it yet. The man needs someone in his life who cares more about his future than his next movie."

Briley props her elbow on the table and drops her chin into her hand, realizing that the conversation has hit a dead end. Timothy is determined to save the addicts of Chicago, one soul at a time, and there's nothing she can do about it. At least not during lunch.

She scans her menu. "I was going to suggest we have a picnic this weekend, but I might have to interview a witness on Saturday."

"See? You work as much as I do."

"But I'm doing it under protest. You seem to enjoy spending time away from me."

"I've heard enough." He shoves the menu aside as he leans toward her, his eyes bright with frustrated affection. "I adore you, Briley Lester, but sometimes I wonder if we're going to make it. You're brilliant and you're beautiful, but you're also infuriating."

She leans forward until her lips are almost touching his. "I'm not beautiful, but thank you. And we *are* going to make it, because in at least one way we're very much alike— neither of us likes to quit."

Chapter Ten

In the back of his limo, Antonio pulls out his cell phone and dials his lawyer's private number. Though Joseph Franklin is sure to be either at lunch or in a meeting, the managing partner at Franklin, Watson, Smyth & Morton answers almost immediately. "Antonio?"

"Joe. I suppose you've heard about my son."

"Of course, I was so sorry to hear the news. I trust you received the flowers we sent."

"I'm sure we did. Listen, I'm calling about a matter relating to Jeffrey's death...but this must be handled, you know, carefully."

In the background Antonio can hear the hum of conversation and the clinking sounds of restaurant service, but Joseph's voice carries clearly: "I'm listening."

Antonio stares out the window, where the stately brownstones and wrought-iron fences of Lincoln Park are sliding by. "The police have made an arrest. I can't believe it, but late this morning they took my daughter-in-law into custody. Erin will be needing a lawyer."

The thick silence of concentration rolls over the line. When Joe speaks again, his voice is guarded. "You want us to defend her?"

"I do. People will expect the family to support her, and you are the family's firm. But I talked to the medical examiner and the chief detective, and the case against her is rock solid. So I want her punished to the fullest extent of the law."

"So you're saying—"

"The fullest extent, you understand? Assign someone to her case, make sure everything's done by the book. But don't allow her to walk free of that courtroom with my son's blood on her hands."

Antonio can almost see the heavy lines of concentration that must be creasing the attorney's forehead. "We'll have to be careful to avoid the appearance of impropriety. Even a guilty client is entitled to an adequate defense."

"I don't think the Constitution says anything about a stone-cold killer being entitled to the *best* defense, does it? So do whatever you have to, but don't let the woman who killed my son walk out of that courtroom without paying for what she did."

The sweet sound of tinkling ice cubes rattles over the line, followed by Joseph's assuring voice. "Don't worry, my friend. As always, we will do everything we can to merit your confidence and trust."

Antonio nods at his grim reflection in the darkened window. "I know you will."

Chapter Eleven

Briley giggles as Timothy's lips, cooled by the ice cream he's just finished, nuzzle the side of her neck.

"That tickles," she says, sliding out of his embrace. "You should warm up those lips before you start breathing down my throat."

His smile widens in approval. "Got any ideas about how I could do that?"

Briley laughs. They are standing in the middle of a busy sidewalk on Chicago's "Magnificent Mile," surrounded by shoppers and employees who, like her, really should get back to work.

She wags a gloved finger at him. "You're going to get me in trouble."

"Sounds promising."

"Come on, walk me back to the office."

Timothy sighs and grabs her hand as they begin to walk. "Thanks for making time for lunch. And for ice cream."

"You're welcome. Maybe we could do it again sometime."

"If we're lucky."

She's about to suggest that they make it a regular date when the tinkle of a cell phone spoils the silence. She groans. "Yours or mine?"

"Not my ring tone. And Dax shouldn't be calling for at least another half hour."

"Ohmygoodness." Briley stops walking and yanks her purse from her shoulder. "My boss. I programmed that ring tone for Mr. Franklin, never dreaming he'd actually call me." She finds the phone at the bottom of her bag and presses it to her ear. "Hello?"

She listens, hears her boss's voice, and strides to a granite planter edging the sidewalk. After dropping her purse on the rim of the planter, she slides the phone between her shoulder and her ear, then rummages for a grocery list at the bottom of her bag. She looks at Timothy, frantically pretending to write on the air.

"No, sir," she tells her boss. "You didn't catch me at a bad time."

Timothy hands her a pen, which she clicks. With his shoulder as a support, she's jotting a client's name on the back of the grocery list when a chill strikes the marrow of her bones.

"Did you say Erin Tomassi?" She grips the phone. "The state senator's wife?"

"The state senator's widow," her boss answers. "And, according to the state's attorney, his killer. She was arrested this morning, so you'll need to get over to the jail ASAP."

Briley winces, not sure she's heard correctly above the sound of tires hissing on the wet asphalt. "You want me to go to the jail? Am I filling in for Morton or Hubbard?"

"What's the problem? Aren't alleged killers entitled to your representation?"

"That's not what I meant. Of course I'll go. But I've never handled a murder case. And *this* trial—"

"We need you to get over there and give us a full report as soon as you can. The Tomassis are highly valued clients, so we need to know what the state's attorney knows. See if you can get a summary of the case and a copy of the police report."

"Right. Okay." Briley disconnects the call and drops the phone back into her purse. She looks at Timothy, aware that most of the sunshine has just gone out of the day.

"What's wrong?" he asks.

"A client," she says, a sense of unease settling over her like a dark cloud. "A murder charge."

He whistles. "That's not your usual gig, is it?"

"No." She frowns at the name on the paper in her hand. "It involves the Tomassi family. This trial is going to be huge, so why did he call—"

"Because you're good." Timothy takes his pen from her grip and puts it back in his pocket, then laces his fingers with hers. "Come on, let's get you back to the office."

Briley walks beside him, her thoughts as clogged as the traffic on the congested street. Something doesn't fit. Franklin, Watson, Smyth & Morton has represented the Tomassi family for years, but never in a criminal case. Antonio Tomassi, the family patriarch, must have been astounded when the state's attorney charged his daughter-in-law with the murder of his son, so he immediately called the family's firm.

But why did Franklin call *her?* She has no experience with murder trials and little experience with the press. And the press will be all over this trial.

Franklin certainly won't keep her on the case. Maybe he needs someone to run to the jail and she's the only associate not tied up in a meeting. Or maybe he's thinking that photos of a female attorney leaving the jail will elicit public sympathy for the defendant. Juxtaposing photos of Briley's solid, unglamorous face with pictures of the elegant Erin Tomassi will make an impression on readers of the morning news.

She halts on the sidewalk and considers what she'll need for her jail visit: pen, paper, a recorder. Fortunately, she carries a digital recorder in her purse and she can get paper at the security desk.

"Can I borrow your pen?" She squints up at Timothy. "I need to take it to the jail."

"You're going *now?*"

"Franklin wants me to get there ASAP, so I might as well catch a cab here."

He pulls the pen from his pocket and drops it into her purse. "So you're off to save the world?"

"Not the world, just one woman. And I'm not going to save her. I'm only pinch-hitting."

"Can you say more?"

She rises on tiptoe and presses a kiss to his cold cheek. "I don't know any more. Besides, I'm sure this is a one-shot deal. This trial's going to be major league, and I'm still in the minors."

Timothy steps to the curb and lifts his hand, signaling to a cab in the right lane. When the cabbie stops, he opens the door and catches Briley's hand. "Off you go." He squeezes her fingers. "Be careful down there."

"Don't worry about me," Briley says, sliding into the backseat. "No one wants to kill the defense attorney until *after* the trial."

As the taxi growls through the traffic on Michigan Avenue, Briley stares out the window and tries to corral her galloping thoughts. This case will undoubtedly end up with John Morton, the firm's most experienced criminal litigant. Last year he handled three high-profile murders and won an acquittal in each case. The man's closing arguments were pure poetry, and rumor had it that he could strike a jury better than anyone in the state. Because he had a knack for ferreting out the hard-liners, his juries were soft enough to eat with a spoon.

If Briley handles this interview well, she might be allowed to sit as second or third chair during the trial. She'll gain valuable experience, and an acquittal would be a feather in her cap, no matter how small her role. If she's going to move up the ladder in this firm, she needs to be involved in more serious cases.

She smiles at the memory of her favorite movie. She's been fascinated by the role of defense attorney ever since watching Atticus Finch defend Tom Robinson in *To Kill a Mockingbird,* but she's never had to defend a client against a murder charge. How will the prosecution play this one? Will they be going for first degree?

An unexpected gust of trepidation blows down the back

of her neck. A first-degree murder conviction could result in the death penalty. Capital punishment in Illinois is reserved for situations with at least one aggravating circumstance, but some of those circumstances might apply in this situation. Briley mentally runs down the list—as a state senator, the victim could be considered a government employee, but that wouldn't count as an aggravating circumstance unless he was killed in the course of his duties. Murder for pecuniary gain is a special circumstance, so if the wife killed her husband to inherit his trust fund, Erin Tomassi's life could be ended by lethal injection.

Briley braces herself as the cab rattles and bounces over a stretch of potholed asphalt. Maybe she shouldn't ask to be a part of this woman's defense team. Tom Robinson's trial devoured Atticus Finch's life and profoundly affected his family. And after all that, plus a guilty verdict, Tom Robinson ended up with a bullet in his back.

When she's finished with this interview, she will be happy to hand the case to John Morton.

The accused killer sparkled the first time Briley saw her, but nothing about Erin Tomassi glitters now.

In a pale green interview room at the Division Four building, part of the sprawling Cook County Jail, Briley comes face-to-face with the firm's latest client. In her V-neck top and elastic-waist pants, the standard jail uniform, Jeffrey Tomassi's young widow huddles in a plastic chair and rubs her bare arms. Since Cook County uniforms are color-coded by security level, Erin is wearing orange—not a good color for blue-eyed blondes.

Briley has never interviewed a prisoner in orange before.

She waits until the armed escort removes the prisoner's handcuffs, then she sets her purse on the table and extends her hand. "Mrs. Tomassi? I'm Briley Lester from Franklin, Watson, Smyth & Morton. I'll be representing you before the judge."

For an alleged murderer, Erin has a surprisingly uncertain look in her eyes. "I—I didn't think I could afford an attorney."

Is she kidding, or is this some kind of act? "I doubt you would qualify for representation by a public defender. Clients above a certain income—"

"The money's not mine." Erin lowers her gaze. "And I don't know why they're saying I killed Jeffrey. I didn't kill him, I *wouldn't* kill him, and I don't want his money. I never did. That's why I signed a prenup before we got married."

Briley waits until the guard leaves and closes the door, then she slips into the chair on the other side of the table, pulls her digital recorder out of her purse, and clicks it on. "Before we begin, I need to warn you—watch what you say here in the jail. Don't talk with the guards, the police, or another inmate about anything even remotely related to your husband's death. Don't doubt that some snitch will rat you out in a minute. Unless you're talking about the weather, the food, or what's on TV, keep your lips zipped."

The woman nods, her eyes reminding Briley of a terrified rabbit's. "How long will they keep me locked up in this place? I don't think I could bear being in here at Christmas."

"Depends upon what the judge sets for bail." Briley slides a borrowed notepad onto the table. "Now—don't tell me what happened. Tell me what they *say* happened. What have you heard from the state's attorney or the police?"

Erin's eyes fill with tears. "They say I killed Jeffrey," she says. "They say I gave him an overdose of insulin while he was asleep. I guess…that'd be first-degree murder, wouldn't it?"

Briley jots on her notepad. "Was your husband diabetic?"

"Yes."

"He took daily insulin shots?"

"He injected himself three or four times a day. He always acted like it was no big deal."

Briley frowns. "How long has it been since your husband died?"

The woman's lower lip quivers. "He died on December 3. The morning after his big fundraiser at the Conrad."

Briley does the subtraction in her head. "Only nine days

ago. Toxicology reports usually take a good six weeks to come back from the lab."

The slender woman rubs her arms again. "I don't know anything about that, but I wouldn't be surprised if Antonio pulled a few strings. The Tomassis always get what they want."

Studying her client, Briley lets the comment slide. "Do you know anyone who would want your husband dead?"

Her shock appears genuine. "No."

"Was your husband suicidal?"

She shakes her head.

"Did the police mention *why* they think you killed him?"

Erin wipes tears from her lower lashes. "All I know is they say he died from an insulin overdose, then this morning they showed up at my father-in-law's house with my name on an arrest warrant. And my juice glass. They kept asking if the fingerprints on the juice glass were mine."

Briley clicks her pen and draws a deep breath. To make such a quick arrest, they must have fingerprints on something more incriminating than a glass. "That's all they asked?"

"They asked if I ever gave Jeffrey his injections. I said no, of course, because I never did."

Fingerprints confirmed on a juice glass. Insulin overdose… They have her prints on a *syringe*. As far as the cops are concerned, this case has been investigated, wrapped, and handed to the state's attorney with a shiny bow on top.

Briley wouldn't be surprised to learn that people are pressuring the state's attorney for a quick conviction. The Tomassis are big names in Chicago, and the senator's fundraising event attracted a lot of media attention. Everyone knew Jeffrey Tomassi was launching his campaign for Congress that night. But if someone wanted to prevent that launch, why wouldn't they kill him the night before?

She exhales in a rush. "Hard to believe that banquet was only nine days ago."

When a question slips into Erin's eyes, Briley smiles. "I

was there—I saw you. When you were dancing with your husband, I thought you looked like the perfect pair."

The widow averts her gaze. "You must have been sitting in the back," she says, her voice strangled. "Appearances can be deceiving."

"So I've learned." Briley notices the gooseflesh on the woman's lower arms. "If I were you, I'd buy a long-sleeved T-shirt at the commissary. They don't spend a lot to heat this building."

Erin rubs her arms again. "I've been warned about that, but I don't have any money. They wouldn't let me bring anything from the house."

Briley pulls out her wallet and slides twenty dollars from the cash compartment. "I'll deposit this in your account before I leave. We don't want you getting sick."

A flush brightens Erin's cheek. "I'll pay you back."

"Don't worry about it. Franklin, Watson, Smyth & Morton wants to take care of its clients."

The woman rubs her nose, then glances toward the painted door. "What happens next?"

"I leave here to go before the judge and inquire about bail. First thing Monday morning, we go to court for your arraignment, where you'll make your plea."

"I didn't do it." Erin's chin quivers as her gaze moves into Briley's. "I'd stand in the middle of Michigan Avenue and shout it at the top of my lungs if I thought it would do any good."

If that statement is meant to impress Briley, it falls far short. "Unfortunately, this building is crammed with women who'd be willing to do the same thing."

"I'm not a murderer. If you could look into my soul, you'd see that." A fresh wave of misery darkens Erin's oval face. "Our marriage may not have been the best, but I'd never hurt Jeffrey. I couldn't."

Briley lifts a warning finger. "We can talk about your marriage later, but don't breathe a word about it outside this room. As for your representation, you can relax. Your father-in-law called our firm, confident that they'd put the best possible lawyer on the job. You'll be working with one of the premier defense attorneys in Chicago."

A worry line appears between the woman's brows. "You're either really overconfident or you think someone else is going to be my lawyer."

Briley smiles as she clicks off her recorder. "I'm only one attorney among many at Franklin, Watson, Smyth & Morton. I go where I'm told, and an hour ago I was told to come down here."

"Are you saying my case looks so hopeless you wouldn't *want* to represent me?"

"You shouldn't want me to be your attorney," Briley answers, pulling her purse onto her lap. "I usually handle lower-profile trials—kids in trouble for shoplifting, assault, vandalism, that sort of thing. I've never defended anyone against a murder charge."

A shadow enters the woman's blue eyes. "So my case will be up for grabs." She drops her head into her hands. "I might as well give up. No one will want to defend me. And no one's going to believe I didn't kill their beloved state senator."

"Don't say that." Briley glances toward the door. Erin Tomassi's helpless act seems sincere, but it's completely unnecessary. Why doesn't she save her theatrics for the judge and jury?

She lifts her purse and stands. "I'm sure my firm's partners will select the attorney best equipped to handle your situation," she says, firming her voice. "Until they do, I'll do my best for you."

She moves to the door and raps on the window, ready to move on.

Chapter Twelve

"Papa? Are you listening?"

Antonio turns from the window and looks at his only surviving son. Jason sits on the other side of the car, in Jeffrey's form, with Jeffrey's eyes. "What did you say?"

Jason covers the mouthpiece of the cell phone. "It's a lawyer from the firm. She wants to know if you're willing to put up bail for Erin."

Antonio shifts his gaze back to the window, watching as the driver steers around a creeping city bus.

Put up money for the woman who killed the light of his life? He'd sooner cut off his right hand. Erin can rot in jail, for all he cares. Better yet, she can die on a gurney. Or even in the electric chair, if Illinois officials can be convinced to use it again.

Jason murmurs a response into the phone, but Antonio turns his thoughts inward. These days, he's finding it hard to care about anything—his work, his daughters, even his remaining son. Jason is a good man, dependable and solid, but he will always be a beta animal. He lacks Jeffrey's intelligence and strength of will. He lacks charisma.

He smiles, remembering the dark-headed twosome who shared a bedroom until they left home for college. As babies, the twins were as alike as two halves of an apple, a perfect binary star, but Jeffrey walked first, establishing himself as the controlling body in their small system. Brighter than Jason, and more naturally inquisitive, Jeffrey delighted his nannies, his teachers, and his girlfriends with his cheerful demeanor and classic good looks. Jason was a pleasant lad, but when standing next to Jeffrey, he always seemed like a faded copy of the original: attractive enough at first glance, but definitely less sharp.

Before the boys turned sixteen, Antonio knew Jeffrey would be the one to lead the family to greatness. Jason would always be a reliable assistant for his brother, an RFK to a future JFK. One brother destined to forge a path, the other to follow and reinforce it. And that's what they did, rising to positions of leadership in student government, college athletics, and the property development business. Three years ago, Jeffrey ran for a senate seat in the Illinois General Assembly and Jason served as his campaign manager. They held their linked hands high at the victory party, two men closer to each other than either could ever be to a wife…for nothing could compete with the intimacy of twins. Antonio understood their relationship and respected it. He often thought his boys could read each other's mind. If that kind of closeness gave them an advantage, so be it.

Outside the car, a cacophony yammers for Antonio's attention—a jackhammer shredding a sidewalk, a traffic cop blowing his whistle, the whine of an approaching ambulance—but none of those things interest him. He lets his head fall back as his concentration dissipates in a wave of fatigue. A cocoon of anguish has enveloped him ever since hearing the awful news, and this morning's announcement has only deepened his grief. Erin's fingerprints were on the insulin bottle, the police said, and also on the syringe.

The sweet, helpless girl he welcomed into his family has murdered his beautiful boy.

He closes his eyes and studies the memory of the last night he spent with his son. He had gone upstairs to see if Jeffrey and Erin were ready to come down, but after letting himself into the hotel suite he heard angry voices. The two of them stood in the living room, both of them dressed in formal wear, but tears streaked a flaming handprint on Erin's cheek. Jeffrey wore a hard look of frustration, an expression Antonio had seen many times.

"What's going on here?" Antonio glanced from his son to his daughter-in-law, waiting for an answer. "Jeffrey?"

"It's a private matter." Jeff tore his gaze from his wife's stricken face. "Is everything ready downstairs?"

Antonio looked at Erin, silently inviting her to give her side of the story, but she lowered her head and refused to meet his gaze. "Everything's ready," he finally answered, slipping his hands into his pockets. He moved toward the sofa table as Erin swiped her wet cheeks with the back of her hand. He offered a handkerchief. "You okay?"

She sniffed and waved away his help.

"Why don't you go fix your face." He jerked his thumb toward the bedroom. "I need to talk to our boy."

His daughter-in-law bowed her head and moved to the other room, her long skirt swishing in the silence. When the door clicked behind her, Antonio rounded on his son. "What are you doing?"

Jeffrey's brows slanted in a frown. "What?"

"You are ten minutes from one of the most important nights of your life, and you've made your wife cry."

A wall appeared behind Jeff's eyes. "Leave it alone, Papa."

"How can I? Someone has to correct you."

Jeffrey moved to the mirror and adjusted his tie. "She's my wife," he said, his voice as cool as an assassin's. "A man's allowed to control his wife."

"In private, sure. But in public, you watch yourself, because people notice every little thing. Everyone knows politics is a dirty business and couples have disagreements during a campaign. But when you are minutes away from a public appearance, you control *yourself.* You tamp down your irritation, you wait to put your wife back in line. When you're in front of strangers, you treat that girl like a priceless porcelain doll."

Jeff smoothed the pleats on his starched shirt. "You

don't have any idea what it's like to be married to a spineless woman."

"Erin may not be as weak as you think. And yes, your mama was strong, but only after I taught her what strength is."

Jeffrey turned away from the mirror. "Erin's about as strong as tissue paper. If I don't keep her on a tight leash, she's going to do something to bring our entire operation crashing down."

Antonio stared, tongue-tied, as the bedroom door opened. Erin appeared in the doorway, her face clean and powdered, her hair shining, her eyes modestly cast down. She looked like a princess—or, better yet, a future First Lady.

"That's more like it." He beamed at his daughter-in-law and hurried to draw her into his arms. After giving her a hug and planting a kiss on her velvet cheek, he stepped back. "You look perfect, my dear, and tonight people are going to stand in line to shake your hand. And Jeffrey is going to treat you with kindness and respect, aren't you, son?"

Beside him, Jeffrey rolled his eyes in bored acquiescence. "You don't have to worry." He flicked a piece of lint from the shoulder of his tuxedo, then stepped around to grip Erin's free hand. "I'm sure we'll look like the perfect couple."

"Yes," Erin added, her voice oddly flat. "We have to knock them dead."

A shiver spreads over Antonio as the memory edges his teeth. Had her words been a warning he'd been too blind to see?

Chapter Thirteen

Joseph Franklin looks up from the open book on his desk when Briley raps on his door. "Miss Lester! How'd it go with Erin Tomassi?"

"Fine…but Mrs. Tomassi was pretty shaken up when we couldn't meet bail. She's dreading the idea of spending Christmas in jail." Briley steps into the office and wanders to the empty space between the guest chair and the doorway. She's been invited to sit before Franklin's desk exactly three times, and she's not likely to extend her record today.

"What was the bail amount?"

"A million even."

Franklin taps the tips of his fingers together. "She couldn't handle a hundred grand?"

"No, sir. The estate's been frozen, so she can't access the joint accounts. I thought her father-in-law might want to help her out—"

"I wouldn't count on any help from Antonio. He called us to represent her, but we may not hear from him again. If the state's attorney assembles a solid case, Antonio isn't likely to continue supporting the woman who murdered his son."

Briley swallows hard. "I—I didn't know he'd had a change of heart. Anyway, Mrs. Tomassi insists she's innocent. I compiled my notes into a case file if you want to take a look."

She holds her breath, waiting for him to say he's assigning the case to one of the partners. If he gives the case to John Morton, she might plead for a spot on the team, even accepting third chair. She won't have much experience to offer, but she could learn a lot while watching a master defend a capital case....

Franklin stares mindlessly at the file folder in her grip, then he lifts his hand in an abrupt wave. "The case is yours, Lester. Give it your best shot."

Briley blinks. "You mean...I'm on the team. Who's first chair?"

"You are."

"But I'm not qualified."

"You're an excellent attorney, you'll provide high-quality legal representation, and you have to start somewhere."

"But my schedule is crammed. The average attorney working on a death penalty case invests nearly nineteen hundred hours before proceeding to trial—"

"We'll clear your other cases." Franklin smiles a grim little grin and returns his gaze to his book. "Keep me informed as to your progress."

Briley back-steps toward the door as a tremor of mingled fear and anticipation rattles her bones. He really means to assign her to this case?

"Mr. Franklin?" She halts, her voice wavering in the spacious room. "You do realize I've never handled a murder trial?"

Franklin has the audacity—or the confidence—to grin at her again. "I'm not worried about you. Female defendant, female lawyer, both about the same age... It's a good fit. So get busy."

"But—" She hesitates, remembering the strobic play of flashing cameras at the senator's fundraiser. The Tomassis are political royalty in Chicago, and the sight of their princess in handcuffs and shackles will draw the paparazzi like Paris Hilton at the Los Angeles county jail. Briley is willing to tackle a death penalty case, but this one will include so many distractions....

"Listen," Franklin says, a muscle flicking at his jaw, "do you remember when you interviewed for this firm?"

She stares, caught off guard by the unexpected warmth in his voice. Why is he suddenly waxing nostalgic?

"I remember—" he points toward the conference table at the side of his cavernous office "—you sitting over there and telling the partners you only had one hero growing up…your father. Do you remember saying you wanted to be like him?"

Still mystified by his motive, she nods.

"I've never forgotten that interview. You set quite a challenging example when you told us your father sacrificed his life on a mission to help someone else. That's why we're here, Briley. That's why we defend our clients. Because we want to make sure every individual who needs a defender gets one." He folds his hands over his book. "Now—do you really want me to give the Tomassi case to Jim Myers?"

Ah…he's baiting her with guilt. Testing her fighting spirit. And he's bluffing, because Myers has even less courtroom experience than she does.

But she can rise to the challenge. With a good support team behind her, she ought to be able to see it through. She is, after all, her father's daughter, and she meant every word she said in that interview.

Briley lifts her chin. "I think I can handle this case."

"Then get busy. And close the door on your way out, will you?"

Briley grips the file, shuts the door, and strides toward the elevator. Her pulse pounds with the knowledge that finally, after three years in this firm, Joe Franklin has noticed her mostly successful record of defending car thieves and child abusers, school bullies and drug users. Maybe he took special note of her only celebrity case, in which she successfully defended a rap star against charges of sexual assault. The client's raunchy video had soured her stomach, but the alleged victim recanted under cross-examination, forcing the judge to dismiss the complaint and free her client.

That afternoon, she'd felt like Ben Matlock's heir apparent.

Maybe she has finally begun to climb the ladder of success. And if it takes the uncomplaining representation of Erin Tomassi to move Briley's office from the second floor to the third, then the partners of Franklin, Watson, Smyth & Morton are about to see the formation of a spectacular defense.

Briley's blood is still swimming in adrenaline when she returns to her desk, but her enthusiasm flickers once she sinks into her chair and gazes at the files stacked pell-mell on her bookshelves. If Joseph Franklin intends to trust her with a high-profile capital case, it can't be because he's been impressed with her record of defending teenage joyriders and drunk-driving businessmen. So why has he assigned her to this trial?

She swivels toward the window and stares at a bland apartment building as her brain arrives at one inescapable conclusion: Her weepy client was right. No defense attorney in her right mind would want this case, because no one will believe Erin Tomassi didn't kill her husband. But lawyers aren't allowed to give up, and associates aren't supposed to complain.

Franklin must not believe the case can be won, so he's allowing Briley to go through the motions of presenting an adequate defense for a political princess. If she makes a mistake, he'll simply assign a more experienced lawyer for the appeal, citing Briley's errors as justification for a new trial. Those errors, if they're flagrant, might be enough to earn her walking papers. By the end of this case, she might be defeated *and* unemployed. And unpopular.

She reaches for the telephone and punches in Timothy's number. He answers on the second ring. "Hello?"

"Remember the Tomassi murder?"

"Of course."

"Guess who's defending the widow."

She hears his quick intake of breath. "No kidding. You got the case?"

"I shouldn't have. No managing partner in his right mind would hand the case to a neophyte, but Franklin gave it to me. That can only mean one thing."

"You're the best woman for the job?"

"Erin Tomassi is guilty and the state's attorney has an airtight case. I haven't seen the police report, but I'm betting Franklin is right."

"You don't know that, Bri. Unless the woman confessed—"

"She says she's innocent. But so does everyone else at the jail."

"Come on, now." A smile slips into his voice. "Don't assume the worst before you even start to work. Give the woman the benefit of the doubt, and give yourself a break. Maybe she's telling the truth."

Briley remains silent, wishing she could believe him. Trouble is, Timothy isn't an attorney. He's a sneakers-wearing Boy Scout with an irresistible grin and an undying belief that some trace of goodness lies in everyone, including his clients. And she'd give up chocolate for a year if he'd forget about his addicts and take a job selling shoes.

"You still there?" he asks.

"Yes."

"Then find out what happened to Jeffrey Tomassi and do your best to defend his wife. Because the alternative is unthinkable."

"I'll do everything I can...but it'd take a miracle to get Erin Tomassi acquitted."

Briley closes her eyes as a memory floats up, a vision of a couple waltzing, swirling through a ballroom in perfect unison. They were smiling at each other, and Jeffrey's arm gripped Erin so tightly... Did something go wrong in their marriage? Something horrible enough to drive one of them to a desperate act?

"This case is going to be huge," she says. "I'll need to hire an investigator and rope in some help around here. Capital cases require a defense team."

"I'm sure the firm will give you whatever you need. They're supportive, aren't they?"

"So far." She swallows hard, reluctant to admit what she needs to say next. "I'll be working a lot. I'll try not to let this case take over my life, but I might have to work a few nights and weekends."

Timothy laughs. "Babe, don't feel like you have to explain yourself to me. Take all the time you need to do your job."

"But I might not be available when you have time off. Unless Dax is able to stand on his own—"

"He's not," Timothy interrupts. "He's doing better, but the boy still gets jumpy when he's around others who are using."

"I thought you were keeping him away from those people."

"I try, but he's in show business, you know? I'd keep him away from booze altogether if I could, but when he goes to parties, every girl who comes up has a drink in her hand."

"Oh." Briley stares at the ceiling, her mind filling with images of parties where dozens of beautiful girls drape themselves over any man in Dax Lightner's reflected glow.

"Hey." Timothy's voice softens. "Don't you worry about a thing."

"I'm not worried."

"You are. I can hear it in your voice."

"Okay." She smiles into the phone. "Maybe I'm a little worried. About you, and about this trial."

"You don't need to fret, kiddo. Jump in with both feet and abandon yourself to the cause. Make your boss and Erin Tomassi grateful that you were bold enough to take the case."

Smiling, she drops her head onto her hand. Timothy has a tendency to turn conversations into pep talks, but he always makes her feel better.

"Stand back and prepare to be amazed," she says. "I'm going to do my best."

* * *

Briley hadn't wanted to go to the fundraiser, but Timothy had insisted. "It'll be fun," he'd said, his eyes sparkling, "and I want to wear my tux. I want to impress you."

So on the second of December she left work early, slipped into a sleeveless gown she'd bought on sale years before, and pulled out a pair of chandelier earrings. She found herself wishing for hair long enough to twist into a glamorous chignon, but the practical chin-length cut that went so well with a suit would have to work with formal wear, too.

Just after dark, a black limo pulled up outside her town house and Timothy stepped out to greet her. Flashing cameras and exclamations from excited onlookers punctuated their arrival at the Conrad, one of Chicago's most luxurious hotels. Briley and Timothy slipped away from the crowd and checked their coats. After entering the ballroom, they found their table, number sixty-seven, located in a quiet corner.

Throughout dinner, she and Timothy made small talk with the other guests: the police commissioner and his wife, the owners of a local drug store chain, a reporter and photographer from the *Chicago Tribune*. Briley enjoyed talking to the reporter until the woman revealed that she was covering the event for the Style section. "I'm here to check out the senator's wife," she said, twisting in her seat as she scanned the front of the room. "They think she's going to be quite the trendsetter in D.C."

"I hadn't heard that," Briley answered, but the woman had stopped paying attention.

Waiters in white jackets whisked the empty dessert plates away as a local politico welcomed the guests and made a series of optimistic predictions about Jeffrey Tomassi's future in politics. While the crowd cheered and clapped, Briley found herself searching the head table for a woman who might be a suitable candidate for national trendsetter.

Only one possibility, really. The matron seated at Jeff Tomassi's left appeared too old to be his wife, but the woman at his right fit the job description. Young enough to inspire women of all ages, she glowed with a rare combination of beauty and approachability. The blonde smiled throughout the long introduction and was one of the first to stand and applaud when Tomassi rose to take the lectern.

During Jeffrey Tomassi's speech, Briley propped her chin on her hand and studied the aspiring candidate. Tomassi repeated all the promises parroted by most politicians, but he was strikingly handsome and tall, at least six-two. Maybe as tall as Timothy.

As the candidate promised brighter days and lower crime rates for Illinois, Briley leaned toward Tim and lowered her voice to a whisper. "Did you know that eighteen American presidents were over six feet tall?"

Tim returned her grin. "And the reason for this comment is?"

"Even Eleanor Roosevelt was six feet tall. Tomassi is tall, too, don't you think?"

"Shouldn't short men run for office?"

"Ask Napoleon." She nudged his shoulder. "How tall are you?"

Tim straightened his spine. "Tall enough to score tickets to this shindig. But maybe not tall enough to run for office."

"Don't worry about it. I don't think I could handle many more of these dinners."

They fell silent as a string ensemble began to play. A murmur of approval rose from the crowd as Jeffrey Tomassi extended his hand to the lovely woman at his side. She stepped out from behind the head table and joined him in the cleared space reserved for a dance floor. And while the strings played Eric Clapton's "Wonderful Tonight," Jeffrey and Erin Tomassi floated over the floor in each other's arms.

Briley fell silent as she studied the dancers moving in the spotlight. How did some women always manage to look so perfect? How, for instance, did Erin Tomassi achieve her unique hair color? Anything that pours from a bottle tends to result in a uniform shade, but Erin Tomassi's hair was a mixture of gold and blond and variant shades in between. It spilled like a waterfall over her shoulders, gleaming and swaying like living silk....

Briley shifted her gaze to the couple's faces—his resolute and handsome, hers soft and graceful. Erin's mouth moved as she said something to her husband. Though Briley couldn't see his answering expression, she did observe his hand flexing over his bride's spine, drawing her closer in the dance.

Chapter Fourteen

While the strings played and her husband hummed in her ear, Erin tried to maintain the stiff smile affixed to her face. "You're holding me too closely." She uttered the words in a voice designed to reach him alone. "Jeffrey, please."

"Relax." He smiled and spun her again, eliciting another burst of applause from the delighted crowd. "They like it when you're relaxed."

"I am relaxed. I'm smiling."

"Not like you were when Dax Lightner looked at you. So step it up, darling, and turn on the charm. Everyone wants to see how you'll handle the pressure as a U.S. congressman's wife."

She turned her face, not willing to look at him, and felt his palm press against her bare back. In a moment, his grip on her hand would crush the bones in her fingers—

She sighed in relief when the music finally faded. Jeffrey released her and stepped back, bowing to the audience and, with a mocking attempt at gallantry, to her. She waved through a veil of tears and turned to go back to her seat. Only in moments like this, when she hid her face from the crowd, could she relax, but soon she'd be on display again, expected to sit and smile and clap and make sparkling conversation with strangers who felt they owned her somehow, so they had every right to pry and pat and soothe her as if she were a china doll to pass around....

Someone must have handed Jeffrey a microphone; she could hear his voice booming out more promises he would keep if elected to national office. National health care! Respect for the environment! A college education for all!

Good grief, he sounded as if he were already running for president. That goal lay at least ten years away, but he and his family had laid careful plans, bridling their ambition until they could sweep into the Oval Office and commandeer space for the entire family in the West Wing.

Unable to bear the sound of Jeffrey's voice another minute, Erin stepped behind the head table and slipped through a gap in the velvet curtain that served as a backdrop. An open door beckoned beyond the empty space, and she ran toward it, not caring what anyone might think about her sudden departure.

On the other side of the door lay a deserted hallway. Safely out of sight, she leaned against the wall and breathed deep to steady her pounding pulse. She had tried her best to please tonight; she had taken extra pains with her hair and makeup, she had chatted gaily with the older man seated on the other side of the lectern. But still Jeffrey had found fault. Naturally, he would. Her efforts were never good enough.

She caught her breath when she heard footsteps approaching through the open doorway. She turned to walk down the hall.

"Erin?"

She glanced over her shoulder when she recognized the voice. Her father-in-law stood behind her, a look of compassionate concern on his face. "Are you feeling all right?"

She forced a smile. "I'm fine. Just…breathless."

"It was warm in there, especially under the lights. Would you like me to take you outside for some fresh air? I could give you my coat—"

"I'll be fine. I'm feeling better already."

"Then let me escort you back inside." He offered his arm, jutting it toward her like the sturdy iron hasp on a length of chain. Reluctantly, she slipped her arm through his, pasted on a smile, and inhaled the refined scent of his cologne.

"What's this?"

She glanced at Antonio's face and saw that he was staring at her upper arm, which bore the marks of Jeffrey's hard grip. "Oh, that." She forced a laugh. "I tripped over the hem of my gown and Jeffrey had to catch me." She smiled, waiting for him to respond, but he stared at her with deadly concentration.

"Maybe you should be careful not to…trip in the days ahead. We have a lot riding on that young man."

Erin lowered her gaze. If she told Antonio the truth, he would correct his son, and later the son would correct his wife. With as much force as necessary to convince her never to speak up again.

"Your son—" she chose her words with care "—is quite forceful about his opinions."

"All great men are forceful." Antonio's dark eyes pinned her in a long and silent scrutiny, then he patted her hand and gestured toward the doorway. "Shall we rejoin the others?"

Still at the lectern, Jeffrey didn't miss a beat of his speech. She sank into her seat and settled her hands in her lap, hoping he hadn't noticed her abrupt disappearance.

But during an applause break, he turned, looked at her, and flashed a knowing smile that made her blood run cold.

Chapter Fifteen

In an office muffled with after-hours quiet, Briley holds a roast beef sandwich in her left hand and makes a list with her right. She's usually home at this hour, watching the news while she eats a prepackaged dinner hot from the microwave, but Timothy's little pep talk has inspired her to begin working on the Tomassi file. Tomorrow she'll check into shifting her current cases to other associates, but now she needs to focus on doing what needs to be done for Erin Tomassi.

That woman, at least, should be relieved to learn that she now has a lawyer. Though she probably won't be thrilled by the firm's choice.

Briley takes another bite of roast beef and considers the first steps she needs to take. Almost immediately, she'll need to assemble a defense team. Current ABA guidelines for death penalty cases suggest that no fewer than two attorneys, an investigator, and a mitigation specialist work concurrently on the case. Not only must they prepare for the guilt-or-innocence phase of the trial, they must be ready for the possibility of a conviction. If the penalty phase of the trial is necessary, the defense team will attempt to mitigate the crime by presenting the defendant's past, social upbringing, good deeds, character witnesses—anything that might persuade a jury to spare her life.

For the first phase, Briley will need copies of the autopsy and police reports, along with an inventory of all items seized when the police searched the crime scene. She'll need to discover what witnesses might be able to shed light on the events of Jeffrey Tomassi's final days, and she'll have to learn what motive the police are ascribing to Tomassi's wife. Why would an openly adoring woman want to kill her husband? As the spouse of a state senator, Erin enjoyed power and prestige. She shared her husband's wealth, which included two homes, one in Springfield and one in tony Lincoln Park. The couple had no children, but Jeffrey Tomassi was close to his father, brother, and four sisters. Presumably the large family had embraced Erin and made her feel at home.

So why would she risk all that by murdering her husband?

Briley draws a question mark in the margin of her legal pad and takes another bite of her sandwich. She'll need to conduct an in-depth interview with her client, which means a trip down to the jail next week. After learning more about the case, she may need to hire a private investigator to track down reasons why other people may have wanted Jeffrey Tomassi out of the way. Joe Franklin is fond of saying that investigators should follow the money trail, so if Erin doesn't inherit her husband's fortune, who does? That person certainly needs to be questioned.

On the other hand—she flips a page—perhaps the medical examiner misinterpreted the evidence and Jeffrey Tomassi suffered an accidental death. She might need a medical expert to testify about insulin injection. Maybe the man overdosed. The family may not want to believe that their rising star could make such an elementary blunder, but stranger things have happened. All Briley needs is the element of doubt. Unless all twelve jurors vote "guilty," her client walks free.

But the state's attorney knows this…and wouldn't have charged Erin with first-degree murder without incontrovertible evidence. Which, presumably, involves a set of incriminating fingerprints on a syringe, and who knows what else?

Briley pulls out the firm's phone directory and looks over the employee roster. She's going to need help on this case, though Franklin hasn't said anything about providing it.

She turns to her computer and types out a quick e-mail, asking Franklin for the full-time assistance of one paralegal, one private investigator, a mitigation specialist and another associate. Given the potential for media interest in this matter, she finishes, I'm sure you can see why I'd feel more adequately prepared with additional staff on the team. With one click, she sends the e-mail, then she telephones the Cook County prosecutor's office to ask for the case file to be sent over. Because the office is closed, her call goes straight to voice mail, but crime—and prosecutors—operate twenty-four hours a day. She might get an answer tonight.

This call will establish the beginning of a long trail of paperwork. As pretrial discovery commences, she will have to provide the prosecuting attorney with the names and addresses of any potential witnesses, copies of witness depositions, any psychologist's or physician's reports she intends to introduce, and a list of evidence she plans to present at trial. The prosecution should provide the same for her, as well as copies of all statements made by the defendant and in the prosecution's possession.

Before she hangs up the phone, she has an e-mail answer from Joe Franklin: Client should be responsible for cost of investigator and any other consultants. Unable to provide full-time assistance for your case at present. Suggest you use staff as they become available.

Briley's stomach lurches. Is the firm *trying* to sabotage her case? The associates and paralegals on this floor are already overworked; none of them will be "available" anytime in the near future. And if Erin can't afford a T-shirt at the jail, how can she pay for an investigator?

Briley chews on her thumbnail, then flips the cover of her address book. Criminal justice standards require jurisdictions to ensure that if a defendant doesn't have money, the court will provide funds for the payment of investigators and experts, as a matter of the defendant's constitutional right to present an effective defense. The court is especially willing to provide funds for persons facing the death penalty.

Franklin, Watson, Smyth & Morton rarely represents indigent clients, but under Illinois's slayer statute, no person convicted of a murder charge can financially benefit from the victim's death. Since the state has filed charges against Erin Tomassi, the banks have undoubtedly frozen Jeffrey Tomassi's estate, including any accounts jointly owned with his wife. The estate will not go through probate until after the murder trial, so for the moment, Erin is essentially penniless. If she's convicted, she'll remain destitute.

Either way, she qualifies for financial help from the state of Illinois. Joseph Franklin may not be wild about the idea of Briley's petitioning the state for a h[...] provide the funds she needs to inve[...] leaving her with no other choice.

Once again, Briley picks up the p[...]

The next morning, Briley pads d[...] clad feet and peeks through a decorat[...] front door. Her newspaper sits on t[...] barely twenty feet away.

Does she dare run out in her robe and socks, or should she wait until she's dressed?

She peers through the glass again, and tries to judge the traffic. She hears no sounds of approaching cars, and nine o'clock is still early, especially for a Saturday.

She flips the dead bolt on the door and pulls on the handle, allowing a stream of frigid air into the foyer. Like a swimmer about to plunge into icy water, she tucks her chin, grips the edges of her robe, and runs across the porch. She scoops up the paper and pivots on the ball of her foot, ready to sprint back inside.

"Hello!" Mrs. Ivins, the older woman who lives next door, lifts her head above the jagged edge of the picket fence and calls out a cheery greeting. "Lovely morning, isn't it?"

Briley glances up at the sky. "Yes," she calls, walking back to the porch as quickly as she can without appearing rude. "Beautiful morning. Going to be a pretty day."

"It's supposed to snow on Sunday." Mrs. Ivins gazes at the winter-dead canes of her rosebushes. "I don't care for the snow, but your father loved it. I've always thought winter was cruel, but your dad used to say it was a promise of better things to come." She blinks and shifts her gaze to Briley. "That reminds me— Are you doing anything special for Christmas? I'm having my open house on Christmas Eve."

Briley shivers and hesitates on the sidewalk. "Um...I haven't decided about Christmas Eve yet. But if I'm here, I'll be sure to stop over."

"By the way," Mrs. Ivins says, "nice picture of you in the paper."

Frowning, Briley twiddles her fingers in a quick wave, then crosses the porch and closes the front door. Mrs. Ivins has to be mistaken about seeing her picture. The woman is eighty if she's a day, and sometimes she talks about Briley's dad as if he were still living in the house....

On her way to the coffeepot, she unwraps the paper. A bold headline dispels every hope of a leisurely morning: Senator's Wife Arrested for Murder.

Forgetting her coffee, Briley slips into a chair at the table and skims the article. The front-page piece centers on the facts of the case, providing details of Jeffrey Tomassi's death and Erin's arrest. But the reporters have been busy. Inside the paper, on pages six and seven, are several affiliated articles. One features the Tomassi family and details the close relationship between the six siblings and their devoted father. Another article records Jeffrey Tomassi's rise to prominence and includes several quotes from political experts who are convinced he was destined for national office, probably "as high as he wanted to go." A shorter article tells the story of Erin Tomassi, a Chicago girl who met Jeffrey at a party and married him not long after. The writer does a good job of implying that Erin married Jeffrey for money, power, or both.

Briley studies a photo of the couple and recognizes the dress Erin wore to the banquet the night Jeffrey died. Jeffrey is flashing a confident grin in that picture; Erin wears a decidedly smaller and more self-contained smile.

She catches her breath as a frisson of recognition climbs her spine. As she'd expected, her picture is featured in the lower half of the page, but it's the small photo that hangs in the foyer at Franklin, Watson, Smyth & Morton. It's a serious-lawyer shot in which she appears unsmiling and severe—completely unlike her glamorous client. A caption beneath the photo announces that Briley Lester will be representing Erin Tomassi in the upcoming trial.

Briley drops the paper to the table and scrapes her hand through her hair. A reporter must have contacted Mr. Franklin late last night, because no one called her for a quote or permission to use her picture.

But they'll be calling soon. And this time around, she'd better handle the media carefully.

This time, the stakes are higher.

Chapter Sixteen

Ten days before Christmas, Briley sits in the high-ceilinged courtroom beside her client, who is shackled hand and foot. Erin Tomassi is still wearing her orange jail uniform, and her long hair appears tangled and unkempt. An ugly purple bruise mars her cheek, a dark oval Briley doesn't remember seeing the last time they met.

Judge Hollister, an older woman wearing rhinestone-studded glasses, motions to her bailiff, then engages the man in a private conversation. She's fast-tracking, trying to clear her call sheet and empty the bullpen before the start of whatever trial is scheduled to begin at nine-thirty. The gallery behind Briley is filled with anxious lawyers, most of whom are checking their watches or reading police reports.

Briley turns to her client and keeps her voice low. "How are you doing at the jail?"

"I'm okay."

"You sure?"

Erin gives her a brittle smile. "I'm tougher than I look."

"If you're having trouble over there…"

Erin glances at the jury box to her left, where a half-dozen other female prisoners await their turn before the judge. "I don't want to make waves."

Across the room, Travis Bystrowski, one of Cook County's leading prosecutors, saunters over with a file, which he drops onto the defense table. "Morning, Ms. Lester. I got your message. I think you'll find everything you need in here."

Briley opens the folder and scans the contents: copies of the police report, the toxicology and autopsy reports, the inventory, and the indictment. "Thank you—and since we'll be working together, why don't you call me Briley." She offers him a polite smile. "Anything you need from us at this point?"

Bystrowski grins and slips his hands into his pockets. "A confession would be nice. Save a lot of taxpayer dollars."

"Why would an innocent woman give you a confession?"

Bystrowski grins and backs away, offering a little wave as he goes.

"Thank you," Erin murmurs, "for taking my case, and believing in me. I'm glad someone does."

Briley gives her client a sidelong glance of astonished disbelief. Could this woman really be so naive?

When the court clerk calls her case, Briley draws a deep breath and stands with her client. The judge looks up when the clerk finishes reading the charge. "Erin Wilson Tomassi," Hollister says, her nasal voice piercing the shuffling from the jury box, "you have the right to an attorney. If you cannot afford one, one will be appointed to you."

"Your Honor, I'm Briley Lester, an associate with Franklin, Watson, Smyth & Morton. I will be representing Mrs. Tomassi."

The judge makes a note and continues: "Mrs. Tomassi, you, or your attorney, have the right to confront and cross-examine witnesses against you. You have the right to a jury trial. You have the right not to incriminate yourself. You have the right to a speedy trial. If you plead guilty, you could be sentenced to death or life in prison without possibility of parole. Do you understand these rights as I have explained them to you?"

Erin glances at Briley, then lowers her head in an abrupt nod. "I do."

"Very good." For the first time, the judge looks squarely at the accused woman. "To the charge of murder in the first-degree, how do you plead?"

Briley clears her throat. "Not guilty, Your Honor."

The judge glances down at her paperwork and lifts a page. "Preliminary trial set for next Monday—"

"We'll waive the preliminary trial, Your Honor," Briley says.

"Then we'll hear pretrial motions in six weeks, on January 26. Any objections?" The judge glances from the prosecutor to Briley, who shakes her head. "Thank you, Counselors, you are dismissed."

Briley gathers the prosecution's case file and her laptop, then stops to address her shackled client. "I'm coming to see you this afternoon," she says, noticing what could be a flicker of relief in the woman's eyes. "Can I bring you anything?"

Erin glances toward the other prisoners in the jury box and shakes her head. "I'd love something to read. Maybe certain paranoid people wouldn't think I was staring at them if I could bury my nose in a book."

Briley grimaces. "I'm sorry, but books are considered contraband. Aren't there any books in the dayroom?"

"A few battered paperbacks." Erin stands as the bailiff beckons to her. "But I'm not sure I dare cross the room to check them out."

"Listen, if someone's bothering you in there—"

"Bothering me?" Erin laughs, but a wild light shines in her eyes as the bailiff approaches to take her away. "I'll see you this afternoon, Ms. Lester. I'll be waiting."

After exiting the elevator, Briley catches the eye of a courthouse security guard and nods toward the daylight beyond the glass doors. "Has it warmed up any outside?"

The guard laughs. "It's colder than a judge's heart out there. But you didn't hear me say so."

She smiles, fastens the top button of her coat, and steps through the tall doors leading to the courthouse steps. She's parked in the garage across the street, so with any luck she'll be able to get to her car before frostbite claims the tip of her nose—

"Miss Lester!"

"Briley!"

She halts, blinking in consternation, as a horde of reporters surges into her path, carrying cameras, recorders, and boom microphones.

Briley glances to her left and right, hoping for a means of escape, but she can see no other way to reach her car. She can see several white news vans parked at the curb south of the courthouse, their satellite dishes extended.

Within a moment, she is surrounded and peering into a sea of wind-chapped faces. The mob thrusts dozens of gadgets in her direction, their motions accompanied by a chorus of insectile clicks.

"Miss Lester!" the closest woman shouts, shoving a recorder into Briley's face. "What can you tell us about Erin Tomassi's case?"

Briley focuses on the parking garage in the distance as the wind slaps her cheeks with frigid fingers. "Erin Tomassi entered a not-guilty plea this morning before Judge Hollister," she says, weighing each word before she speaks it. "That's it for now."

"Can you tell us how you plan to defend her? Your personal theory of the case? Is it true that Jeffrey Tomassi was having an affair with a flight attendant?"

Briley glares at the male reporter who released the barrage of questions. "We are not prepared to make further comments at this time. Now, if you'll excuse me, I believe I have the right to cross the street unimpeded."

A couple of the reporters grin and step aside, but the impudent man keeps yelling as she pushes her way down the remaining steps. "Have you subpoenaed Jeffrey Tomassi's phone records? What about the twin brother? Is it true that Jeffrey and Jason frequently exchanged roles to fool unsuspecting women?"

Briley lowers her head and steps into the street, more willing to trust the oncoming traffic than the rabble of reporters.

Chapter Seventeen

Briley hands cash to the parking lot attendant, takes her receipt, then pulls out of the garage and into traffic, careful to avoid the fresh wall of snow piled at the curb. Flurries blow past her windshield, shimmying and dancing to the thump of rap music from a vehicle in the next lane.

She braces her elbow against the door as a traffic light turns red and her car crawls to a halt behind a green Hyundai. At this rate, she'll never get back to the office before lunch, and she needs at least an hour to review Bystrowski's file before she heads to the jail. After studying the material and speaking to her client, she ought to be able to formulate a defense strategy.

Though Franklin and others in the firm would probably advise her to delay as much as possible, she can't help thinking about Erin Tomassi spending the holidays in jail. The "old wine defense"—delaying a case as long as possible—might benefit a defendant who is out on bail. But her present client doesn't look like the sort who will be able to handle a long stint behind bars. Her fragile demeanor, that porcelain skin...not even the shapeless jail uniform can disguise the fact that Erin Tomassi looks like a pampered princess. And the hardened inmates of the Cook County Jail tend to resent princesses.

Even Briley could find it easy to resent Erin Tomassi. Despite the article that portrayed Erin as a girl from the working class, she obviously traveled an easy road after marrying Jeffrey Tomassi. The newspaper had mentioned two homes, a housekeeper, and a jet-set lifestyle that kept the Tomassis busy flying from one five-star hotel to the next.

Briley can't remember the last time she stayed in a five-star hotel. And, being single, she's had to work for almost everything she owns.

A smile crawls to her lips as a voice rises from her memory. "And who crowned you the Queen of Everything?" her father would chide whenever she complained about working around the house. "Get off the couch and help me with the dishes. Then we can sit down and tackle your algebra."

A car honks, startling her out of her reverie. She steps on the gas and her car lurches forward, carrying her through the intersection and back to her place at the Hyundai's rear bumper.

No, Erin Tomassi doesn't look like she grew up scrubbing dishes. She won't have to work at the Cook County Jail, either, but she might find the routine tedious. No afternoon teas, no formal dances, no shopping trips, unless you count the occasional jaunt to the commissary to buy shampoo and underwear.

Still, Briley can't help but feel a small stirring of sympathy for her client. She can't think of anything more horrible than spending the holidays locked up...unless it's spending Christmas alone in the dorm at boarding school. She's done that, and she would never want to do it again.

She wouldn't wish that kind of loneliness on her worst enemy.

Chapter Eighteen

Erin shuffles into the interview room and stands without moving until the guard releases her handcuffs and shackles. Briley Lester is already sitting at the table, several stacks of papers spread before her. Her face seems to be in a fully uptight and locked expression, a look that doesn't exactly fill Erin with confidence.

After the guard leaves, she rubs the bones of her wrist and approaches the table. "Thanks for coming," she says, sliding into a plastic chair. "I didn't really expect to see you again so soon."

The lawyer looks up, surprise in her eyes. "Why? I said I'd come."

Erin lifts one shoulder in a shrug. "After a few days in this place, you learn not to expect too much."

Ms. Lester tilts her head, as if urging her to explain, but Erin looks away, unwilling to spell out the obvious. The woman didn't want this case; apparently no one at her firm did. So Erin's been stuck with a reluctant lawyer, one who will go through the motions and shake her head in regret when the court finds her guilty of murder.

So here they are, beginning the attorney-client dance. Other than "I didn't do it," she has no idea what she's supposed to say to this woman.

The sound of voices intrudes on the silence, an inaudible exchange of taunts and retorts that grows louder as a prisoner and two guards move down the hallway. Erin presses her hand to her forehead as the shrill sound of female cursing seeps through the concrete walls, accompanied by the jingle of chains and the creak of a guard's leather belt. Finally, the noisy procession moves away, but not before reminding Erin of what appears to be an inevitable future.

After an awkward moment, the attorney clears her throat. "I've been reading the police report," she says, folding her hands. "And I can see why they felt they had enough evidence to make an arrest. Your home was sealed tight— video cameras covered the front and back doors and your security system was armed and functioning properly. No one tripped the alarm that night. The video cameras didn't pick up any signs of an intruder. So apparently you and your husband were the only two people in the house."

Erin shivers as a subterranean tremor passes through her. "I never blamed Jeffrey's death on an intruder. If the police are trying to make me look like a liar—"

"They're not. At least you're not on the record as saying someone broke in. But if you didn't kill your husband, and he didn't kill himself, then someone else injected him with that overdose. Simple logic tells us that much."

"I didn't kill him."

"Your fingerprints are on the syringe. How'd they get there?"

"I don't know. I never handled his medical supplies, and those syringes come in a paper wrapper. If my prints are on a syringe, someone put them there."

The lawyer's mouth dips in a cynical smile. "You're kidding, right? I need you to be honest with me."

"I *am* being honest—I don't know what happened. After the banquet, we came home and I went to bed. I took a sleeping pill. In fact I took a double dose."

"Isn't that dangerous?"

"I didn't care." Erin lowers her gaze to the tabletop, where some unimaginative prisoner has scratched a series of vulgar suggestions. "I felt dead. A bomb could have gone off, and

I don't think I'd have heard it. The next morning, I woke up and went into the kitchen. When I finally checked on Jeffrey, he was dead."

"The medical examiner estimates the time of death at about 2:00 a.m.," Ms. Lester says, glancing at a paper in one of her stacks. "What time did you go to bed?"

Erin rubs her temple with her fingertips, trying to remember. "We came home…around midnight. I had a headache. I went to bed about an hour later."

"Did your husband go to bed before or after you?"

"Maybe a little after, but not much. He was tired, and he never let me go to bed without him."

Erin's pulse skips a beat when the lawyer shoots her a questioning look. "He never *let* you?" Ms. Lester asks.

She shrugs. "Jeff had strong opinions about certain things. He wanted us to be together…nearly all the time."

The lawyer consults her notes again. "What did you do between midnight and one? Did you talk about the evening? Did you argue?"

"I put away our formal wear and got ready for bed."

The lawyer stares at her, then blinks. "It takes you an hour to change clothes?"

"They were expensive clothes." Erin attempts a smile, but the effort feels more like a facial twitch.

"Erin." The lawyer shoves her papers aside and leans forward, her eyes widening. "I know you barely know me, but I'm your attorney. You can tell me anything, and I need you to tell me *everything* you can remember about that night. We might find some clue you've overlooked—something to give us an insight into what your husband was thinking and feeling. You don't want to spend the rest of your life in prison because he made a careless mistake, do you?"

Erin presses her lips together as tears sting her eyes. "His name was Jeffrey…and he rarely made mistakes."

Ms. Lester straightens and picks up her pen. "So tell me what happened after you and Jeffrey got home."

Erin studies her hands as a tear rolls down her cheek. "We had an argument. Jeffrey had been irritated with me all day. The argument started before the fundraiser began. He was yelling at me in the hotel suite when his dad came up to see if we were ready."

"What was the argument about?"

"I think—I think it started because I forgot to pack his silk socks."

Surprise flickers over the lawyer's face like heat lightning.

"Oh, I don't blame him for being upset. I meant to pack his socks, but in all the excitement I grabbed an ordinary nylon pair. We were busy in the suite all day, talking to party leaders and all, so we only had a few minutes to dress before the banquet. Jeffrey got upset when he couldn't find his silk socks. Like I said, it was all my fault."

The lawyer gives Erin an uncertain look. "You got into a fight...over socks."

Erin nods. "Jeffrey doesn't handle disappointment well. Anyway, when Antonio came upstairs, he asked me to leave the room. I did, but I stood at the bedroom door and heard him warn Jeff about being hard on me in public. That only made Jeffrey even more furious, so we argued again while we were waiting for the event to begin. Later, while we were dancing, he said he wasn't finished with me." She looks away as shame bubbles up from the secret place in her heart. "I knew I was going to get it when we got home."

"Wait a minute. What do you mean, 'get it'?"

Erin presses her hands to her flaming cheeks. In the five years she's been married to Jeffrey Tomassi, no one has dared ask this question. Evidence of his brutality has been viewed by hotel maids, family housekeepers, campaign workers, various relatives, even her father-in-law. All sorts of people have glimpsed her bruises and heard Jeffrey's shouting; they have seen the black look in his eye when he turned to her, upper lip curled and fist clenched....

But in the winding and torturous length of their marriage, no one has ever asked what he did when they were alone together.

"I don't think you want to know," she whispers, keeping her gaze lowered.

"I wouldn't ask if I didn't want an answer," Ms. Lester says, her voice clipped. "Let me put it this way—were you an abused wife? Did that man hit you?"

Without speaking, Erin closes her eyes and grips the hem of her prison shirt. She lifts it, knowing that her ribs are still faintly colored with greenish bruises.

She can't help hearing the other woman's quick intake of breath.

"Are you saying Jeffrey Tomassi did that on the night he died?"

Erin nods.

"That was nearly two weeks ago." Ms. Lester narrows her eyes. "Did the matrons see this when you were admitted? When they searched you?"

Erin feels her cheeks flame. "I told them I fell up the stairs."

"And they believed you?"

"They seemed to."

"Did your husband hit you often?"

Erin swallows. "As often as he liked."

"Do you have proof? Photographs? Were you ever treated at a hospital for your injuries?"

Erin drops her shirt. "Jeff was always clever. He hit me where it wouldn't show. He had me wear long sleeves when my arms were bruised. Once he broke my ribs, but he wouldn't let me go to the hospital."

"You should have gone." The words fall like rainwater from the lawyer's lips, spoken without understanding.

"That would only make things worse." Erin meets Ms. Lester's horrified gaze. "I was surrounded by people who knew what Jeffrey was doing. But they adored him and wouldn't allow anything to harm his image. It was easier to ignore me.... Besides, I filled a useful role."

"What, the candidate's punching bag?"

"Something like that. As long as Jeffrey could come home and take his frustrations out on me, they were pretty much spared from his tantrums. No one would ever admit it, but I think they were relieved I was around. He had this one friend…Terry Rhodes, who helped with the campaign… Anyway, Terry once saw him hit me. He turned and walked out of the room."

A livid hue spreads over the other woman's face. "No woman deserves to be beaten. You should have been an equal partner in his team—"

"How old are you, Ms. Lester?"

The question catches the lawyer by surprise. Her eyes widen and a blush deepens the color on her cheeks. "I'm almost thirty. And please, call me Briley."

"I'm twenty-eight. But right now I feel about ten years older than you…Briley."

The attorney leans back in her chair and crosses her arms as thought works in her eyes. "We could make a case for Jeffrey's being emotionally disturbed. He may have looked polished on the outside, but a man who beats his wife has obvious mental problems. We could theorize that he purposely injected himself with a massive dose of insulin because he was overcome with remorse for the way he treated you that evening."

Erin shakes her head. "I'm not sure you should mention those things."

"Why not?"

"I thought lawyers were supposed to be bright."

Briley exhales in a rush. "If you're thinking the abuse provides a motive…"

"Doesn't it?" Erin's voice cracks as she offers a truth she hasn't dared verbalize until this moment. "I can't tell you how many times I've wished Jeffrey were dead. I have, and I know it's wrong. But I didn't kill him. Murder is a mortal sin, and I'd never hurt anyone on purpose. I can't even kill a bug."

Briley lowers her hand to Erin's arm. "You need to let me be the lawyer. Let's get the facts of the case on the table, then we'll formulate a strategy. But first, I need to know everything about you and Jeffrey—where you met, how you got together, when his violence began. Can you take me back to the beginning?"

Erin dashes more wetness from her eyes, then takes a deep breath and nods.

Chapter Nineteen

Briley steps through the gates of the Oak Woods Cemetery and strides down the paved road that leads to her father's resting place. She breathes in the woodsy scent of the evergreen wreath in her arms, then shifts her gaze to study a group of tourists gathered around the red granite tombstone of Jesse Owens.

No crowds will ever gather around her father's memorial; his circle of influence did not extend far beyond Chicago's West Side. But he was everything to her—mother, father, pastor, teacher, adviser. She couldn't follow him into the ministry—she could never submit to a God who abandoned his servants at their most vulnerable—nor could she ever give herself as completely as he did. But there's no denying she is who she is because of what happened to him.

Her father's cemetery plot rests under an aging red cedar, its branches dusted with snow. She bends to brush a layer of powder from the top of the simple gravestone, then props her wreath against the granite face. After glancing around to be sure she won't be disturbing any other mourners, she steps back and takes a deep breath. "Hey, Dad. Sorry it's been a while."

In the distance, she hears the roar of passing traffic on East Sixty-seventh Street. No one will bother her, though. No one ever does.

"I have a new case—a murder trial. I wouldn't be surprised if one of the partners swooped in and took it from me, but so far they've left me alone. I'm a little nervous. The victim was high profile and the evidence against my client is pretty daunting. But there are extenuating circumstances...and you always told me never to judge a woman until I've walked a mile in her stilettos."

She smiles as the cedar rustles in evergreen applause. "I've got to put together a theory of the case, something I can believe well enough to sell to the jury. Trouble is, I'm not sure what I believe. My client seems sincere, but fingerprints don't lie. And the state's attorney has video proof that the husband and wife were alone that night. One of them had to do it, right? Either the husband or the wife?"

Beside the pathway, a streetlamp begins to glow, activated by the gloom seeping from a bruised and swollen sky. They should have snow tonight, a deep blanket of it.

"I know I'll figure something out," Briley tells her father. "Sure wish you were here. Timothy's not around much these days. We're still together, but he's taken on a new client, a movie star who's really messed up. He's not only an addict, he's also spoiled rotten. Apparently he needs Tim's approval to go to the bathroom."

Voices rise from somewhere beyond the crest of a hill, probably a tourist group making their way back to the main gate. They are cold, night is approaching, and this is no place for an unarmed woman to be alone after dark.

"I love you, Dad." She reaches out to adjust a drooping poinsettia petal in the wreath. "I miss you. And I'll be thinking of you at Christmas."

Chapter Twenty

Briley walks to her car with a more determined step on Tuesday morning. Since Timothy was unavailable last night, she spent the hours before bed doing online research. She learned that while the battered-woman's-syndrome defense is not often effective in getting women acquitted, in several cases it has been used to win a verdict of manslaughter instead of first-degree murder.

She unlocks her car and slides into the driver's seat. The problem with her situation is that Erin Tomassi says she did not kill her husband. If she continues to insist that she didn't administer the fatal injection, Briley may not be able to place the fateful syringe in her client's hand without impeaching Erin's testimony. And if Erin is proved to be a liar, the jury won't believe a thing she says.

She is three blocks from the jail when her cell phone rings. Without reading the caller ID, she hits the hands-free answer button on her steering wheel. "Hello?"

"Good morning, Ms. Lester."

For a moment, she can't place the voice. Then she groans. Travis Bystrowski. Who else would sound so confident and chipper at this hour?

"What can I do for you, Mr. Bystrowski?"

"Just thought you'd want to know that yesterday we interviewed a housekeeper who works for Antonio Tomassi. The woman reported seeing bruises on your client's back and ribs."

"So?" Briley turns at an intersection. "The matrons at the jail saw the bruises, too."

"Ah, but the housekeeper told our interviewer that Mrs. Tomassi claimed to receive those bruises in a fall on the stairs—but the stairs in Mrs. Tomassi's house are covered in very expensive, very plush carpeting. The housekeeper did a little snooping and asked her boss to confirm that fact."

Briley sighs. "Sounds like hearsay to me."

"The housekeeper came to us because she's convinced your client got tired of being beat up. Seems the woman really liked Jeffrey Tomassi."

"So did most of Chicago. And your point is…?"

Bystrowski laughs. "I'm trying to give you a break, Briley. Correct me if I'm wrong, but isn't this your first capital case?"

She scowls as she steers around a slow-moving pickup. "I'm not as green as you think."

"Just wanted to welcome you to the big leagues. By the way—" he pauses, his voice shifting to a more somber note "—I thought your name seemed familiar, so I looked you up. Wasn't your father Daniel Lester?"

Despite the steady blast from her car's heater, a chill travels down her spine. "You always do research on your opponents?"

"I was in law school when your dad was killed. Our criminal law professor asked us to follow the trial."

Briley bites the inside of her lip, unnerved by the thought of her father's case being used as part of a law curriculum.

"Anyway, I wasn't surprised to hear that Daniel Lester's daughter had become a lawyer. I am surprised to find you working as a defense attorney. I would have bet that you'd opt for the truth-and-justice side of the courtroom."

"Life is anything but predictable, Mr. Bystrowski."

"Would you relax? We're not sitting across the aisle from each other yet. I'm trying to help you out."

She brakes at an intersection and glances in the rearview mirror, half expecting to see Bystrowski smirking in the backseat. The car behind her honks when the light changes. "Maybe I opted for defense because of the bigger paycheck," she says, proceeding through the slush-covered crosswalk. "Or maybe I like trouncing overconfident prosecutors who overstep their bounds."

"Now I've offended you." A conciliatory note fills Bystrowski's voice. "And I'd better let you get busy. If you need anything from my office, you let me know, okay?"

She hesitates. "Will do."

"But be careful with that abused-wife defense. The American Psychiatric Association doesn't recognize it. I don't know if you want to take the risk."

She pulls into the parking lot across the street from Division Four of the Cook County Jail. "Thanks, Counselor. I'll be sure to keep that in mind."

Which is more sympathetic—an abused woman who suffers in silence, or one who rises up to defend herself?

Briley drops her purse and briefcase onto the conveyor belt at the jail's security station and considers various angles of the battered-woman defense. Bystrowski's mention of the APA's not accepting battered woman's syndrome means nothing. The jury box won't be filled with members of the APA. But if she makes Erin's status as a battered wife a vital part of her case theory, the prosecutor could bring in an expert witness to debunk anything she says about battered women. If she's successful in convincing the jury that Erin ultimately acted in self-defense, the odds are good that they'll still convict her of manslaughter, which translates into years of prison time.

So maybe she shouldn't use the abuse to mitigate Erin's alleged actions. Perhaps the domestic violence could be portrayed as a symptom of Jeffrey Tomassi's disturbed mental state, a state that ultimately led him to take his own life through an insulin overdose. The scenario is plausible, but how does she reconcile Erin's fingerprints on the syringe with her statement to the police? She told a detective she never gave her husband insulin injections.

Briley signs in at the visitor's center, walks through the air puffer, and makes banal conversation about the weather as the guard leads her to the chilly interview room. She keeps her coat on as she pulls a notepad, recorder, and pen from her briefcase, then she rubs her bare hands together. The state of Illinois must be doing its part to save energy by keeping the jail thermostat set at sixty.

The door opens, and a guard leads her client into the room. Erin stands motionless as the guard removes her handcuffs and shackles, then she pushes her hair away from her face and sits across from Briley. She looks better this morning, less wan and washed out, but she doesn't return Briley's smile. Instead, she props her elbows on the table and drops her head into her hands.

Briley glances toward the door. "What's wrong? Are you having trouble with one of the other inmates? With a guard?"

Erin's shoulders rise and fall. "I need to tell you something," she says, not meeting Briley's gaze. "And you're going to think I'm crazy. But I'm not, honestly I'm not—unless all crazy people go through what I'm experiencing." She releases a hollow laugh. "Sometimes I think I must be insane—otherwise, why would I have married Jeffrey? I loved him, but it takes more than love to make a marriage work."

Briley settles back in her chair, quietly wishing she had invited one of the more experienced associates along for this interview. Maybe all murder defendants declare themselves to be insane during the third interview. Maybe tomorrow Erin will claim to have found Jesus. Maybe these dramatics are nothing unusual, and Briley should prepare for even more outlandish claims in the days ahead.

She pulls her notepad and pen closer. "Why don't you begin at the beginning?" she says, smoothing the skepticism from her voice. "I'm here to listen, and I want to understand you. Only by knowing your entire story will I be able to put the pieces together and present the best possible defense."

Erin shakes her head. "I'm not sure where to begin."

"Well, what kind of family did you have? Where did you grow up? What were your goals and aspirations?"

"My family? I'm not even sure the word applies." Erin folds her arms across her chest and draws a deep breath. "My father died when I was young. I had an older brother, but he didn't live with us, so I barely knew him. The neighborhood was quiet, run-down."

Briley struggles to hide her surprise. The newspaper article was right about Erin's working-class origins. Somehow she'd pictured this woman growing up in a fully staffed white colonial surrounded by manicured green lawns. "Sounds lonely."

"It was. I would have gone crazy if not for my invisible friend. My mom used to tease me about her, but Lisa Marie was around when my mom was indisposed, so I guess it's only natural that I came to depend on her."

Briley jots the name on her legal pad. "Lisa Marie is what you called your invisible friend?"

"Yes."

"What did you mean by 'indisposed'? Was your mother an invalid?"

Erin chuffs softly. "She was a drunk. We lived on food stamps and welfare, which probably explains why I was attracted to Jeffrey. I never knew any luxury growing up, and Jeff and his family offered the kind of stability I'd always dreamed of."

"Where'd you meet him?"

"Chicago State. One night after class, I went to a party with some friends. Jeffrey was there. We met, we talked. After that, we were almost always together."

Briley makes a note and glances at her client. Erin is wearing an inward look of deep abstraction; wherever she's gone, she doesn't want to leave. "What are you thinking?"

The woman shudders slightly and rubs her arms. "I was thinking about Lisa Marie. I remember being surprised when I realized Mom couldn't hear her—after all, I heard her voice in my head all the time. But as I got older, Mom told me I was stupid to keep pretending. So I stopped talking to Lisa Marie, but she didn't stop talking to me."

Briley's pen halts on the legal pad. Is this woman trying to make a case for schizophrenia? "Are you saying—" she proceeds with caution "—that your invisible friend *still* talks to you?"

Erin rakes her hand through her hair. "I told you it sounds crazy."

"That's reassuring. I'm no psychiatrist, but I've heard that crazy people think they're perfectly sane."

Erin stares at her, then manages a brief smile. "Okay— yes, I still hear her, but only in my dreams. Sometimes I'll go to sleep and she'll be waiting to talk to me about something. When I was a teenager, she knew all about Mom and how things were at home. When I'd want to run away, Lisa Marie would calm me down and tell me that things would be worse on the street. I learned to listen to her. Her advice was always better than my mother's."

Briley presses her lips together. She can't remember much from her college psychology classes, but surely there's some part of the human mind that reasons with the other parts when they're under stress. This is probably a normal function, like the conscience reminding us of the consequences of unlawful behavior....

Still, an interview with a forensic psychologist is definitely in order. The firm keeps a file of experts in the field, but if Briley calls a shrink to testify, the prosecution will call an expert of their own. Net result: zero gain.

She clicks the end of her pen in a burst of nervous energy. "Do you know what Lisa Marie looks like?"

Erin frowns. "In my dream, she looks like me. That probably means something, but I've never seen her any other way. She doesn't morph into anything, if that's what you mean."

"I don't mean anything. I'm only trying to understand."

Briley snaps the end of her pen again. "Did Lisa Marie speak to you the night Jeffrey died?"

"I told you, I was out cold from the sleeping pills."

Briley smiles. "So if you're not still dreaming of her…"

"That's just it, I am. Weeks go by and I don't see her, but I dreamed of her last night. She told me something, then she said I should tell you. You're going to think I'm making this up, but I'm not, I swear I'm not."

Briley braces herself. "And what are you supposed to tell me?"

The corners of Erin's mouth tighten. "She did it. After I went to sleep that night, Lisa Marie killed Jeffrey."

Chapter Twenty-One

Antonio Tomassi steps off the elevator and into a branch of the Cook County State's Attorney's Office, a space crowded with L-shaped desks, steel-and-vinyl chairs, and myriad human bodies. Fluorescent lights flicker overhead while the air vibrates with the hum of fax machines and computers. Tired-looking men and women work behind desks, either tapping on keyboards or squinting at papers as they tilt their heads to hold telephones against their shoulders. Every one of them looks like central casting sent them to play the role of anonymous civil servant.

Without glancing behind him, Antonio gestures to Jason. "Yes, Papa?"

"Who is the man we need to see?"

Jason steps forward and pulls a slip of paper from his pocket. "Travis Bystrowski."

Antonio steps into the room, narrowing his gaze as he scans the nameplates on several doors opening off the main area. He knows better than to expect the state's top dog to try his son's case, but he hopes the man has assigned the trial to someone with experience and a hunger for justice—

He points to a door in the far corner of the room. "There. Bystrowski."

"A Polack." Jason shakes his head. "Wouldn't you know we'd draw a Polack?"

"Shut up." Antonio lifts a warning finger. "You don't say a word in that room, understand? You listen and let me talk."

Without waiting for his son's response, Antonio shoul-

ders his way through the sea of government workers and
cheap furniture. The door to Bystrowski's office is closed,
but through the frosted glass he glimpses a human form
behind a desk. He raps on the door.

"Come in."

Bystrowski—a young man with short hair and a lean
look—glances up from his reading when Antonio steps
through the doorway. "Can I help you?"

Antonio removes his hat. "My name is Antonio Tomassi,
and this is my son, Jason. I understand you are the prosecutor assigned to my son's case."

Bystrowski's brow furrows until the name registers.
"Tomassi—Jeffrey Tomassi." He stands and offers his hand.
"May I extend my sympathies to you both? And yes, I'll be
prosecuting the case."

Antonio shakes the man's hand, then gestures to the
chairs crowded against the wall. "May we?"

"Certainly." Bystrowski waits until Antonio has been
seated before he settles back in his seat. "How can I help
you, gentlemen?"

Antonio looks around, taking in the diplomas on the back
wall, the newspapers piled in the corner, the nameplate pro-
claiming Travis Bystrowski an assistant state's attorney, the
cigarette stubs in the ashtray. A half smile tugs at his mouth
as he points to a length of curled ashes. "Are state's attorneys allowed to smoke in public buildings?"

"Um, no." Bystrowski has the decency to flush as he
dumps the ashtray into the trash. "I often work late, and if
I'm alone up here—"

"Don't worry, Mr. Bystrowski, your secret is safe with
me." Antonio smiles, without humor. "We want to support
you in any way possible. We want justice for Jeffrey."

Bystrowski glances from Antonio to Jason, as if he
doubts the sincerity of their stated intention. "That's what
the state wants, as well. How much do you know about our
progress with the case?"

"We know Erin has been arrested."

The attorney nods. "That's correct. She was arraigned yesterday, and pleaded not guilty."

Antonio barely resists the urge to spit. "She killed him, of course. Who else could have?"

"The evidence certainly points to her," Bystrowski says. "The police found no indication of a break-in. And her fingerprints were on the murder weapon."

"The trial will be concluded quickly, then? No surprises from the defense?"

"Well—" Bystrowski spreads his hands "—the defense can try to sell any cock-and-bull theory to win sympathy for the defendant. Sometimes, particularly if the defendant has money, they can hire expert witnesses that can convince a jury of almost anything."

"You need not worry about the defense attorney," Antonio says, satisfaction warming his face. "The woman is inexperienced in these matters."

Bystrowski gives him an uncertain smile. "You know Briley Lester?"

Antonio shrugs. "I know she is no threat. Not only is she unskilled, but Erin has no money for experts and such. Jeffrey gave her everything, and she killed him for more."

Interest flickers in Bystrowski's eyes. "We've been unable to confirm details of your son's will."

"I'll be sure my lawyer gives you a copy." Antonio gestures to Jason. "See that it's done, will you? But though Erin stood to inherit their considerable joint assets, she cannot inherit if she killed him, right? Such injustice should not be allowed."

"The Illinois slayer statute prohibits a murderer from profiting from the crime," Bystrowski says. "So yes, you're right. If Erin is convicted of killing your son, she cannot inherit the estate. It would go to whomever is next of kin."

Antonio nods. "That would be Jason. It is only right that Jeff's estate should go to his twin. My boys were as close as a hand and glove. It is *not* right—" he pauses as a rise of feeling chokes his words "—that they should be parted."

Bystrowski remains silent until Antonio gains control of his emotions, then he folds his hands. "Mr. Tomassi, I promise I will do everything I can to put your son's killer behind bars."

Antonio meets the prosecutor's gaze head-on. "Behind bars is not enough, my friend. I want a life for a life, one fatal injection for another. That is justice, and that is what I will have."

Chapter Twenty-Two

Briley gapes at her client in a paralysis of incredulity. "Your invisible friend," she repeats, "killed your husband."

Erin's face disappears behind her hands. "I know you think I'm only looking for a way out. But I'm not crazy. I'm trying to tell you the truth."

Briley takes a deep breath and feels a dozen different emotions collide. So long, battered-woman's defense; hello, insanity plea.

The steady pulse of an approaching headache begins to pound at her temple. "Erin," she begins, "when I came in today, I was thinking that we might have a good chance of convincing the jury that your husband committed suicide. Even though the police report says your fingerprints are on the syringe and the insulin bottle, that's not inconceivable if a husband and wife share the same bathroom."

"But it's not the truth." Erin drops her hands and looks across the table, her eyes gleaming with determination. "I'm telling you the God's honest truth, because I want to be completely transparent with you. I don't know anything about defending someone in court, but I want you to know what actually happened. Whether or not you believe me, the truth is that I didn't know what happened until last night."

"Until Lisa Marie told you. In a dream."

Erin nods.

Briley squeezes the bridge of her nose. She should have listened to her college adviser and minored in psychology. Right now, she could use a crash course in delusions and body language…or maybe an expert opinion on why a client would invent an implausible story when a believable defense could be stitched together using most of the available evidence.

"We're going to bring in an expert." Briley looks into the woman's resolute blue eyes. "I want you to talk to a psychologist. But if we bring someone in, the prosecution is going to counter with a psychologist of their own. Say whatever you like to the examining doctors, but know this—if you're lying, they're likely to see right through you. I'd advise you to tell them the truth, in the simplest terms possible."

"I'm not a liar." Erin speaks with quiet firmness. "I may be weak and cowardly, but I never even lied to Jeff, and telling *him* the truth got me into more trouble than you can know."

"You lied to the prison matron." Briley tilts her head. "And to your father-in-law's housekeeper. You told them that you fell going up the stairs."

A flush rises from Erin's neckline, blotching her pale complexion. "I—I forgot about that."

"Every word you say matters." Briley picks up her pen again. "Let's talk about your relationship with your husband. What convinced you to marry Jeffrey Tomassi?"

Erin shifts her gaze to the wall. "Jeffrey was working for his father when we met. I was a senior in college, but he seemed so polished. Mature. I couldn't believe he was interested in me."

"In college, did you date many other men?"

"I hardly dated at all. I wanted to concentrate on my studies. But once I started dating Jeffrey, I was doing something with him almost every night. I finally had to tell him I couldn't see him on weeknights because I had to study. That only seemed to make him more persistent. Before I knew it, he proposed."

"And you accepted?"

"Not right away. I adored him, but I wanted to be independent for a while, so I turned him down. After graduation, I started an event-planning business, and Jeffrey was my first client. I arranged a birthday party for his father, and at the event Antonio welcomed me like I was already one of the family. Jason seemed to like me, too, as well as the girls. They were all so warm and friendly, so *Italian*—they showed me everything a family could be. So when Jeffrey proposed again, I accepted."

"When did you marry him?"

"Five years ago, in September. If I'd been wiser, I might have realized that every time I refused him, he became more determined to have me—not in a romantic sense, but like a possession. We hadn't been married a week when he asked me to quit my job. I didn't want to, but he bought the brownstone in Lincoln Park and said taking care of the house would take up all my time. I wanted to please him, so I disbanded my little company and dedicated myself to making Jeffrey happy."

"What did he do to make *you* happy?"

Erin blinks. "Well…he'd say he did a lot. He gave me a beautiful home, hired a housekeeper and a gardener. When we entertained, I was supposed to bring in a cook and a decorator and a party planner—and that irritated me, because I am good at that sort of thing. It didn't take me long to realize he didn't trust me to handle the smallest detail."

"Was he attentive? When you were alone together, did he behave as though he loved you?"

Erin manages a tremulous smile. "Jeffrey loved me…like he loved his Bentley. He loved owning me. If I complained about us not spending meaningful time together—time where we talked or did something I wanted to do—he would say that I had everything a woman could want, so what right did I have to complain?" Her gaze drops to the scarred tabletop. "After a couple of years, he began hitting me to reinforce whatever lesson he wanted to teach. And I learned. I learned to keep quiet and do what I was told."

Briley bites her lower lip, barely managing to quell the anger thrumming beneath her breastbone. Men like Jeffrey

Tomassi shouldn't be allowed to marry. If they managed to get to the altar before revealing their true colors, they should be incarcerated after the first blow.

She'd join Bystrowski's team if it meant she could lock men like Jeffrey Tomassi away.

"It's a good thing—" she clicks her pen in a flurry of frustration "—you didn't have children. Imagine how frightened you'd be for them." When Erin's chin quivers, Briley knows she's hit a sensitive spot. "During the marriage…were you ever pregnant?"

Erin presses her hand to her face, her eyes bright with repressed tears. "I wanted a baby more than anything," she whispers in a ragged voice. "I knew I'd have to be careful to make sure he didn't hurt our child, but I was sure he wouldn't. After all, Antonio adored his children—he revered them, gave them everything they asked for. And he desperately wanted a grandson. He dropped hints every time we were together."

Briley pulls a tissue from her purse and hands it to her client. "So…?"

Erin takes the tissue and sniffs. "I have a brother. He's thirty-two, he has Down syndrome, and he lives in an adult group home. I don't see Roger often, but I'd never do anything to hurt him."

Briley lifts her chin. Erin has mentioned the brother before, but only in passing. She nods as the pieces fall into place. "Let me guess—Jeffrey wasn't exactly thrilled to hear about your brother."

Erin snorts. "He was furious. If I'd told him about Roger *before* the wedding, I think he would have called the entire thing off. Maybe that's why I didn't tell him until our first Christmas, when I was making out our shopping list."

"That's a shame. Other politicians have been up front about relatives with disabilities. No one would have criticized Jeffrey. They might have actually praised him for caring about people with special challenges."

"That's what I thought, but Jeffrey wasn't about to care for Roger until I convinced him that it'd be better for us to place Roger in a private group home than have his story leaked to the press. I hated the thought of hiding my brother away, but Jeffrey was terrified by the idea that we—that I— might have a baby with a genetic problem. After he found out about my brother, he convinced himself that my genes were defective. He wanted a child—he thought it'd be a plus to have a son on the campaign trail—but he forced me to go to a geneticist before he'd even consider the idea. He told me that if the tests proved my DNA was free from genetic diseases, we could have a baby." She shakes her head. "He had it all planned. If everything worked out, our baby would be six or seven by the time Jeffrey was ready to run for president. I knew he could imagine himself standing before a crowd with a child on his hip, promising to put new blood in the White House."

"Where did you fit in that picture?"

Erin's mouth twists. "I suppose he either saw me standing beside him, waving like the perfect little wife...or dead." She pillows her head on her arms and wearily closes her eyes. "That's why your suicide theory won't ring true to anyone who knew Jeffrey. His father, his siblings, his closest advisers—they all know how determined he was to win a congressional seat and then tackle the White House. Some people joke about such things, but Jeffrey was dead serious. He wanted to win. He did not want to die."

Chapter Twenty-Three

Antonio slows his step as he comes down the winding staircase, his eyes gravitating to the twenty-foot spruce in the foyer. The decorators have done exceptional work: the tree shines and sparkles with hundreds of lights, dozens of blown-glass bulbs, and a boxful of traditional Tomassi Christmas ornaments. Next to the tree stands the *ceppo,* a wooden pyramid with shelves.

He pauses on the bottom step to scan the battered "tree of light," one of the family's few remaining Old Country traditions. A nativity set rests at the bottom, and a star hangs from the uppermost point. When his children were small, small gifts of fruit, candy, and glitter-encrusted pinecones crowded the interior shelves. He mounted candles at the ends of each shelf, and tiny pennants fluttered in the candles' warm breath.

No one rolls pinecones in glitter anymore; none of his children would appreciate an apple or orange for Christmas. But they have continued one Italian tradition, a ritual that far surpasses anything the Americans have invented. Instead of writing selfish letters to Santa, Antonio's children write letters to their papa to tell him how much they love him. These letters are placed under his plate before Christmas dinner, and during the meal Antonio pretends that he's unaware of the missives hidden under his meal. Then, just after the serving of the panettone, he discovers the letters—aha!—and reads them aloud so that everyone can share in the joy.

Jeffrey always wrote the best letters. Jason is an adequate

writer, at best, and the girls are sweet and grateful, but Jeffrey had a way of making Antonio feel young and hopeful. Every year his letters grew richer, while Antonio's hopes for his favorite son grew brighter—

He steps off the lowest stair and approaches the *ceppo*, then fingers the silver star dangling from a ribbon. Grief strikes like a blow to his stomach, forcing him to drop the ornament and step back while he gasps for breath.

This Christmas will not be like any other. Despite tradition and his five remaining children, brooding sorrow will saturate this holiday. As painful as grief is, the most horrible aspect of this tragedy is feeling impotent in the face of intolerable injustice. Antonio is used to being obeyed; he orders and people run to do his bidding. Yet the American system crawls toward judgment, careful to give killers the protection and consideration they did not offer their victims.

But he will not sit idly by. He will let the American court proceed with its plans, but he will work behind the scenes. He will do whatever he must to be certain Jeffrey's death is avenged.

Flushed with the prospect of action, Antonio strides into his study, closes the door, and picks up the phone.

Chapter Twenty-Four

How can a perfectly rational twenty-eight-year-old woman believe in a murderous phantasm?

The question hounds Briley, even popping into her brain when she wakes on Wednesday morning. When no obvious answer springs to mind, she knows she's in for hours of reading and research.

When she slides behind her desk at the office, she finds an urgent e-mail from her boss: Need you to meet with us on the Majestic Elevator matter. How's 9:00 a.m.?

She glances at the computer clock. She's already late. She should have checked her e-mail before leaving the house.

Five minutes later she's in Franklin's office, listening to Jim Myers recap a recent deposition of an elevator mechanic. She glances from Myers to Franklin, not sure why she's been summoned when a far more pressing case waits on her desk.

When Myers finishes his report, she waves for Franklin's attention. "I'm not exactly sure why I'm here." She smiles at Myers, not wanting him to think that she's complaining about him.

"I want you to assist Myers on this one," Franklin says, peering over the top of his reading glasses. "We need to depose the plaintiff's coworker, because he witnessed the accident. I'll be sending you to do that."

"Me?"

"The guy's a hardnose. I think he'll tone down the machismo if we send a woman to take the deposition."

Briley looks from Franklin to Myers. Have any of the

other female associates had to face this kind of subtle sexism? On a purely practical note, however, the man might have a point. "I'd be happy to help," she says. "But this is the first I've heard of the matter."

Franklin looks at Myers and jerks his thumb in her direction. "Fill her in, will you?"

Myers crosses his leg at the ankle. "We're defending the Majestic Elevator Company in a lawsuit filed over a year ago. The plaintiff is a twenty-four-year-old guy who slammed into a pair of elevator doors while horsing around with his buddies on the sixth floor of his apartment building. He popped the doors off their tracks and fell down the shaft, breaking both legs and an arm."

"Ouch." Briley grimaces. "That can't be his interpretation of the event."

Myers grins. "Of course not. He would have us believe that he barely touched the doors and they flew open, forcing him to be sucked in by the evil elevator monster that lives in the shaft."

"Sarcasm—" she struggles to hide a smile "—can hurt you."

"Not in here, it can't." He punches her shoulder. "Lighten up, Lester. You know some of these cases are ridiculous. Since when are companies supposed to protect people from that kind of stupidity?"

"Are you sure the guy's pals didn't pry open the doors and throw him down the shaft?" She frowns. "If that's what happened, maybe *pals* isn't the right word."

"I'm arguing that he was negligent because he and his friends were drunk and they were playing tackle football in the sixth-floor lobby." Myers jiggles his bent knee, a testament to the uncontrolled energy of young men. "He's lucky he survived."

"I still don't see how the elevator company had anything to do with his injuries. Is he saying there's a problem with the design, the maintenance, or both?"

"So far they're beating around the bush on that, but the plaintiff's attorney claims Majestic was negligent because the doors shouldn't give way when a klutz like his client tries to plow through them. But any hard blow can knock the sliding doors off their track. What is Majestic supposed to do, surround the elevator with a vault?"

Briley shakes her head. "Seems to me he should be suing the building owners. Don't they maintain the doors?"

"The owners, a mom-and-pop landlord, are codefendants. They say, of course, we're the ones with the maintenance contract, so it's our problem. And the plaintiff's lawyer probably figures Majestic has deeper pockets. They install most of the elevators in the Midwest."

Franklin gives Myers a satisfied smile and turns to Briley. "Got that?"

She nods.

"Give Nancy your avoid dates so we can coordinate with the plaintiff's attorney." Franklin taps the arm of his chair, then lifts his hand. "By the way, Ms. Lester—how are you coming with the Tomassi case?"

Briley clears her throat, surprised by his reference to her case. "Erin Tomassi's arraignment took place Monday morning," she says. "She pleaded not guilty. I kicked off informal discovery by interviewing her at the jail, and met with her again yesterday. I'm beginning to wonder if I ought to consider an insanity defense."

Her boss's mouth takes on an unpleasant twist. "Do you think she might not be competent to stand trial?"

"She certainly seems competent. But I'm going to have her evaluated by a forensic psychologist. We'll see what the shrink says before formulating a case theory."

She waits, braced for an objection—the approach is too expensive, too time-consuming, or too complicated—but Franklin says nothing else. Nor does he thank her for her efforts and state that he'd better assign the case to someone more experienced.

Instead, he reaches for the coffee decanter and pours himself another cup. "Thanks, everyone." He nods at them above the rim of his mug. "Good work all around."

Myers falls into step with Briley as she leaves the boss's office. "Sorry about all this. I told Franklin I'd be happy to take the elevator guy's deposition, but he wants you to do it."

"I don't mind, but I hope it doesn't interfere with my current case. Franklin seems to think I can handle it alone, but I'm not so sure. I need to do a lot of research, and there are people to interview—"

Myers stops and lowers his voice. "Is your client really crazy?"

Briley shakes her head. "I don't think so. I get this feeling that she watched an episode of *Law & Order* and decided to use one of the plots for her defense. She has developed…a delusion."

Myers gapes in pleased surprise. "What kind of delusion are we talking about?"

"You wouldn't believe me if I told you." She gives him a rueful smile. "I was half hoping Franklin would transfer the case to someone else. I'd be a little disappointed, but in the long run it'd be a relief to walk away from this one."

Myers grins. "I could tell you were ticked when he said he wanted you to take our witness's deposition."

She shrugs. "I'll fit it in, if you can get me a summation and a list of questions. How long will it take, a couple of hours? A full morning?"

"In a perfect world, sure. But the guy lives in Washington State, so you'll lose at least two days in travel time."

Two days of travel and a day for the deposition means three days away from home, her murder case, and Timothy. "That's three days." She meets Myers's gaze. "I can't be gone three days."

"Why not? You like Starbucks. I hear Seattle has one on every corner."

"Can't we do the deposition by phone or video link? It'd

be a lot less expensive for our client, plus we've got the holidays to consider—"

"They don't mind paying for the advantage of face-to-face. They want your reading of the witness and his credibility, plus you've got that female thing going for you. When you smile, Lester, you can be quite disarming." Myers grins. "Want me to book your flight?"

She exhales through clenched teeth. "Thanks, but I'll do it myself."

And as she walks away, she considers the possibility that in a week or two she may feel as trapped and miserable as Erin Tomassi.

How is a woman supposed to have a personal life with a work schedule like this?

Briley retreats into her office, grateful for a few hours of uninterrupted time in which to work on her theory of the Tomassi case. She opens the file and studies the police report, which includes a copy of the crime scene's fingerprint analysis, a report remarkable primarily because no fingerprints save those of the victim, the accused, and an unknown third person, probably the housekeeper, were found at the crime scene. Furthermore, the syringe found in the trash can revealed only one set of prints—and the partial print on the plunger is an exact match for Erin Tomassi's left thumb.

The evidence is so tight, she might need wire cutters to unravel the prosecution's case.

She shuffles through the papers in the folder and finds the statement filed by Detective Mark Malone. In a conversation recorded the morning after the murder, Erin Tomassi told Malone that she never administered her husband's insulin. Unless she killed Jeffrey, there is no reason for her thumbprint to be on the plunger of any syringe, especially one found in the trash and not in the special receptacle for the safe disposal of used needles. *If the victim had self-admin-*

istered the overdose, Malone wrote, *his prints should have been on the wrapper, the cap, and the syringe. They were not.*

In her law school days, Briley dreamed of defending an *innocent* client in her first murder trial. Too bad those dreams have gone the way of her belief in Santa. Sighing, she consults her notes. Despite Bystrowski's warning, she ought to give the battered-wife defense serious consideration. After all, the concept of necessity usually supersedes that of immediacy. If Erin believed her husband would one day kill her in a fit of temper, she had the right to defend herself even though she was not under direct threat.

But did that give her the right to kill him while he slept?

Selling that concept to a jury would be difficult. First, she'd have to produce credible and sympathetic witnesses who would testify to the abuse Erin suffered. Given the hero-worship surrounding Jeffrey Tomassi, such witnesses might be hard to find.

Second, she'd have to establish that Erin feared for her life, and Erin is probably the only person on earth who could testify to that. Third, she'd have to establish Erin's credibility, and Erin has already lied to Antonio Tomassi's housekeeper about the source of her bruises. If Briley calls the housekeeper or a jail matron to testify about the signs of abuse they witnessed, she'll expose her client as a liar. Fourth, she'd have to call expert witnesses to testify about the psychology of battered woman's syndrome, but a preliminary Westlaw search revealed that the field is rife with "experts" whose theories are nothing but junk science and patently unprovable. Bystrowski would pick them off like ducks in a shooting gallery.

Finally, murder as self-defense rarely results in a get-out-of-jail-free card. Other women who claimed the battered-woman defense have been found guilty of manslaughter and sentenced to prison time.

Briley turns a page in her trial notebook. When one case theory presents too many obstacles, or doesn't fit with the evidence, it's time to consider another. Mental illness? Always risky, no matter how many voices the defendant hears in her dreams. A trial based on a plea of insanity has to be divided into two phases: the first phase determines the defendant's guilt or innocence of the crime; the second determines whether or not the defendant is sane. If Erin Tomassi is judged guilty and then insane, she could be sent to a mental hospital for years.

If sanity is not an issue… Briley considers the arguments of diminished capacity and intoxication. Erin told Detective Malone she took a double dose of Ambien, and some sleep aids have been known to cause parasomnia—behaviors like sleepwalking and unconscious eating. The sleepwalking defense has been used in murder trials, but does it apply in this case? A quick search of the Illinois criminal code reveals that intoxication is not a valid defense for criminal conduct unless the intoxicated condition was "involuntarily produced." Erin willingly took the sleeping pills…but she couldn't have known that they would produce parasomnia.

Briley slips out of her office and walks to the law library at the end of the hallway. The firm owns an impressive collection of law books, most stacked on floor-to-ceiling shelves, but hundreds exist in digital editions. A large conference table occupies the center of the room, a computer monitor waiting at each seat. William Hughes, the law librarian, looks up when she enters the room.

"Good afternoon, Ms. Lester," he calls, one hand rising to adjust his bow tie. "Can I help you find something?"

"It's Briley." She scans the intimidating shelves. "What do you know about sleepwalking as a murder defense?"

"Murder? That's not your usual purview, is it?"

"No," she answers, her voice dry. "But apparently Mr. Franklin thinks I'm up to the challenge."

William rolls his chair toward the closest computer and sets to work, his fingers clattering the keyboard. "Seems to me that defense was recently addressed by a medical doctor after a rather bizarre murder. A man stabbed his wife forty-four times, then pulled on gloves and dragged her to the pool, where he held her underwater until she drowned. A neighbor saw the drowning and called the police. By the time the cops arrived, the man had changed clothes, wrapped up the evidence, and tucked the bundle in the trunk of his Volvo. The police took him to the station, where he magically awoke and claimed no memory of the murder. But he did remember to mention he was a frequent sleepwalker."

Briley watches over the librarian's shoulder as he enters search words in the LexisNexis database. An instant later the monitor fills with case digests and a law review article analyzing the "sleepwalking defense."

William looks up at her. "You want this printed or e-mailed?"

"Was the defendant acquitted?"

"Guilty of murder in the first-degree. The jury couldn't get past the fact that he stopped to put on gloves. Sleepwalkers aren't supposed to engage in complex actions."

"E-mail it to me, please." Briley taps her chin as the document disappears. If Erin Tomassi has a history of parasomnia, Briley might be able to convince a jury that a woman could fill a syringe and inject her husband in the middle of a deep sleep. A dutiful wife might even commit such a subconscious act in an effort to be helpful. Though the actions are slightly complex, Erin has undoubtedly witnessed her husband doing the same thing hundreds of times. Furthermore, like a guileless sleepwalker, she made no effort to disguise her crime—she didn't hide the syringe, wipe her fingerprints off the bottle, or flee the scene.

Sleepwalking might be a workable defense.

"My client says she took Ambien," she says. "Anything on that?"

William chuckles. "You've hit the mother lode. Ambien has been used as a defense ever since Patrick Kennedy crashed his car into a security barricade near the U.S.

Capitol. He blamed it on a mixture of Ambien and some other drug."

"Remind me." Briley slides into the chair next to the librarian. "I'm fuzzy on the details."

He taps on the keyboard, then points to the computer monitor. "Right here. The congressman attributed his car crash—and his insistence that he was rushing to a vote at 2:45 a.m.—to a combination of Ambien and Phenergan."

He grips the mouse and clicks through a series of articles. "Ambien has been blamed for everything from sleepers' driving, eating, cooking, and having auto accidents, but most investigations reveal that the patient didn't take the drug properly. The label clearly says Ambien shouldn't be mixed with other medications, and shouldn't be taken unless the patient has set aside at least seven hours for sleep."

"My patient didn't mix medications," Briley says, thinking aloud. "And she didn't take it until she was ready for bed. So one could argue that the parasomnia was an involuntary reaction."

William leans back and uses one finger to smooth his mustache. "Did she do anything between taking the pills and going to sleep?"

"Besides examining the bruises the husband inflicted on her rib cage? I don't think so."

The line of William's mouth tightens. "I meant, did she do anything to set up the crime? To prepare for it?"

"I'm sure she didn't." Briley studies the last screen again, then nudges his shoulder. "Can I have a copy of that article, too?"

"Sure. Say…" He turns, his brown eyes crinkling at the corners. "You wouldn't happen to be working on the Tomassi case, would you?"

"Did Franklin send a memo around?"

"I guessed. The Tomassi family has been a client of this firm for years, so I expected one of our attorneys to defend the wife." The corner of his mouth twists as he looks back at the screen. "I didn't think it'd be you."

"Trust me, I was as surprised as you are."

"Who did they assign as cocounsel? Who's your research assistant?"

Briley stares at him. So, she isn't the only one to be surprised by Franklin's stinginess with the firm's resources. "They gave me squat," she says. "And the client's estate is frozen. I'm going to petition the court for funds to hire a private investigator and a forensic psychologist."

"Count me in." William gives her a broad smile. "I've been a fan of the Tomassis for years. I'd like to help."

Briley studies him. "Were you a fan of the husband or the wife? Because if it's the husband—"

"I don't like politicians. Blue-eyed angels, though, are right up my alley."

She stiffens. "Are you planning to help me or hit on my client?"

William drops his jaw. "I'm shocked, Counselor, to hear you suggest such a thing. You can trust me to be a complete professional during the trial. But after you get the widow acquitted, I might drop her a note to see how she's doing." He shakes his head when a photo of Erin Tomassi appears on the computer screen. "She is drop-dead gorgeous, no pun intended."

Briley pushes away from the table, a little disconcerted to think of the sweater-vested librarian fixating on her client. "I'll take you up on that offer to help. I could use a fresh pair of eyes." She stands and picks up her legal pad. "Let me know if you think of a surefire way to convince a jury that our blue-eyed angel's not a cold-blooded killer."

Chapter Twenty-Five

"Hold on a minute, will you?" Dr. Pamela Lu, one of several doctors Briley is consulting for her case, turns away from the phone. Briley is afraid the psychologist is pausing to laugh out loud, but the woman coughs instead. "Sorry... tickle in my throat," she says, coming back on the line. "So, your client says an alter killed her husband?"

Briley swivels her chair toward the window. "Is that what you'd call Lisa Marie? Erin refers to her as an invisible friend."

"Alter, invisible friend, different names for the same thing—a phantom." The doctor's voice is low and raspy, probably the result of a cold or too many cigarettes. "Has she ever been treated for DID?"

"And that is—?"

"Dissociative identity disorder. What we used to refer to as multiple personalities."

"I don't think so."

"Any mental problems at all?"

"None I know of, but I'm only beginning my investigation. I have learned one thing—she was a battered wife. I've seen the bruises."

"Any chance they were self-inflicted?"

Briley blinks, stunned by the question. "I don't think so. She's not a happy woman, but I don't think she's self-destructive."

"Hmm. So what's your overall impression of this woman?"

Briley considers the question. "I don't think she is mentally unbalanced—she seems quite poised when you first meet her. But when she began to tell me about her invisible friend, I figured she was either mentally ill or trying to be clever. That's why I need you to sort things out."

The doctor coughs again, then clears her throat. "She's at Cook County Jail?"

"Right. Can you fit her in this week? I know we're coming up to the holidays—"

"I'll make room for a session on Friday, but you'll have to get me clearance to see her. This trial's going to be in the spotlight, isn't it?"

Briley closes her eyes. "I'm afraid so."

"That's fine. I'll refrain from any public comments until after the trial concludes. Any idea what sort of defense you'll be using?"

"I'm not forming an opinion until after I read your report. I'm considering diminished capacity. She did take a double dose of Ambien on the night of the murder."

"Any way to prove that?"

"Unfortunately, no. No one did a blood test at the scene."

"Bad break for you—or maybe not, depending on whether or not she's telling you the truth." The psychologist rustles a few pages, then clears her throat again. "All right, Ms. Lester, I'll examine your client and prepare a full report. You should receive it sometime after the holidays."

"And you'll be available to testify? Right now, we have a trial date of March 16. I'm thinking the trial will take at least a week."

"I'll put it on my calendar. I assume you have a list of my usual fees."

"I do. Thank you."

"Oh—Ms. Lester?"

"Yes?"

"Find out what you can about your client's childhood. Interview the parents, if possible."

"Won't you ask Erin about her history?"

"Of course, but we're on a tight schedule. If you can get

me background facts, I'll be better able to sort out any fabrications I might hear. Together, we'll figure out what's actually going on in your client's head."

Briley agrees, then disconnects the call and leans back in her chair. The sounds of laughter and merrymaking spill through her open door, evidence of the Christmas party under way in the office kitchen. She ought to be in there with the others, munching on holiday cookies and downing cups of eggnog. If she weren't working on this case, she would be trading quips with Jim Myers and counting the minutes until she could go home to prepare dinner for Timothy.

But she's trapped behind her computer, her skirt wrinkled and her shoes hiding somewhere beneath the desk. She could leave anytime, but she has reams of paper to peruse and dozens of options to consider. This case she can't slough off.

She props her head on her hand and studies the book on her desk: *The Illinois Criminal Code of 1961*. She'd give her right arm if she could employ something other than a psychological defense. If she claims temporary insanity or diminished capacity, she'll be admitting that her client committed the crime. But with no other suspects and Erin's fingerprints on the syringe, what else can she do?

The phone on the kitchen counter is ringing when Briley steps through the doorway at six-thirty. She drops her purse on the table and runs forward. "Hello?"

"Hey, beautiful. I figured you'd be home."

"Just walked into the house." Smiling, she settles the phone between her ear and shoulder while she pulls out a bar stool. "So…are you able to come over tonight? I rented that Lars von Trier film you wanted to see."

She knows what Timothy's answer will be the moment she hears him sigh. "I'm sorry, babe, but I can't. Dax has been having a bad day. He got some awful news this afternoon, and he's going to be alone tonight. Which means I really shouldn't leave him."

Briley knows she ought to feel sympathetic; she ought to ask about Dax's awful news. But she's spent the entire day talking to librarians and psychologists and court clerks, so all she wants to do is crawl through the telephone line and strangle a certain spoiled British actor.

"Gee," she says, her voice bitter in her own ears, "considering how you put your client's needs above mine, one might think you are romantically involved with Dax Lightner."

"That's not fair, Bri. You know what my job involves."

"I know you have trouble drawing boundary lines. You're supposed to be on call for emergency situations, but you're babysitting this guy twenty-four hours a day."

"Sometimes that's what it takes. An addict never knows when he's going to be tempted."

"Then leave him at home and come over tonight. Dax can call you if he has a problem. Who knows? He might learn that he can stand on his own two feet."

"I can't leave him alone, but I might be able to come…if you wouldn't mind me bringing him along."

Briley gapes in astonished silence. Dax Lightner, movie star, hanging out at her house? Some women would sell their firstborn children for the opportunity, but she can't think of anything less appealing.

Still, if she wants to see Timothy…

She blows out her cheeks in surrender. "Okay, bring him. But don't bring the entourage. I was looking forward to a quiet evening."

"Are you cooking?"

"I'll feed you both, so don't worry. Can you make it by seven-thirty?"

"I'll— We'll be there. Thanks, Bri, for understanding."

She clicks the phone off and drums her fingernails on the counter. Timothy is a uniquely gifted man, but he can't seem to prevent people from taking advantage of him. He's like her father in that way, which is probably why she was attracted to him in the first place. But she can't marry a man like her father, so Timothy is either going to have to change or she's going to strangle him, which means she'll end up being interviewed in jail by Dr. Pamela Lu while some inexperienced bozo from the firm defends her....

No, thank you. She's not going to murder anyone; she's not going to jail. But Timothy is going to learn how to set boundaries.

"Hi, sweetheart." Timothy steps over the threshold and plants a quick kiss on Briley's cheek. She smiles as he enters the house, but her smile fades when a bearded stranger in a ball cap and sunglasses grips her shoulders and swoops in for an air kiss.

"Hello, luv." His stubble scrapes her cheek.

"Hello, Dax," she answers, her voice flat. She allows him to pass, then checks the sidewalk to be sure no paparazzi are hiding in the shrubbery.

"Something smells great," Timothy calls, heading toward the kitchen. "I hope you didn't put yourself out for us."

"No problem." She closes and locks the front door. "This dish is easy."

Her dinner—a tossed salad and a cranberry chicken entrée—waits in the middle of the kitchen table, with three plates set on three place mats. She watches, disbelieving, as Dax takes the middle seat. Does the man always expect to be the center of attention?

If the movie star's choice bothers Timothy, he gives no sign of it. He slides into a chair and sniffs at the chicken. "Smells delicious, Bri. I hate that you went to so much trouble."

She moves to the cupboard for glasses. "I didn't mind." Not for him, at least.

Dax plucks a cherry tomato from the salad bowl and pops it into his mouth. "So." He grins at her as he chews. "Timothy tells me you're a lawyer. Any juicy cases lately?"

She forces a smile as she fills three glasses with ice. "I don't like to bring my work home with me."

"My girl's not a gossip," Timothy says. "And she doesn't read the tabloids."

"Then maybe she'll like me." Dax laughs, looking to Briley for approval of his joke. "I'm glad you don't read that trash."

Now she can die happy. Briley sets a glass in front of Timothy. "What would you like to drink? Tea? Soda?"

"I'll grab a diet soda from the pantry. Dax will have the same."

"Right," Dax says, his British accent much softer than in the movies. "Nothing alcoholic for me—our Tim's a stickler about such things. When I'm around him, I have to be letter perfect in my sobriety."

"That's why you hired me." Timothy hands him a diet soda. "You wanted someone who would be tough."

"Yeah, but even a tough guy can have a moment of weakness." Dax winks at Briley. "Isn't that right, Bri?"

"It's Briley," she corrects him. "And Timothy's right—if you hired him to do a job, you should be glad he's conscientious about it."

"I'm glad, all right. If not for my conscientious sober companion, I'd probably be sitting in a bar, drowning my sorrows and on my way back to rehab."

Briley pulls two bottles of salad dressing from the refrigerator and sets them on the table, then looks around. Silverware, napkins, dressing, and drinks—has she forgotten anything?

"You're going to be fine," Timothy tells Dax, his voice calm as he pours diet soda into his glass. "You just might have to find a few new friends."

Dax turns wide eyes on him. "I like you a lot, Tim, but I don't think I can settle into your idea of a social life. People expect to see me out and about with starlets on my arm, not—" he waves his drink toward Briley "—eating home-cooked dinners with bookish lady lawyers."

Briley freezes behind her chair. She's reasonably sure she should be offended, but how is she supposed to react?

"Now I've done it." With a wince of phony remorse, Dax pats her hand. "Didn't mean anything by that, luv. I'm sure you're a good solicitor and a marvelous cook."

Briley sinks into her chair, picks up the serving fork, and stabs the entrée. "Timothy, would you please pass me your plate?"

He gives her an apologetic look, then offers her his plate. She drops a chicken breast onto it, then drops another onto Dax's plate. The movie star stares at the cranberry-glazed meat, then picks up his knife and gives it a tentative poke. Finally, he looks at her. "I'm sorry, but I don't usually eat this sort of thing. Do you have any sprouts?"

Briley forces a smile. "Are you vegetarian?"

"No. But the things I'm usually served are…leafier, I suppose. And the meat is chopped into little bits."

"Then why don't I teach you?" Briley lifts her knife and fork. "This is a knife." She brandishes the blade before Dax's startled gaze. "You use it to slice the meat. You use the fork to lift the meat to your mouth. It's actually a simple procedure."

Across the table, Timothy muffles a laugh.

"Sorry." Dax picks up his own silverware. "Didn't mean to offend."

As Dax dutifully cuts his meat, Briley eats in silence, resenting the fiasco her dinner is becoming. She and Timothy should be sharing confidential details about their day. She is dying to tell him about her frustrations with Franklin, and she wants to hear about his trials as a celebrity chaperone. She doesn't want to experience those trials firsthand.

She is about to stand and serve dessert when the doorbell rings. She glances at Timothy. "Are we expecting anyone?"

He shakes his head. "I'm not."

"That'd be the girls." Dax swipes at his mouth with his napkin and pushes away from the table. "I gave them the address in case they wanted to drop by."

Briley watches in amazed horror as the star strides to the

front door, flips the dead bolt, and throws the door open. Two young women stand on the porch, a blonde and a brunette, both of them looking as though they have been spray painted with iridescent spandex. They greet Dax with squeals and kisses, then the blonde pulls a bottle of champagne from her bag.

"That'd be my cue," Timothy says, moving toward the door.

Briley blinks back tears of frustration as the threesome invades her living room. Dax moves to the CD player and changes the radio station from soft rock to rap, then cranks up the volume. Timothy confiscates the bottle of bubbly, but not before the blonde has popped the cork and proclaimed her readiness to party.

Timothy had better check her designer bag—no telling what else she has stashed inside.

Briley turns her back on the living-room rave and focuses on cleaning her kitchen. Her perfect evening has been ruined, all because Timothy doesn't know how to maintain boundaries between his personal and professional lives. Her father had the same problem—he was always bringing home strays, feeding them at the table, and bedding them down on the sofa. Briley remembers a childhood filled with ringing telephones, urgent summonses, and strangers—one of whom ended up taking her father's life and reputation.

Her heart has already been broken once. She may not survive if it is shattered.

Chapter Twenty-Six

A do-gooder in a jingling Santa hat stops outside the Division Four interview room and catches Erin's eye through the reinforced square window. The round-faced woman has been visiting inmates for the past week, distributing travel-size bottles of shampoo, conditioner, and body lotion. A month ago, Erin would have disdained the offer of a one-ounce sample of an off-brand shampoo. Now she's tempted to stop her interview and beg on her knees before the volunteer's squeaky cart.

She shakes her head, ruefully and wordlessly explaining that she can't step out and partake of the Christmas bonanza. She has to sit here and have her psyche analyzed, first by her lawyer's psychologist, then by the prosecutor's.

She crosses her arms and shifts her gaze to the petite Asian doctor who has been interviewing her for the past hour. She knows it's important to cooperate, but though Dr. Pamela Lu is pleasant and professional, her questions are beginning to irritate.

"My childhood?" Erin says. "I've already told you about my parents."

"And now I'd like to talk about you. What do you remember about growing up on the West Side? What was your childhood like?"

Erin lets her gaze rove over the painted cinder-block walls. "I'd say it was fairly normal. I mean, every family has its share of quirks, right?"

The doctor's left brow shoots skyward. "What were your family's quirks?"

"Oh…alcoholic mother, deceased father, retarded brother, lonely daughter. No dog, only a couple of stray cats that mostly lived under the house. No cable television, which meant my cultural education was limited to school and the major networks."

Dr. Lu scratches on the notepad in her leather folio. "Any regular visitors to the home? Uncles, neighbors, maybe older cousins?"

Erin shakes her head. "Not even an Avon lady. My dad died when I was three, and Mom didn't stay in touch with her family. I had friends at school, of course."

Dr. Lu hesitates, then folds her arms on the table and leans forward. "You know you can be honest with me, right? I'm working for your benefit."

"But you're preparing a report for the court. So it's not like what I tell you is confidential."

"Unless I'm called to testify, I'll be sharing my opinions with your attorney, not the court. Everything you tell me is attorney-work product and is privileged. Do you understand?"

Sighing, Erin nods.

"Now, I need to know something personal, and you needn't be worried or embarrassed to admit it. Do you recall any time in your childhood when you might have been touched by an older person in an inappropriate way?"

Erin recoils, arching away from her interviewer. "No."

"Are you positive? These experiences are often repressed—"

"Look, Doctor, I know what you're getting at, but I was not molested. Just because I lived in a poor neighborhood doesn't mean you can assume I was a sexual victim."

The petite woman stares thoughtfully at Erin, then looks down to make another note. Erin can't help feeling that she's somehow disappointed the psychologist.

"Your invisible friend," Dr. Lu says, moving on. "You told your lawyer about Lisa Marie. Do you still hear from her?"

"From my lawyer?"

"From Lisa Marie."

A flush heats Erin's cheeks. "If you've talked to my lawyer, then you know I do."

"Let's discuss that for a while. When you hear this voice—"

"I never said I heard a voice."

"How, then, do you know she's still with you?"

"I dream of her." Erin looks away, knowing her heated face must be as red as a tomato. "I see and hear her in my dreams, but they're not like ordinary dreams. It's usually just her and me, on a swing or maybe sitting across from each other at the kitchen table. That's when we talk."

"What does Lisa Marie look like?"

"Like me, I suppose. But she wears her hair shorter."

"Why?"

"Why does she look like me?"

"Why does she prefer short hair?"

Erin blushes, knowing the doctor must think her dense, dull-witted, or both. But when every word has the potential to shape your future, you have to be careful with what you say. "I… Because Jeff liked long hair, I suspect."

"Which do you prefer, longer or shorter hair?"

"I really don't care!" Erin laughs to cover her annoyance. "In this place, it's safer to have short hair. Nobody can drag you by your hair if there's nothing to grab on to."

The psychologist makes another note. "If it's safer to have short hair, why are you still wearing yours long?"

Erin stares across the table, at once hurt and astounded. "Because I want to get out of here! Because I didn't kill my husband and I don't belong in jail."

The doctor doesn't seem at all perturbed by Erin's outburst. "When you talk, what sort of things does Lisa Marie tell you?"

Erin shifts her position. "She used to warn me about Jeffrey, tell me not to get him upset. A couple of times she told me to leave him, but…I couldn't."

"Does Lisa Marie ever become angry with you?"

"I don't know. She used to shout at me, but then she'd calm down and tell me that things were going to be okay. She said she wouldn't let him hurt me—not if she could help it."

"And yet Jeffrey *did* hurt you, didn't he?"

"Not seriously."

"You don't call broken ribs serious?"

"He never hurt me as badly as he could have." She holds the doctor's gaze, determined to make her point. "I knew he wouldn't dare leave any visible marks when we had to be out in public. No black eyes, no broken bones, nothing permanent. He'd have a hard time explaining that to the press."

"So he…what? How did he abuse you?"

Erin crosses her legs and struggles to get comfortable in the hard plastic chair. "Can we take a break? We've been at this a long time."

"Do you need to use the restroom?"

Erin hesitates. She'd say yes just to get out of this chair, but that'd mean calling a guard, putting her wrists in handcuffs, being escorted to the toilet.…

"I think I need to stretch my legs."

"By all means." Dr. Lu gestures to the space around the table. "You can talk and walk, if you like."

Erin stands and faces the door, hoping for a glimpse of the woman in the Santa hat. If she concentrates, maybe she'll be able to hear that squeaky cart approaching.

"You were about to tell me how Jeffrey abused you," Dr. Lu says, her voice slow and patient.

Without looking at the doctor, Erin tucks her hair behind her ear. "Verbally, of course, but only in private. When we were alone, he called me every name in the book, things I wouldn't call my worst enemy. He'd punch me in the stomach or slap my face with the flat of his hand. Sometimes he'd punch the back of my head.… I guess he figured my hair would cover any mark, and his fist wasn't hard enough to fracture my skull. I think he enjoyed knocking me off my feet."

"Did you tell anyone about this abuse? Your mother, maybe?"

Erin laughs and walks toward the door. "Are you kidding? I can't think of anyone less equipped to help. Even if Mom had wanted to take me in, she wouldn't have been able to stop Jeffrey from swooping down and dragging me back home. Mom was afraid of the Tomassis. She said they had connections with organized crime. She was terrified of ending up in some back alley with her throat slit. She used to say the Tomassis didn't get mad, they got even."

"Your mother honestly believed your in-laws might kill her?"

"Believe me, she wasn't exaggerating," Erin answers, her tone dry. "My father-in-law has always been kind to me, but I've seen him in the company of men who looked like they chewed glass for breakfast. Maybe I have an overactive imagination, but I knew not to ask about certain things in the family. I felt it in my bones."

"Did you ever see evidence of illegal activity?"

"No. But that doesn't mean there wasn't any."

Dr. Lu remains silent as she scratches on her notepad. "Did you ever feel threatened by other people in your life? Neighbors, authority figures, teachers?"

Erin shoots her a black look. "I'm not paranoid."

"I didn't say you were." The doctor smiles. "Let's move on to a more pleasant topic. What was your major in college?"

"Business, with a minor in psychology."

"I might have guessed. When you undertook the study of psychology, were you hoping to find a reason for Lisa Marie?"

Erin frowns. "What do you mean?"

"Obviously—" the doctor gestures in a sweeping motion "—you are being haunted, in a sense, by this figment from your childhood. Lisa Marie seems to play the role your mother should have played. She warns you, she guides you, she comforts you. As you studied all the ways the human mind attempts to smooth out the bumps in life's road, did you ever think that Lisa Marie might be a mother-substitute?"

Weary of pacing, Erin drops back into her chair. "She is nothing like my mother. Besides, she's not real."

"She's real to you, isn't she? If she's not real, what is she?"

"Look." Erin's voice goes hoarse with frustration. "I don't know what she is. What I do know is I didn't kill my husband and Lisa Marie says she did. If that means I'm crazy, then maybe I am." She turns to the wall as a lump rises in her throat. "What if I am? Could I be doing things and not even know I'm doing them?"

Dr. Lu says nothing for a long moment, then she closes her notebook. "Erin," she says, "before the night of your husband's death, did Lisa Marie ever mention killing Jeffrey?"

Erin flinches. "No."

"On that night, did you know she intended to kill—"

"I would have argued with her."

"Why? She was trying to protect you."

"But murder is wrong. And killing is never the answer. Look at me—I'm in jail because she killed him."

"The morning after, when you woke up—did you suspect that Lisa Marie had killed Jeffrey?"

Erin's heart contracts with anguish. "I told you, I didn't know anything about Jeffrey's death at first. I only knew I didn't kill him. I couldn't."

"Because you were asleep."

"Yes."

"But when you sleep...isn't that when Lisa Marie comes out?"

Erin claps her hands over her ears as a low wail rises from someplace deep within her. She can't do this anymore; she can't give answers she doesn't know. If they can't believe her, they won't believe her. So why is this woman asking the same questions over and over again? She's trying to confuse things, to make her say something they can use against her in court, and that pale-faced defense attorney who hired this shrink doesn't have the slightest clue about what she's doing....

"Relax, Erin." Dr. Lu props her arms on the table. "That's enough for now. You look tired."

Erin wipes her tear-splashed cheeks. "I don't claim to understand it," she whispers, her voice breaking. "But I didn't kill Jeffrey. I couldn't kill anyone."

"Just tell me this…" Dr. Lu leans forward as if to share a confidential whisper. "Has Lisa Marie ever acted to help you before?"

Erin covers her mouth with her hand. "I—I don't know."

"Do you think she might have?"

For the briefest instant, the image of a face appears in Erin's mind—a pale man with blood running from a wound in his forehead. "There was some trouble at college…and I've always wondered. But I don't think so."

The psychologist slides her folio into her lap, then tilts her head and speaks in a soothing voice. "Can I talk to Lisa Marie now?"

In a flash, Erin understands what the doctor wants. If this were a movie or TV show, Erin's face would twist in a spasm and another personality would emerge, maybe a wise-cracking temptress with an alluring smile and a fondness for makeup, tight skirts, and violence....

She lifts her head and looks the psychologist in the eye. "Sorry, Doctor."

"Because I'm not allowed…or because you don't want me to?"

"Because," Erin answers, "I don't know how you can talk to a dream."

Chapter Twenty-Seven

Two days before Christmas, Briley drives out to Austin, a once-elegant suburb on Chicago's West Side. After checking the address, she pulls up outside an aging frame house and parks at the curb. A rusty mailbox affixed to the front porch lacks a cover, and a screen door hangs at an odd angle. The painted steps are peeling, and the lowest one protests as she climbs toward the front door. Though several houses on this street are gaily decorated, no wreath hangs on the door, no electric lights line the sagging porch.

So…this is the house Erin Tomassi once called home. No wonder she was eager to leave the place.

Briley presses the doorbell, but hears no chime or buzzer. After a moment, she wrestles the screen door open and raps on the wood behind it.

She waits in a quiet so thick the only sound is the roar of a jet in the distance. Then she hears the rattle of a chain lock and the click of a dead bolt.

The front door opens. An older woman stands in the doorway, her eyes as narrow as her frame. Her wiry hair matches the color of day-old snow and stands at attention on her head. "What do you want?"

"Eunice Wilson?"

"Who wants to know?"

Briley pulls a business card from her pocket. "My name is Briley Lester, and I'm a defense attorney. I'm representing your daughter, Erin Tomassi, in a murder trial."

Mrs. Wilson takes the card and studies it, her face set in

a grim look that contains no suggestion of surprise. She lifts her gaze and stares at Briley, then steps forward and pushes the sprained screen away from the doorway. "Come on in, then. Mind the cat. Don't want him slipping out and getting himself killed."

Briley bends to block the green-eyed tabby winding around Mrs. Wilson's swollen ankles, but the animal seems content to remain with his mistress. When the door has closed behind her, Briley widens her eyes in the shadows of the foyer and barely avoids stepping into a litter box against the wall. The place smells of cigarette smoke, ammonia, and stale furnishings; the rug looks as though it hasn't been cleaned in years.

"In here," Mrs. Wilson calls, tightening the belt of her robe as she leads the way to a living room. Fraying blinds cover the windows, a paltry defense against the bone-rattling cold. Another slant-eyed cat lounges on the couch, its paws tucked beneath its chest, but as Briley approaches, the animal leaps up and scurries away.

"Have a seat," the woman says, sinking into a patched recliner. She props one elbow on the leatherette armrest and fixes Briley in her pinched gaze. "What's that you said about Erin?"

Briley settles on the end of a couch cushion, removes her gloves, and tries not to think about the cat hair that will soon be clinging to her dark suit. "Your daughter is on trial for the murder of her husband. It's my job to defend her."

A radiator against the wall hisses, nearly drowning out the sound of Eunice's snort. "I wouldn't blame Erin for killing the snob. Rich young man, thinkin' he can order her around just because he's got a hunk of his daddy's money. I never did like him much."

Briley pulls her notepad from her briefcase. "Do you mind if I ask you a few questions? You might be able to help me prepare Erin's defense."

From someplace within the bowels of the recliner, the

woman produces a package of cigarettes. She shakes out a smoke, then pats her pockets. "Go on, shoot. Ask what you like."

Briley glances at her notes. "Erin mentioned that she grew up in this house. When did you move here?"

The woman pulls a lighter from her pocket, flicks it into flame, and touches the quivering yellow streak to the end of her cigarette. After inhaling, she takes another long drag and dangles her hand off the armrest. "I moved here—" she squints, as if peering into the past "—when I was twenty. When I married Carl Wilson."

"Carl was Erin's father?"

"Yeah. She never really knew him, though."

"Where is he now?"

Eunice snorts. "Graceland Cemetery. He fell off the L platform coming home from work—or at least that's what they told me." She takes another drag and gives Briley a bright-eyed glance, brimming with wry humor. "He was a good man, just couldn't drink and walk a straight line. But nobody ever gave me the goose bumps like he done."

"Well." Briley searches for a segue into her next question. "How old was Erin when her father passed away?"

"Practically still a baby—she was about three and a half. Roger was five. Both of 'em awful young, so it was good they were too little to realize all that was goin' on."

Briley looks away as a host of familiar feelings bubbles up from her own memories. She and her client have something in common, then—early loss resulting in a single-parent household. After her father died, did Erin also experience guilt and confusion? Did she toss and turn at night, worrying about losing her only remaining parent? Just because a young child can't verbalize her emotions doesn't mean they aren't powerfully present.

She gives the wizened woman a brief, distracted glance. Any child would worry if she had Eunice Wilson for a mother. The woman seems about as reliable as a tabloid headline. At least Briley's father was dependable…until the night he died.

When Eunice coughs, Briley blinks the images of the past away. "Erin tells me she had an invisible friend when she was small."

"You mean Lisa Marie?"

"So you knew. You knew her name."

"Good heavens, yes. Erin talked about Lisa Marie like she was a real person. Nearly drove me crazy for a while, especially after Roger went away."

"What do you mean?"

"Roger? He was retarded, you know. After Carl died, a social worker took him and put him in a special home. I didn't argue, because I didn't know how I was going to take care of two kids, one of 'em Down's, without a husband."

Lucky Roger, getting away from this place. Briley forces a smile. "Caring for only one child must have made things easier for you."

"I wouldn't say that. Life was never easy with Erin. She was too doggone picky." The woman exhales a stream of smoke through her mouth. "Lisa Marie didn't like chicken. Lisa Marie didn't like to wear blue. Lisa Marie wasn't sleepy at bedtime. Lisa Marie didn't want to go to school. Hard enough to please one kid without having to please her imaginary pal, too."

"Did Erin eventually outgrow that…phase?"

"Outgrow Lisa Marie?" Eunice purses her lips around her cigarette again. "I wish she'd outgrowed it. She kept talking about Lisa Marie at ten, eleven, twelve, never givin' up. One day I got so sick of hearing about that little brat that I hauled off and slapped Erin. After that—" She closes her eyes, squinching them in what looks like an involuntary spasm.

"Mrs. Wilson?" Briley leans forward. "Are you all right?"

The woman's features relax, then she lowers her head in a slow nod. "I slapped my kid," she repeats, keeping her eyes closed. "Knocked her across the room and into the wall. I didn't mean to hit her so hard, but all that talk about Lisa Marie nearly drove me batty." Eunice opens her eyes and looks at Briley, lifting her hand. "After a minute, I knew she was okay, because she raised up and looked at me. But when she did—" she inhales deeply on her cigarette, sucking in nicotine like a starving woman "—this may sound crazy, but I coulda sworn a different person glared out at me through Erin's eyes. Erin had *never* looked at me so mean and hateful. I don't think she's ever had that much hate in her."

Briley waits for the story to continue, but on her legal pad she makes a note: *suffered abuse at mother's hands, too. A pattern?*

Eunice releases a tired laugh. "When I knew she wasn't hurt, I left the room. I don't know how to explain it, but I had a feeling that something inside Erin would hurt me if I tried to hit her again."

Briley looks down at her notes, not certain how to proceed. This story might help explain Erin's delusion, but Eunice Wilson is not going to make a good witness. Instead of eliciting sympathy from the jury, she might convince them that the apple hasn't fallen far from the tree.

"Did you ever come up with an explanation for Erin's reaction?" Briley asks, determined to remain reasonable. "Obviously, the person looking back at you couldn't have been anyone but Erin. But if your perceptions were altered because you'd been taking some kind of medication, or drinking—"

"A mother knows her own daughter." Eunice's brows arch into indignant triangles. "And that thing—whatever it was—inside Erin was *not* my girl. Scared me spitless, it did, so the next week I took her down to the church revival and asked them to cast out the demon."

Briley breaks every rule of decorum and stares. "You did *what?*"

"I took her down to the church on the corner," Eunice says, her gaze drifting to a memory Briley can barely imagine. "I took her down, sat with her through a whole lotta hoo-ha, then dragged her down front and had them lay hands on her. They did a lot of prayin' and singing' and shoutin', and I hoped that would take care of Lisa Marie for good. But when we got home, Erin went straight to her room and slammed the door. The next day, she went to school and came home actin' like nothing had happened. Except before she went to bed, she drew me a picture of herself and Lisa Marie, holding hands on the playground. Her way of tellin' me she wasn't lettin' go."

"Mrs. Wilson…" Briley pauses, not certain how to continue. "Were you drinking during those years?"

The woman tips her head, resentment in her eyes. "No more'n usual."

"Well…do you think it might be fair to theorize that Erin clung to Lisa Marie because she felt she was unable to depend on you?"

Eunice sucks at the inside of her cheek for a minute, then draws on her cigarette and exhales twin streamers through flaring nostrils. "I was always here for that girl." She punctuates every word with nicotine-stained fingers. "You ask her, she'll tell you. I was always here."

And probably passed out on the couch. Briley glances around, imagining what life must have been like in this dingy house. She sees nothing to contradict Erin's dismal account.

"Did you know," she asks, changing the subject, "your son-in-law and his family? Did you spend much time with Jeffrey Tomassi?"

Eunice flicks the smoldering end of her cigarette into an empty peanut can on the floor, then waves her hand like some glamorous movie star. "I was lucky to get invited to the wedding. They put some old woman in charge of me. I couldn't go to the toilet without that broad tagging along to be sure I wasn't going to embarrass the family."

"Did you like Jeffrey? Did Erin seem happy with him?"

The woman tastes her cigarette again, her eyes narrowing in contemplation. "I didn't like him, but Erin isn't real open about her feelings. She's more like her father than me. He was always reserved, but yeah, I'd say she seemed happy with Jeff. Happier with him than with me."

Briley makes a note on her legal pad. No wonder the girl invented an invisible friend. With few friends, an alcoholic mother, and a quiet nature, Erin had no confidante but Lisa Marie.

Until Jeffrey Tomassi came along.

Chapter Twenty-Eight

On the second day of the new year, Briley raps on Jim Myers's open door. "Just wanted to check in," she says, waving when he gestures for her to enter. "Seattle's wet, your elevator witness fully corroborated your version of the accident, and I ordered regular turnaround from the court reporter. She said you should receive a copy of the deposition in the next couple of weeks."

"Wait a minute," Myers calls as Briley turns toward her office. "Come in, let's talk about it."

"Can't." She flaps her fingers in a wave. "I've got records to review, reports to read, and e-mail to answer."

She exhales in exasperation when she finds her computer in-box overflowing. Along with the usual spam, urban myths, and interoffice memos, she discovers several important messages: Franklin wants a report on the status of the Tomassi case, Bystrowski wants a receipt for the documents he's messengered over, and the court clerk wants to confirm her hearing for pretrial motions on January 26—only four weeks away.

Briley grits her teeth as she deletes offers to help her lose weight, increase her libido, and deliver a thirty-million-dollar bequest if she'll send a measly ten thousand to a foreign bank account. If Franklin hadn't asked her to fly to Seattle to take that deposition, she could have stayed on top of all this correspondence. If she hadn't lost two days in travel time, she might have already finished her status report. And if she hadn't spent New Year's Day flying from one side of the country to the other, she might have enjoyed a wonderful holiday with Timothy.

Her finger freezes above the delete key when she recognizes a familiar name: Pamela Lu writes that she has completed her evaluation of Erin Tomassi and would be happy to meet and discuss it. If Briley will call her office at the earliest possible opportunity…

Briley dials the number before she finishes reading the e-mail. Relieved to find the doctor in her office, she greets the psychologist and asks if she's free for lunch.

"Do you know Los Dos Laredos on Twenty-sixth Street?" Dr. Lu asks in her throaty voice. "I'm craving an enchilada, so if you'd like to join me around noon…"

"I'll be there."

Briley hangs up and settles back in her chair. Los Dos Laredos isn't far from the Cook County Jail, so while she's in the area she should stop and deposit another twenty dollars in Erin Tomassi's commissary account. The last time Briley checked, her client had only five dollars' credit. She'll need more before her trial is finished.

By the time Briley drives to Twenty-sixth Street, finds a parking place, and visits the jail, Dr. Lu has already settled in a booth and ordered tortilla chips. Briley slides into the seat across from her and apologizes for being late, then notices a large manila envelope on the table. "Is that for me?"

"My evaluation, along with a transcript of my session with your client. You'll also find the results of a standard personality test."

"Thank you." Briley sets the envelope on the seat and picks up the list of daily specials. "What's good here?"

"Everything," Dr. Lu says, setting her menu aside. "You can't go wrong with Mexican food in this part of the city."

Briley orders an enchilada platter with rice and gratefully accepts a glass of water from the waitress. When the woman has gone, she unwraps her straw and gives the petite psychologist her full attention. "So, let me have it straight out—is my client insane?"

Dr. Lu's mouth curls in an expression that barely deserves

to be called a smile. "Do you always cut to the chase before the food arrives?"

"I haven't much time, nor do I have much help on this one. I need to settle on a credible case theory as soon as possible."

"Okay, then." The doctor folds her arms. "At first I thought your client was a sure candidate for dissociative identity disorder. She fits most of the criteria—the presence of two or more distinct identities, occasions when each identity apparently takes control of the subject's behavior, blackouts and memory loss, and the lack of a physiological explanation like alcohol abuse or seizures. The typical DID patient will talk about having heard voices, or a voice, in her head since childhood, and your client *almost* fits that profile."

"Why almost?"

"Because DID is the result of childhood trauma, usually sexual abuse. Dissociation is a creative way of keeping the unacceptable memories out of sight while allowing children to maintain an emotional attachment to the abuser. Your client, however, insists she was not sexually abused. So either she has totally repressed this information, perhaps within another alter, or she's telling the truth and doesn't fit the profile for DID."

"If you interviewed her again, do you think you could somehow dig out a memory of the past abuse?"

"You're assuming abuse is present. Why do you think it is?"

"Because she's a grown woman who still believes she has an invisible friend. That *has* to be DID, doesn't it?"

Dr. Lu lifts one shoulder in a shrug. "It's possible. But even if you're right, it might take years of therapy before we're able to uncover the alter who is safeguarding the traumatic memories. Unless you have evidence that could point us to an individual who might have abused your client, I wouldn't know how to begin."

Briley drops her straw into her glass. "Erin says Lisa Marie speaks to her in dreams. Don't people with DID have flashbacks in dreams? Isn't that enough to prove that Lisa

Marie is associated with some traumatic memory from Erin's childhood?"

Dr. Lu reaches for her coffee mug. "I could testify that Lisa Marie *might* be an alternate personality resulting from a previous trauma, but I could never affirm that as fact. The prosecutor would chew me up, because I could just as easily testify that there's no clear evidence to indicate Erin's delusion is the result of trauma."

Briley sorts through her thoughts. While the doctor's belief that Lisa Marie might be an alter might help establish reasonable doubt, "could be" statements never cut it in court. The prosecutor would be on his feet in a flash, and the judge would rule the statement inadmissible. "Dr. Lu—" she looks the woman directly in the eye "—if Lisa Marie is not a product of DID, then what is she?"

The psychologist sips from her mug and smiles across the brim. "To use Erin's own words, Lisa Marie is an invisible friend."

Beyond exasperation, Briley exhales in a rush. "Adult women do not have invisible friends."

"Maybe they should. How is your client different from the lonely widow who spends all day talking to her Yorkie? Or the romance reader who fantasizes that she's lying in the hero's arms when her portly husband comes home? By keeping Lisa Marie alive, your client found a way to survive in a pressure-filled public arena. The verbal and physical abuse she suffered only intensified her need for a confidante. Since she felt she couldn't trust her mother or anyone in the Tomassi family, she relied upon her best friend from childhood. Until recently, her delusion was harmless, even beneficial. Unfortunately, other people are rarely willing to see the benefit of a good delusion."

"So you're saying I should forget about mental illness and seriously consider the Ambien defense. Diminished capacity."

The doctor tilts her head. "That's not bad, but you'd be placing the murder weapon directly in your client's hand. Are you sure you want to do that?"

Briley barks out a laugh. "It's not like I have many choices. The *evidence* puts the murder weapon in my client's hand. Unless… Do you believe… Did Erin say something that's led you to believe she'd be incapable of murder?"

"I think—" the psychologist pauses as the waitress approaches with two steaming platters "—I think it's highly unlikely that Erin Tomassi killed anyone. Her personality test reveals that she's not a schemer, not the sort to prepare for murder. She wants the people around her to live in harmony, and she may be one of the most phlegmatic people you or I will ever meet. If Jeffrey Tomassi hadn't been given an overdose of insulin, she might have borne his abuse for years without uttering a peep. Look how she endured her mother's indifference."

Briley leans back in the booth, more confused than ever. "Maybe I should tell Travis Bystrowski to indict Lisa Marie."

"Might as well tell him to arrest the tooth fairy. What I'm saying, Counselor, is that I don't believe your client is capable of planning and carrying out the murder of her husband. I'd testify to that in court. On the other hand, I can't swear that Erin Tomassi suffers from DID. As to whether Lisa Marie is a genuine delusion or a desperate attempt to evade a murder conviction…I'd have to vote for the former. I don't think your client is naturally duplicitous. The prosecutor's shrink, of course, is likely to disagree with everything I've just said."

"Anyone," Briley says, thinking of former clients, "is capable of surprising those who know them best. I can't tell you how many mothers have assured me that their children simply couldn't have committed the crimes they were accused of, but I knew those kids were as guilty as Cain."

"No one is perfect, but few people are as bad as they can be." Dr. Lu picks up her fork. "If I were you, I'd choose to believe in Erin Tomassi's innocence. I can't speak to the evidence, but I'd stake my professional reputation on my belief that your client has done nothing to deserve the death penalty." She nods at Briley's steaming plate. "Now, enjoy your lunch before it gets cold. I didn't ask you to come all the way down here to eat a cold enchilada."

Chapter Twenty-Nine

Erin sidesteps through the lunch line, keeping her gaze pinned to her tray as much as possible. Behind the sneeze guard, a plastic plate moves from gloved hand to gloved hand as bored cafeteria employees scoop up a spoonful of hash, an apple, and a sandwich from serving bins. The food goes on the plate; the plate moves down the line until it lands on Erin's tray, next to a glass of yellow pseudo-punch. She lifts the tray and is about to turn when the big woman to her right gives her a shove. Erin lurches forward, managing to hold on to her tray only by some kind of miracle. But the motion spills the punch, drenches her meal, and splashes her uniform.

A uniform she won't be allowed to change until next Saturday.

"Too bad," says the woman, a barrel-chested behemoth called Big Shirley. "Guess you should pull your nose outta the air and watch where you're goin'."

Erin draws a ragged breath and forbids herself to tremble. Ignoring the boisterous whoops from the crowd gathered around the first two tables, she skirts the center of the cafeteria and heads toward an empty space near the back of the room.

How many more days of this can she endure?

Careful not to turn her back on the crowd, she slides onto the bench and drops a napkin into the pool of punch on her plate. The sandwich is soggy, the white bread now stained the color of apple juice, but she'll eat every bite. If she doesn't gulp down her food, the wolves will begin to circle, eventually attacking and helping themselves to everything on her plate.

She grabs the apple and tucks it beneath the elastic waistband of her pants, hoping to hide it until later. She's devouring the hash when a shadow falls across her plate. She looks up to see Big Shirley and Wilma standing at the end of the table. Wilma, who stands five foot ten and is at least a welterweight, is moving her jaw and curling her mouth as if she's planning to spit.

Erin closes her eyes, not wanting to watch.

"Hey, Princess," Shirley says. Her voice is soft, and terrifying in its intensity. "Aw, lookee that. The Princess had an accident with her tray."

Erin opens her eyes as gremlins of panic nip the back of her neck. Something tells her it wouldn't be wise to ignore these two.

"What'd ya do, Princess?" Wilma asks, her rough voice a pitiful imitation of Shirley's. "Pee in your plate?"

Erin narrows her eyes, pretending indifference even as anxiety squeezes her pounding heart. "You know what happened."

"*Moi?*" Big Shirley widens her eyes and looks at Wilma. "Is she accusing me of something?"

Wilma leans two hands on the table and slants forward, her bulk casting a long shadow over Erin's tray. "I think she's saying you're uncouth."

"We can't have that." Shirley glances toward the doorway. "We gotta have couth. So no one's allowed to spill around here."

Like moths drawn to a light, other inmates leave their places and approach Erin's table. She can see them from the corner of her eye; she can smell the tension, hear it crackling in the air.

"Why don't you leave me alone?" She picks up her sandwich and attempts the glare she's been rehearsing in the darkness of her cell. "Go back and eat with your friends."

"I would—" Big Shirley draws close enough for Erin to smell the acrid scent of underarm perspiration "—but my friends are feelin' a little uncomfortable with a princess in their midst."

"I never said—" Erin begins, but Shirley's big hand slams her head to the tray. A shower of lights sparks through her field of vision and something slices into her tongue.

"Lick it up," Shirley commands, her grip like a vise on Erin's neck. "Eat, Your Royal Highness."

Erin tries to answer, but in her hunched position she can't draw enough air into her lungs to push out the words. The wet sandwich is oozing into her left eye, the wet napkin is cold against her face, and punch is running into her nose. Her face missed most of the hash, but apparently someone found a fresh supply, for a wet gob of the stuff lands in her hair, smelling of potatoes and corned beef. When she tastes the metallic tang of blood, she realizes she has bitten her tongue.

"Eat it!" someone calls, and the air fills with the sound of female fury. "Eat it, eat it, eat it!"

Erin struggles, striving to reach Shirley, to connect with anyone, but the hand at the back of her head does not budge. A sob rises in her throat, breaking from her lips in a gurgling rasp, but still no one comes, no whistle blows, no representative of sanity appears. This place is off the radar, removed from reasonable society, a limbo where law and order are restored as a last resort and decency is unknown....

Food pelts Erin's head, her shoulders, her arms. She lowers her hands to her sides and weeps, surrendering to the humiliating indignity. Jeffrey's brutality, as bad as it was, was never like this. That was man against woman, but this...this feels like the worst kind of betrayal.

The hand on her scalp contracts, grips her hair, and pulls her head up, nearly lifting Erin from the bench. Her hands rise, flailing at the arms holding her prisoner, and in that instant a fist swings toward her midsection.

The welterweight.

Realizing the hopelessness of her situation, Erin gives up the struggle and succumbs to the darkness.

Chapter Thirty

Briley stops by Kate Barnhill's desk on her way to her office on Monday morning. "Hey, there." Kate pulls off her reading glasses and gives Briley a speculative smile. "You look like you had a relaxing weekend."

"I did." Briley tosses her head and grins. "Believe it or not, Timothy had the weekend off, so we went to the theater Saturday night and watched old movies all day Sunday."

"What show did you see?"

"*The Lion King.*" Briley sighs at the memory of the extravagant production. "If you haven't seen it, it's a must. It's simply spectacular."

"By the way—" Kate's eyes light with calculation "—you haven't told me what your boyfriend does. With the hours he keeps, he must be…what, a hospital resident?"

Briley shakes her head. "Not even close."

"He can't be a lawyer. I know you. You're not that fond of the law."

"You're right on that score." Briley sets her laptop case on Kate's desk. "I hate being secretive, but his work is sort of confidential."

"What, his position?"

"His client list."

"Wait." Kate lifts a finger. "He's a personal trainer."

Briley laughs. "He's a sober companion. Addicts pay him to stick by them until, you know, they can handle life without drugs."

Kate's face goes blank with surprise. "You're kidding. That's a job?"

"A pretty good one, too. He earns more than you'd think."

"As much as a lawyer?"

"About as much as a slow-moving associate. The money's good, but the hours are awful and the training's a nightmare."

"Wow." Kate drops her glasses to her desk. "How do you train for a job like that? Take counseling classes?"

"You overcome an addiction yourself." Briley pulls her laptop case from the desk and gestures down the hall. "I'd better get busy."

"Wait." Kate digs through some papers on her desk, then hands Briley a note. "I took this off the answering machine. The call came in yesterday morning."

Briley glances at the name. "The Cook County Sheriff's Office? They called on a Sunday?"

"The infirmary. Apparently your client ended up there this weekend."

Briley grimaces. "This case is killing me. I feel so lost, and the clock is ticking. I have a pretrial hearing in three weeks, and I've barely begun my investigation. I filed a petition to get money from the court, but that petition's been held up…. I'm afraid I'm going to have to file for a continuance."

"You need me?" Kate smiles. "All you have to do is ask."

"Could you give me a hand? William's agreed to help, and Franklin said I could use staff members if they were available—"

"I'll make myself available," Kate says. "Just tell me what you need, and I'll get to it. I think it's awful that they've left you alone to handle this case."

"Thanks." Briley waves the phone message. "I guess I'd better go see what happened to my client."

Ten minutes later, she is on the phone with a nurse at the jail. The nurse remembers Erin Tomassi, and assures Briley that her client has returned to her cell.

"Was she badly hurt?"

"A few bruises, that's all. Nothing unusual. Sometimes the women get into fights. Not as often as the men, but still…"

"Why'd they fight?"

"Like they need a reason. You ever seen a pack of wolves around a baby moose? That's what it's like in there. The strong ones circle the new ones, the weak ones. If the newbies don't toughen up, they go down. Your girl, though—she gave as good as she got. She broke Big Shirley's arm."

Briley blinks. "She did what?"

"I didn't see it, but boy, did I hear about it. Apparently your girl put up with a lot, but when Wilma almost knocked the wind out of her, she came to life and punched Wilma right back. Then she spun around and snapped Shirley's arm across her knee. Broke it like a twig."

"You sure you're talking about Erin Tomassi? Small blonde, probably wears a size four?"

The nurse chuckles. "Yeah, I was surprised, too. But now the others will think twice before picking on her."

Briley runs her hands through her hair, distressed by the thought of Erin suffering abuse even behind bars. "So you think she'll be okay from now on?"

"I said they'd think twice. I didn't say they wouldn't come after her. Listen—" the nurse lowers her voice "—you could ask the sheriff to place her in isolation, but you'd be doing her no favors. Sooner or later, she'll have to come out, and then the others will resent her even more. She's better off toughing it out where she is. Trust me."

Briley has no choice.

Briley slips out of her office and heads down to the law library. William is working at his desk, but he looks up when she enters the room. "Ms. Lester." His smile lifts the corners of his mustache. "How goes the war?"

"Slow but sure," she says, dropping into a nearby chair.

"Have you had a chance to look over your copy of the transcript of the conversation between Erin and Dr. Lu?"

"Spent the better part of Saturday morning reading it. Also did a bit of background research on my own."

Briley makes a face. "I didn't mean for you to spend personal time working on this."

"No problem—it was fascinating." With a flourish, he pulls several pages from a file in his desk drawer and begins to read. "Erin Wilson Tomassi graduated from Chicago State University in 2003. Business major. Honor roll. Pledged no sororities, but in the yearbook she is featured on a page for student government leaders."

Briley laces her fingers. "Thanks, but I've got all that."

"You may not have this—in the transcript, your client mentions something about trouble with the school, so I did some checking. Turns out that in September 2000, a Douglas Haddock filed a complaint with student security against sophomore Erin Wilson, claiming she injured him in an assault. The next day he dropped the charges, so school officials never notified the police."

"What sort of injury was it?"

"No record of the details. When Haddock dropped the charges, the school didn't pursue the investigation."

Briley makes a note on her legal pad. "Any current leads on Doug Haddock?"

"I searched him on the Internet. Haddock graduated in 2001 and is living in Kankakee with his wife and two kids. He runs a printing company down there." He hands Briley another sheet of paper. "Everything you need, even his current address and a map."

"Thanks, William." She gives him a grateful smile. "You've saved me a ton of work."

"No problem." He slips his hands into his cardigan pockets. "So, chief—what's next on our agenda?"

Briley picks up the map and turns it sideways, trying to get her bearings. "I think I need to visit Kankakee."

* * *

Keenly aware of the passing hours, Briley clears her desk after lunch and heads toward the parking lot. Kankakee lies about an hour south of Chicago, and once the traffic thins on the interstate she finds herself relaxing behind the wheel. She hasn't made an appointment with Mr. Haddock, but she did call the Quick Print Company to confirm that he'd be in town and at work this afternoon.

The young woman who answered the phone assured her that Doug Haddock hadn't missed a day of work in three years. "He's a great guy," the woman said after Briley introduced herself. "So if you're thinking about suing him—"

"I don't sue people," Briley interrupted, keeping her voice light. "I'm a defense attorney, and no, your boss isn't in trouble. I just need a few minutes of his time."

"Then come on in," the woman chirped. "I'm sure Doug would be happy to help."

The man sounds like a real salt-of-the-earth type. Why, then, did his encounter with Erin Wilson result in a complaint to student security?

After entering Kankakee, Briley finds the Quick Print Company in a strip mall at the edge of town. She enters the building and smiles at the girl behind the counter, a pretty young woman wearing an apron over jeans and a polo shirt. "Can you help me? I'm looking for Doug Haddock."

The young woman glances over her shoulder, then grabs a pad and pencil. "If this is about an order, I can help you."

"It's not about an order. I need to see Mr. Haddock."

The girl's face screws up into a question mark, then clears. "You're the lawyer."

"Yes."

"Just a minute, I'll get Doug."

While she waits at the counter, Briley breathes in the scents of ink and oil and freshly cut paper. Somewhere in the distance, a printer clacks with rhythmic regularity, while a humming copy machine against the wall spits copies into a multilevel tray.

A moment later, the girl returns, followed by a shaggy-haired man who appears to be in his early thirties. His brows are knotted in a frown, but his face clears as he gives Briley a polite smile. "I'm Doug Haddock. Something I can do for you?"

"I hope so." Briley slides her business card over the counter and waits while he reads it.

"You're an attorney?"

"From Chicago. I'm representing Erin Tomassi on a murder charge."

He tosses her card back over the counter. "I don't know anyone by that name."

"I believe you knew her as Erin Wilson. You were in college together at Chicago State University."

Briley watches as memory hardens his eyes. "I didn't know her well."

"You filed a complaint against her with the school authorities."

"I dropped that complaint."

"Please, Mr. Haddock." Briley sets her purse on the counter and leans toward him. "I'm not here to make trouble for you. But I need some honest answers."

"I don't want to get involved in any trial, and I don't have time to go up to Chicago."

"If you don't have knowledge of the present case, you won't have to. But I need to understand a few things about my client's history, and I believe you can help me."

Haddock turns to the young woman who's pretending not to listen from a few feet away. "Nona, I'll be in my office."

"Okay, Doug."

Briley feels the prick of the young woman's eyes as she steps behind the counter and follows Haddock to a small office at the back of the building. He lifts a stack of real estate brochures from the only guest chair and offers her a seat.

"Thanks."

He settles himself behind the desk and picks up a pencil. "What can I tell you? I really didn't know Erin Wilson. I met her at a party one night, she came back to my dorm. Next thing I know, she's breaking a lamp over my head. I had to get stitches—cost me ninety bucks to get sewn up at the emergency room." He lifts an uneven section of hair and points to his forehead. "See that scar? Three stitches to close up the gash she left me with. That's thirty bucks a stitch."

Briley peers at the faint red line. "Why did she hit you?"

"How should I know? The girl was crazy. She came on all sweet and clingy at the party, but she sure changed once she got back to my room. It was like she was a different person."

"Did you ever date her again?"

"Why should I date a wildcat?"

"I assume that's a no." Briley pulls her notebook from her purse. "Did you have a roommate?"

His eyes narrow. "Why?"

"I thought maybe your roommate drove you to the emergency room. You must have been in quite a bit of pain. And head wounds bleed like nobody's business."

"Tell me about it." He grunts. "After I got stitched up, I filed the complaint, because I wanted my ninety bucks reimbursed. But a few hours later, I was ready to let it go. Considering all the other shenanigans that went on in my dorm, three stitches was really no big deal."

"You were willing to forget about ninety bucks after only a couple of hours?" She whistles. "Your college budget must have been a lot more flexible than mine."

"Uh…I must have figured my insurance would cover it."

Briley searches the man's eyes. He may be telling the truth, but it's not likely that a man who can still remember the cost per stitch would easily forgive a debt.

Briley hesitates, pen poised over the paper. "Your roommate's name?"

Haddock frowns. "He wouldn't remember any of this."

"Maybe not. But Erin remembers the incident—just not quite the way you do. Mostly she remembers that a young man made trouble for her in her sophomore year."

Haddock shakes his head. "You know, I'm not sure I remember that guy's name. I moved off campus the next year."

"That's fine, then." Briley closes her notebook. "I'm sure the college will have a record of dorm residents. They should be able to find your roommate's name and address in only a couple of minutes."

"John Savage." Haddock lifts his head. "I just remembered. I think he was from Elgin."

"Thank you, Mr. Haddock." Briley stands and offers her hand. "I appreciate your cooperation."

On the drive back to Chicago, Briley calls William, who uses the Internet to track down two John Savages in Elgin, Illinois. Only one is the right age, so Briley recites his number into the car's hands-free system and hopes she's found the right man.

Unbelievably, Mr. Savage picks up on the first ring. "Yeah?"

"I'm looking for the John Savage who used to room with Doug Haddock at Chicago State," Briley explains. "Do I have the right number?"

The man laughs. "Sure do. Are you his wife or his girlfriend?"

"Neither, I'm a defense attorney. A few minutes ago I was talking to Doug about the night Erin Wilson hit him over the head with a lamp. He said you drove him to the emergency room."

"Oh, man." Savage groans. "Has she finally pressed charges against him?"

"Actually, I'm defending Erin in another matter. I'm trying to gather a few details about significant events in her history."

"I really didn't know her." The man hesitates. "Actually,

I've always felt bad about that night. It's been preying on my conscience."

"Oh?" Briley reaches for the digital recorder in the passenger seat and clicks it on. "You want to tell me about it? I'm recording this, by the way."

"This isn't— I'm not going to get Doug in trouble, am I?"

"That's not likely. Erin is too busy dealing with her current problems to worry about something that happened in college."

When Savage hesitates, Briley wonders for a moment if she's lost the connection.

"We were all at this bar," Savage finally says, "and Doug spies Erin, who was just his type, a real hottie. We talk to her awhile, and when she's not looking, Doug slips her a roofie."

Briley tightens her grip on the steering wheel. "He didn't."

"Yeah, he did. The girl gets as high as a kite, then we all go back to the dorm and the girl—Erin—passes out. Doug puts her on the bed and goes into the bathroom. I don't want anything to do with what he's planning, so I'm in the corner, rummaging in the minifridge for a beer and planning to leave. But the next thing I know, Doug's stepped out of the bathroom and the girl is awake, up, and swinging a lamp like it's the bottom of the ninth and bases are loaded."

Briley turns on her blinker and slants toward the exit lane. "I'm sure Doug was surprised."

Savage grunts in affirmation. "That's the understatement of the year. The girl runs out the door while Doug writhes on the bed, carrying on like she's killed him. He's bleeding like a stuck boar, but when we get to the E.R. they clean up the blood and we see that the wound is really just a slice. I think it only took three or four stitches to sew him up."

"And…what happened to Erin?"

"We never saw her again. Doug was so ticked about the money he went down to file charges with campus security, but later I told him that she must have seen him slip the drug into her drink. She couldn't have swallowed it, or she'd have been out cold for hours. So he dropped the charges and we tried to forget the whole thing."

A moment of silence spills over the line, then Savage clears his throat. "I know it was a lousy thing he did."

"It was a lousy thing you *both* did," Briley says. "Because you helped him carry her to your room, you could have been charged as an accessory to attempted rape."

Another interval of silence, then Savage adds, "Whoever said confession was good for the soul…was wrong."

"It's not the confession that makes you feel better." Briley stops at an intersection and stares at the traffic ahead. "It's forgiveness…and for that, you need to talk to Erin Wilson."

She thanks him for his time, then disconnects the call and turns toward the office. Dr. Lu may not believe Erin is capable of violence, but Doug Haddock and John Savage have witnessed a display of her temper, and so have several inmates at the Cook County Jail. Hard to believe that violence could reside in a woman so retiring and shy, but deep character often comes out when people are under pressure.

How deeply buried is Erin's violent streak?

Chapter Thirty-One

In the doorway of the interview room, Erin rubs her wrists after the guard removes the handcuffs. At the table, her lawyer is already seated and frowning at a page filled with handwritten notes.

Well…at least the woman has been doing *something* while she rots in jail.

She pulls out the cracked plastic chair at the opposite side of the table. "Hi," she says, her voice flat. "Long time, no see."

Finally, Briley looks up and meets her gaze. "How are you feeling? I heard you were involved in some trouble this weekend."

The lawyer knew? And yet she did nothing. Obviously Erin's name is not at the top of this woman's priority list.

She pushes a stray hank of hair out of her eyes. "I'm surviving. Nobody's about to vote me Miss Congeniality, but—" She shrugs. "I shouldn't complain. I can stand this place for as long as it takes to get through the trial."

The lawyer smiles, but with a distracted, inward look, like a parent who's afraid to make promises she can't keep.

Erin looks away. "Did you have a nice Christmas?"

"Um…yes. And you?"

Erin rolls her eyes. "Jolly. The Baptists came in and sang carols. New Year's was fun, too. In honor of the holiday, someone taped a poster of fireworks to the cafeteria wall. We got to stare at it for almost ten minutes before someone ripped it down."

Briley says nothing, but beneath the smooth surface of

her face Erin sees a suggestion of movement, as if opposite impulses were battling beneath a protective layer. Finally, Briley's impassive expression twists in a guilty grimace. "I know it's been a while since I've come out to see you—"

"Twenty-one days," Erin says.

Briley presses her lips together. "You may not believe this, but I am working hard on your case. I've had to do most of the footwork myself. I've also had to try to keep my boss happy, and he shipped me off to Seattle for three days—"

"I'm not complaining." Erin winces at the lawyer's defensive tone. "I know you're busy. I don't expect you to put your life on hold because of me."

"Listen." Briley's eyes soften. "You don't have to always settle for the bottom of the barrel. You're my client, and I am going to do whatever I can to help you. Unfortunately, you're not going to see most of my efforts on your behalf."

Erin shifts her gaze to her hands. "Let's just get down to work, shall we?"

Briley takes an audible breath, then gestures toward the scrawled legal pad on the table and picks up her pen. "I've been conducting a background investigation. I've come up with some interesting information—and some contradictions I need to ask you about."

Erin rubs her chilly arms. "I don't know that I'd call my life *interesting*."

"A lot of people would. You've been given a lot of opportunities, met a lot of influential people...."

"Those were Jeffrey's friends." Erin hunches forward in her chair. "If not for him, I would never have gone anywhere or met anyone."

"I met your mother." Briley's faint smile holds a touch of sadness. "I learned...we actually have a lot in common."

Erin stares, momentarily speechless with surprise.

"I grew up in a single-parent home, too," Briley continues, "but it was my mother who died when I was little. My father managed to stick around until I was fifteen."

"Did he abandon you?"

"He was taken." When Briley looks at Erin this time, something fragile has entered her eyes. "An ex-con killed him, five days before Christmas."

"I'm so sorry."

"So am I."

When Briley swallows hard, Erin senses a fleeting camaraderie. For a moment, at least, they are not lawyer and client, but women bound by the shadow of loss.

An instant later, the lawyer returns. Briley flips the page on her legal pad and props one elbow on the table. "Yesterday I had an interesting encounter with a man you knew in college. Do you remember meeting Doug Haddock or John Savage? They were students at Chicago State at the same time you attended."

Erin sifts through fractured memories. "Were they in one of my classes?"

"They claim they met you at a bar. I don't know if the bar was memorable, but before the night was over, you sent Doug to the emergency room. He says—and his friend verifies—that you hit him over the head with a lamp."

Erin grips the table as surprise siphons the blood from her brain. "They said I did *what?*"

"Surely you remember." Briley's eyes scan Erin's face like laser beams. "Doug filed charges against you with campus security. You mentioned that trouble to Dr. Lu."

Erin shakes her head, as stunned as if she'd been zapped with a cattle prod. "I remember the trouble, but I never understood what I was supposed to have done. I got a letter telling me to report to the campus security station, but by the time I got there, the guard on duty told me the charges had been dropped. He said it must have been some kind of mistake, so I figured that's all it was—a mistake."

The lawyer's eyes narrow. "You don't remember meeting Doug Haddock?"

Why is this so important? At the look in Briley's eyes,

Erin struggles against a surge of momentary doubt. She has seen a man's face, the forehead streaked with blood.... No, that must have been a dream. She shakes her head. "I met lots of guys."

"You went back to the dorm with this one and his friend. Apparently you three got pretty chummy."

"I don't remember that."

Briley taps her pen against the tabletop. "The roommate, John Savage, says Doug slipped you a roofie. You passed out soon after arriving at the dorm."

"If I passed out, how could I remember anything? Honestly, I don't recall either of those guys. Maybe a picture would jog my memory, but right now those names mean nothing to me."

Briley glances at her notes. "The roommate, Savage, says you woke up and hit Doug in the head with a lamp. What I'm wondering is how you could do that if you were unconscious...and why you don't remember anything." She leans back, a speculative look on her face. "Has anyone ever told you that you walk in your sleep?"

Baffled, Erin shakes her head. "No."

"Have you ever awakened in a strange place? Ever had memory lapses you can't explain?"

"No!"

Her voice is sharper and louder than before, but the lawyer doesn't flinch. Instead, she underlines something on her legal pad. "I suppose I should share this story with Dr. Lu. It could establish grounds for a workable defense."

Unnerved by the sudden change in topic, Erin huddles in her seat. "What kind of defense are you talking about?"

"The case theory I want to use claims you aren't guilty because you were unaware of your actions. The 'sleepwalking' defense has been used before—sometimes it works, sometimes it doesn't. In your case, I think it'll work. But I'll have to file a brief and argue that the parasomnia is involuntary, even though you took sleeping pills—"

Erin's breath catches in her lungs. "You think I did it."

"That's not what I said."

"You want to tell the jury I did it."

"That's not what I'm saying at all."

"It is! You want to say I did it, but I didn't. I didn't walk in my sleep, and I didn't kill Jeffrey."

"How do you know that?"

Erin sits motionless, stunned at the inscrutable expression on her lawyer's face. Briley Lester has been working hard, all right, trying on one defense after the other because she doesn't believe Erin's story about Lisa Marie. If her own lawyer can't believe her, who can?

After a painful moment of realization, Erin stands and moves toward the door. "I'm ready to go back to my cell."

"I wouldn't advise you to walk out now. We have other matters to discuss."

"Why? You don't believe me, and I'll never be acquitted if you don't. If I'm willing to trust the lawyer who warned me she wasn't good enough to handle my case, why can't you believe in me?"

"The law doesn't work like that. And I never said I wasn't good enough."

"It's what you meant." Erin pounds on the door. "Guard! I'm done in here."

"Stop it." Briley stands and strides to her side. "There are rules, you know. It's improper for an attorney to voice her personal belief in a client's innocence. In the courtroom, that could be construed as inappropriately attempting to sway a jury."

"I didn't ask you to voice your belief to a jury." Erin spits the words like stones. "I asked you to believe in me. Obviously, you don't."

Briley leans closer, lines of concentration deepening under her eyes. "I don't know how much you know about the crime-scene evidence, Erin, but we're not going to be able to pin this murder on anyone else. In your bathroom trash they found a syringe marked with your fingerprints, no one else's. Your partial thumbprint is on the plunger, as clear as day. And you know what they say—seeing is believing."

"Maybe they've got it backward. Maybe believing is seeing."

Briley exhales in a rush. "You're making no sense."

"I'm making perfect sense. I didn't kill Jeffrey, but you're so blinded by what you *see*—"

"If you didn't kill Jeffrey, then who did? And don't give me that song and dance about Lisa Marie, because apart from you she doesn't exist."

The lawyer's declaration rings in the silence, and Erin cannot answer. How can she explain? She knows Lisa Marie better than anyone, but she's never been able to explain the friend she cannot see or touch or hear except with her heart....

Her lungs squeeze so tight she can barely draw breath, but she forces words over her tongue: "If you use that sleep-walking defense, everyone in the courtroom—my father-in-law, my brother-in-law, my sisters-in-law—they'll all think I killed Jeffrey. They'll think I wanted him dead, and I didn't. Yes, he was abusive, but I didn't want to kill him. I only wanted him to stop hurting me. I would have been happy to leave him if I could. He would have been better off without me, because I never knew how to make him happy."

When a tear drops onto Erin's cheek, Briley's voice softens. "The parasomnia defense doesn't assign blame. Our position will be that you cannot be held accountable for the murder because it was committed while you were asleep and incapable of reason."

Erin looks out the window and searches for the guard. "Doesn't matter. The family will know there's blood on my hands. And they won't let me get away with murder." She looks at the woman beside her. "Have you ever been afraid for your life, Briley?"

The lawyer blanches. "Surely you don't think they will—"

"Jeffrey was the favorite son." Erin presses her palm

against the reinforced glass in the door. "The one who would be president. They pinned so many dreams on him, the man practically clinked when he walked."

A guard steps into the hallway, and she catches his attention. She taps the glass, signaling her readiness to leave. As he strides forward, pulling handcuffs from his belt, she drops her forehead to the chilly window frame. "I didn't kill my husband, but I guess it doesn't matter. If you can't prove someone else did, my life is over."

Chapter Thirty-Two

"Hey, beautiful." Briley lifts her hands from the computer keyboard as Timothy steps through her office doorway and drops into her guest chair. "How's your day been so far?"

"What are you doing here?" Grinning, she steps out from behind her desk and moves to the door, then glances down the hall to see if anyone has noticed her unexpected visitor. Timothy would have had to pass Kate's desk, but Kate wouldn't care if Briley entertained a personal visitor for a few minutes.

She closes the door and leans against it. "I don't believe it. You came here to ask about my *day?*"

He tips his head back and grins at her. "I was in the area. Dax has a doctor's appointment, so he'll be tied up for a while. I thought I'd pop in and see how my favorite girl's doing."

She gives him a look of pained disbelief, then walks to her desk and leans against the edge. "You should have called."

He laughs. "Do I need an appointment to see you?"

"No, but a little consideration would be nice." She crosses her arms. "I don't have as much leisure time as you and Dax. I spent most of the morning at the jail, and this afternoon I have to work on my case theory. Plus I'm expecting a call from the prosecutor's psychologist."

"But you're not on the phone now."

"Thanks for pointing out the obvious." She feels a smile slip onto her face. Sometimes she finds it hard to stay upset with this man.

She leans forward and gives him a quick kiss, then points to the laptop on her desk. "I'm sorry I can't talk, but I'll be tied up until six. After that, I'm all yours."

"Okay, but by six I'll be on duty with Dax. He's entertaining some producer, so the pressure tonight will be intense."

Briley sighs. "Honestly, how much longer is it going to take?"

His eyes flash a gentle warning. "What?"

Feeling reckless, she plunges ahead. "Is the man ever going to stand up for himself? This 'I need to be with Dax' routine is getting a little old."

"You know what my job entails—I have to be available for as long as my client needs help. We're building a relationship based on trust. No one's going to listen to a sober companion they don't know and respect."

"I only wish you would set a few boundaries. Even in your line of work, you have to protect time for yourself."

Laughter lights Timothy's eyes as he slips his hands into his coat. "You're still upset about the night Dax came for dinner. He got rid of the girls, didn't he?"

"After ruining our night. And I'm not mad about that anymore. I'm worried."

"About what?"

"About us." There, she's said it. She didn't mean to, didn't want to bring up the fact that since Timothy started working for Dax they seem to be traveling in two different directions. She has always reserved time for him, but he doesn't seem to think it's necessary to do the same for her.

"Briley." Tim stands and places his hands on her shoulders. "I know you're under a lot of stress, but take a step back and think about this. We're both in the same kind of work— we want to help people. You use your knowledge of the law, I use my knowledge of addiction. Because I've been in that dark pit, people trust me to be there for them…just like your clients trust you."

Briley's mind burns with the memory of Erin Tomassi

pounding on the interview-room door, desperate to escape her lawyer's plan. Why has that picture sprung into her head? Her present case has nothing to do with her personal life, nothing at all.

She looks up into the dark pools of Timothy's eyes and breathes in the scent of leather. "You don't have to give so *much.* I know when to cut things off with my clients. I try to walk out of here at six and plan on no more than a couple of hours' work at home every night. This is a busy time of my life, but when I'm with you, I'm with you completely. I'm ready to focus on *us*…but you're not likely to be around."

Timothy's mouth shifts just enough to bristle the two-day stubble on his cheek. "Life doesn't come tied up in nine-to-five packages, Bri."

"And a career doesn't have to take over your life. If you want a relationship, if you want a family, you're going to have to learn how to maintain a professional distance with your clients."

"Professional." He pronounces the word as if it were an expletive. "You think I'm not *professional?*"

"Don't act like I've just insulted you. I don't know where you draw the line as a sober companion, but there are so many other things you could do. You could be a counselor or work in a rehab center. You could go to jails and talk to prisoners about how to beat addiction. You wouldn't have to become personally *involved*—"

He releases his grip on her shoulders. "Good grief, it sounds like you want me to wear a tie and sit behind a desk. I'd hate that."

"That's not what I said. I'm saying you could find a job that doesn't demand a complete surrender of your private life."

"But I haven't given up my private life. I'm with you now, aren't I?"

"But you shouldn't be!" Briley glances at the clock, her frustration rising with every passing moment. "I grew up with a father who was always looking out for other people.

Every time the phone rang, he would run out the door, carrying groceries to some family or going off to pay some single mother's electric bill. He'd apologize every time, telling me he'd be right back, but the phone calls never stopped coming, until the night he didn't come home…and the world is still full of needy people." She stops, her hand going to her throat, as a sudden lump strangles her voice.

Timothy studies her, his eyes moist and concerned, then he bends to kiss her cheek. "I'll be going, then," he says, releasing her. He moves toward the door. "I'm sorry I interrupted your work."

"Don't go away mad, please."

"Just go away, right?" He releases a hollow laugh. "I understand, Briley. Maybe more than you realize."

"Timothy, that's not—"

The door closes with a definite click.

By the time she wipes the wetness from her cheeks and hurries into the hallway, he has disappeared.

With less than two weeks remaining before she has to return to the courtroom, Briley opens her laptop and smiles at the members of her defense team—a motley crew, by the firm's usual standards. For a trial with this kind of notoriety, she ought to have a couple of interns, a paralegal, and another associate by her side, but Franklin keeps insisting that no one is available to assist her.

She smiles at Kate and William. These two, at least, have been generous with their time.

They are in the library, sorting through all the material received in pretrial discovery. Four cardboard boxes wait on the conference table, recent arrivals from the state's attorney's office. Each box holds dozens of folders containing information, some of it redundant, from the prosecutor or the police investigators: an inventory of all evidence gathered at the crime scene and photographs of the collected evidence; names and addresses of potential witnesses, along with copies of recorded statements from those witnesses; statements made by Erin Tomassi during interrogation; the autopsy and toxicology reports from the medical examiner's office; and copies of an evaluation from the psychologist Bystrowski hired. Briley has shipped several similar boxes to the prosecutor's office.

Kate is studying a list of physical evidence gathered by the police, including bagged hairs, trash from the master bathroom, the sterile wrapper that once held the presumed murder weapon, bottles of insulin, and the personal sharps disposal unit from under the vanity sink.

"Two cotton-tipped swabs from the trash," she reads, making a face. "Good grief, did they catalog *everything?*"

"Nothing's too trivial to scrutinize in a murder trial," William answers, his voice dry. "I'm surprised they didn't empty the trap on the sink and catalog every hair."

"There are lots of random hairs listed by location," Kate says. "Most of them from the bed, but a couple from the carpet and one from the closet."

"Be glad they didn't go through the vacuum cleaner bag." Briley shakes her head. "I know they have to be thorough, but only two people were in the house that night."

"They found three sets of fingerprints," William reminds her.

"Meet the housekeeper." Kate holds up a fingerprint card. "Shirley Walker went down and got her hands inked. So all the prints belonged to people who should have been there."

"Too bad." William picks up another folder. "If another person had been in the house, wouldn't that get our client off the hook?"

"Any mysterious third person would have to be invisible and walk through walls," Briley says, her voice dry. "No one set off the alarm, remember? And the video cameras don't reveal anyone else entering or leaving the house."

For several minutes, they read in silence, each team

member sorting through the files and making notes. After skimming the witness statements, Briley has a strong hunch Bystrowski will build his case around a motive of revenge. "For several reasons," she tells the others. "First, Bystrowski will say Erin had reached her limit with the abuse. Because he knows I could use the abuse to our advantage, he'll want to establish that Erin acted with malice. To do that, he'll say she knew Jeffrey was cheating on her, so she killed him. It's not the most elegant case theory, but it's simple. A jury won't have any problem understanding it." She looks at her two assistants. "But can he make it stick?"

Kate shrugs. "Why not? People have killed for far less."

William tweaks the end of his mustache. "How do we know the senator was cheating?"

"Bystrowski has a statement from the man's girlfriend." Briley waves the appropriate page. "And judging from what I've heard about Jeffrey Tomassi, I doubt she was his only paramour."

Kate snorts. "We could subpoena half the women in Chicago if we wanted more proof. The man wasn't subtle about his infidelities."

"He was sly, though." The corner of Briley's mouth twists. "According to this statement, Jeffrey usually used his twin's name at hotels. In fact, once he was downtown engaging in a tryst while his brother stood in for him during a televised charity event. What a toad."

"Now I understand why our client killed him," Kate says. "Any rat who'd do that simply couldn't love his wife. He reminds me of this guy I used to date—"

"Our client *allegedly* killed her husband." Briley cuts her off, not willing to discuss matters of the heart while they're working. She hasn't heard from Timothy in a week, so he must have been more upset by their last meeting than she realized. "And, by the way, Erin insists she didn't know her husband was cheating. I'm not sure she bore him malice. Like a lot of abused wives, she felt the abuse was somehow her fault."

William holds up his legal pad and shows Briley a numbered list. "So…what's our defense going to be? Mental illness, battered-spouse syndrome, parasomnia, or something we haven't covered yet?"

"I have a plan, but let's discuss it." She shoves a folder aside and opens a document on her computer. "The prevalent definition of legal insanity says a person is not responsible for criminal conduct if at the time of such conduct, as a result of mental disease or defect, he lacks the capacity either to appreciate the criminality of his conduct or to conform his conduct to the requirement of law."

"Break it down." Kate taps the stem of her glasses against the table. "Mental disease or defect—what about Erin Tomassi's invisible friend? Does delusion qualify as mental disease?"

Briley shakes her head. "I tried to convince Dr. Lu that we had to be dealing with a split personality, but she wouldn't confirm that diagnosis. Bystrowski's shrink said the same thing. Erin may be delusional, but so are a lot of perfectly sane people."

"So you form a case around parasomnia," William suggests. "How does Dr. Lu feel about the sleepwalking defense?"

Briley glances at her notes. "She's not thrilled about it. If Erin went sleep-jogging a couple of times a week, we'd stand a better chance of convincing a jury. But I've only been able to document one other case of parasomnia in her history—if that's what you call waking in the middle of a drug-induced stupor with enough energy to fight off your would-be rapist and flee the scene."

"Have you completely written off self-defense?" Kate asks. "That preacher's wife who killed her husband with a shotgun claimed abuse as a defense and was only convicted of voluntary manslaughter."

William snaps his fingers. "I remember that one. The wife was sentenced to two hundred and ten days and released after serving a couple of months."

"Sixty-seven days," Briley says. "Self-defense is still a possibility. But the problem with all of these arguments is that they put the syringe in Erin's hand. She keeps resisting, because she still insists she didn't inject her husband. I can't walk into that courtroom with a hostile client."

"Maybe she'll fire you," Kate says, smiling.

Briley sighs. "She's stubborn, but she's not stupid. If she fires me, she knows she'll get a public defender—someone who's likely to be overworked, underpaid, and even more understaffed than me. Plus her trial will be postponed, which means months of waiting in jail."

Kate leans back in her chair, a frown puckering the skin between her eyes. "Denial is a powerful emotion. Maybe part of your job is going to be helping her realize what happened that night."

"I still like the suicide argument," William says. "Jeffrey Tomassi was a lowlife who abused his wife and cheated on her. He might have had an attack of conscience."

"That's a problem," Briley says. "The Tomassi family is adamant that Jeffrey wasn't suicidal. If the prosecution puts all those grieving siblings and cousins on the stand…" She shakes her head. "We'd be talking tragic opera. Not a good idea."

"Accidental death?" William asks. "Maybe he got careless."

"Fingerprints," Briley counters. "The fingerprints on the syringe are hers, not his. And Erin's on record saying that she never gave her husband insulin injections."

"So…" Kate tugs on the blond hair at her collar. "What's it going to be, Counselor?"

Briley stares at William's list. "Every theory has a hole in it. As much as I hate to go against my client's wishes, I think we have the best chance of mitigating a first-degree murder charge with the parasomnia defense. Erin is innocent because she could not form intent while asleep. Sleepwalking is the only way we can explain her fingerprints on the murder weapon."

William draws a deep breath. "Even if you get her off, some people will never buy that theory. To them, she'll always be guilty of murder."

"What other choice do I have? Fingerprints don't lie."

"Sometimes they do," Kate says. "I once saw a TV show where a secret agent used a gummi bear to replicate and plant a fingerprint."

Briley frowns, not sure if she's joking. "Any other thoughts?"

"Just one." William presses his hands together. "The most incriminating piece of evidence is the syringe with our client's fingerprints on it, right?"

Briley nods.

"Well…what if that evidence were thrown out?"

"Excluded? How?" Briley clamps her mouth shut, wishing she felt more confident. A more competent attorney, one with actual experience in a capital case, would know more than the law librarian.

William wags a finger. "Was the evidence properly obtained? Did the police have a warrant when they entered the house?"

"I don't think they need a warrant to enter when they've been called because of a suspicious death," Briley says. "And until a death is ruled suicide or accident, any scene is considered a crime scene."

William shrugs. "I'm wondering if they asked Erin for permission to search the residence."

Briley bites her lower lip. "You may have something there. I'll speak to my client. If they didn't ask—"

"You could get the evidence thrown out." William smiles and tweaks the corner of his mustache. "You could blow them out of the water."

Briley rests her chin on her hand. If she attempts to get the evidence excluded and doesn't succeed, she may become the laughingstock of the Cook County courthouse. On the other hand, one never knows what argument might sway a judge. If she hits the books and digs around on Westlaw, she may be able to find a legal precedent....

She smiles at the others around the table. "Wish me luck, then. If this works, we may annihilate the state's case with just one motion."

Chapter Thirty-Three

On Thursday morning, Briley slides into her car and drives to an interview she's been dreading. She's not certain if she'll learn anything useful from Erin's brother, but at some point, every desperate lawyer trolls for information.

In a northern section of Austin, Roger Wilson's group home lies on a street that has managed to retain a hint of its stately dignity. Briley parks on a pitted section of asphalt and studies the sprawling two-story Victorian as she locks her car. She crosses the sidewalk and opens a peeling iron gate, careful to latch it behind her. A gently curving sidewalk leads her through a sea of winter-dead grass to the front door, where a hand-painted sign presents a smiley face and a command: ring the bell. She does.

She stands on the front porch, shivering in the frigid wind, until a white-haired man in a cardigan opens the door and welcomes her to the house.

"I called earlier," Briley explains, stepping into the foyer. "I'm here to see Roger Wilson."

"You must be the attorney. I'm Floyd McKee." The man smiles, reminding her of the genial Grandpa on *The Munsters*. "Roger is in the dayroom. If you'll come with me…"

Briley follows her host to a large room with wide windows overlooking the bare side lawn. Three adult residents sit in the room, two of them engaged in watching an *I Love Lucy* rerun. Another resident sits alone, working a jigsaw puzzle on a TV tray. He is dressed like Floyd: dark slacks, cardigan sweater, and white shirt, though his face is unlined. If fashion sense is inheritable, these two could be father and son.

"Please excuse the holiday decorations," Floyd says, gesturing to the Christmas tree in the corner of the room. "I know the season has passed, but my young friends like the lights."

Briley pauses before the tree, which has been adorned with plastic bulbs, Popsicle-stick ornaments, and paper cutouts.

"Roger?" Floyd walks over and rests his hand on the puzzle-worker's shoulder. "You have a visitor. This young woman is a friend of your sister's."

Roger looks up, his wide forehead crinkling. "Is Erin coming to see me?"

"She can't come today." Briley steps forward and gives him a smile. "I'm Briley. May I sit and talk with you a few minutes?"

Roger looks to the older man, who reaches for a folding chair. "Make yourself comfortable," he tells Briley, setting the chair on the other side of the TV table. "You can help Roger with his puzzle. And may I take your coat?"

Briley shrugs out of her coat and hands it to Floyd, then sits. Roger gives her an absent frown and returns his attention to the puzzle pieces scattered over the tray.

This interview isn't going to be as straightforward as she had hoped.

"This is a pretty puzzle," she says, tilting her head to see it better. "What will it be, a seascape?"

Roger's brows knit in puzzlement. "It's the beach."

"Of course. The beach." She picks up a straight-edged piece and looks for a match. "I'm sorry Erin couldn't come with me today. Do you remember living with her when you were younger?"

Still intent on his puzzle, he shakes his head.

"That's too bad. Does she visit you here?"

Roger holds a puzzle piece before his eye, as if he could see through it. "She comes to see me. Sometimes."

Floyd, who has been standing behind the other two residents, steps toward them. "We haven't seen Erin in a couple of years," he explains, his smile apologetic. "Last time she stopped by, she said it was hard for her to get away. With a husband in politics, I suppose I can understand."

"Her husband was...quite demanding." Briley gives Floyd a pointed look. "I don't suppose Roger reads the newspapers?"

"We don't even take a paper." Floyd's expression remains neutral, though he has to be curious about Erin's case. "He has no idea about—the matter that brings you to see us. I don't let my young friends watch the evening news, either."

"A good idea." Briley smiles at Roger. What did she hope to find here? "Erin asked me to come see you," she says, trying to catch his gaze. "She misses you."

Roger sets another puzzle piece into the center of the tray, then looks at Floyd, his eyes glowing. "My sister misses me."

"I'm sure she does," Floyd answers, pulling over another folding chair.

Briley's heart sinks when the older man sits down. This is not going well; Roger is less communicative than she'd hoped. She ought to tell him goodbye and be on her way, but now that Floyd has taken a seat, she'll need to talk for at least a few minutes or he'll think her rude.

The older man laces his fingers. "Such simple souls." He crosses his leg at the ankle, doubtless settling in for a nice long conversation. "You might not think they are deeply devoted, but Roger adores his sister. He keeps several pictures of her up in his room."

Briley glances at her watch. "Does his mother ever come to visit him?"

The older man's face shifts back into a neutral expression. "Why don't you ask Roger?"

Briley turns, about to repeat the question, but Roger has his answer ready. "Christmas," he says, poring over the puzzle with a new piece in his hand. "Mama visits at Christmas."

For a moment Briley sits in awkward silence, not knowing what else to say. On the other side of the room, Ricky explodes into Spanish as he scolds Lucy for overspending. The two men watching television laugh.

"Plato," Floyd says, resting his folded hands on the cushion of his belly, "held that we are born perfect and then split in half by Zeus. So we spend the rest of our lives searching for our missing half, our soul mate."

Briley's thoughts immediately dart to Timothy. She swallows the lump that rises in her throat and picks up another puzzle piece, a bit of green ocean.

"I don't buy into Plato's theory," Floyd continues, shifting his focus to the men in front of the television, "but often I look at my friends and wonder if some genetic accident robbed them of the selfish streak most people exhibit from infancy. They're not perfect, but they're generally much sweeter than ordinary people." One corner of his mouth turns up, and his blue eyes gleam as he grins at Briley. "Maybe they've had most of the selfishness yanked out of them."

Briley snaps her puzzle piece into place and watches as Roger's mouth curves into an approving smile. "I wouldn't know," she says. "I don't have much time for mysticism. Or religion, for that matter."

"You're a skeptic, then."

She shrugs. "A realist. But I can appreciate people who have the time and willingness to consider things like souls…and sweetness."

She snaps a blue piece of sky into place, and smiles when Roger gives her another grateful grin.

Chapter Thirty-Four

As swollen clouds threaten to engulf the top floor of the courthouse, Briley and her client wait for Travis Bystrowski to arrive in the courtroom. Erin has been given a clean jail uniform for this appearance, but her face is thinner than it was a month ago, with shadowed blue eyes taking up most of the available space. Shackles bind her ankles and hobble her steps; handcuffs clink every time she lifts her arm.

Though a defendant has the right to attend any hearing related to her case, some defense attorneys do not bring their clients to hearings concerned with matters of law. Briley, however, thought it important for the judge to get a good look at Erin Tomassi. Looking at her, the judge will see not a scheming killer, but a woman who is more doormat than diva.

"How are you doing at the jail?" Briley asks, grateful for an opportunity to speak to her client outside that depressing interview room. "Are things getting any easier for you?"

Erin snorts softly. "I've learned how it feels to be an unwelcome minority." She rubs a hand over her thin arm. "Some of the women despise me because I'm white. Most of them think I'm some kind of a snob."

Briley peers at a dark spot on Erin's jawline. "Is that another bruise? Did someone else hit you?"

The corner of Erin's mouth dips. "I'm learning to keep my head down and not look anyone in the eye. And I pray a lot."

Suddenly embarrassed by her freedom, Briley lowers her gaze. "How do you pass the time in there?"

"You don't. Time passes *you*."

Briley straightens when she spies Bystrowski coming through the double doors. "Here we go."

A moment later, the prosecutor extends his hand to Briley. "Good to see you, Counselor. I trust you received all of our materials?"

"Yes, thanks." Briley sinks back into her chair, noticing that the prosecutor didn't think to greet her client. "I trust you received our files, too."

"If I hadn't, you'd have heard about it."

He drops his briefcase on his table and pulls out a chair. Briley glances at the clock on her cell phone and hopes they won't have to wait long for the judge.

"I have an offer for your client," Bystrowski says, opening his briefcase. He pulls a sheet of paper from a folder and hands it to her. "Save the state time and money, plead guilty to voluntary manslaughter, and we'll send Ms. Tomassi to Decatur women's prison for twenty years. It's medium-security, not hard time."

Briley knows nothing about Decatur, but she could live with a manslaughter conviction. Twenty years, however, is a long time, even with the possibility of parole. "I'll have to confer with my client," she says, scanning the offer.

"No." Erin speaks in a jagged whisper. "I did not kill my husband."

"Are you sure?" Briley lowers her voice. "We could negotiate the sentence."

"No." Erin lifts her chin and meets the prosecutor's gaze straight on. "No deal."

Briley looks at Bystrowski and shrugs. "Your offer is refused."

"Don't you want to take a couple of days to think about it?"

"You should be grateful we're saving the state's valuable time."

His gaze narrows. "You can't possibly believe you can pull off an acquittal."

"I believe there's more to this case than meets the eye. My client did not intentionally kill her husband."

"I didn't kill him unintentionally, either." Erin leans forward and meets the prosecutor's gaze. "I know you don't believe me, but it's true. I didn't murder—"

"Shh." Unnerved by her client's outburst, Briley drops her hand to Erin's arm. "That's enough, Mrs. Tomassi." Maybe she should have urged Erin to waive her right to attend this hearing.

Briley waits, hoping Bystrowski will counter with another offer, but the prosecutor only gives her an incredulous look and sits at his table. "Looks like we're going to trial."

Three minutes later, Judge Milton Trask sweeps into the courtroom and takes his seat on the bench. He is an older man, with jowls that hang in flaps like the muzzle of a hound, but his eyes snap with curiosity and directness.

The court reporter, a thin woman in black slacks, slips in behind the judge and sits at her table, immediately opening her laptop.

After greeting the two lawyers, the judge turns to his case file. "Oh, yes," he says, pulling a folder from his briefcase. "The state senator."

"Your Honor..." Bystrowski stands and hands Briley a list of official charges. "The state is charging Erin Wilson Tomassi with first-degree murder in the death of her husband, Jeffrey Tomassi, an Illinois state senator, on December 3 of last year."

The judge looks at the page with the air of a man who has seen such charges many times before. "And the pretrial motions?"

"The defense has a motion pending." Briley stands, offering the prosecutor a copy of the motion she filed the previous week. "Your Honor, the defense moves to exclude any and all evidence gathered at the Tomassi house on the day of Jeffrey Tomassi's death."

Bystrowski rolls his eyes. "The state objects. Police detectives have every right to investigate a suspicious death."

"As I stated in my motion, Jeffrey Tomassi's death was not considered suspicious at the time of the investigation," Briley argues. "The detectives had no reason to rummage through my client's home without her permission."

"But they asked permission, Your Honor. The search was good. The police did everything by the book."

"Did they?" Briley arches a brow and looks at Bystrowski. "I don't recall seeing a signed statement in the police report. Or any mention of recorded assent."

"Young woman." The judge's granite eyes lock on her. "Ms. Lester, you are to address the court, not opposing counsel. Do you understand?"

Briley swallows hard. "Yes, Your Honor."

The judge shifts his gaze to Bystrowski. "Do you have evidence of permission to search, Counselor?"

When the prosecutor's face goes the color of bleached paper, Briley knows he has no proof.

"Not at hand, Your Honor."

"But you've known about this motion for a week." The judge folds his hands. "Am I correct in assuming that evidence of permission to search does not exist?"

Bystrowski's nostrils flare. "Apparently…that is an accurate assumption."

"Then I'm afraid I'll have to exclude—"

"I gave him permission."

Erin's voice is so low that at first Briley is certain she's hearing things. But when she looks down, she sees that Erin is biting on her thumb. She's also looking directly at the judge. So she *did* speak. She opened her mouth and destroyed everything Briley is trying to accomplish.

"Y-Your Honor…" Briley's head swims with words, none of which want to cooperate with her stammering tongue. She needs to object, but with what argument? Should she invoke the Fifth Amendment and her client's right not to incriminate herself? Or should she simply state that the defendant is naive and has a fool for an attorney?

Too late. Judge Trask casts Briley a disbelieving glance before addressing her client. "Mrs. Tomassi, did I hear you correctly? You gave the police permission to search?"

Erin lowers her head in an abrupt nod. "One of the policemen who showed up right after the ambulance asked if he could look around. I said he could. That's the same thing, isn't it? Granting permission?"

"It certainly is."

Briley suppresses a groan as Trask drops the copy of her motion. Why didn't he just wad it up and toss it over his shoulder? "Motion to exclude is denied. And, ma'am—" he transfers his gaze to Erin "—in court, you are usually best served by letting your attorney speak for you. Do you understand?"

A dark, painful red washes up from Erin's throat. "Yes, sir."

Unable to look at the judge, Briley lowers her head to her hand. She should have kept her client under control; she should have explained what she was trying to do. In attempting to impress the judge with Erin's vulnerability, she has made a fatal mistake.

The prosecutor wouldn't have been able to prove anything without the fingerprint-covered syringe. The judge would have dismissed the case.

She rakes her hand through her hair and gives Bystrowski a *Can you believe it?* look. Maybe Erin should reconsider that insanity defense.

Judge Trask glances from one lawyer to the other. "Are any other motions pending?"

"Yes, sir." With great reluctance Briley stiffens her spine to address one other important piece of business. "The defense has also filed a motion to take the death penalty off the table. Illinois requires special circumstances before the option of capital punishment can be presented to jurors, and none of those special circumstances apply in this case."

Bystrowski's mouth dips into an even deeper frown. "The state disagrees, Your Honor. We believe this case qualifies under at least two special circumstances."

"Really?" Briley shoots back. "Name them."

"Ms. Lester." The judge casts her a sharp look. "You are out of order."

"I'm sorry, Your Honor." Briley lowers her head in what she hopes is an apologetic posture.

Bystrowski continues. "Illinois allows the death penalty for cases where the murder was committed for pecuniary gain," he says. "Erin Tomassi stood to inherit her husband's fortune if he died. Second, as a state senator and public servant, Jeffrey Tomassi qualifies as a government employee. Special circumstances must apply in this case."

"As a wife, Erin Tomassi already shared her husband's fortune," Briley argues. "That statute was created to punish murderers-for-hire, which is not the situation in this case. And the government-employee provision was intended to protect police officers, firemen, and even state's attorneys as they go about their duties. Jeffrey Tomassi was not working while he slept."

"Your Honor, when is a state senator not working?" Bystrowski counters. "Public officials do not keep office hours. They are continually serving the people. Earlier that night, Tomassi attended an event for his constituency—"

"He attended a fundraiser for his next campaign." Briley's nervousness disappears, replaced by a rising indignation. "On that night, he wasn't thinking about his place in the Illinois state senate, Your Honor. He was dreaming about a spot in the U.S. Congress."

"Where he would still be serving the people of Illinois!"

Judge Trask holds up his hand. "I've heard enough from both of you." He studies a page of the case file for a moment, then looks up. "Within the next ten days, I'd like each of you to send me a brief with your points and authorities. I will withhold my ruling on the death-penalty motion until the trial. Until then, I advise you to proceed as if this is a capital case. Now…is there anything else?"

Briley crosses one arm over her chest and struggles to cool her simmering temper. "The defense has nothing else, Your Honor."

Bystrowski shakes his head. "Nor does the state."

"Then I'll see you on the sixteenth of March."

As the judge walks out, the court reporter in tow, a corner of Bystrowski's mouth twists in a cynical smile. "I'll see you ladies in a few weeks, then."

Briley waits until the prosecutor closes the heavy court-room door, then she turns to her client. "Erin…things did not go well for us today."

Erin stares at her, her eyes like bits of brilliant blue stone. "What do you mean?"

Briley closes her eyes and struggles to find a way around the unspoken accusation on her tongue: *Are you trying to sabotage your trial?*

"I told you I've never tried a capital case," she finally says. "Maybe you need a better lawyer."

"I don't think I can find a better lawyer."

Briley turns, about to suggest that Erin try the yellow pages, then she realizes her client is smiling.

"You've worked hard," Erin says, her hand coming to rest on Briley's arm. "I heard passion in your voice today, and that's what I need in a lawyer. You've never done this before? Neither have I. But you can't quit on me now. I won't let you."

Briley draws a deep breath, then pats Erin's hand. Something in her wants to respond with a quip about putting that statement in writing because it'll be useful during the appeal, but this is not an appropriate time for teasing.

A deputy is approaching. It's time for Erin to go back to jail.

Chapter Thirty-Five

From the way Shirley Walker keeps jiggling her leg, Briley deduces that the housekeeper is nervous.

"Thank you for coming in," she says, stepping out from behind her desk. "Can I get you a cup of coffee? Some water?"

"No, thank you." Mrs. Walker smoothes out a wrinkle in her dark jeans. "If we could get on with this, I'd appreciate it. I still have two houses to clean this afternoon."

"Of course. I appreciate your time." Briley pulls over a guest chair and sits directly across from the white-haired woman. She smiles, hoping to put Mrs. Walker at ease. "I'm sure you know I'm not allowed to tell you what to say if you're called to testify. In any case, I wouldn't want you to say anything that isn't the truth."

The woman bobs her head in a quick nod. "I've seen *Law & Order*."

"Good. If the prosecutor calls you as a witness—and I'm sure he will—he'll begin by asking your name and where you live. Then he'll want to know how long you worked for the Tomassis. He'll probably ask you to describe your relationship with them."

The woman nods again but remains silent.

Briley folds her hands. "Can you answer that question now?"

"Which question?"

"How would you describe your relationship with Jeffrey and Erin Tomassi?"

The woman rubs her jeans again. "Mr. Tomassi was

always nice to me. He paid on time, he didn't leave a big mess, and he didn't speak sharp to me."

"And your relationship with Mrs. Tomassi?"

The beginnings of a smile lift the corners of Mrs. Walker's mouth. "We were friends. Erin was sweet, and she never took my help for granted. Some mornings, if she didn't have to rush off with him, she'd stay and help me clean. She didn't think nothing of getting up on a chair to take down draperies or running a comforter to the dry cleaner. She wasn't afraid of hard work."

Briley jots a note on her legal pad. "Were you around the Tomassis enough to get a feeling for the state of their marriage?"

"You mean…were they happy?"

"Yes. Did you see evidence of happiness?"

Mrs. Walker's frown deepens. "Nobody smiled much in that house, at least not when he was around. He was polite, but not what you'd call warm, and sometimes he spoke real sharp to her. She was always polite to him, but a few times I walked in and caught her crying at her desk. No, I couldn't say I saw much happiness in that house."

"Did you ever hear Erin threaten her husband? Did she ever say anything to you about leaving him or wishing she were free of him?"

"No, never. Nothing like that."

"Very good," Briley says. "Try to keep your statements centered on the facts. Don't elaborate. And relax—you're going to do fine."

The woman's face softens in an expression of relief. "I wouldn't want to say anything to hurt Erin. She doesn't deserve any more pain."

Briley stands. "I haven't decided if I'll call you to testify, but if you're needed, someone from the court will call to let you know when you'll need to appear at the courthouse. You'll have to arrive early and go through the metal detectors. Sometimes it's good to bring a crossword puzzle or something to read, because trials usually involve a lot of waiting around."

"That reminds me." The woman pulls several envelopes from her purse. "I've been gathering the mail for Mrs. Tomassi. Will you be seein' her anytime soon?"

"Probably later today." Briley takes the mail and skims the return addresses—mostly bills and credit card offers. With no one living in the house, she should probably send these to Antonio Tomassi or some other family member.

"And there's this." Mrs. Walker hands Briley a slip of paper with a name and number written on it. "This doctor has called twice. He says he needs to speak to Mrs. T about something."

Briley frowns at the unfamiliar name. "This is a physician? Was Erin seeing him about something?"

"I don't know. All I know is, he's left two messages on her machine."

"I'll pass the word along. Thank you, Mrs. Walker, for your help."

After the housekeeper leaves, Briley pulls out her list of witnesses and places a check next to the woman's name. She may not have to call Mrs. Walker, but she needs to be ready in case Bystrowski decides to put her on the stand. She also needs to prepare Dr. Lu, and she may have to subpoena Douglas Haddock....

The judge has allowed only seven weeks to prepare for trial. Briley would ask for an extension—and would probably get one—but every day she waits is another day Erin spends in jail. The memory of the bruise on her client's jawbone spurs her to look for Dr. Lu's phone number.

Postponement is not a viable option.

Chapter Thirty-Six

Erin shuffles into the interview room and waits like a hobbled animal as the guard unlocks her handcuffs. The room is chilly, unlike the communal area where most of the inmates lounge around the television and moan about their men and their incompetent lawyers. That space stinks of sweat and fury, but this place is as cold as a tomb.

She chafes her wrists and sinks into a plastic chair, then lets her head drop to the table. Her eyelids fall, and in the silence she can almost imagine herself back in her kitchen, her cheek against the cool granite countertop.

Hard to believe she's still here. Harder to believe that by this time next week, her fate should be settled. Her trial begins Monday, so Briley is coming to the jail today, eager for one last chance to prepare her client…who doesn't dare hope for acquittal.

She steels her nerves when the door opens and screeches in protest. She hears her lawyer murmur to the guard, Briley's quick steps on the concrete floor. Then something slaps the table.

Erin opens her eyes and lifts her head. "What's this? You're bringing me junk mail?"

"It's about the only thing not on the contraband list," Briley answers, but if she meant to joke, the words fall flat. Erin shuffles through the envelopes—three credit card offers, a notice from the Republican party, a real estate brochure about homes for sale in Chicago's affluent Oak Park area, and a couple of utility bills.

Erin slides the envelopes back across the table. "You can toss it all, as far as I'm concerned."

Briley picks the bills out of the pile. "Do you think your father-in-law would take care of these? I'm sure he'll want to maintain the property."

"Because I'm not going home?" Erin attempts a careless grin, but her mouth only twitches with uncertainty.

"Of course you are…eventually." The lawyer gives her an artificial smile and opens her notebook. "I've prepped our witnesses, I've talked to our team, I've fashioned our case theory, and put the prosecution on notice. Once I run all this by you, we'll be all set."

"Okay."

Briley draws a deep breath and stands. "I'm recommending that we plead not guilty by reason of involuntary intoxication. Illinois law requires that you be examined by at least one psychologist named by the prosecuting attorney, but we've already covered that, so we're good to go."

Erin stares, her protest wedging in her throat.

"I know what you're thinking," Briley adds as she begins to pace, "and I know you weren't drunk. But you took two Ambien, so you were intoxicated by the drug. The law says that involuntary intoxication is a defense if it causes the same symptoms required by the insanity defense."

Erin listens with rising bewilderment. "What are you talking about?"

"We have gathered good information on Ambien and the side effect of parasomnia—sleepwalking. You cannot be held responsible for something you did while you were asleep because you would be unable to form mens rea, or intent."

Erin stares at her lawyer. "That won't work."

"It's time for you to start being reasonable. We've talked this through."

"Apparently you weren't listening. I don't want any defense that implies I killed my husband."

"But the state has irrefutable evidence. *Your* fingerprints, not Jeff's, are on the syringe."

"So what? I'm sure there were several syringes in the sharps bin. His fingerprints had to be on those."

"The police report says the syringe in evidence was found at the top of the trash. The fact that it was—proof that you didn't try to hide it—is further affirmation of parasomnia. Only someone who wasn't concerned about deception would have dropped it there."

Erin lowers her head to her hand. "I know you don't believe in Lisa Marie—"

"Erin—"

"But I didn't kill Jeffrey. Why can't we go to court, tell the truth, and get justice?"

The lawyer turns away, frustration evident in every line of her body. She's probably been hoping Erin would never mention Lisa Marie again, but how can she hide the truth?

"You think it's that simple?" A bitter edge lines Briley's voice. "I used to think that practicing law would be straightforward. That cases would be black and white. That every time I stood with a client, he would be either innocent or guilty, and the jury would always recognize the truth."

The lawyer's words tremble in the stillness, as if they were rising from some raw and secret place.

"But you know what?" Briley releases a bitter laugh. "In no time I learned that law isn't about justice. Too often it's about clearing the judge's crowded calendar and pretending that unstable clients are responsible citizens. It's about convincing a guilty woman to settle for ten years in prison instead of a lifetime sentence without possibility of parole."

"Who are you talking about?" Erin's teeth chatter. "Don't you believe me?"

"Who is Lisa Marie?" Briley's eyes flash as she whirls around. "Where does she live? I'm no psychologist, but there's only one answer to this riddle—Lisa Marie lives inside your mind. Therefore, *your* hand reached for the insulin bottle. *Your* fingers filled the syringe and injected your husband. Lisa Marie is not tangible. She's not able to confess to the court. *You* are the one the jury will see. *You're* the wife with a motive. And if we don't succeed in our defense, you're the one who'll go to prison or face the death penalty. *You*."

Erin gulps hard, tears slipping down her cheeks. "But I didn't kill anyone. And if you won't believe me, I don't know how I'm going to convince a jury that I didn't do it. But I didn't."

A melancholy frown flits across Briley's features. "It won't be enough to deny that you injected your husband. In the face of such strong evidence, we're going to have to show that someone else had opportunity, motive, and access. As long as Bystrowski is holding that damning syringe, you're asking me to do the impossible."

Erin wipes her dripping nose with the back of her hand. "The prosecutor has to prove his case, right? Then let him prove it. But don't say I did it, because I didn't. If you tell them I injected Jeffrey, I might as well take that plea bargain the prosecutor offered. I might as well give up."

"You can't give up. You deserve your day in court…and I'm going to see that you get it."

Erin looks across the table and notices for the first time that shadows lie beneath Briley's eyes, dark, puffy circles. The woman has been losing sleep.

"Briley," she whispers, dropping her head onto her outstretched arm, "I'm not a fool. I'm terrified by the thought of spending the rest of my life in jail. But I'm even more frightened by the thought of facing the Tomassis with Jeffrey's blood on my hands. I don't know how my fingerprints got on that syringe, but you have to believe me when I tell you that I'd kill myself before I'd kill Jeffrey. I know I'm innocent, and I know you can help the jury see the truth."

The lawyer shakes her head, then crosses her arms and

leans back against the wall. "You're killing me. You're making this so much harder than it has to be."

Erin lifts her head and peers out through bleary eyes. "How hard is it to tell the truth?"

Chapter Thirty-Seven

"Ladies and gentlemen of the jury, as Judge Trask informed you, my name is Briley Lester and I'm representing Erin Tomassi, the defendant in this case."

When someone raps on her office door, Briley stops rehearsing and glances at the clock—8:00 p.m., so everyone but the workaholic associates should be long gone. *She* should be long gone, but somehow it seemed important to remain in the office where she could focus on the upcoming trial.

"Come in?"

She nearly drops her note cards when Joseph Franklin opens the door and leans into her office. He gives her a casual smile. "A fax came in for you. I thought you might want to see it."

Briley takes the document and scans it. The document is a letter opinion from Judge Trask. He's ruled on her motion to void the death penalty for Erin Tomassi's case, and he's ruled against her.

She groans. "I can't believe it."

"You can't be surprised," Franklin says. "Trask is a real law-and-order judge. I thought you knew that."

She shakes her head. "I was hoping for better news." Though she has prepared for this outcome, her workload has just tripled. Now that the death penalty is officially hanging over Erin's head, Briley will have so many more things to consider....

"You all set for Monday morning?" Franklin asks. "Anything I can do to help?"

Briley shakes her head, not trusting her voice. Why is he finally asking about her case? After working her ragged, remaining out of touch, and answering her questions through assistants and secretaries, *now* he wants to lend his support?

Franklin props a hand against the door frame. "How's our client holding up? Did you find her cooperative?"

"I found her stubborn." Briley leans against the edge of her desk in an effort to appear relaxed. "I visited her this morning. She still insists she didn't kill her husband, but I'm afraid the evidence is going to bury us. I'm still trying to find a defense we can agree on."

Franklin gives her an apologetic smile. "Don't let the tough ones break your spirit. I stopped by to tell you not to be crushed if this case doesn't go the way you'd like it to. As you know, the Tomassis have been clients of this firm a long time, so of course they turned to us in their hour of crisis. But Antonio wants justice. If the evidence points squarely to his daughter-in-law..." Franklin straightens and folds his arms, giving Briley an eloquent shrug. "I hope you hear me saying that you shouldn't be worried about your standing at this firm if your client is convicted. Do your best, of course, as I'm certain you will. But know that we won't think less of you if the jury doesn't come back with a manslaughter conviction."

Briley nods, her mouth dry.

"All right, then." He smiles and gives her a jaunty salute. "Break a leg Monday morning."

Briley makes a face at her boss's retreating back as he closes the door. In the three years she's worked at Franklin, Watson, Smyth & Morton, she has never heard a partner give an "It's okay to lose" speech to an associate. The lawyers of this firm are usually determined to win.

If Franklin considers a verdict of manslaughter unlikely, her chance for an acquittal must be virtually nonexistent.

Briley refuses to read the newspaper in the days just before the trial, knowing that William and Kate will tell her about any important new developments in the case. She's seen far too many articles portraying Jeffrey Tomassi as a saint and Erin as a gold digger. She can only hope any potential jurors have avoided the papers, as well.

She intends to spend the weekend browsing through a garden catalog, but when she stands by her frozen flower beds, the images of lilacs, peonies, and hostas refuse to bloom in her imagination. She blows out a frosty breath, tucks the catalog under her arm, and hurries back into the warmth of the house, reminding herself that spring is only a few weeks away.

Feeling restless and irritable, she curls up on the sofa and clicks the television remote, but finds nothing of interest. She ought to be reveling in a few hours of personal time, but her thoughts keep drifting toward the coming trial. Though she feels well prepared, she could certainly rehearse her opening remarks and review her trial notebook. She has already made notes on every possible defense strategy, planning to choose one once she discerns Bystrowski's approach, but perhaps she has overlooked something important....

She starts when her cell phone rings. She frowns at the unfamiliar number, then answers. "Hello?"

"Ms. Lester?" The man's voice is vaguely familiar. "This is Floyd McKee. I'm so sorry to disturb you on a Saturday."

She struggles to place the name. "Mr. McKee?"

"From Roger Wilson's group home. Listen, we tried to keep Roger away from the TV, but this morning a special report caught us by surprise. Mrs. Tomassi was on the news and Roger saw everything. He's been upset ever since, and since he can't call the jail, I thought maybe you could say something to comfort him."

Briley presses her hand over her face. What does she know about comforting childlike men? And if Joseph Franklin is right about her chances of success next week, she ought to tell this man that his sister will be going away for a long time...maybe forever.

"Floyd, I don't think—" She stops when she realizes no one is on the line. She hears shuffling sounds, a soft murmur, then a thick voice. "'Lo?"

"Is this Roger?"

"Yeah?"

"This is Briley, a friend of Erin's. Do you remember me? I helped you with your puzzle."

Roger remains silent for a moment, then a torrent breaks forth. "I saw Erin on the TV and she was crying with her hands tied up with bracelets and the police were taking her away." He is weeping now, the sound awful enough to break a heart of granite. "I don't want Erin to go away to jail. That's where bad people go, and Erin is not bad. Erin is good. She is kind and she brings me cookies and puzzles."

When these words are followed by a loud clunk, Briley assumes he has dropped the phone...or thrown it.

She hears the muffled sound of tortured sobs, then Roger is back on the line. "Please, lady, will you help Erin? Don't let them put her in jail."

She listens, tears welling in her eyes, until she regains control of her voice. "I'll try my best, Roger. I'll do what I can for your sister."

"You promise? 'Cause it's not good to break a promise."

"I promise. I do."

"Mr. Floyd wants to talk to you."

Briley inhales a deep breath as the older man comes on the phone. "Ms. Lester, I hate to bring this up, considering the circumstances, but I'm concerned about Roger's account."

"His what?"

The man clears his throat. "A payment of twelve hundred dollars a month. We usually received it from Mrs. Tomassi's accountant, but we haven't recorded any payments for this calendar year. The account is now thirty-six hundred dollars overdue. I hate to say anything, considering the circumstances, but if we're not able to bring this account up to date—"

"Wait a minute— Your home is privately funded? I thought you were affiliated with a public agency."

"We do receive some support from the community, but not much. Our residents are primarily supported by relatives or trustee accounts."

Briley groans. All of Jeffrey's and Erin's accounts were frozen at the time of Jeffrey's death. They will remain frozen until the end of Erin's trial, and if she is sent to prison, the monies will go to the Tomassi family.

Briley doubts Antonio Tomassi will want to support Roger Wilson.

"What happens," she asks, "if Roger's support is cut off?"

Floyd draws in a quick breath. "I—I guess he'll have to leave. Seems a shame, since this has been his home for years, but we have continual expenses and a waiting list. The medical bills alone…"

"I understand."

After clicking off the phone, Briley sits in a melancholy fugue, feeling as though she has swallowed some lumpy object that keeps pressing against her breastbone.

What will happen to Roger if Erin is sent to prison? Without her financial support, he'll have to rely on the state—not the kindest or most accommodating provider. Though Floyd McKee is a nice man, he can't afford to run a charity. Roger has found a nurturing home, a place where he can watch *I Love Lucy* and enjoy Christmas lights in March. Wresting him from that home would be cruel.

Briley walks to the kitchen and stares into the refrigerator, but food will not assuage this pain. She needs to talk. She needs Timothy.

Without thinking, she dials his cell phone number. He answers on the second ring.

Thank goodness.

"Timothy." She smiles from the sheer joy of saying his name.

"Bri?" Surprise rings in his voice. "What are you doing?"

"Nothing…I'm just sitting around the house. If you have some free time, I thought maybe we could get together this weekend—"

"I'm in L.A., Bri. Dax is filming a commercial out here."

His answer is a stab in the heart.

"We've been in California a couple of weeks," he continues, obviously unaware of her stunned response. "I'm not sure when filming will wrap up. They keep coming up with alternate ideas."

Her face twists. "Okay, then. I'd better let you go—"

"What's wrong?"

Of course he'd realize she was upset. He knows her voice, knows the peaks and valleys of her moods. He doesn't have to see her to know that something is terribly, awfully wrong.

Her eyes clamp tight to trap a sudden flood of tears, but they overflow and spill over her lower lashes. For a moment she can't speak, then she throws dignity to the wind and tries to verbalize her feelings. "It's…this case. I really blew the pretrial hearing, and the judge ruled against my motion to take the death penalty off the table. The trial starts Monday and everyone expects me to lose. And Erin has this brother in a home for adults with Down syndrome. If she goes to prison, he'll have to leave. And I have no idea where he'll be able to go."

She hiccups a sob, waiting to hear Timothy say that she shouldn't expect to win her first murder trial.

"You're going to do a great job," he says instead.

She hiccups again. "What?"

"I believe in you, Bri. I've always believed in you, because you care about people. You care about your client."

"But the evidence is stacked against us. And Erin hates the only credible defense I've been able to develop. She keeps saying she didn't do it."

"Do you believe her?"

Briley swallows the next hiccup as she considers his question. Does she believe a woman who hears voices in her dreams? She'd sooner believe in the tooth fairy, but maybe Timothy has a point. She hasn't accomplished anything by openly doubting Erin's story.

"If everyone in Chicago thinks Erin Tomassi killed her husband," he continues, "she doesn't stand a chance. Everyone in Hollywood thought Dax would slip back into addiction, but you know what? He didn't…because someone believed in him."

Briley draws a deep, trembling breath. "I want to believe her. But the evidence—"

"You're a preacher's kid," Timothy says, a smile in his voice. "Don't you remember what faith is? It's believing in something when everyone around you doubts. It's believing in someone because you know they wouldn't lie to you."

With a shiver of vivid recollection, the mention of her father carries Briley back to December 1994 and the awful months that followed. She stopped reading newspapers then, too, because every day brought new stories about her father's murder, his relationships, his involvement with addicts and ex-cons. Reporters broadcast the murderer's side of the story on television and in the papers, while no one listened to the brokenhearted girl who found herself all alone in the world.

Her blood soars with the unexpected memory. Years have passed, but the passion to make things right still flames within her breast. And this time, Erin Tomassi is her client. Like Briley's father, Erin tells the truth, even when the results are disastrous.

"Can you have faith in Erin Tomassi?" Timothy asks. "Because I have faith in you."

"You know," she whispers, closing her eyes, "I think I can."

Chapter Thirty-Eight

After leaving her car in the five-story parking garage across from the Cook County courthouse, Briley crosses to the hulking gray stone building at the corner of Twenty-sixth and California. A fleet of news vehicles is parked along the curb, each van sprouting cables that snake across the sidewalk and up the courthouse steps.

Briley slips on her sunglasses and keeps her head down, not wanting to attract media attention while she's trying to focus her thoughts.

At the courthouse doors, a veritable flood of humanity merges from all directions, the somber suits of government employees and lawyers mingling with the street clothing of jurors, witnesses, and reporters. Briley lingers at the edge of the courthouse steps until she spies William Hughes in the crowd. Somehow he has obtained the firm's permission to attend the trial. He won't be entitled to sit at the defense table—an honor reserved for those who have passed the bar exam—but he can sit in the first row of the gallery and offer any assistance she might need.

She smiles, finding comfort in the sight of a familiar face. "William!" She waves to catch his attention, then falls into step beside him as they move toward the entrance.

"So?" He gives her an uncertain smile. "Did you sleep at all last night?"

She shakes her head. "I tried to put the trial out of my mind this weekend, but I couldn't stop revising my opening statement. Last night I ended up drinking warm milk to help me sleep, then I dreamed of Napoleon and Waterloo." She takes him in with one glance. "You look nice, by the way."

"Thanks." He lifts the edge of his overcoat and pats the lapel of the suit beneath. "Thought maybe it'd be best to leave the cardigan at home, seeing as how I'll be representing the firm."

They slow their steps as the crowd funnels through a single hallway that ends at a pair of metal detectors. The people around them begin to remove watches, shoes, and heavy jewelry. Anything metal must be placed in a plastic bin.

"Just like the airport," William jokes as he takes off his belt. He pulls his cell phone from his coat pocket and drops it into the tray with his belt and shoes. "Americans strip down pretty easily these days."

Briley gives him a quick smile, but she's not feeling up to small talk. They probably won't accomplish much more than seating a jury today, but the right jury can make all the difference. She's never selected a jury for a murder case, but the firm still wouldn't approve funding to hire a jury consultant. So she'll be on her own, with only William and her instincts to help her choose the best jurors for this trial.

She slides off her shoes and drops them into a plastic bin, then sets it on the conveyer belt beside her briefcase. Ahead of her, a security guard barks commands and instructs all arrivals to remove their outerwear and jackets. She slips out of her coat and suit jacket, noticing that the young man behind her, sans coat, is wearing obvious gangsta attire.

She hopes he's not heading toward her courtroom.

William's smile vanishes when the security guard gestures to him. With the posture of a brigadier, William marches through the machine and waits for his bin to roll through the X-ray machine.

Briley follows, nodding in relief when she passes through without setting off the alarm. When she and William have collected their belongings, she leads the way past the snack shop and the bulletin board where printouts of the day's court calls are tacked in fifteen rows, three pages deep. While they wait outside the elevator, a single-file line of prospective jurors passes, their eyes wide as a deputy herds them from one holding pen to another.

"Seventh floor," she tells William when they enter the elevator. "Judge Trask's courtroom."

They ride up in the heavy silence generated by a group of somber strangers, and exit at the seventh floor. But when she steps into the hallway, Briley grabs William's arm as her knees turn to gelatin.

Standing before the courtroom's double doors is Jeffrey Tomassi.

Chapter Thirty-Nine

In a surge of fierce satisfaction, Antonio smiles as he watches the defense attorney's knees buckle. "Look." He nudges Jason. "The woman is nervous. She knows her client is doomed."

Jason glances at the man and woman huddled in the hallway, then he takes his father's arm. "Come, Papa. We should go inside."

Antonio jerks free of Jason's grip. "We have all day to sit. I want to stand here...and let them know Jeffrey will not be forgotten." He lifts his chin as a photographer approaches, camera in hand. He stares, silently granting the man's unspoken request for a shot, but a deputy runs over and reminds the stranger that photography is not allowed in the courthouse.

Antonio sighs in resignation. He glances behind him to be sure his daughters have come out of the restroom where they went to repair their makeup. The youngest is pale; the oldest has red-rimmed eyes. All of them look like grief-stricken women, as they should.

"No tears," he reminds them. "Keep your chin up and pray for justice. Now...let us go inside."

Like the stately patriarch his father once was, Antonio leads his children into the courtroom.

Chapter Forty

William pats Briley's hand. "Are you all right?"

She pulls herself off the wall, hoping that no one else noticed her stumble. "Is that…? That's not…?"

"The resemblance is remarkable, isn't it?"

"But that's not Jeffrey."

"It's Jason Tomassi, Jeffrey's brother."

Briley straightens and releases William's arm. "Amazing likeness."

"Almost close enough to be identical, but I hear they were fraternal twins."

Briley takes a deep breath to calm her leaping pulse. "I did some checking up on Jason, just to be sure he didn't have any reason to profit from his brother's death. They went to college together, and apparently they had some kind of secret language. Used to drive their frat brothers nuts."

She steps forward on legs that threaten to tremble beneath her weight.

"Are you sure you're okay?" William asks, walking beside her.

"I'm fine. I…had forgotten how alike they were." She pauses several feet away from the courtroom doors, allowing the Tomassis to enter undisturbed. When Jeffrey's family has moved down the aisle, she grips her briefcase and steps through the doorway.

After they pass the family, William jerks his head toward the Tomassi men. "Could Jason have a reason for wanting his brother dead?"

Briley shakes her head. "Not likely. Jason was with his girlfriend the night Jeffrey died, so he has an alibi. Don't worry, I made sure the police checked him out. If Erin is convicted, Jeffrey's estate goes to his brother."

"I assumed Jeffrey's lavish lifestyle was financed with his daddy's money."

"That's a good assumption. Apparently the Tomassi family patriarch gives his children a lump sum when they get married. Jeffrey used his to buy the house in Lincoln Park and still managed to invest a good amount."

William grins. "Mr. Franklin always says you should follow the money."

The comment hangs in the air as Briley makes her way to the counsel table. Has she done enough to follow the money? The estate leads directly to Jason, but there's no evidence to implicate him in the crime. Furthermore, at this point it's not her job to play Columbo. Her job is to defend Erin.

She steps through the swinging gate set into the wooden bar and sets her briefcase on the defense table. William sits in the gallery behind her, and she reminds him to reserve that seat for the duration of the trial. "If I need something," she tells him, "I want to be able to glance over my shoulder and know you're there."

She looks up, distracted by the sight of a familiar face in the crowd. Shirley Walker, wearing a dark suit and heels, is heading straight for her.

To spare the woman the embarrassment of being stopped by a deputy, Briley steps into the gallery. "Mrs. Walker. Did you get my message? We won't need you today. We probably won't need you until later in the week."

The housekeeper takes Briley's hand. "I didn't come down here to testify. I came to give Erin my support. And to give you a message for her."

"What's that?" Briley smiles, though an inner alarm bell begins to clang. If the woman has just remembered something important...

"I had Erin's calls forwarded to my house, so when Mrs. Tomassi's doctor called again, I picked up the phone and spoke to Dr. Phillips. He said it's important that Erin call him as soon as possible. I didn't tell him, of course, about her being locked up. Apparently he doesn't watch the news."

Briley sighs, remembering the slip of paper in her briefcase. It had been among the letters she carried to the jail last week, but the note must have dropped to the bottom of her bag. "Thank you, Mrs. Walker. I'll give Erin the message."

"Thank you, dear. We can't be too careful about our health, you know." The woman pats Briley's shoulder and moves to a seat on the second row.

Briley looks up as a door to the left of the judge's bench opens. A bailiff appears and leads Erin into the courtroom. She has been allowed to trade her orange uniform for the ivory suit Briley bought her, and today she has chosen the bright blue blouse to provide a spot of color. As her client walks forward, Briley notices that the blue is a perfect match for Erin's eyes.

"Nice choice on the outfit," she says, meeting Erin at the defense table. "I was hoping you'd like the clothes I picked out."

Erin runs her hands over the pencil skirt. "This is a lovely suit, but I'm afraid it'll be dirty by the time the trial is over."

Briley smiles, preferring not to explain that she chose ivory for a reason. She wants her client to appear virtuous, and an ivory suit is a tad more subtle than Virgin Mary robes.

"I can pick up something more practical later," Briley says. "Maybe something in yellow."

"Can't you get something from my house?" Erin's eyes fill with helpless appeal. "It's not that I don't appreciate the outfit, but it's not mine. I'm so out of my element, it'd be nice if I could at least wear my own clothes."

Briley leans over to pat her hand. "I understand. But your house is a crime scene, and it won't be cleared until after the trial. Let's see how things progress. If all goes well, you should be wearing your own clothes in a week."

When a murmur moves through the gallery, Briley turns to see Travis Bystrowski and his assistant approaching. "Buckle your seat belt," she says, keeping her voice low, "here comes the opposing team."

After Bystrowski settles at the prosecution's table, Briley walks over and extends her hand. "Good morning, Counselor," she says, her voice artificially bright. "Ready to go another round?"

"Always ready for you." The prosecutor smiles as he takes her hand, but Briley can't shake the feeling that his remark is an intentional insult. He's reminding her that she's in the big leagues now, and sorely inexperienced.

She tilts her head toward the doorway that leads to the judge's chambers. "Shall we go in and greet Judge Trask? I'm ready to get this show on the road."

He extends his hand in a gallant gesture. "Ladies first."

She strides forward with a confidence she doesn't feel, then raps on the door to the judge's office. A hearty "Come in" gives her permission to proceed.

Judge Trask, already wearing his robe, is downing a bottle of water when Briley and Bystrowski enter. He keeps swallowing until the container is empty, then he wipes droplets from his lips. "Good morning, Counselors." He tosses the plastic bottle into the trash. "Anything I need to know before we begin?"

The judge looks at the prosecutor. "Mr. Bystrowski?"

"The state is prepared," he says. "We're ready to commence with voir dire."

The judge glances in Briley's direction. "Ms. Lester, did you receive everything you needed in discovery?"

She struggles to find her voice. "As far as I know, Your Honor."

"Good. Anything else, then?"

"Yes, sir," Briley says.

When both men look at her, she steels herself to roll the dice again. "In light of your recent ruling," she says, knowing she's taking a risk, "the defense would like to move that a particular piece of evidence be excluded. A syringe was taken from my client's bathroom without a warrant. In this situation she had a reasonable expectation of privacy—"

The judge lifts his hand. "Didn't we cover this at the pretrial hearing?"

"No, sir. The motion I made at that hearing had to do with whether or not my client gave her consent for a search. My present motion is based on the fact that the home wasn't a crime scene until the medical examiner declared Jeffrey Tomassi's death suspicious—an event that occurred several days after the search on December 3. On that day, my client cooperated fully, calling 911 for her husband and giving police permission to search the bedroom where the victim's body was found."

"The people object, Your Honor." Bystrowski gives Briley a *You're kidding* glance. "The police don't need a warrant to search if consent has been given."

"But the police had no reason to search the master bathroom," Briley argues. "The victim was discovered in the adjacent bedroom, where he expired. Given that citizens have a reasonable expectation of privacy in the most protected areas of their homes—"

"Preposterous, Your Honor. The police had a right to search any room in the house."

Judge Trask fixes Briley in a steely-eyed gaze. "Interesting gambit, but you're assuming the crime occurred in the bedroom, and we don't know where the man was attacked. I will not grant your motion on the basis of assumption, therefore anything found in the house is admissible if permission to search has been granted. Your motion to exclude is denied."

Briley sighs. "Thank you, Your Honor."

"All right, then." The judge picks up a copy of the prosecution's witness list and compares it to Briley's. "Any idea how long this trial should take?"

"We'll need three days," Bystrowski says. "Our case is simple and straightforward."

Briley nods. "We'll need a day or two. Our defense is equally simple. But if my client is convicted, we'll need several days for the penalty phase of the trial."

"Understood." The judge waves the papers in his hands. "And is this the proper order?"

"Yes, sir."

"Then let the games begin."

When the judge grabs another bottle of water from a minifridge behind his desk, Briley realizes they've been dismissed. She and Bystrowski exit the judge's chambers and take their seats at their respective tables.

A moment later, the bailiff calls for order.

"All rise."

Briley stands with the crowd as the bailiff announces, "This honorable court is now in session, the Honorable Milton Trask, Judge, presiding. Be seated, please, and come to order."

As the judge enters and takes care of a few housekeeping matters, Briley studies the faces of the men and women in the jury pool and wishes she had more time to consider them. From the fifty people filing in through a front door, she and Bystrowski must choose twelve jurors and two alternates. Because this is a death penalty case, she and the prosecutor are both allowed twenty peremptory challenges.

Beside her, Erin seems listless and anxious. Knowing that such behavior can influence jurors' opinions, Briley takes a legal pad and a pen from her briefcase and slides them to her client. "By the way," she whispers while the jurors are listening to the judge, "because jurors get suspicious when we put our heads together, write any comments you'd like to tell me on this paper. It's less distracting."

Briley listens to the judge's instructions and makes a note on her legal pad when one of the jurors looks confused.

She needs intelligent jurors, people who can follow a line of reasoning and come to the correct conclusions.

Voir dire will continue for a couple of hours, and before they actually strike the jury she and Bystrowski will be given the opportunity to repeat the judge's questions and ask follow-up questions of their own. She will not emphasize the possibility of capital punishment; instead, she'll stress that not every guilty verdict deserves a death sentence. She might ask whether or not these jurors have faith in something that contradicts the laws of science and reason....

She'll have to be careful with that last query, but she really wants to know.

She needs jurors who can believe in phantoms.

When the judge dismisses the court for lunch, Briley reaches for her briefcase, then halts in midgesture. She usually spends the midday recess in a nearby restaurant, pre-occupied with the trial, but Timothy's words keep haunting her: *You care about people. You care about your client.*

Does she? In three years of practicing law, Briley has never given a thought to where her clients eat lunch. She looks up and sees a deputy approaching to escort Erin to wherever the "custodies" are fed. "I'd like to have lunch with my client today," she says, using her firmest voice. "Maybe you could find us an empty interview room?"

The man stammers in surprise, but Briley proceeds as though she does this every day. "Wills," she says, pulling two tens from her wallet, "will you run out and grab us some burgers? We're going to eat with Erin today."

"I'll have to talk to the judge," the deputy says. "This is highly irregular."

"Please check with him, then." Briley folds her arms on the table. "We'll wait right here."

Five minutes later, the deputy returns with an answer. "Judge Trask says you can eat here, in the courtroom, or in the bullpen. But if you eat there, you'll be on one side of the bars and your client on the other."

"What an appealing option." Briley rests her chin in her hand and smiles. "I guess we'll have a picnic here. Deputy, would you like to join us for a burger?"

The invitation flusters the man. He backs away, both hands raised, and gestures to indicate the doorway. "I'll just stand there and wait."

"Suit yourself."

Once the man is back in his usual spot, Briley shakes her head. "He has to be starving."

"He looks nervous," Erin adds. "Maybe he's afraid I'm going to run away."

"You wouldn't get far. There are more cops per square foot downstairs than at any place in the city."

Erin glances at her hands, then gives Briley a sidelong look. "Are things not going well? Is that why you wanted to talk to me?"

Briley winces in regret. Has she kept herself so aloof that Erin can't believe she might simply want to talk? "Things are fine," she says. "I just thought it'd be nicer for you to eat in here than in the holding cell."

Erin smiles. "You're right about that."

"And I knew I'd enjoy your company." Briley keeps her voice light, but the deeply appreciative look in Erin's eye shames her.

While she is searching for a safe topic of conversation, Briley remembers the message in her briefcase. "I keep forgetting—" she pulls the slip of paper from beneath her laptop "—despite your housekeeper's best efforts to remind me. Apparently this doctor called your house and left a message. Mrs. Walker pulled it off the machine."

After taking the paper, Erin reads the name. "Dr. Phillips?"

"Doesn't the name ring a bell?"

She nods in delayed recognition. "Of course. With every-thing that's happened, I forgot about going to see him."

Briley stands when William enters with their lunch. "I was about to send out a search party."

"I had to run up the back stairs," William says, panting. "The reporters are everywhere. They're not getting much, but they're sure doing a lot of fishing."

"The Tomassis," Erin says, nodding. "I'm sure they'll be speaking to the press—when the time is right, that is."

William halts before the gate in the bar and lifts his gaze to the high ceiling. "Wait—we're eating in *here?*"

"The judge said we could," Erin answers, grinning. "Pretty fancy, huh?"

William shakes his head. "Just don't drop any crumbs on the table. I'll get rid of the trash before people start coming back in." He sinks to the first pew and stares at Briley. "What will people think when they smell onion and bacon burgers?"

"Maybe they won't notice." Briley accepts a burger from William, then looks back at Erin. "This doctor who called— I hope you weren't seeing him for anything serious."

"Dr. Phillips is the geneticist Jeffrey asked me to see…you know, before he'd consider having a baby." Erin's eyes glitter with unshed tears as she unwraps her hamburger. "I can't believe I'm hearing from him now. I gave him a DNA sample eight—no, ten weeks before Jeffrey died. I remember noticing that the leaves had just begun to change when I went to his office."

Briley glances at William. "Doesn't exactly want to make you nominate Jeffrey Tomassi for father of the year, does it?"

"I can't blame Jeff for being cautious." Erin's voice dissolves in a rough whisper. "After all, if my genes *were* defective, I wouldn't want to pass them on to an innocent child. I'm flawed in so many ways—"

Briley slams her hand onto the table. "Good grief, Erin, stop it. You're not flawed, but your husband was a jerk." She takes a ragged breath, barely managing to tamp the irritation rising within her. "From this moment on, I don't want to hear you put yourself down. Your husband was wrong to make you doubt yourself. Your mother was wrong to ridicule you. You're not stupid, you're not crazy. You're an intelligent woman, and it's time you stood up for yourself."

Erin presses her hand over her mouth as her eyes fill with tears. Briley is afraid she's gone too far until William waves a snack bag toward their client and breaks the awkward silence. "Would you like some…chips?"

The question is so ordinary and innocuous that Erin laughs and Briley manages a wavering smile.

"Thank you." Erin accepts the bag and looks at Briley. "What you just said…it's almost as if you believe I'm going to make it out of here."

"You are going to make it." Briley speaks with a confidence she's far from feeling, but what did Timothy say? *Faith is believing when everyone else has doubts.* So she'll believe. For Timothy. For Erin.

She turns sideways in her chair. "When I entered law school, I saw things as black or white, right or wrong, fair or unjust. I believed in lining up the facts and assembling a case theory from what I could see, hear, and authenticate. But if you say you didn't kill your husband, I'm going to fight to prove you didn't. And I won't quit until you walk out of this courthouse a free woman."

Erin doesn't answer, but a glint of wonder fills her eyes.

And that glint speaks volumes.

Chapter Forty-One

Briley settles back in her chair and tries to keep her face composed in pleasant lines as the state's attorney stands to give his opening statement. Fourteen carefully selected jurors have been seated in the box, and Briley takes comfort in knowing that Bystrowski is about as pleased as she is with the result.

Behind the counsel tables, dozens of observers, reporters, and members of the Tomassi family have jammed the gallery. Most of the Tomassis, like guests at a wedding, have chosen to sit on one side of the courtroom—the prosecution's.

Briley's gaze roves over the men and women who are part of the extended Tomassi family. Did they show this kind of loyalty to Jeffrey during his marriage? Erin says she tried to confide in her sisters-in-law about the abuse, but they wouldn't listen. Were they convinced Jeffrey could do no wrong?

"Ladies and gentlemen of the jury," the prosecutor says, unbuttoning the top button on his coat, "my name is Travis Bystrowski, and I'm presenting this case on behalf of the citizens of Illinois. An opening statement—what I'm delivering now—is like the photo on a jigsaw puzzle box. It gives you an idea of what you're going to see once we put all the jumbled pieces of a case together. Some of the pieces may seem confusing, but if you'll be patient and bear with me, in time you'll see the big picture.

"What is the big picture in this case? It's simple. The state will prove that the woman seated at the defense table, Erin Tomassi, purposely murdered her husband with premeditation and malice. Why? Because her husband, Jeffrey Tomassi, had a problem with his temper. Because he loved his wife and didn't want a divorce. And because he wanted to run for a seat in the U.S. Congress. Erin Tomassi wanted no part of her husband's future life, and staging his death to look like an accident or suicide was the only way she could end the marriage and maintain her claim on Jeffrey's fortune."

He rests his elbow on the lectern, undoubtedly attempting to appear relaxed and charming. "Ladies and gentlemen, over the course of this trial you will hear testimony that might lead a reasonable person to believe the Tomassi marriage endured a fair amount of domestic discord. We are willing to grant that the marriage was unhappy, but unhappiness is never an excuse for murder. The law provides women with several means of escape from an unsatisfactory marriage—divorce, separation, even legal protection. If the defendant truly felt threatened, she could have sought marriage counseling, but she did not. Erin Tomassi could have moved out of the family home. She could have filed for divorce and a restraining order. But she did none of those things.

"Instead, with malice and cunning, she attacked her husband while he slept. While he lay helpless in their marriage bed, she injected him with a massive overdose of his own medication, knowing that within moments he would be unable to respond or call for help."

Bystrowski steps to the side of the counsel table, casually resting his hand on its surface. "Unfortunately, her plan succeeded. When she woke the next morning, Erin Tomassi did all the right things—she called 911, she wept, she claimed she had no idea what had happened to her husband. But the evidence demonstrates another reality, an inescapable truth. Erin Tomassi knew what an insulin overdose would do, and she knew it would be hard to detect. If not for the toxicology reports, if not for a vigilant father and a diligent medical examiner, she might be sitting on a beach right now, soaking up the sun and spending her husband's fortune.

But medical reports do not lie, science does not mislead, and we have apprehended the killer. After you hear the presentation of the evidence, you will understand why the state has charged Erin Tomassi with first-degree murder. It is your duty, ladies and gentlemen, to ensure that justice is enacted in this courtroom."

In a silence that is the holding of breaths, Briley waits until Bystrowski takes his seat, then she stands and walks toward the lectern. "The prosecution," she begins, "has told you a story and described it as the picture on a puzzle box, but I'd like to tell you a story that results in a far different picture. It's the story of a young girl from a rough part of town, a young woman who was swept off her feet by a handsome and charismatic young man. That girl is the defendant in this case, Erin Wilson Tomassi. All she ever wanted out of life was a happy home, children, and an opportunity to help other people. With Jeffrey Tomassi, she thought she had found someone who wanted the same things.

"Erin hadn't been married long before she discovered that Jeffrey Tomassi was not quite a knight in shining armor. His words became sharp, his glance hard. He began to grip her arm more tightly than was necessary, and even to push her when she didn't move quickly enough.

"Then he began to hit her." Briley pauses, waiting for her words to sink in. "Jeffrey Tomassi was careful never to injure his wife where others might see. He learned to aim for the thighs, the soft part of the belly, the ribs. Erin learned to stifle her cries in order to protect her husband's reputation. She kept silent, because she had no one to intervene on her behalf—her father was dead, her brother mentally challenged, her mother an alcoholic. The Tomassis—a large, warm family who had welcomed Erin with open arms—turned a deaf ear when she tried to tell them about the violent abuse that had invaded her marriage.

"So she learned to suffer in silence. And one morning, after a particularly bad beating, Erin woke early, tiptoed out of bed, and crept into the kitchen. When Jeffrey didn't appear to demand his breakfast, she went to check on him…and found him dead. She called 911 in a panic, she tried to administer CPR, she rode with the ambulance to the hospital. She sat in the morgue, shocked into grief, waiting for someone to explain why her strong and healthy husband stopped breathing in the middle of the night.

"Erin Wilson Tomassi did not murder her husband." Briley looks down the first row of jurors, meeting the gaze of each somber individual before shifting to the next person. "The prosecution says they can prove Erin is a killer. They say she killed him because murder was her only way out of an unhappy marriage. But we will demonstrate that Erin *couldn't* kill him. On the night in question, she had been badly beaten. She was in so much pain that she went into her bathroom and took a double dose of sleeping pills. She went to bed and didn't wake until morning. She did not murder him. Why do I say that? Because no matter how many times Jeffrey hit her, she still loved him."

Briley pauses beside the lectern, knowing that the jurors are looking in Erin's direction when they look at her. "Erin Tomassi did not commit murder. Perhaps the victim injected himself, perhaps an intruder entered the house. Jeffrey Tomassi's death may have been a suicide, a murder, or an accident. We don't know, because we don't have all the facts. We may never have all the facts. But our duty in this courtroom is to tell Erin's story. After hearing it, you'll understand that my client did not, could not, kill anyone."

The prosecutor calls his first witness.

Briley opens her trial notebook and picks up a pen as Detective Mark Malone steps out of the gallery and takes the stand. Bystrowski begins his examination, first laying a foundation to establish the cop's expertise and experience, then he begins to question him about the morning he examined Jeffrey Tomassi's body. The detective testifies that rigor mortis had set in by the time he arrived, so the man obviously died sometime during the night. He also testifies about the alarm system, the security cameras, and the video-tapes that did not reveal any intruder. When Bystrowski asks, Malone tells the jury that the police took several hair samples from the crime scene and the crime lab later reported that DNA from the samples matched Jeffrey Tomassi and his wife. Finally, Bystrowski asks about the syringe discovered in the bathroom trash—a syringe marked with a partial print from Erin Tomassi's thumb.

While Bystrowski goes through the routine of having the evidence marked for identification and entered into evidence, Briley looks at her client. Erin has been mostly silent during the trial, her eyes centered either in her lap or on the witness box. She does not, Briley notices, look at the jury, as if she's afraid of what she might see in their eyes.

Briley needs to tell Erin to keep her chin up and look more confident. She makes a note on her legal pad: *Fake it till you feel it.*

Bystrowski leaves his latest evidence bags with the clerk, then steps back to the lectern. "Detective, in your examination of the many objects gathered at the crime scene, did you find anything to indicate that anyone other than the victim and the defendant were present at the scene?"

"We found a few other latent fingerprints, which were subsequently identified as the housekeeper's. Nothing else."

"Thank you, Detective." The prosecutor nods at the jury, then moves back to his counsel table.

Briley's pulse quickens when the judge looks her way. "Ms. Lester, you may cross-examine the witness."

Conscious of the pressure of dozens of curious eyes, she stands and moves to the lectern. "Thank you, Detective Malone, for your fine work on this case. In your examination of the Tomassi home's exterior, you testified that you saw no footprints in the flower beds. Do you recall if those areas were covered with mulch?"

The policeman tugs on his shirt collar. "I'm not sure."

"Let me show you this photo. Perhaps I can refresh your memory." She pulls a photograph from her folio and glances at the judge. "May I approach?"

"You may."

"Now, Detective—" Briley shows the photo to the man in the witness box "—do you recognize this property?"

"Yes, it's the crime scene."

"I should remind you, sir, that we haven't established that a crime has been committed. Can you identify this property by address?"

The detective checks his notes. "It's 944 Montana Street in Lincoln Park. Home of Mr. and Mrs. Jeffrey Tomassi."

"Thank you. Now, if you will, please examine the leafless shrubbery next to the front door. Isn't that mulch on the ground?"

The detective props his reading glasses on the end of his nose, sucks at the inside of his cheek, and grunts. "Looks like it."

"It is, isn't it? And isn't it true that pine bark mulch wouldn't reveal an intruder's footprint if one existed?"

The cop scowls at her. "We checked the ground-floor windows. No one forced an entry."

"You didn't answer my question. If an intruder entered that house through an unlocked window, he wouldn't leave any footprints, would he?"

"He might not have left a footprint, but if he'd been in that bedroom, he would have touched something. He would have left some trace of his presence. Fingerprints, at least."

"Unless he was wearing gloves."

The detective's scowl deepens as Bystrowski stands. "Objection, Your Honor. Where's the question?"

The judge gives Briley a warning look. "Objection sustained."

"Thank you, Your Honor, I do have a question. In your examination of the windows, Detective, do you recall noticing if any of them were unlocked?"

Malone's face goes blank for an instant. "I don't recall."

"Did you check the windows?"

"We looked for signs of a break-in. We found no evidence of forced entry."

"So you never actually tested the windows, correct? To see if any of them were unlocked?"

"No, we didn't test the windows."

"Did you spend much time examining the kitchen?"

Malone yanks on his tie. "No, ma'am. We found the victim in the bedroom, so we designated that as the crime scene. Nothing in the kitchen appeared out of place. Ditto for the guest room and the living room."

"Did you empty the trash cans throughout the home? Did you go through the trash compactor?"

"We saw no need to turn the house upside down."

"Later, when you read the autopsy report—a document stipulated to be admissible by me and the prosecutor—did you find yourself wishing you had checked the kitchen compactor? Or the trash cans outside?"

"Lady," the detective drawls, "I don't know what you mean."

Briley forces a smile. "Have you read the autopsy report?"

"Yes. So?"

"According to the medical examiner's report, what was Jeffrey Tomassi's cause of death?"

The cop drapes both arms over the chair's armrests. "Insulin overdose."

"So don't you wish you'd checked those other waste receptacles? Isn't it possible that you left the house without discovering the actual murder weapon?"

The cop eases back in his chair, his irritated expression shifting into one of bored tolerance. "What if Santa Claus did it? That'd be mighty convenient, but highly unlikely."

Briley ignores a wave of twittering from the jury box. "Detective Malone, you testified that you found a sharps disposal unit. Where did you find it?"

"Under the bathroom sink."

"And in it you found how many syringes?"

"Twenty-two."

"How do you know the syringe displayed here as state's exhibit one was the murder weapon? Why couldn't the murder have been committed with one of the twenty-two in the sharps receptacle?"

The detective holds Briley's gaze as he knuckles small sparkles of sweat from his upper lip. "Mrs. Tomassi's prints were on the syringe in the evidence bag."

"That doesn't mean this particular syringe was used to kill Jeffrey Tomassi, does it? Or that his wife administered the fatal dose?"

"Then it must mean she's a liar, because she told me she *never* gave her husband injections."

Briley closes her eyes and remains facing forward so that the jurors can't see her grimace. She has broken the cardinal rule, the one drummed into every trial lawyer's head: never ask a question if you're not sure of the response. She wasn't expecting the cop to be so clever.

"Your Honor," she says, her voice strangled, "the defense moves to strike Detective Malone's last answer as unresponsive."

Trask tilts his head. "The jury will disregard that last answer."

"Detective—" she forces a smile as she focuses on the grinning cop "—one set of fingerprints on a single syringe doesn't inconclusively prove that you've found the murder weapon, does it?"

His smile fades a degree. "No. But it sure sets that syringe apart from the others."

Sensing trouble, Briley moves on. "What else did Mrs.

Tomassi tell you that day? Did she relate the events of the morning and the previous night?"

"Yeah— Yes. She said they got home late. She took sleeping pills and went to bed."

"The sleeping pills...did she specify what type they were?"

When he gives her a confused look, she knows he's intentionally giving her a hard time. His report was far more specific. "The brand name, sir?"

"Ah, yes. Ambien."

"Thank you." Briley glances at her notes. "Previously, you testified that Mrs. Tomassi gave you permission to search the house."

This time, the detective does not look at Erin. "Yes."

"Did she seem reluctant to grant permission?"

"She was upset. I don't think she gave the question much thought."

"Are you always able to read the minds of the people you interrogate?"

"Objection, Your Honor." Bystrowski rises. "Counselor is badgering the witness."

"I'll withdraw the question." Briley gives the detective a more sincere smile. "This permission you received from Mrs. Tomassi—was it tape-recorded?"

"No."

"Written, then. As a conscientious officer of the law, you knew that any evidence you discovered without permission could be excluded from a trial. So you had her sign a document, right?"

The man looks away as his face reddens. "No."

Briley widens her eyes, feigning surprise. "Then how is it that we have evidence from the Tomassi home?"

The cop glares at her. "Because I gathered it."

"Isn't it true, Detective, that all the evidence from the alleged crime scene has been allowed into this trial solely because Erin Tomassi personally told the judge that she gave you permission to search?"

"Objection!" Bystrowski is on his feet again. "Counsel is out of line, and she knows it."

"Objection sustained," Trask rules, frowning down at Briley. "The jury will disregard that last question."

The cop crosses his arms and stares at the back wall, refusing to meet Briley's gaze.

"I'll withdraw the question." Briley inhales a deep breath, content that she has given the jury an important piece of information about her client's integrity. "How many years have you been interviewing homicide suspects, Detective Malone? Was it ten?"

"That's right."

"Given your extensive personal experience with suspects in murder cases, when you interviewed Mrs. Tomassi, did you suspect her of being the sort of woman who would pick up a syringe and give her husband a fatal overdose?"

When she turns and sees a smirk on Bystrowski's face, she realizes she's made an egregious mistake. She's asked a leading question to which Bystrowski ought to object, but he's keeping silent, giving the detective yards of rope to wrap around her neck. Now that she's opened the door, he can claim that Erin was as cool as Lizzie Borden or as friendly as Ted Bundy....

Time slows to a crawl as she turns to face the witness stand. She holds her breath, watching as the detective looks at the expectant prosecutor and shakes his head in what looks like slow motion.

"No, I didn't." His answer reverberates in Briley's ears, filling her with relief. She's about to smile her thanks for being an honest cop, but Malone can't resist a parting shot: "But first impressions can be deceiving."

"Indeed, they can be." Briley exhales in a rush as time resumes its normal pace. She smiles at the jury. "Sometimes a situation is not at all what it appears to be. Thank you, Detective," she says. She walks away, determined to cut her losses. "Thank you very much."

* * *

The medical examiner, Dr. James Drew, squints at the item in the evidence bag. "Yes, that's a typical insulin syringe."

Bystrowski turns the bag for the jury to view. "Based on your examination of the evidence, are you able to conclude if this is the murder weapon?"

The man's dark brows shoot toward his forehead. "In order to make such a conclusion, we have to weigh all the elements of the crime scene."

"What particular facts about this syringe did you consider?"

Dr. Drew leans an elbow on the witness chair. "Twenty-two syringes were found in a sharps disposal unit. Police records indicate that this syringe was found by itself, in a regular trash can. Logic tells me that as a diabetic who gave himself daily injections, Mr. Tomassi had almost certainly developed the habit of disposing of his needles in a sharps receptacle. Obviously, whoever threw this syringe into the trash did not share that habit."

"Objection, Your Honor." Briley rises. "The witness is drawing conclusions."

"I'll allow it." Trask inclines his head. "Mr. Bystrowski, you may continue."

Bystrowski crosses one arm over his chest and studies the doctor with an air of thoughtful contemplation. "Can you be certain that whoever administered insulin with this syringe wasn't giving him the usual nighttime dose?"

"I am quite certain the injection was intended to be fatal." The medical examiner looks at the jury, his eyes grave. "The dose administered to Jeffrey Tomassi was more than enough to kill him. In cases of accidental insulin overdose, the patient usually slips into a coma, but a massive overdose can end a life in a matter of hours. I have no doubt that whoever injected the victim intended to kill him."

Briley stands again. "Your Honor, move to strike as un-responsive. The witness did not answer the question."

The judge inclines his head in a slow nod. "Objection sustained. The jury should disregard that last statement."

But it doesn't matter. The jury has heard the medical examiner's opinion, and Briley can see acceptance in their eyes. They're believing every word the man says.

The prosecutor thanks the medical examiner, then nods in Briley's direction. "Your witness."

Briley glances at her notes, then stands. "Dr. Drew," she begins without any preamble, "would the average person know how much insulin is required to kill someone?"

The medical examiner frowns. "I don't believe the average person would know—but a diabetic's spouse isn't really an average person."

"A simple yes or no will do." Briley gives him a stiff smile and moves to the lectern. "Detective Malone has testified that Mrs. Tomassi never gave her husband injections. Would a wife who never deals with her husband's insulin know the difference between a coma-inducing overdose and a fatal one?"

The M.E. shrugs. "I have no idea how much the defendant knows about diabetes treatment. But a quick Google search of the Internet could provide a definite answer."

Briley stifles a grimace. "You are a medical doctor, correct?"

"All medical examiners in the state of Illinois are medical doctors. Most are also certified in anatomical and forensic pathology."

"That's good to know. We will value your expert opinion all the more."

"Objection." Bystrowski stands, frustration evident in the line of his hunched shoulders. "Is counsel planning to ask a question?"

Before the judge can admonish her, Briley looks directly at the medical examiner. "After Mrs. Tomassi took two Ambien and fell asleep, could someone have planted her fingerprints on that syringe? If she were in a deep, drugged sleep, isn't it possible she might remain unaware that someone was manipulating her hand?"

"Objection, Your Honor." Bystrowski is on his feet again. "Calls for speculation on the part of the witness. We don't know if Mrs. Tomassi took two Ambien, one Ambien, or any pills at all."

Trask gives Briley a reproving look. "Objection sustained. Either drop the question or rephrase it."

"I'll rephrase." Briley returns her attention to the man in the witness box. "Dr. Drew, is Ambien an effective sleep-inducer?"

He nods. "Indubitably."

"Does it promote *deep* sleep? The sort of sleep in which a person might not be aware of being moved?"

The medical examiner glances at Bystrowski before speaking to the jury. "Yes, depending upon the individual, of course. People react differently to various drugs."

"Is Ambien so effective that a double dose might have put Mrs. Tomassi in such a deep sleep that she would remain unaware of someone manipulating her hand?"

"I suppose so."

"Could Jeffrey Tomassi have injected himself with an overdose, wiped the instrument clean, and placed the syringe in his wife's hand?"

"I have no idea—"

"Can you think of any reason to conclude that this scenario absolutely *could not* have happened?"

"Anything's possible, but what you're describing is highly unlikely."

"Many things are unlikely, sir, but still they occur. Such a scenario is possible, isn't it?"

The M.E. sighs. "Yes."

"Thank you. Now, can you tell the jury what prompted you to look for signs of an insulin overdose? It's my understanding that this is not a common cause of death."

Dr. Drew transfers his gaze to the crowd of Tomassis in the gallery. "The toxicology reports revealed the cause of death."

"Is this the report?" Briley pulls a signed and dated copy of the report from her folder and offers it to the medical examiner.

He scans the stapled pages. "Yes, that's the toxicology report. As you can see, the insulin levels are extraordinarily high."

Briley retrieves the document and pretends to study the first page. "How long does a toxicology report usually take to prepare?"

The medical examiner shrugs. "Four to six weeks."

"But this report is dated December 10, only five workdays after Jeffrey Tomassi's death." She furrows her brow. "How did you happen to receive it so quickly?"

The medical examiner glances at his hands. "I'm not sure."

"Have you a guess? What set this case apart from all the others that routinely move through your office?"

The man draws a deep breath. "I don't know exactly what happened, but I believe Antonio Tomassi may have called in a few favors."

"He pulled strings in your department?"

The doctor shakes his head. "I'm not a politician, Ms. Lester. But Jeffrey Tomassi was."

Briley glances at the jury, hoping that they are beginning to see the big picture. If the jury can begin to view the Tomassis as wealthy, pushy politicians, she'll have a better chance of winning sympathy for Erin. "During your investigation—" she turns back to the doctor "—did you have occasion to speak to Antonio Tomassi?"

"I spoke to him after my investigation. My assistant spoke to him at the point of intake."

"Would you mind sharing the gist of that first conversation?"

"Objection." Bystrowski stands. "The witness should be asked only about what he knows, not what someone told him. Furthermore, the content of that conversation is covered by doctor-patient privilege."

"Dr. Drew is not Antonio Tomassi's physician," Briley counters.

Judge Trask lifts a warning finger. "The hearsay objection is sustained. The objection regarding privilege is overruled."

Briley takes a step closer to the witness box. "Dr. Drew, do you know of a conversation between your assistant and Antonio Tomassi?"

"Yes."

"What do you know of the conversation between your assistant and Antonio Tomassi?"

"Objection!" Bystrowski is on his feet again. "This is still hearsay, Your Honor."

The judge looks at Briley as if he would read her mind if he could…and she wishes she could let him. William spoke to the M.E.'s assistant; she knows what transpired after Jeffrey died. She wants Dr. Drew to admit that Antonio Tomassi went to the morgue and made veiled threats. She wants the jury to see what the Tomassis are really like.

"I'll allow it," Trask says, nodding in Briley's direction. "But the jury needs to understand that this testimony is not offered as proof of the matters asserted."

Briley turns to the man in the witness chair. "What can you tell us about the conversation between Antonio Tomassi and your assistant?"

The medical examiner's lips thin with irritation. "As best I can recall, Mr. Tomassi wanted to know the autopsy findings as soon as possible. My assistant assured him we would handle the case in an expeditious manner and asked if his son had any medical conditions that could have been life-threatening. At that point, Mr. Tomassi said his son had been a diabetic."

Briley blinks, distracted by the answer. "So—so that's how you knew to check the insulin levels?"

"Correct. If we hadn't known—" He lifts his hands. "Someone might have gotten away with—"

"That's all I have for this witness." Briley turns on the ball of her foot. "Thank you."

The judge nods at the prosecutor. "Any redirect, Mr. Bystrowski?"

"Yes, Your Honor. Dr. Drew—" Bystrowski steps in front of his counsel table, in full view of the jury "—do you or the police have any medical proof that the defendant took two Ambien as she claimed?"

"To my knowledge, Mrs. Tomassi was never tested for the presence of drugs in her system."

"So you have only her word to support this statement?"

The medical examiner smiles at the jury. "That's my understanding."

"Thank you, sir."

The judge looks at Briley, silently asking if she has anything further. When she shakes her head, he folds his hands. "The witness may step down."

The trial progresses throughout the afternoon, and Briley rides an emotional roller coaster as Bystrowski calls witness after witness. Jeffrey Tomassi's doctor testifies that the decedent had managed his diabetes successfully for more than twenty years, undercutting her theory of accidental death. Allegra Tomassi, a cousin of the deceased, testifies that a jubilant Jeffrey called her after asking Erin to marry him, and that he had been "deeply, passionately in love with the woman." A priest at the family's church testifies that Jeffrey would never have divorced his wife because he believed marriage was a divine institution intended to last a lifetime. And since the church considered suicide a mortal sin, Jeffrey would *never* have considered taking his own life.

When it's time to cross-examine the priest, Briley is tempted to ask if the man knew about Jeffrey's affairs or his insistence that Erin use birth control. But the prosecutor hasn't raised those issues, and she doesn't want to offend any Catholics who might be sitting in the jury box. So the priest gets a free pass, though she may want to recall him later.

Terry Rhodes, Jeffrey Tomassi's campaign manager, testifies that on the night of December 2, Jeffrey had been upbeat and optimistic about the future.

"Did you ever know the victim to be depressed?" Bystrowski asks.

"No," Rhodes answers. "I've never met a more determined man than Jeffrey Tomassi. He was planning to win the coming election, and he had dreams far beyond the U.S. Congress. He would have fulfilled those dreams, too. He was that kind of man—he reached out and took what he wanted."

Briley crosses her arms and struggles to keep her disappointment from showing in her face. She had hoped the possibility of suicide might provide the jury with reasonable doubt, but after this testimony they may not even consider the idea. Bystrowski is methodically eliminating all possible answers for Tomassi's unexplained death—except premeditated murder.

Still, she has to take a chance.

"Your witness." Bystrowski nods at Briley as he returns from examining Terry Rhodes. His head is angled away from the jury, so they can't see the smug expression on his face.

Briley hesitates, then stands. "Mr. Rhodes, how would you describe the state of the Tomassis' marriage?"

A flicker of uncertainty moves across the man's features. "They appeared happy."

"Really?" Briley looks at Bystrowski, knowing that eventually he will try to establish abuse as Erin's motive for murder. Erin has mentioned Terry Rhodes; he has seen Jeffrey's brutality. Will he bear witness to it?

Briley steps out from behind the defense table and turns to survey the gallery. On the left side of the room, behind the prosecution's table, rows and rows of well-heeled Tomassis watch the proceedings with tight expressions. On the other side, dozens of reporters take notes and mind their digital recorders. Where are the people who will speak for Erin?

She lifts her chin and walks to the lectern. "Mr. Rhodes, did you spend much time with Jeffrey and Erin Tomassi together? As a couple?"

Rhodes glances at the men and women in the jury box. "Yes, I did. Like I said, they seemed happy enough."

"Would you characterize your relationship with Jeffrey as close?"

"Sure." Rhodes crosses one leg. "We were good friends."

"Did he confide in you?"

Rhodes adopts a thoughtful look. "He did. Probably more than anyone else, except perhaps his brother."

Briley smiles. "Since you were so close, were you aware that Jeffrey had a habit of beating his wife?"

She holds her breath, waiting for the objection. The domestic violence hasn't been established, so Bystrowski ought to be on his feet...unless he is planning to introduce the abuse later.

Rhodes draws in his chin and glances at Bystrowski. A buzz rises from the gallery on the prosecution's side, while delighted gasps rise from the reporters behind Erin.

The judge calls for order. When the courtroom has quieted, Briley relaxes and repeats her question. The prosecutor was probably planning to save this revelation, preferring to use Rhodes to reinforce his contention that Jeffrey couldn't have committed suicide. But while Bystrowski may want to portray the victim as an innocent choirboy, Briley wants the jury to know the truth. If Rhodes denies the abuse, anything he says can be called into question.

Rhodes glances at the floor, then lifts his head and looks Briley in the eye. "I never saw any evidence of violence."

Her jaw drops in pretended surprise. "Really? Did you never see Jeffrey strike Erin?"

Rhodes looks at Bystrowski again, but Briley steps in front of the prosecutor's table, blocking the witness's line of vision. "Mr. Rhodes? Did you ever see Jeffrey Tomassi hit his wife?"

Rhodes leans forward as a dusky flush rises from his collar. "I saw something once. It certainly didn't happen often."

"How do you know? Were you with the couple twenty-four hours a day?"

"I was with them a lot." He glances from Briley to Bystrowski, then sighs. "Look, I know he beat on her, okay? I even tried to comfort her once, but she blew me off. I figured she had learned to live with it because, like I said, it didn't happen often. Jeff had a quick temper, that's all. A lot of powerful people do."

Satisfied, Briley turns toward the defense table. "I have no additional questions for this witness."

Chapter Forty-Two

Briley glances at her watch, alarmed by signs of fidgeting among the jurors. The day has been long and the jurors are restless, but Judge Trask seems intent to get this trial finished as quickly as possible. Bystrowski has called almost every witness on the list he sent over for discovery, but the hour is so late—

"Your Honor," Bystrowski says, standing, "the prosecution would like to call Douglas Haddock to the stand."

Briley turns as the man comes through the double doors at the back of the courtroom. He does not glance at the defense table as he strides forward.

Erin grips Briley's wrist. "Who is that?" she asks, hissing through clenched teeth.

In order to keep the jury from being distracted by whispering, Briley writes her answer on her legal pad and slides it toward her client: *You don't know him?*

Erin shakes her head.

Briley leans back in her chair. She can understand why Bystrowski might call the man to testify, but why would Haddock agree unless compelled by subpoena? She glances around the courtroom, seeking some clue, but every eye is fixed on the shaggy-haired man who doesn't seem at all reluctant to enter the witness box.

Haddock takes the oath and blinks beneath ragged bangs as the prosecutor rises. "Mr. Haddock," Bystrowski begins, "do you know a woman named Erin Tomassi?"

The witness leans forward and bumps the microphone with his chin. "Um, I used to. In college she was Erin Wilson."

"How well did you know Ms. Wilson?"

"Not well, actually. But one night she sent me to the emergency room for stitches."

The jurors gasp, and several look at Erin with accusation in their eyes.

Briley stands to object. "Your Honor, this testimony is irrelevant and prejudicial. One isolated incident does not, cannot, establish character or habit."

The judge tents his hands in a moment of consideration, then he nods. "I hear what you're saying, but I believe the testimony has probative value. I'll allow it."

Travis Bystrowski can't resist shooting Briley a triumphant look. He locks his hands behind his back and gives his witness an approving smile. "What happened that night?"

Haddock folds his hands like a proper schoolboy. "We met at a bar. She was drinking—she was drunk, actually—and we were hitting it off. So I took her back to my dorm room and hung a tie on the door, if you know what I mean. Everything was fine, but then she hauls off and hits me in the head with a lamp. I backed away, seeing stars, and she ran out of the room. My roommate had to take me to the hospital for stitches."

Bystrowski gapes as if astounded by this bit of news. "Later, did the defendant offer any sort of explanation?"

"I never saw her again. Never wanted to. That was one freaky girl."

"Your Honor!" Briley is on her feet again. "I must protest this characterization of my client!"

"Objection sustained." The judge looks at Doug Haddock. "The witness should confine himself to relating facts."

Bystrowski doesn't miss a beat. "Did you do anything to the defendant—anything that might provoke such a reaction?"

"No way. I thought she was into me. I thought we were going to have a good time and then, blam!"

Bystrowski casts a look of well-mannered dislike in

Erin's direction, then returns his attention to his witness. "Would you say Erin Wilson Tomassi possesses an explosive temper?"

"Objection!" Briley stands, exhaling in frustration. "Counsel is leading the witness."

"Objection overruled."

She watches in disbelief as Haddock wags his shaggy head. "That's a good way to describe it. Explosive."

Briley's had unfair judges before, but Trask is railroading her client. Is he on Tomassi's payroll, too?

"Were you surprised," Bystrowski continues, "to learn that Erin Wilson Tomassi had been charged with the murder of her husband?"

Haddock chuffs. "I wasn't surprised at all. After what I went through, I felt sorry for the guy who married her."

"Thank you, Mr. Haddock. I have no further questions for this witness."

Briley springs to her feet. "Mr. Haddock—" her heels click over the hard floor as she barrels toward him "—do you recall the occasion when you first learned that Erin Tomassi had been charged with murder?"

His forehead crinkles. "Um…maybe it was on the news?"

"All right, perhaps it was." She crosses her arms and draws a quivering breath, barely mastering the anger threatening to rattle her. "Do you recall a conversation you and I had a few weeks ago, when I visited you at your place of employment?"

The man tilts his head as if struggling to remember. "I remember."

"We talked about this incident with the lamp, didn't we?"

"Yeah."

"Do you remember taking an oath a moment ago? A vow to tell the *whole* truth?"

He squints. "I do."

"Then let's continue the story of the girl and the lamp. This time, let's share the whole truth with the jury."

He screws his face into a question mark. "What truth are you talking about?"

Briley draws a quick breath. How should she handle this? Doug Haddock never gave her the entire story; she needed John Savage to fill in the blanks about the roofie and how Erin acted in self-defense. But Savage isn't here, and he's not on the witness list. She could call him to testify, but she'll need time to reach him.

The odds of getting Doug Haddock to disclose his crime are about a million to one. Perry Mason had no problem getting criminals to confess in the courtroom, but she's not Perry Mason.

"Mr. Haddock," she continues, speaking more slowly now, "isn't it true that Erin Wilson Tomassi was *not* 'into you'? And she wasn't drunk that night, yet she was under the influence of a drug because you slipped a roofie—otherwise known as Rohypnol, or the date rape drug—into her drink when she went to the ladies' room. Isn't that true?"

Haddock's expression shifts to one of aggrieved horror. "I would never do a thing like that."

Briley pins him with a sharp look. "You testified that Erin Wilson assaulted you without cause. Did you report this assault?"

"I did. I reported it to campus security."

"What was the result of your report? Was Erin expelled from school? Reprimanded in some way?"

Haddock lifts one burly shoulder in a shrug. "I doubt it. The next morning, I'd cooled off and figured she wasn't worth the hassle. I called the security office and had them drop my complaint."

"Isn't it true that you dropped your complaint because you didn't want to be accused of taking a barely conscious woman back to your room with the intention of raping her?"

"That's not true. Who's saying that it is?"

Briley grits her teeth, fighting the urge to fling her answer in this man's face. She cannot lose control, nor can she respond to this witness by telling him to shut up because she's the lawyer and she gets to ask the questions.

"I'm sorry, Mr. Haddock—" she lifts her chin "—but the rules of evidence do not permit me to answer your question. If they did, I'd be happy to explain."

As Bystrowski roars out another objection, Briley wraps herself in the rags of her dignity and retreats to the defense table.

Briley sits at the defense table, hunched over her trial notebook. The day has been long and emotional, leaving her mind thick with fatigue. She has experienced a few victories, but they seem small and inconsequential when compared with her many blunders.

She rests her chin on her hand and stares at the door through which Erin and the bailiff disappeared at the end of the day. Erin actually thanked her before leaving, which only proves that the woman has no idea how much trouble she's in.

"You still here?"

She glances over her shoulder to see who's spoken. The room has finally emptied, but here comes Bystrowski, probably eager for a chance to gloat.

"I'm here," she says, closing her notebook so he won't be tempted to read over her shoulder. "I thought I'd go over my notes for tomorrow."

He walks through the swinging gate and grins at her. "Come on, Briley, 'fess up. I know what you're feeling— I felt wrung out at the end of day one of my first capital case, too. I wanted to crawl into a hole and not come out."

She tilts her head, amazed by his honesty. "You mean the great Bystrowski gets beat up, too?"

"I mean, you win some, you lose some…and some days you should've stayed in bed." He picks up a folder someone has dropped on the floor by his table, then taps it against his palm. "Gotta study for tomorrow. You should go home and get some rest."

"Maybe I need to study, too."

"You're doing fine." He heads toward the door, waving the folder at her as he goes. "The press is still pretty thick out front, if that's what you're worried about. You could go out the side entrance if you want to avoid them."

The man has read her mind. Briley exhales a deep breath, slips her trial notebook into her briefcase, and stands to put on her coat. The courtroom, always impressive, is even more intimidating in the silence. She turns from the carved wood of the ornate judge's bench and trudges toward the double doors, dwarfed by the soaring ceiling and ornate pilasters.

In the wide hallway, she looks left and right. A couple of men in trench coats stand at the end of the space, and a woman is coming up the wide stairs. Since those stairs and the elevator will take Briley to the public lobby on the first floor, she turns left and walks to a narrow staircase that leads to an unimposing side entrance most often used by lawyers in a hurry.

She opens the fire door and enters the stairwell, her thoughts as heavy as her steps. Not only did she make several stupid mistakes today, but she's begun to believe that Judge Trask is deliberately favoring Bystrowski. He's an experienced jurist, so he'll be careful not to do anything too obvious, but she's going to have to make sure all her objections remain on the record. If they lose and this case goes before an appellate court, other judges will be weighing in on her objections and Trask's rulings....

She slows on the sixth-floor landing when she hears a door close overhead. Someone else has entered the stairwell...probably another weary lawyer who's eager to avoid the reporters out front. Or maybe it's Bystrowski, looking for her. She stops, expecting to hear someone call her name, but the person above her halts in midstep...as if listening.

Why would anyone do that? She's imagining things.

Briley shakes her head and continues down the stairs. She ought to scan the newspaper to see what other trials are being held here this week. She's been positively myopic since beginning this case, with no time for anything but reading and thinking—

Her heart begins to pound when she hears the footsteps again. What are the odds that some other lawyer waited so late to leave the building? The other person could be a judge or a clerk, but why are his or her steps keeping time with Briley's?

She quickens her pace and continues down the staircase, passing the fifth-floor landing. The air here is heavy, cold, and still, filled with a hushed malevolence that chills her to the marrow.

On a whim, she exits at the fourth-floor landing and hurries into the hallway. She passes several doors and breathes a sigh of relief when she spies the ladies' room.

Briley darts into the restroom and hurries through the small lounge. Her pumps clunk against the tile floor, an ordinary, comforting sound. She slips into one of the stalls and latches the door, then stands in the silence, her hands pressed to the painted surface. Every muscle tenses when she hears the door open, followed by the comforting splash of running water.

She takes a deep breath and forbids herself to tremble. Some secretary is rinsing out a coffeepot or washing her hands, that's all. No one is pursuing her, nothing has gone wrong.

Still, she waits until the water stops running and the door opens again. Then she exhales a deep breath and unlatches the door, knowing that William and Kate will hoot when they hear how thoroughly she's managed to spook herself.

She steps out of the stall and flinches when she sees herself reflected in the restroom mirrors. Her face is as pale as Erin's, her eyes are as wide, her makeup is long gone. She steps forward and lowers her head to search for a lipstick at the bottom of her purse.

Without warning, someone rushes at her from the next stall. Briley squeaks out a gasp, but a hand claps over her mouth, a hand clad in leather.

A masculine form wrapped in a trench coat shoves her against the tile wall. A red ski mask covers the facial features, but the words are clear as the intruder spills vile breath into her face. "She's not worth it," he growls, flinty eyes burning through slits in the knitted fabric. "So let the slut die."

Briley's thoughts skitter in panic as the gloved hand lifts, leaving the taste of leather on her lips. She is easing toward the safety of the nearest toilet stall when a fist rockets from out of nowhere and slams against her temple. The blow sends a flurry of white dots into her field of vision and knocks her off her feet. She blinks, and finds herself staring at a pipe attached to the bottom of a sink. She reaches for something solid, feels a crumpled paper towel beneath her fingers, and tastes blood on her tongue. A distant radiator begins to clank and hiss, and one thought runs through her mind before the room goes black. Is this what Erin experienced every day?

"Ouch." Briley grimaces as a uniformed security guard hands her an ice pack for the lump at the back of her head.

The EMT kneeling by her side holds up two fingers. "How many?"

"Two," she says. "And I've already named the president and the mayor of Chicago. I'm fine, I just want to go home."

"Not so fast."

The security guard steps aside as a man in a trench coat approaches. Briley blinks up at him and sighs when she recognizes the face. "Detective Malone. Fancy meeting you here."

"Twice in one day, even." As the EMTs pack up their gear, the cop sinks to a chair and pulls his tablet from his coat pocket. "First off, are you okay?"

"I'm fine." Briley lifts the ice pack and smiles with a bravado she doesn't quite feel. "I bit my tongue and got a bump on the head. That's it."

Malone clicks his pen. "Want to tell me what happened?"

She shrugs as she looks around the hallway, searching for

signs of a red ski cap. "I was in the side stairwell and thought I heard someone following me. I ducked into the restroom on the fourth floor and waited until the coast was clear. Apparently I'm not so smart. The guy just opened the door so I'd *think* he was gone, then he hid in the next stall. He caught me when I came out. He knocked me on the head and I passed out. Next thing I know, a cleaning lady is slapping my wrist and waving smelling salts under my nose."

"Did you get a look at your assailant?"

Briley leans forward and lowers her voice. "If I did, do you think I'd tell you? I don't think the guy would want me to rat him out."

Malone leans forward, too. "If you don't give me a few details, how are we supposed to catch the bad guy?"

She leans back in her chair. "It was a warning. Pretty scary, but that's all. He didn't even take my purse."

"But he threatened you." The detective's squint tightens. "Want to tell me what he said?"

She hesitates. "It was a warning…about my client. Apparently I'm supposed to take a dive on this one."

"Really." Malone pockets his notebook. "I have to tell you, Counselor, usually it's the prosecutor who gets threatened. Why do you think the shoe's on the other foot this time?"

"Not my job, Detective." Briley lifts the ice pack from her head and drops it onto Malone's knee. "And now, if you'll excuse me, I have homework to do."

"You're not driving, are you?"

Briley stands and takes a step, then hesitates as the room sways around her. She reaches for the closest solid object—Malone's shoulder—to steady herself.

"Come on," he says, taking her arm. "Let me drive you home."

They are halfway to the elevator when Briley looks up at him. "Rancid breath," she says. "Red knitted ski cap. Brown trench coat. Male, maybe five-eleven or six foot. And honestly, that's all I can tell you, except…"

"Except what?"

"Except maybe you should check out the Tomassis."

Malone rewards her with a quick smile. "Good enough, Ms. Lester. That's a start."

Chapter Forty-Three

When the prison van rumbles to a halt on the second morning of Erin's trial, she leans forward and tries to peer out the narrow window in the back door. Yesterday she had to walk past a crowd of reporters and photographers, but today the driver has parked closer to the side door of the courthouse building. Yesterday this spot must have been occupied...either that, or the driver took a bribe and fully intended to parade his passengers in front of the waiting paparazzi.

When a guard unlocks the door at the back of the van, she shuffles forward, the links in her shackles clinking as she awkwardly manages the step down to the asphalt. Blinking in the sting of the frigid lake wind, she breathes out a breath and hurries through the ensuing frosty cloud. Prisoners are not given coats for this brief transfer, and the jail uniform provides little protection from a Chicago winter. Following her escort, Erin tries not to think about the many coats waiting in her closet at home—the red wool trench, the brown mink, the green stadium jacket. Right now, she'd give her right arm for any of them.

Half a block away, a handful of reporters are waiting behind a security fence, cameras in one hand, Starbucks cups in the other. She looks away, but one of them has recognized her. "Hey. That's Erin Tomassi! Hey, Erin, look over here!"

She lowers her head and concentrates on her shuffle until she is safely inside the courthouse, where a pair of uniformed deputies waits in the hallway. They greet her escort and joke about the weather, paying her no more attention than if she were an inanimate object. Without a word or even a glance at her face, one of them takes her arm and leads her to the elevator.

She leans against the back wall and closes her eyes for the duration of the ride upstairs. The elevator stops on the seventh floor. The deputy steps off, tugging at Erin as if she were a dog on a leash. She tries to walk at his side, but the shackles around her ankles will not let her keep pace with the man.

Finally they reach the holding area connected to Judge Trask's courtroom. Erin steps over the threshold and inhales the aromas of warm food and fresh coffee. Her defense team has gathered around a table against the wall: Briley; William, the man who works at Briley's firm; and a middle-aged blonde Erin has never met.

Briley, who is eating a breakfast burrito, looks up, sees Erin, and nearly chokes on her food. With an effort, she swallows. "What happened to you?"

The deputy turns to Erin, looking at her face for the first time. A flicker of compassion moves in his eyes, then he moves aside so she can enter the iron cage that takes up half the room. Once she steps over the threshold, he kneels to remove her shackles and handcuffs.

While he works, Erin meets Briley's gaze. "I tried to use the phone last night. I needed to call my doctor, remember?"

The unfamiliar woman's face is blank with shock, while William's mustache twitches above the newspaper he's reading.

When she is free, Erin moves to a bench and looks pointedly at the newcomer, who is holding an outfit swathed in dry cleaner's plastic. "I'm Erin Tomassi. I don't believe we've met."

"S-sorry," the woman stammers, a blush brightening her face. "Kate Barnhill. I'm a paralegal at the firm. I've brought you some clothes."

"Kate's been helping me." Briley drops her unfinished

breakfast on the table and peers at Erin. "Are you okay? We could get an extension if you need to see a doctor."

Erin shakes her head. "It's only a few scratches."

"And the mother of all bruises," Kate adds. "Looks like someone took a baseball bat to your cheek."

"It was a fist," Erin says. "I waited over an hour in line for the phone. I was nearly there when Big Shirley cut in front of me. I gave her a dirty look—or so she says. Next thing I know, she's pounding on me and all her friends jump in to help her out."

Briley stares at Erin for a long moment, then looks at Kate and William. "What do you think? Do we cover that bruise with makeup?"

Kate studies Erin, her eyes alive with speculation. "If you hide that bruise, you might miss a great opportunity to win the jury's sympathy."

"On the other hand," William says, "leave it, and some of the jurors might think she's strutting around the jailhouse picking fights. Is that the image you want to project?"

"I don't think," Briley says, speaking slowly, "that Erin looks like she *struts* anywhere."

"What about you?" William asks. "If that lump on your head weren't covered by hair, would you want the jury to see it?"

Erin frowns when Briley shoots him a warning glance. "What lump?"

"It's nothing," Briley says, shrugging. "I fell." She peers at Erin again, then winces. "Are you *sure* you're okay?"

"I'm fine." Erin flashes a smile, though the effort makes her face ache. "The one thing I don't want is an extension. I don't want to spend a single extra day in that place."

"So we leave it," Briley says, though her voice is a long way from confident. "Did you ever make that phone call?"

Erin rolls her eyes. "What do you think?"

"You want me to call the doctor for you? Maybe he could explain what he wanted."

Erin studies her hands, which are scraped and bruised from last night's brawl. "You can try. With those new privacy laws, I don't know if he'll tell you anything."

"I'm a lawyer." A teasing smile flickers across Briley's face. "I have ways of making people talk."

Chapter Forty-Four

Shirley Walker, Erin and Jeffrey Tomassi's housekeeper, appears even smaller and older behind the oak railing of the witness box. In comparison, Travis Bystrowski looks like a giant as he reinforces the fact that Erin was an unhappy wife by quizzing the housekeeper about the Tomassi marriage.

"All that poor girl wanted was a baby," Shirley says, touching a tissue to the corners of her eyes. "And he didn't want one."

Briley studies the jury. Four of the women visibly soften at this remark, but most of the men sit with blank and unreadable faces. She's been watching the jury all morning, trying to discern how they're feeling about her client. What are they thinking about Erin's scratched and bruised features? Do they see her as a victim, or some kind of hellcat?

When Bystrowski concludes his examination, Briley approaches the lectern with a smile. "Mrs. Walker, how many years have you worked for Jeffrey and Erin Tomassi?"

"I've been with them since they first married." Shirley settles her hands in her lap. "They've never had any housekeeper but me."

"You worked at their house, what...once a week?"

"That's right. I cleaned every Tuesday."

"Did you know them well?"

"I knew Erin real well," Shirley says, her eyes bright behind her glasses. "Him, not so well. But she confided in me quite a bit. I got the feeling she didn't have anyone else to talk to."

"Did you like her?"

"Yes, I still do." As if to prove her point, Shirley leans forward and sends a smile winging toward the defense table.

"Tell me, Mrs. Walker—in all the time you spent with Erin, did you ever see her do anything intended to hurt someone else?"

"Heavens, no." Shirley's lower lip trembles. "That girl wouldn't hurt a fly."

"How can you be so sure?"

"Well, once we found this kitten in the gutter in front of their brownstone. I brought it inside, thinking I'd take it to the humane society as soon as I finished cleaning, but Erin picked it up and started lovin' on it. Next thing I know, she's feeding it milk and tuna and calling it Tinker Bell. I thought maybe she'd finally found something to help her feel a little less lonely, but the kitten was gone when I came back the next week. Erin said Jeffrey wouldn't let her keep it." The woman frowns. "I only hope he took it to the humane society instead of dropping it in a Dumpster. I wondered about that, but didn't have the heart to check."

Concerned that Shirley may have given the jury another reason to believe Erin killed her husband, Briley moves on. "That's an interesting anecdote, but it doesn't really establish Erin Tomassi's character. After all, people can love animals and resent other human beings, can't they?"

The housekeeper blinks behind her glasses. "I suppose so."

"Did Erin ever say anything about resenting her husband? Or anyone else in particular?"

Shirley hesitates, then shakes her head. "I don't think so. That girl was more sad than hateful. But I never heard her say a bad word about her husband or anyone else, and generally people who resent other people talk bad about 'em. But Erin isn't the gossipy type."

"You testified that Erin was unhappy in her marriage and that Jeffrey often raised his voice to his wife. Did you ever hear Erin yell back at him?"

"No."

"Did you ever see her strike out at him, even in jest?"

"Heavens, no. Erin isn't the type."

"Not a fighter, then? Not a brawler?"

"No." Shirley's forehead crinkles as she glances toward the battered woman at the defense table. "I don't know what happened to her, but I know she's not the sort to pick fights. Especially not with her husband. He was so much bigger than her."

"Thank you." Briley glances at her notes. "What sorts of things did you do at the Tomassi home?"

"You mean...what did I clean?"

"That's right."

Shirley shrugs. "I vacuumed all the carpets, dusted the entire house, scrubbed the kitchen sink and counters, cleaned the bathrooms, changed the sheets in the master bedroom, and put fresh flowers on the foyer table. Erin loves fresh flowers in the foyer."

"Did your duties include cleaning the windows?"

A smile gathers up the wrinkles by the woman's mouth. "Sure. I did the windows about once a month."

"Did you raise and lower them, or just clean them on the inside?"

"I usually cleaned the inside."

"Did you ever have occasion to raise the windows?"

"Well...sometimes when the weather was nice, I raised them up to let in some fresh air."

"Did you always lower the windows before leaving the house?"

"Well...no."

"Objection." Bystrowski stands, a look of weariness on his face. "While this is fascinating, it's also irrelevant."

"I have a point, Your Honor," Briley says. "If I may be allowed to continue, my reasoning will become clear."

Judge Trask nods. "Objection overruled. Get to your point, Ms. Lester."

Briley turns to the bewildered housekeeper. "Is it possible,

Mrs. Walker, that after opening some of the Tomassis' windows, that you might have left a window unlocked?"

The housekeeper's smile dissolves. "Why— I didn't mean to."

"But on the days when you left and some of the windows were still open...someone might have closed a window without locking it, correct? And it remained unlocked for an indefinite amount of time?"

Her face goes pale as uncertainty creeps into her expression. "You mean...I might have let the killer in?"

Briley braces for another objection, and Bystrowski does not disappoint. "Objection—unresponsive. The witness did not answer the question."

Trask sighs and pinches the bridge of his nose. "Objection sustained. The jury will disregard that last remark."

Briley tries her best not to smile. Mrs. Walker leaped to the appropriate conclusion, and the jury followed her. She turns toward her witness again. "Emptying the household trash cans—was that another one of your duties?"

"Yes."

"Did you often see syringes in the trash?"

"Every once in a while."

"Did you find these in the bathroom trash bin? Or did you ever find them in other areas?"

"The kitchen," Shirley says. "Sometimes Mr. Tomassi would test his blood in the kitchen and give himself a shot at the sink."

"Did he carry that syringe into the bathroom and dispose of it in the special sharps receptacle?"

"Shoot, no, he couldn't be bothered. He'd drop it into the trash compactor. I learned to be real careful when emptying that machine. I didn't want to get stuck with a needle. Those syringes come with plastic caps for protection, but Mr. Jeffrey never bothered to put them back on."

"May I approach, Your Honor?"

The judge motions her forward.

Briley walks to the courtroom clerk and picks up the bag marked State's Exhibit One. "Mrs. Walker—" she holds up the evidence bag "—does this look like one of the syringes you occasionally saw in the trash compactor?"

Shirley nods with great enthusiasm. "Yes."

"And for the record, will you state whether or not the cap is on the needle?"

"It's missing." Shirley directs her gaze toward the jury. "No cap on that one."

Briley smiles at the witness. "Thank you, Mrs. Walker."

For some reason—probably because he looks so much like his dead brother—Erin tenses when the prosecutor calls Jason Tomassi to the stand. She sits beside Briley, her face pale, her eyes downcast, and her arms locked across her chest. Her right foot betrays her anxiety and begins a rapid-fire tap-tap-tapping on the carpeted floor.

Briley's own pulse begins to pound as the prosecutor establishes Jason's identity and relationship to the deceased. She tilts her head and imagines Jason Tomassi's face covered by a red ski mask. How tall is he? What would his voice sound like in a ragged whisper?

As much as she'd like to ponder the matter, she needs to focus on the trial.

Bystrowski launches into a series of questions obviously intended to undermine the housekeeper's benign opinion of Erin's character. "Mr. Tomassi," Bystrowski says, "were you surprised to hear that your sister-in-law had been arrested for the murder of your brother, Jeffrey?"

"No," Jason answers, his expression tight and grim. "That woman is as crazy as a coot."

"Objection!" Briley stands and narrows her gaze at Jason. "The witness stand is not a venue for expressing personal opinions."

"Overruled." The judge looks at Bystrowski. "I trust there's a valid point to this line of questioning."

"Yes, sir," the prosecutor says. He looks at his witness. "You may continue."

Jason shrugs. "There's not much to say. Jeffrey loved Erin, but the more I got to know her, the more I thought she was a few bricks short of a load."

"For the record, could you explain the metaphor?"

Jason scrubs the stubble on his cheek, then leans forward, a picture of earnestness. "At first I thought she was naïve. She always seemed kind of quiet and shy, sort of distracted. Then Jeff began to tell me—"

"Objection." Briley stands. "This is hearsay. The witness does not have direct knowledge of these facts."

"Objection sustained," the judge rules. "Mr. Tomassi, you may testify only about what you yourself heard or know. The jurors should disregard that answer." Trask points at Bystrowski. "Continue, Counselor."

The prosecutor faces his witness. "Mr. Tomassi, were you and your brother close?"

"Very. We were twins. When we were kids, we spoke in a special language no one else could understand."

"Did your close relationship continue into adulthood?"

"Yes. Jeff confided in me about everything—including things he didn't share with his wife."

"Really? Was there some kind of problem between him and his wife?"

"Jeffrey had doubts about Erin—"

"Objection, Your Honor." Briley stands, struggling to mask her frustration. "This is hearsay and speculation. We cannot know what Jeffrey Tomassi thought about his wife."

Judge Trask narrows his gaze and studies the witness. "Objection overruled," he says, nodding at Jason Tomassi. "I'd like to hear this."

Briley sinks back to her chair, her irritation increasing when she realizes that her hands are trembling. Is his voice affecting her on some subconscious level... or is she simply paranoid?

The prosecutor motions to his witness. "Please continue."

"Well," Jason goes on, "after a while Jeff began to wonder if Erin was mentally unstable. He said she talked to herself, and she had a tendency to rage when things didn't go her way. He was worried about how she'd handle being in the public eye as a politician's wife."

"If he didn't think she could handle her role as a politician's wife, why'd he continue in his political career?"

"Because politics was his passion." Jason transfers his gaze to the jury. "I'm not saying my brother didn't love Erin—he did. But he's been planning to run for national office ever since junior high. He was our eighth-grade class president, and he's loved politics ever since. Erin knew all this before they got married. He was honest with her about his priorities."

"I see. Do you have an opinion as to why the defendant might have killed your brother?"

"Objection!" Briley rises. "Opinions are not facts, Your Honor."

The judge's voice booms from the bench. "Objection overruled. I want to hear this." He nods at Jason Tomassi. "You may continue."

"Yes," Jason says. "I have an opinion."

"Would you care to share it with the court?"

Jason clears his throat and glances at the jury. "I believe my sister-in-law killed Jeff because she was tired of politics. The night Jeff died, they'd just come from a big fundraiser and Erin obviously didn't want to be there. I think that night—and seeing how well Jeff was doing—convinced her that she was in for years of that sort of thing. Something in her must have snapped."

"Objection, Your Honor." Briley stands again. "The witness is not a psychologist. He cannot know the defendant's mental state."

The judge tips his chin in Briley's direction. "Objection sustained."

Briley sits, but the damage has been done. The jury knows Jason Tomassi thinks her client is crazy.

Bystrowski turns away from the lectern and flashes a grin in Briley's direction. "Your witness, Counselor."

Briley takes a moment to consider her options. None of Jason Tomassi's opinions should be in the record; the jury shouldn't have heard any of his testimony. She can move to strike, and the judge might actually be reasonable, but if she strikes Jason's testimony she can't cross-examine him on the issues he raised. The elephant has walked through the room; can she pretend no one saw it?

She gathers her notes and steps out from behind the defense table. "Mr. Tomassi, you've testified that you and your brother were close. How often did you see each other after he married Erin?"

Jason shrugs. "Several times a week. If Jeff didn't have an event to attend, we ate dinner with our father every Friday night. And we played racquetball together every Wednesday morning if Jeff was in town."

"That sounds like fun. Did you, by chance, make time for lunch together, as well? Or did Jeffrey play a quick game, shower, and run off to work?"

Jason's eyes spark with indignation. "He took time. He'd shower at the gym and then we'd spend the rest of the morning together."

"That's nice. So you loved your brother, correct?"

Jason may have adored his brother, but the look he gives Briley is far from loving. "Yes."

"Mr. Tomassi, are you a licensed psychologist?"

"No."

"Are you a therapist? A psychiatrist? Did you, perhaps, take more than a basic psychology course in college?"

The witness shakes his head.

"We need a verbal answer, sir."

"No."

"Do you ever talk to yourself?"

Jason looks out at someone in the gallery, then turns his head. "Well…sure."

"Really? Don't you think that's a little *crazy?*"

He forces a laugh. "I don't do it all the time."

"Speaking in a special twin language—isn't that just a little *odd?* A few bricks short of a load, to use your own metaphor?"

"Objection." Bystrowski stands, his eyes hot. "Counsel is badgering the witness."

"I'll withdraw the question, Your Honor." Briley glances over her shoulder and searches for Antonio Tomassi. There he is, red-faced and determined, right behind the prosecutor's table. She smooths her face into pleasant lines and walks closer to the witness stand. "Mr. Tomassi, on the occasions when you saw Erin and Jeffrey argue—or, as you testified, you saw Erin go into a *rage*— what did she say? And may I remind you that you are under oath?"

Jason blinks. "I can't remember every word."

"Surely you can give us the gist of the conversation."

He shakes his head. "I don't recall."

"Perhaps your memory is more attuned to the visual. When you saw Erin raging, did she storm about? Did she get physical with your brother? Or did she threaten him?"

Jason shifts in the hard oak chair. "She got angry, that's all."

"Did she pace back and forth? Throw things? Curse?"

Jason gives Briley a blank look, but his eye twitches. The man must suspect that he's crossed the line into perjury…or he's thinking about the last time he stood this close to her.

A sudden chill climbs the ladder of her spine as she peers into his eyes. "Not remembering much about your sister-in-law, are you? Then let's talk about your late brother. What did Jeffrey do when *he* became angry? Did he hit Erin?"

Jason manages a theatrical grimace. "I've never seen him hit her."

"No? Then surely you've seen the bruises. Mrs. Walker testified that she occasionally saw bruises on Erin's body. Did you ever see bruises on your sister-in-law?"

"I did not."

"That's right, she took pains to keep them covered. Did Jeffrey do the same thing?"

"What?"

"Did your brother ever experience bruises from these alleged *rages* of Erin's?"

He shakes his head. "How should I know?"

"Indeed, how could you? You played racquetball with him every Wednesday morning. You both showered at the gym. And you two were close, so close you even spoke in your own special language, right?" Briley pauses to let the obvious inconsistencies sink into the jurors' minds. "Let's be honest, Mr. Tomassi. Erin never hit Jeffrey, did she? She knew better. She was afraid to argue with him. She never resisted your brother, because she was terrified that resistance would only increase his brutality."

"Objection!" Bystrowski stands, one corner of his mouth twisting in a derisive expression. "Counsel is testifying, not asking questions."

Trask nods. "Sustained."

The thin line of Jason's mouth clamps tight and his throat bobs as he swallows. "My brother never brutalized his wife."

"How do you know? Did he confess this in your secret language?"

"Your Honor!" The scrape of Bystrowski's chair cuts into the dialogue. "She's badgering the witness and opening the door to hearsay."

"I'll withdraw the question." Breathing hard, Briley moves toward the defense table and struggles to maintain her momentum. This man is a pitiless liar, maybe a brute, and she needs to thoroughly discredit him. The jury shouldn't— can't—be allowed to believe a word of his testimony.

"Mr. Tomassi—" she turns toward the witness box "—are you married?"

Apparently relieved by the change in topic, Jason tosses a grin at the jury. "Not yet."

Briley refuses to smile. "Do you believe marriage is *the* most important human relationship between two people?"

He hesitates. "Yeah. Yes."

"Do you believe a husband and wife ought to be loyal to each other above all other relationships?"

"Sure."

"Should a husband and wife defend each other, cling only to each other, and honor each other in all things?"

Tomassi's forehead crinkles. "I feel like I'm in church."

"That's not an answer, sir."

"Yeah, okay. I do."

"Then does a man who insists on valuing his political career above his relationship with his wife violate a sacred trust valued by millions of people?"

For an instant, she almost feels sorry for Jason Tomassi. Apparently he has never given marriage a great deal of thought, but the jurors certainly have. Voir dire revealed that eight of the twelve are married, and three of them have been married more than fifty years.

When an audible murmur of disapproval rises from the jury box, Jason hears it. "My brother," he says, glaring at Briley from beneath lowered brows, "didn't deserve to die without even a chance to fight back. He would never have taken the cowardly way out, and only a coward would kill him while he was asleep—"

"The defense has no further questions for this witness," Briley says, turning back to the defense table. "Thank you, Mr. Tomassi."

Chapter Forty-Five

During the lunch recess, Briley, Kate, and William huddle in the courtroom to compare notes. Erin sits at the end of the counsel table while a deputy stands at the door. The scent of coffee hangs in the air, mingling with the peppery scents of Chinese food. Briley watches William, noticing that he has no trouble managing his chopsticks with one hand while he holds a folded newspaper in the other.

"Nothing in the news about your assault." He tosses the paper aside. "That's good, at least."

"You're pretty good with those chopsticks," she quips, slipping her feet out of the pumps that have begun to restrict the circulation to her toes. "You must eat a lot of Chinese."

He shrugs. "Born just outside San Francisco's China-town. I learned how to eat with sticks at an early age."

"Well?" Kate shoots Briley a questioning look over the top of her latte. "Are you going to put our client on the stand?"

Briley glances at Erin, who hasn't said more than five or six words since Judge Trask dismissed the court. She might be in pain from the beating she took last night, or perhaps Jason Tomassi's testimony upset her. Briley would like to know what she's feeling, but right now she needs to focus on the trial.

"What do you think, Coach?" William lowers his voice. "Before we dismiss today, you're going to have to switch to offense. So what's our game plan?"

Briley screws up her face. "I hate sports analogies."

"Sorry." William lifts both hands in an apologetic gesture. "But we need to pin this down. Bystrowski's winding up."

"I know." Briley pulls out her trial notebook, in which she has outlined three possible approaches. "The problem isn't that I don't have a plan—the problem is that I have too many. And Erin isn't happy about any of them."

William and Kate both turn to look at the client, who is munching on an egg roll and staring at nothing.

Briley sighs. A more experienced attorney might know exactly what to do in this situation, but despite hours of preparation, she isn't sure her client can handle the pressure of a hostile cross-examination. The woman is fragile, especially now, and tears on the stand might lead the jury to think she's putting on a show for their benefit. On the other hand, if she cries in the right way and at the right moment, a few tears might convince them she is a grieving widow who has no idea how her husband died.

Only one thing is certain: if Briley puts Erin on the stand, she will not ask about Lisa Marie. If the jury thinks she's unbalanced enough to believe in an invisible friend, they'll have no trouble believing she's unstable enough to kill an abusive husband.

"Some of the firm's attorneys," William offers, "believe the defendant should testify no matter what, because no juror is going to acquit unless they hear the defendant say 'I didn't do it.' Others aren't willing to take the chance. I mean, what if the client gets up there and loses his cool?" A blush colors his cheeks as he looks over at Erin. "Not that *you* would do that."

Erin manages a weak smile, then stabs a plastic fork into a carton of kung pao. "I've never had any cool to lose."

"Erin's done real well in rehearsal." Briley sends her client a reassuring smile, then picks up a spare quarter and rubs her thumbnail over the serrated edge. "I could almost flip for it," she says. "Heads, she testifies. Tails, she doesn't."

"I vote for putting her on the stand." Kate crosses her arms. "First of all, you'll be able to address the injuries to her face. No one's explained them, and the jurors want to know what happened. I can see questions in their eyes."

Briley makes a note on her legal pad. "That's a good point."

"Second," Kate continues, "Erin's a calm and reasonable person. When the jury sees how soft-spoken she is, they're bound to realize the brother-in-law was lying through his teeth when he said she picked fights with Jeffrey."

"Jason's testimony is forcing our hand," Briley admits. "But I don't think any of the jurors believed him."

"I wouldn't be too sure about that." William waves a chunk of fortune cookie for emphasis. "Think about it— having a twin testify is almost like having the victim call for justice from the grave. I think the jury is going to give Jason's testimony a great deal of weight."

"But Jason is nothing like Jeffrey," Briley protests. "Jason may look like his brother, but he doesn't have the same appeal. He doesn't have Jeffrey's charisma."

Kate nods. "I have to agree with William. Jason may have fabricated his story, but he held those jurors in the palm of his hand. And in case you haven't noticed, the Tomassi men draw a lot of favorable attention just by breathing. Jason may be a liar, but he's also an Adonis."

"Even the old man is good-looking," William admits. "They've all got that Italian-machismo thing going for them."

The trio falls silent and eats, the silence broken only by the tick and buzz of fluorescent bulbs. Briley is wondering if any of the others have considered the possibility that Jason might be the man who assaulted her, when William unfolds the fortune from his cookie and peers at the tiny type: "The soul that gives is the soul that lives."

Kate makes a face. "What is that supposed to mean?"

"Fortunes aren't supposed to be interpreted. You're supposed to accept them in all their profundity." William shifts his gaze to Briley. "It's almost time. So…are you still going with parasomnia? Or are we going to try to pin this one on whoever killed JonBenet?"

Not wanting to unnerve her client, Briley gives William a warning glance, but Erin is focused on eating, her fork dipping into the cardboard carton as if she hasn't had a decent meal in weeks.

Briley props her chin on her hand. If only the stakes weren't so high. In her previous cases, a mistake in judgment might result in a sentence of a few extra months or years. In this case, Erin could pay for Briley's mistakes with her life.

"I'm considering," she says, keeping her voice low, "the cockroach defense."

Kate gives her a skeptical look. "What's that?"

"It's used when you have no clear option, so you settle for crawling all over the other side."

William snorts. Briley glances at her client, afraid she'll see a stricken look on Erin's face, but apparently the woman isn't following the conversation.

"Are you serious?" Kate asks.

Briley shrugs. "Halfway. If I throw up every defense I can think of, something might stick."

"Or it'll all land at your feet with a big splat," William says. "Since that's the most likely scenario, I think you should stick with diminished capacity."

"Based on…?"

"The sleeping pills," he answers. "That's a viable defense. Precedents have been set, defendants have been acquitted."

"Maybe." Briley taps the end of her pen against the table. "I just keep thinking about Lisa Marie and wondering whether Erin would be better off spending a few years in prison or an indefinite period in a mental hospital. But some of those places can be worse than jail."

"Do you think—" Kate glances at Erin "—the Tomassis know about the invisible friend?"

Briley shakes her head. "Jason would have mentioned Lisa Marie if he knew. That testimony would have bought our client a one-way ticket to a hospital for the criminally insane."

"Unless the family doesn't *want* her to be mentally ill."

William cracks open another fortune cookie. "After all, the mentally ill can be cured, and cured patients are eventually released from the hospital. Something tells me the Tomassis want Erin to suffer for more than a few years."

Briley closes her eyes, not wanting to admit that William is most likely right. "Mental illness," she says, "is not an acceptable defense. Except for Erin's attachment to an invisible friend, she is as sane as we are."

Kate nods, then speaks in a barely audible whisper. "But if that attachment led to murder, shouldn't she be convicted and sent away for treatment? Have you ever thought about what might happen if next year Lisa Marie kills a neighbor? Or a child?"

Panic wells in Briley's throat as she stares at Kate. "Not until now."

"Relax, you're forgetting about the shrink." William offers Briley a bit of the broken cookie. "She tested your client and found her completely harmless, remember? You can have her counter Jason's testimony about Erin being unstable. The doc will say she's merely imaginative."

Relief washes over Briley as she waves the cookie away. William is right; there's no cause for worry. Her client is neither insane nor guilty, and Briley needs to be steadier in her resolve. If she wants the jury to believe in Erin's innocence, she must believe in it, too.

"I plan to use Dr. Lu," she says, "and I'm going to let her address all the issues we've discussed, including Erin's so-called delusion. The only thing that concerns me is the possibility that Bystrowski will go on a fishing expedition during cross-examination. I don't want the jury to hear that Erin thinks her invisible friend committed the murder."

She looks up, seeking William's and Kate's approval, and finds it in their eyes.

Kate points to the quarter in Briley's hand. "You gonna flip that thing or not?"

Briley tosses the coin into the air, catches it, and turns it between her palms. Then she lifts her right hand, but doesn't look at the quarter. "It's heads." She meets Kate's wry gaze. "We're putting Erin on the stand."

William strokes his mustache. "Are you absolutely certain?"

"You bet. In fact, I'm going to call her first. Might as well lay our cards on the table and go for broke."

William's uncertain look morphs into a horrified expression of disapproval. "But what if you lose?"

Briley leans closer. "Then I hope Erin gets a far better lawyer to handle her appeal."

After the lunch recess, the prosecution officially rests its case.

When the judge looks toward the defense table, Briley stands. "Your Honor," she says, bracing herself on the desk, "the defense would like to request a directed verdict for acquittal. We contend that the prosecution has failed to present sufficient evidence to prove beyond a reasonable doubt that the defendant is guilty of the crime with which she has been charged."

The request is routine, and she doesn't expect a favorable answer. So she's not surprised when Judge Trask leans forward and gives her a smile that is ten percent politeness and ninety percent challenge. "The defense's motion for a directed verdict is denied. Counselor, call your first witness."

Briley swallows hard. "The defense calls Erin Tomassi to the stand."

Bystrowski and his team sit motionless, frozen in a tableau of astonishment, as the court clerk repeats the name and stands to administer the oath. Erin walks forward with stiff dignity and shivers as she maneuvers around Briley. Her heels clunk against the wooden platform beneath the witness chair. But when the clerk asks if she swears to tell the truth, the whole truth, and nothing but the truth, her response is loud and clear: "I do."

Briley glances at her notes. If all goes well, she will help Erin present her story without tears or histrionics or any mention of Lisa Marie.

When Erin appears comfortable in the simple oak chair, Briley steps behind the lectern and looks directly at her client. "Mrs. Tomassi, do you understand the nature of the charges you are facing here today?"

Erin nods, her face somber. "I do. I've been accused of killing my husband, Jeffrey."

"Did you? Did you take a syringe and inject your husband with an overdose of insulin?"

"No." Erin's voice wavers as she looks at the jury. "As God is my witness, I didn't. I would never hurt anyone if I could help it."

Briley steps to the side of the lectern, relaxing her posture and her approach. "Thank you, Erin. Let's go back and review some of your personal history. Have you ever been in trouble with the law?"

Erin blushes. "Not until this."

"Not even a parking ticket?"

"No."

"No period of teenage rebellion?"

She lifts one shoulder in a shrug. "I had no one to rebel against. My father died when I was young, and my mother didn't seem to care what I did."

"Why didn't your mother care?"

Erin lowers her gaze. "She drank a lot."

"Growing up, did you have siblings? Someone to keep you company?"

"I have a brother, Roger. But social services took him away before I started school."

"Why did they take him?"

"He has Down syndrome. Apparently my mother wasn't able to properly care for him."

"Does he live with your mother now?"

"No, he lives in a supervised group home."

"That must be expensive. How does Roger pay for his living arrangements?"

"Jeffrey—my husband—and I pay the bill every month."

Briley watches the jury to be sure they are absorbing this testimony. They have to see Erin as a generous person, not a cold-blooded killer. "Let's talk about your relationship with your husband. How long were you married to Jeffrey Tomassi?"

Erin tilts her head. "Five years."

"Did you love him?"

"Yes…yes, I did, though our relationship was often… difficult."

"How was it difficult?"

"Jeffrey was a difficult man to please. I tried, though, because when he wasn't happy, I couldn't be happy. When he lost his temper, he would hit me."

"You have a bruise and scratches on your face now." Briley softens her tone. "Surely you don't want us to think your husband caused those."

"No." Erin's hand creeps to the worst welt on her cheek. "Last night at the jail…apparently some of the women don't think I have the right to wait in line for the telephone."

"Some of the other inmates beat you up?"

She nods.

"For the record, Erin, we'll need you to answer verbally."

"Yes."

"You seem to frequently be a victim. Do you go around picking fights?"

Erin shrinks visibly, her shoulders hunching as she draws into her self. "I don't fight with anyone. I hate violence. Always have."

"I see." Briley surveys the jury. All fourteen of them are focused on the woman in the witness box. "Erin, do you think it's fair to describe yourself as an abused wife?"

Erin's eyes narrow as a flush colors her cheeks. "I don't

like those words, but I suppose that's what I am. Or was. I suppose that's what I was."

"If you were being abused and mistreated, why didn't you walk away from the marriage?"

A disbelieving smile crosses Erin's face. "You don't walk away from the Tomassi family. Besides, Jeffrey told me he'd never let me leave. He said he'd do anything to track me down and make me regret the day I thought about walking away. I knew he wasn't kidding, so I never even considered leaving."

Briley paces behind the lectern, giving the jury time to ponder Erin's answer. "Did your husband ever strike you in public?"

"No. Jeffrey would never let anyone see behind the mask. No one, that is, except his brother and a couple of other close friends. Jason saw Jeffrey smack me several times. But he never said anything to me about it."

"Erin." Briley stops pacing. "Why did you marry Jeffrey Tomassi?"

"Because I loved him." Erin looks at the jury, but only for a moment, as if she were afraid to let her gaze rest on the questioning countenances in the jury box. "When Jeffrey and I were dating, I thought he was perfect. He was thoughtful, handsome, charming, and he wanted to take care of me."

"Did you marry Jeffrey for his money?"

"No. I never wanted his money, though I was attracted to his lifestyle. But Jeffrey asked me to sign a prenuptial agreement, and I agreed. I understood I would never have any claim on the money he brought to the marriage."

Aware that some jurors might consider money a motivation for murder, Briley pushes ahead. "If you are acquitted in this trial, what will you do with your inheritance?"

Surprise flickers in Erin's eyes. "Jeffrey's money?"

"Yes."

"But I don't have any right to that. I signed a prenup."

"A standard prenuptial agreement applies if a couple

divorces," Briley says, keeping her voice matter-of-fact. "As a widow, aren't you entitled to your late husband's assets?"

Erin shakes her head. "Our contract wasn't standard— the Tomassis wanted to guard their money. Our agreement states that if Jeffrey dies, I don't get anything that originated with the Tomassi estate. Besides, I don't want their money. The family can keep it."

"Objection, Your Honor." Bystrowski is on his feet again, his eyes gleaming with interest. "This is hearsay. The agreement must speak for itself."

Briley shakes her head. "This testimony is necessary to explain Mrs. Tomassi's motives. Her understanding of the agreement is relevant to this line of questioning."

The judge sits quite still, his eyes narrow, then he nods at Briley. "Objection overruled. Continue, Ms. Lester."

Briley smiles in relief, grateful that today, at least, the judge seems to be favoring her side of the argument. Now to drive the point home. "Erin," she asks, "do you know who will inherit Jeffrey's portion of the estate?"

Erin looks at the line of Tomassis seated on the front row of the gallery. "I…I suppose Jason does. I don't know. I never handled the money. Jeffrey told me to let our accountant deal with our finances."

Briley steps closer to the witness box. "Let's talk about December 2, the night Jeffrey died. According to Detective Malone's testimony, you told him that you went to the fundraiser for Jeffrey's congressional campaign, and there you had an argument with your husband. Do you remember what the argument was about?"

Erin lowers her head. "Jeffrey was upset because I forgot to pack his silk socks. Later, I told him I had a terrible headache and didn't want to sit at a head table in front of all those people. I asked if I could go lie down in the hotel suite, but he said no. I had to sit through his speech, and then we had to dance."

Briley moves closer. "Did you argue with him at the event?"

"I didn't dare. I started to cry though, out of sheer frustration, and Jeffrey grabbed my arm. He squeezed it so tightly he left a mark."

"Did anyone see him grab you?"

"I don't think so. We were standing behind a velvet curtain, and everyone else was in the banquet hall. Jason or Antonio might have been around, but I wasn't looking for them. I was trying not to lose sight of Jeffrey."

"Why?"

"I was afraid."

"Of what?"

"Afraid that if my attention wandered, he'd hit me. Maybe not at that exact moment, but later, when we got back to the house. He always let me know if I did something to upset or disappoint him."

Briley turns to the jury. "Erin, do you read what reporters write about you?"

"Sometimes."

"Have you ever read that you usually watch your husband with 'a wide-eyed look of adoration'?"

Briley turns in time to see her client blush. "Yes."

"That's not true, is it?"

"Objection," Bystrowski stands. "Your Honor, counsel for the defense is supposed to be questioning the witness about facts, not soliciting comments on gossip columns."

"I'll withdraw the question." Satisfied that the jury has taken her point, Briley retreats to the lectern. "What happened when you and your husband arrived at home in the early hours of December 3?"

Erin shudders slightly. "I was exhausted, so—"

"Mrs. Tomassi," the judge interrupts, "you'll have to speak up. Move closer to the microphone, please."

Erin obediently slides her chair forward. "I was exhausted," she repeats, her voice ringing through the sound system, "and Jeff was all wound up. He was on the phone, calling his brother and some other staffers, so I went into the bathroom and took a double dose of Ambien. I hoped I'd be asleep by the time he got off the phone. I figured maybe he wouldn't take things out on me if I were unconscious."

"Do you know why Jeffrey was wound up?"

"Objection!" Bystrowski stands, vexation evident on his face. "Counsel is asking for personal opinion, not facts."

Judge Trask rubs a hand over his face, then lifts a finger. "Objection overruled. I want to hear this."

Briley repeats the question. "Can you tell us why your husband was wound up?"

Erin winces. "I— Do I have to say?"

Briley steps forward and rests her hands on the railing of the witness box. "Erin," she says, filling her voice with as much intensity as she can muster, "I know this is painful, but you have to tell the jury the truth."

Erin shivers, reminding Briley of a puppy that's been kicked too many times. "Could you repeat the question?"

"Certainly. Will you please tell the jury why your husband was wound up?"

Erin stares into the empty space between the judge's bench and the attorney's lectern. "He was wound up... because he'd just beaten me."

"Beating you...excited him?"

"Objection, leading!" Bystrowski roars this time, accenting his cry with a knock on the table.

But Judge Trask, who hasn't taken his eyes off Erin in the past several minutes, replies automatically: "Overruled."

Briley glances at the jury. Like the judge, they are watching Erin, and several of the women have tears in their eyes.

Rather than repeat the question, Briley simply looks at Erin and waits.

Erin nods, her lower lip trembling.

"Let the record show," Briley says, her own voice breaking, "that the witness has nodded in assent." She reaches out to squeeze Erin's arm, then thinks better of the impulsive action and takes a step back. When she is certain her own emotions are under control, she begins again. "After you took the sleeping pills and lay down, did you speak to your husband again?"

"No. I closed my eyes and pretended to sleep. I could hear Jeffrey talking to his brother as I drifted off. The next thing I knew, the sun was up."

"You didn't wake until morning?"

"That's right. I got out of bed and left Jeffrey alone—I didn't want to bother him. I went into the kitchen and made breakfast, then put his meal on a tray and carried it into the bedroom. Jeffrey still wasn't awake, so I left the tray on the dresser and went back into the kitchen to eat my breakfast." She rubs her arms as if she's caught a sudden chill. "He hates being rudely awakened."

Briley studies the jurors' faces. Most of them are wide-eyed and intent upon Erin. Are they imagining themselves in her position? Are they experiencing the horror of that abusive relationship? Juror number four is clutching a hand-kerchief, as if she expects to burst into tears at any moment, and juror number eight has her hand pressed over her mouth. Two men in the back row, however, have crossed their arms, a sign of defensiveness.

Either the men are not buying this story or they're guarding against emotional involvement.

"Erin—" Briley turns to face her client "—I know this is painful, but can you tell us what happened next?"

Erin rubs her arms again. "When I heard the clock strike nine, I began to worry. I knew Jeffrey and Jason had a rac-quetball court reserved for nine-thirty, and Jeffrey was usually up in time to shower and shave before heading to the gym. So I went into the bedroom to wake him up. But when I got there—" her voice quivers, and tears gleam in the depths of her eyes "—I saw that he was gray and his lips were blue. I went over and shook him, but his skin was cold. That's when I ran for the phone and called 911."

Briley strides toward the defense table and picks up a

copy of a cassette tape. "Your Honor," she says, delivering the tape to the court clerk, "this is a copy of the 911 call Erin placed that morning." She looks at the jury. "With the court's permission, we'd like to play it for you now."

The judge looks at Bystrowski. "Any objection?"

The prosecutor shakes his head. "We have stipulated that the tape is a copy of the 911 call in question."

As the clerk prepares to play the tape, Briley leans against the lectern and folds her hands. What is *wrong* with her? A few moments ago she almost lost control, almost wept in the middle of a direct examination. She couldn't have made a more egregious mistake if she'd jerked handsome juror number six from the box and launched into an impromptu tango in the middle of Judge Trask's courtroom.

Professional lawyers remain in control of their cases, their clients, and their emotions. She's been working too hard, that's all; she's been under too much pressure. She's even been mugged.

Fortunately, as Wills would say, they have entered the home stretch.

Chapter Forty-Six

Erin closes her eyes as the sound of her own panicked voice rips the curtain that has protected her from memories of that cold December morning. The woman on the other end of the line was calm, eerily so, and Erin had to repeat herself before the dispatcher seemed to understand the urgency of the situation.

"He's cold, he's blue, he's not breathing," Erin had said, pacing in the bedroom.

"Can you feel a pulse?"

Erin halted in midstep. Touch Jeffrey? Wake him up? He always got so angry when she disturbed him....

But this wasn't sleep, this was something else. Something wrong.

"Just a minute. I'll check." Clutching the cordless phone, Erin crept toward her husband's sleeping form. Jeffrey lay flat on his back, the covers pulled up to his chest. She caught her breath as she leaned forward and pressed two fingers to the side of his neck. The flesh felt like chilled leather. Nothing moved beneath the skin, no pulse, no breath, no life.

Frantically she jabbed at his shoulder, as if she might restore some loose connection and set everything to rights. "There's nothing," she told the emergency operator. "No pulse, no breath. He's cold and blue."

"Do you know how to do CPR?"

"Maybe, but you have to send someone!" Erin's voice broke. "He'll kill me if I mess this up. You need to send someone who knows what they're doing."

"I've already dispatched the rescue squad, ma'am. But you can help us if you calm down. Can you get him flat on his back?"

"He's already flat. He's...stiff."

The phone slipped from Erin's fingers as the truth struck with the ferocity of a blow. Her husband, her lover, her tormentor is dead. The center of her life throughout five years of marriage is gone.

And the thought of freedom brings unspeakable relief in its wake.

"Erin?"

Briley Lester's voice draws her back to the present. She lifts her head and sees the black microphone, the smooth grain of the oak railing, the box filled with more than a dozen sets of curious faces. She sees her lawyer, wide-eyed and alarmed. "Yes?"

Briley inclines her head, her eyes snapping with concern. "You okay?"

"Yes."

The lawyer seems to doubt this, but she turns toward the judge. "The defense has no further questions at this time, Your Honor."

Erin grips the armrest of her chair as the tall prosecutor stands. But instead of stepping out from behind the table, Travis Bystrowski simply looks at her with challenge glittering in his eyes. "We have no questions at this time," he says. "But we reserve the right to recall this witness."

The judge voices his approval, and Erin is free to step down.

Chapter Forty-Seven

"Your Honor, the defense calls Dr. Pamela Lu to the stand."

As the petite psychologist enters the courtroom and walks toward the clerk, Briley gives her nervous client a smile.

"How'd I do?" Erin whispers, the corners of her eyes crinkling.

Briley scratches a note on her legal pad. *You did fine. Now you can relax for a while.*

Briley glances at Bystrowski as the clerk administers the oath. His postponement of Erin's cross-examination caught her by surprise; she had been braced for a sharp counter-punch. What is he planning?

After Dr. Lu settles in the witness chair, Briley stands and moves to the lectern. "Dr. Pamela Lu, what is your occupation?"

"I'm a forensic psychologist. I have earned degrees in forensic psychology and medicine."

"So you've earned two Ph.Ds?"

"One M.D., one Ph.D."

"And those degrees equip you to do what?"

"Examine suspects and convicted criminals, then offer testimony about their physical and mental states. I am typically engaged to help lawyers determine whether or not a suspect is capable of forming the necessary mens rea for a crime."

"In other words, you help lawyers determine if defendants have malicious intentions, correct?"

The doctor glances at the jury and smiles. "Yes, that's right."

"Do you work for prosecutors, as well as defense attorneys?"

"Absolutely."

"Are you being paid for your testimony here today?"

"I am being paid for my time. No one has told me what to say."

"Were you engaged to examine the defendant, Erin Tomassi?"

The doctor glances at the defense table where Erin sits. "Yes, I was."

"Why were you hired to examine her?"

"Such exams are standard for a murder case. A conviction of first-degree murder requires that the killer form an intention to commit the crime. Because of several factors—Mrs. Tomassi's status as an abused wife, the involvement of sleeping pills, the possibility that the death was an accidental overdose—the defense wisely questioned whether Mrs. Tomassi was able to form the necessary intent to kill. Furthermore, after a brief interview with Mrs. Tomassi, I thought it might be possible that she suffers from a delusion."

"Delusion?" Briley glances at the jury to make sure they're following the testimony. "What do you mean by *delusion,* and why should Erin Tomassi suffer from one?"

Dr. Lu steeples her fingers. "In psychological terms, a delusion is a strongly held belief that contradicts demonstrable reality…and, after further investigation, I don't believe Mrs. Tomassi clings to any delusions. Her grip on reality is quite firm."

"So you believe she's mentally competent?"

"I do."

"What made you think she might suffer from a delusion?"

The psychologist smiles, obviously understanding that these things must be painstakingly explained to the jury. "Mrs. Tomassi," she says, her voice calm and soothing, "was a solitary child and an unhappy wife. It'd be perfectly natural for her to seek an outlet for her innermost thoughts. In childhood she entertained herself by talking to an imaginary friend. In adulthood, Mrs. Tomassi occasionally finds comfort by talking to that same friend. But she knows she's not talking to an actual person."

Briley looks at the jury and feigns surprise. "Isn't that sort of thing—well, isn't it crazy?"

"I don't think it's much different from a man or woman who talks to the family dog. We humans are social creatures—we yearn to project our emotions and feelings onto whatever is around to hear us. Remember the Tom Hanks character's attachment to Wilson, the volleyball, in *Cast Away?* Unfortunately, as a child, Erin Tomassi had no pets, no close friends, and her only sibling, a brother, was moved to a facility for special-needs children. To ease her loneliness, she invented an imaginary friend."

"Did you examine the defendant to ascertain whether or not this so-called attachment was a symptom of something more serious? After all, most of us have seen movies about people with multiple personalities...."

"What used to be called multiple personality syndrome is now referred to as dissociative identity disorder, and no, Erin Tomassi does not suffer from DID. This condition is found in people who have endured terrible trauma as children, usually sexual abuse. As a child, Mrs. Tomassi was neglected, not abused. I found her to be a pleasant, unassuming woman suffering from grief and confusion as a result of her husband's sudden death and her own incarceration."

Briley locks her hands behind her back and studies the jury. Most of them are wearing confused expressions that clear somewhat as each juror reaches a level of understanding. When she is reasonably certain the jurors believe that Erin is neither irrational nor insane, she faces the psychologist again. "Dr. Lu, are you aware of the prosecution's theory claiming that Erin Tomassi killed her husband with a massive injection of insulin and then calmly tossed the syringe into a nearby wastebasket?"

"I am."

"Based on your examination of my client, are you able to support this scenario?"

The doctor's mouth twists in a smirk. "No. After suffering at her husband's hands, Erin took a double dose of Ambien that night. Under normal conditions, it's highly improbable that she'd be able to rouse herself at all."

"But her fingerprints are on the syringe. Can you think of a way to explain *that?*"

Dr. Lu's eyes narrow. "Frankly, I can only think of one."

Briley shifts her position to keep an eye on the jury, because they must understand this element of her defense. "What is your explanation for a locked house, a sleeping wife, and a dead husband?"

The doctor scans the jury box before replying. "Medical literature documents several cases in which the prescription drug Ambien caused irrational episodes in patients—many have climbed out of bed and strolled to the kitchen for a snack, some have walked outside, others have even unlocked their cars and gone for a drive. While under the influence of the drug, it's entirely possible that Erin Tomassi got out of bed, filled a syringe with insulin, and gave her husband an injection. Under the control of her subconscious, she may have even acted out of an impulse to assist him. While we cannot be sure of her unconscious motivation, there is no evidence to suggest or support malicious intention."

"How can you say that with such certainty?"

"Because she made no effort to conceal her activity. She did not wipe her fingerprints from the syringe or the bottle. She made no effort to hide the syringe. She simply got back into bed, pulled up the covers, and went to sleep."

"Must a person possess malicious intent in order to be convicted of first-degree murder?"

A hush falls over the courtroom, the almost palpable silence of waiting.

"In this country, yes."

Briley smiles. No matter what happens in this trial, that statement should be enough to prevent Erin from being sentenced to death by lethal injection.

"Thank you, Doctor. We have no further questions for this witness." She lifts her chin as she returns to the defense table. Let Bystrowski grill Dr. Lu during the cross. He may leave the jurors wondering if Dr. Lu is qualified to question a cat, but he'll never convince them that Erin deserves to die.

"Miss Lester?"

During the midafternoon recess, Briley turns and sees a tall, thin man standing in the aisle of the gallery. A tuft of thinning white hair spills onto his forehead as he smiles and extends his hand. "Kenneth Sparks, M.D. You asked me to testify on behalf of the defense."

"Thank you for coming...and for working with Kate." She steps forward, grateful that he remembered to show up. She called his office over a dozen times, begging for an hour in which she could help him prepare his testimony, but the doctor insisted he was too busy. Finally she sent Kate, who booked a patient appointment and reviewed the doctor's testimony in one of his exam rooms.

"I'm so sorry I wasn't able to meet with you," he says, shaking her hand, "but your assistant apprised me of the issues involved. I've testified in court many times."

"But not in *this* case." The words slip from Briley's tongue, a spillover of her frustration.

He waves her concerns away. "Don't worry. I reviewed Mrs. Tomassi's chart before coming over."

She is about to tell him he'll be free to leave after his testimony when a door at the front of the courtroom opens, revealing Erin and her escort. "Excuse me," Briley says, turning. She meets Erin at the defense table, then leans down to whisper in her ear. "Your doctor's arrived."

Erin turns toward the gallery. "Which doctor?"

"Dr. Sparks."

The bailiff barks a command: "Be seated and come to order."

Briley opens her trial notebook as Judge Trask assumes his place on the bench and waits for the shuffling to cease. After the bailiff brings the jury back in, Briley rises and moves to the lectern. "The defense calls Dr. Kenneth Sparks to the stand."

The doctor strides forward, offering a brief nod of acknowledgment to the watchful jury. After being sworn in, he folds his hands and adopts an almost paternal pose. The effect is a good one. Without saying a word, his demeanor and confidence have done a lot to establish his testimony as trustworthy and credible.

"Dr. Kenneth Sparks," Briley begins, "you are a family physician in Chicago, correct?"

"My office is in Lincoln Park," he says, looking every inch the kindly grandfather. "I've been practicing medicine in that community for thirty years."

"Are you acquainted with the defendant, Erin Tomassi?"

"She's one of my patients."

"Have you treated her often?"

"I've seen her on several occasions. Annual checkups, that sort of thing."

"Do you ever recall seeing Mrs. Tomassi when she came to your office for something other than a checkup?"

His mouth spreads into a thin-lipped smile. "I remember one specific occasion. Mrs. Tomassi presented with pain in her side and difficulty breathing. An X-ray revealed two broken ribs."

"Did she mention how she obtained those broken ribs?"

"She told me she fell down the stairs."

"Did this seem strange to you?"

The doctor shrugs. "She had other contusions which seemed to support her story—bruised knees, elbows, and a large bruise at her jawline. I asked how she came to fall down the stairs, and she said something about having two left feet. I specifically remember sitting beside her and asking if there was anything else I should know. She insisted that all was well."

Briley studies the jury. "I have to ask, Doctor—was Erin Tomassi's husband with her during that visit?"

A tremor touches the man's pale lips. "Yes, Senator Tomassi was with his wife. I asked if he wouldn't be more comfortable in the waiting room, but he insisted on remaining with his wife. He was quite...determined."

Briley proceeds carefully, not wanting to cast blame on the doctor for not intervening aggressively. She needs to keep him—and the jury—on her side. "After that particular examination, Dr. Sparks, were you able to draw a conclusion as to the cause of the injuries to Erin's bruised knees, elbows, face, and broken ribs?"

The doctor's valiant attempt at remaining professional is marred by a sudden thickness in his voice. "I wish I had been able to speak to her alone. I had my suspicions, but that's all they were—suspicions. On the surface, Erin seemed a lovely, content woman and the senator a devoted husband."

Briley turns to the jury box and scans the fourteen faces. Are they hearing what she wants them to hear? Do they understand?

"Dr. Sparks—" she softens her tone "—did Erin Tomassi come to see you about six months ago?"

"Yes. She came alone and said she was unable to sleep. I prescribed zolpidem tartrate, commonly sold as Ambien."

"Did she say why she was having trouble sleeping?"

"I didn't ask."

"After you gave her the prescription, did she complain of any side effects from the drug?"

"Not to my knowledge."

"Are you familiar with published literature in which others have complained of side effects when using Ambien?"

"Yes. Some patients have exhibited parasomnia while taking the drug."

280   *Angela Hunt*

"For the less medically inclined among us, can you define *parasomnia?*"

"Literally, the word means 'outside sleep.' Parasomnias are odd or unusual activities that occur while an individual is sleeping. These include sleepwalking, sleep talking, nighttime terrors, REM behavior disorders, and nocturnal dissociative disorder."

"Dr. Sparks—" Briley steps closer to her witness "—are you aware of the prosecutor's theory that Erin Tomassi intentionally injected her husband with an overdose of insulin while he slept?"

The man tilts his head. "Yes, I read the papers."

"Hypothetically speaking, if a woman swallowed a double dose of Ambien, went to sleep, woke in the middle of the night, injected her husband, tossed the syringe in the trash can, and went back to bed, would you blame the woman or the drug?"

"Objection." Bystrowski stands and shakes his head. "Calls for speculation."

"Objection sustained."

Briley turns back to her witness. "If a woman behaves in an unpredictable manner after taking a double dose of Ambien, would you consider the drug a possible trigger for her actions?"

The doctor smiles. "I don't see how you could rule it out."

"Thank you, sir. The defense has no further questions for this witness."

Briley moves toward her counsel table, but the prosecutor wastes no time in launching a counterattack.

"Dr. Sparks—" Bystrowski doesn't even bother to move to the lectern "—how long have you been practicing medicine? Thirty years?"

The doctor nods, sending a sheaf of white hair into his eyes. "That's correct."

"In your long practice, Doctor, how many times have you prescribed zolpidem tartrate?"

"Impossible to know without checking every chart in my files."

Bystrowski takes off his glasses. "More than a dozen times? More than a hundred?"

Dr. Sparks narrows his eyes at the prosecutor. "Since the drug was introduced in 1993, I've probably prescribed it at least fifty times per year."

Bystrowski pauses to crunch the numbers. "Seven-hundred-fifty scripts? Does that number sound plausible?"

"Yes."

"To seven-hundred-fifty different patients?"

"Well, give or take a hundred. Some of those are refills."

"All right, then. Of these six-hundred-fifty patients, how many have exhibited signs of odd nightly activities? In other words, how many of your patients have turned into sleep-walkers and sleep talkers?"

Dr. Sparks spreads his hands. "Impossible to tell. Unless a problem is reported to me, I remain unaware of it. Some-times these events are so mild that no one notices them. Or a wife may become so accustomed to her husband's wan-dering around in the dark that she thinks nothing of it."

"But you have heard reports of sleepwalking?"

"Among my patients?"

"Yes."

"How many times?"

"A few."

"I need a number, sir."

"I couldn't give you a number."

"Less than twenty?"

"That sounds about right."

Bystrowski leans on the lectern and shifts his gaze to the jury. "How many of those less-than-twenty sleepwalkers and sleep talkers have become sleep *killers?*"

Dr. Sparks gives the prosecutor a glare that should have singed Bystrowski's eyebrows. "Apparently that number will depend upon the outcome of this trial."

At the defense table, Briley stirs uneasily. She should have booked an appointment with the doctor and paid for two hours of the man's time. If she'd known he was going to play into Bystrowski's hands, she could have manufactured a headache.

The prosecutor gazes at the jury as if perplexed. "If unwanted nocturnal activity is common with people who take Ambien, why is the drug still on the market?"

The doctor's mouth puckers with annoyance. "Parasomnia is not common among patients who take the drug correctly—people who allow plenty of time for sleep while they avoid alcohol and other prescription medicines."

Bystrowski crosses to his counsel table and glances at his notes. "When you recited possible side effects for Ms. Lester, you mentioned something called nocturnal dissociative disorder. Can you define that condition for us?"

Dr. Sparks leans an elbow on the witness box. "It's when the patient disassociates from his true self—sort of a mental disconnect."

"Really. Are you familiar with published literature that details a case like this?"

The doctor sucks at the inside of his cheeks while his eyes lock with Briley's. Her uneasy feelings shift to a deeper and more immediate fear: what is he about to say?

"Well," the doctor begins, "I've read case reports of at least two men who killed their wives while in the grip of nocturnal dissociative disorder."

Briley studies Bystrowski, who, wide-eyed and gaping, is pretending he's never heard this bit of information. His associate at the counsel table, however, is reading something in a notebook and smiling in self-congratulation.

Bystrowski has done his homework. He has Dr. Sparks on the hook, and all that remains is to reel the old man in....

"Really?" the prosecutor says. "Were these two men convicted and sent to prison?"

"Objection!" Briley rises in a flash, her mouth going dry.

For an instant, she's too stunned to respond, then her brain floods with words. "Assumes facts and circumstances not in evidence, Your Honor. This is prejudicial and irrelevant."

"The witness is a medical expert," Bystrowski argues. "And counsel for the defense opened the door to this line of questioning."

Trask measures the prosecutor with a cool, appraising look, then he nods. "Objection overruled. The witness will answer."

"I'll repeat the question," Bystrowski says. "These two men who killed their wives while experiencing a parasomnia—were they convicted of these crimes?"

"One was." The doctor looks at the jury. "In 1997, Scott Falater murdered his wife by stabbing her forty-four times and then holding her underwater in the pool. He claimed to have no memory of the event because he was sleepwalking, but police found the murder weapon and Falater's bloody clothing hidden in the trunk of his car. Furthermore, the man put on gloves before picking up the knife to kill his wife. Because he showed premeditation and took evasive actions, the jury found him guilty of first-degree murder."

Briley holds her breath. Maybe this testimony won't hurt her. Falater's case is nothing like Erin's; in fact, Bystrowski may have underscored her point.

The prosecutor glances at Briley, his expression unreadable, then he presses his hands together and turns to the doctor in the witness stand. "We've heard testimony that your patient, Erin Tomassi, took a double dose of Ambien in the early morning hours of December 3. Would you say she was taking the drug correctly?"

"Unfortunately, no. I would never advise doubling the dose."

"Interesting, though, that she'd take a double dose of a drug known to cause problems with sleep on the night she kills her husband." Bystrowski pauses to wipe his lenses on a handkerchief, then returns his glasses to his nose. "Doesn't her behavior strike you as a little *convenient?*"

"Objection." With an effort, Briley pushes herself up from the table. "How this behavior strikes the doctor is irrelevant."

The judge swivels his chair toward the witness stand. "I see your point, Ms. Lester, but I'm going to allow the witness to answer."

The doctor glances at Briley, then stares at the prosecutor. "I'm afraid I don't understand what you mean."

"It's not a difficult question. I'm only saying the scenario is terrifically tidy. Our long-suffering battered wife just happens to take a notorious sleep aid—incorrectly—on the night she kills her husband."

"Objection!" Briley stands again. "The prosecutor is assuming facts not in evidence."

When an indignant buzz rises from the gallery, Trask waits, his heavy cheeks falling over his collar, until the room has quieted. "Objection sustained. Mr. Bystrowski, you know better." He turns to the jury. "Ladies and gentlemen, you should disregard that last remark. And let me remind you that comments from counsel are not evidence. Evidence is what you hear from witnesses under oath."

"I'll withdraw the question." Bystrowski backs away. "I have nothing else for this witness."

Briley steps out from behind her table. "Redirect, Your Honor?"

When the judge nods, Briley walks toward the doctor with a confident smile. "You mentioned two men who killed their spouses while allegedly in the grips of a sleeping disorder. The first man was convicted because he attempted to cover up his crime. Do you recall what happened to the second man?"

The doctor's eyes are more focused now, as if he's realized the harm he's done and is willing to make things right. "I do."

"Would you share that result with the jury?"

One corner of Dr. Sparks's mouth twists upward. "In 1981, a man named Steven Steinberg stabbed his wife twenty-six times with no memory of the event. But because the prosecution could find no evidence of premeditation or defensive evasion, the jury acquitted the man."

"Thank you, Dr. Sparks."

Briley returns to her counsel table and studies the jurors as the doctor descends from the witness box. She *had* them, all fourteen of them, when she finished direct examination, but the state's attorney's snide summation may have wrested them from her grasp. A single believer in Erin's innocence can keep her client out of prison, but as her gaze roves over the jury box, Briley can't find a single juror who will look her in the eye.

While Judge Trask prepares to adjourn for the day, Briley pushes away from the defense table and digs in her purse for her car keys. She is not lingering in the courtroom tonight; she is not taking the rarely used staircase. She may have to run a gauntlet of reporters, but anything is better than facing another man in a ski mask. She is planning to meet Kate and William at a restaurant for an over-dinner post-mortem, then she needs to get home so she can review her notes and work on her closing remarks.

As she pulls out her wallet and sunglasses case, a small slip of pink paper flutters to the floor. Erin bends to pick it up.

Briley waits until Judge Trask stands to leave, then she sets her keys on the table and stuffs her wallet back into her purse. "Okay, I'll see you tomorrow morning—"

"Please." As the bailiff approaches, Erin presses the pink paper into Briley's palm. "You promised to call for me."

Briley glances at the handwritten phone message and recognizes the geneticist's name. How can Erin be worried about her ovaries while Briley is struggling to save her life?

"Listen—" she hurries, aware that the bailiff has pulled handcuffs from his belt "—I know having a baby once meant a lot to you, but I really don't think we need to be distracted right now."

"Briley." Erin's blue eyes brim with tears. "I know you're trying to focus, and I appreciate it, but when I get out of jail—*if* I get out of jail—I want to move forward with my life. And to do that, I need to know what's wrong with me."

"Who said something was wrong?"

"Dr. Phillips. He said it was important that I call him. Why would he say that if something weren't wrong?"

Erin stands and extends her wrists. Briley studies the name and number as the bailiff fastens the handcuffs. She's had her fill of doctors today, but if she calls tonight, maybe this Dr. Phillips won't be in his office. She can leave a message, meet her obligation, and be off the hook.

"All right, I'll phone him for you." She slips the message into her suit pocket. "But I can't promise anything. He may not be at his desk."

"That's okay, at least he'll know I'm still around."

Briley watches, her heart sinking, as Erin submits to the shackles and shuffles away.

It's a small thing, this favor. Taking a few minutes for a phone call doesn't mean she's violating her boundaries and becoming personally involved.

She grabs her briefcase and stands as an inner voice hoots at her rationalization. Despite her best intentions, she's becoming more like her father every day.

Chapter Forty-Eight

The skirling wind skitters past Briley, tossing hair into her face and whipping her skirt tight around her legs. Wishing she'd taken the time to fasten the buttons, she clutches at the edges of her coat and rushes toward the warmth of the restaurant.

The door jingles as it slams behind her. She looks up to find herself in a dimly lit diner, one that has probably prospered more on account of its proximity to the courthouse than on the merits of its food. Ignoring the overburdened coatrack by the cashier's stand, she thrusts her cold hands into her pockets and strides toward the booth where her volunteer staff is waiting.

Kate has both hands wrapped around a cup of coffee. "Hey," she says, pausing before she takes a sip. "Have a seat and let's dish."

"Food first." William waves for the waitress's attention. "I'm starving."

While Kate and William huddle over their menus, Briley pulls out her cell phone. She punches in the geneticist's number, then crosses one arm to wait for an answer. The waitress hands her a coffee mug; Briley thanks her with a smile and points to her companions. Let them order first.

"Hello?"

Briley startles when a voice rasps in her ear. "Dr. Phillips?"

"Speaking."

She covers her free ear to block some of the noise. "I'm Briley Lester, calling on behalf of Erin Tomassi. Apparently you've been trying to reach her for several days."

She expects him to hesitate—after all, how many patients must this doctor have?—but he responds immediately. "Yes, it's important that I speak to Mrs. Tomassi as soon as possible."

"I'm sorry, but that's going to be difficult. Mrs. Tomassi is unavailable. I am her lawyer, however, and I could carry a message to her."

"Is she...?"

"She's incarcerated."

"Oh, my." The man's shock and horror roll over the phone line. "I'm so sorry to hear about her trouble. I had no idea she was *that* Tomassi..."

"You understand why it's been difficult for her to return your call. You can, however, speak to me and I'll relay the message."

"It's just— Well, we usually discuss this sort of information only with the patient. The privacy laws. You understand."

"I do."

"But this is so unusual, and I want to publish this information in an article I'm preparing. I won't use her name, of course. I wonder...is there any way you could obtain Mrs. Tomassi's permission for me? Then I could relay the information to you, and you could pass it on and get her approval."

Briley turns sideways to shield her face from Kate and William, who are watching from across the table. "My client is concerned that there's something wrong with her DNA," she says, lowering her voice. "Is that a correct assumption?"

"I really shouldn't give the information over the phone," the doctor hedges. "But if you can come to my lab at the hospital—"

"I'm in court all week. I'm sure your project is important, but I'm fighting for my client's life."

"How about this evening? I can meet you anytime."

She glances at Kate, who is pointing to the waitress. "A bowl of soup," Briley whispers, her hand over the phone. "Whatever they have will be fine."

"Ms. Lester?"

"Still here, Doctor." She shakes her head at William, who is mouthing *Anything wrong?*

What's *not* wrong? In the middle of her first murder case, a trial that could go either way, her client has asked her to track down an eager-to-publish geneticist who probably sleeps in his lab coat and eats peanut butter crackers for dinner. And because Erin looked so pitiful with her bruised cheek and scratched face, Briley has decided to go out on a freezing winter night when she could be practicing her closing in a luxurious bubble bath at home....

"All right." She returns her attention to the phone. "If you'll give me your address, I'll come by tonight. First I'll have to swing by the jail and get an authorization form signed by Mrs. Tomassi, so look for me around eight."

She jots the address on a napkin, thanks the doctor for his time, then tucks her phone and the napkin into her coat pocket.

"What's that about?" William asks, his face a study in concern. "Who's Phillips? Not another shrink, I hope."

Briley shakes her head. "He's a geneticist. And this has nothing to do with the trial, it's a personal favor for Erin. I don't know why I let myself get talked into these things."

"You'll learn." Kate dumps another sugar packet into her coffee cup. "In no time at all you'll be as down-to-business as the best of 'em at Franklin, Watson, Smyth & Morton."

Briley sips from the steaming coffee the waitress poured for her, then sighs and closes her eyes.

"We understand," William says, correctly interpreting her weary expression. "Bystrowski mopped the floor with Dr. Sparks."

Briley's eyes fly open. "It wasn't that bad...was it?"

"He killed with the word *convenient*," Kate says. "Hard to argue with that, especially in the Google age. Some juror is going to realize that Erin could have heard about those Ambien murder cases and decided to implement the same defense. She goes to the doctor, gets a prescription, has it filled a couple of times.... She doesn't even have to actually take the pills. It's a great plan, but it makes her look awfully cold-blooded."

"A scenario with first-degree written all over it," William says, his eyes flat and hard.

"Gee, thanks for the encouragement." Briley reaches for the bucket of peanuts on the table. "So, any suggestions? I'm nearly out of fresh ideas."

"Character witnesses?" William suggests. "What about Antonio Tomassi?"

Briley shakes her head. "We have to save character witnesses for the penalty phase, but I wouldn't call that man in any case. Have you been watching him? He thinks she's guilty."

"Are you sure?" Kate frowns. "Hard to believe a father-in-law could turn on his son's wife like that."

"I'm sure," Briley answers. "But we're going to need to dig around in Erin's past to see if we can dredge up old teachers, friends, anyone who could testify about the good she's done. I might have to ask for a continuance, since we don't have a mitigation specialist—" Her voice catches as the events of the past few weeks collide in her head like the scattered puzzle pieces on Roger Wilson's tray. They shift, they spin, then they fall into place, revealing a picture she's been too distracted to see.

She stares across the booth at Kate and William, her mouth open.

William freezes in the act of cracking a peanut shell. "What?"

"The firm," Briley whispers. "They didn't put me on the case because they believe in me. They put me on this one because they're sure I'll lose."

Kate makes a face. "Now *that's* crazy talk."

"No, it makes perfect sense." Briley swallows hard. "Tomassi is an important client, and he wants Erin punished—you said it yourself, Wills. That's why I'm handling this trial alone, and that's why Franklin wouldn't assign another associate to help me. Not that you two haven't been terrific, but if Tomassi wanted Erin acquitted, the firm would have put one of the partners on this case, and you know it. They would have assigned one of the partners and given him a death penalty team."

"Acquitted?" William drops his jaw. "No one, not even Mr. Franklin, has dreamed of getting that woman *acquitted*. She did it, Briley. She killed her husband. You'll be working a miracle if you can save her from lethal injection or life in prison."

"You're wrong about that, Wills." Briley gives him a tight smile. "I don't think she did it. And I want her to walk out of that courtroom a free woman."

A faint glint of humor fills William's eyes. "Now *you're* talking like a crazy woman."

"I don't think the firm set you up to fail." Kate shakes her head. "That's unethical."

"If they were actively manipulating my case, maybe. But they haven't done that. Erin's getting her defense, the firm is getting paid, the judicial process is being satisfied. The law doesn't say a defendant is entitled to the *best* representation. It only says she's entitled to representation. That's what I am—understaffed, inexperienced, rookie murder-trial representation."

William lifts his coffee cup. "And here I thought you were moving up the ladder of success."

"I'm not sure I'll even be *on* the ladder after this." Briley presses her hand to her stomach as a sludge of nausea roils in her gut. "I can't believe I didn't see it until now. If I win, Antonio Tomassi will be unhappy, so the partners will be unhappy. If I lose, Antonio will be satisfied and the story will be broadcast on every channel and written up in every political blog. No client will want to hire me…and the firm may not want to keep me, despite Mr. Franklin's assurances." She winces as her phone buzzes in her pocket.

Kate folds her arms. "Someone has lousy timing."

"It's not a call, it's a reminder." Briley pulls out her phone and shuts off the alarm. "I have to swing by the jail and visit a hospital tonight, so I need to get moving."

The waitress returns, bearing a tray with their orders. Briley looks at the steaming bowl of soup and pushes it toward William. "I'm not hungry. I'm going to run these errands, and then I'm going home. Maybe I'll come up with a brilliant idea while I'm rehearsing my closing."

"You need a test audience?" William's eyes shine with a hint of flirtation, but Briley's not in the mood for flirting. Not with Timothy in California and her trial in the tank.

"Sorry, but I'll have to take a rain check." She gives William a purely platonic smile, then buttons up her coat and heads out into the night.

A security guard directs Briley to Dr. Steven Phillips's lab, which is off a long, nondescript, basement hallway with polished tile floors and what appears to be a nearly endless succession of windowless doors.

She hesitates outside the door marked "S. Phillips," then pulls it open. A black-topped table beyond the door reminds her of high school, and an Asian man in glasses turns at her approach.

"Hello," she says, looking past him. "I'm looking for Dr. Steven Phillips."

"That's me. You must be Briley Lester." The man smiles as he steps forward, his hand extended. "Don't let my name throw you. I was adopted by an American family."

"Ah." She gives him a polite smile. "I don't want to keep you, and I still have work to do tonight, so—"

"This shouldn't take long. Do you have the signed authorization from Mrs. Tomassi?"

"Right here." Briley pulls the handwritten form from her briefcase and hands it over. She hopes the doctor appreciates the effort it took to get that authorization. Due to the late hour, she had to go to the jail, call the warden's office for special permission to see Erin, go through Security, wait for Erin to be brought out of her cell…

The doctor scans the page, then slips it into his pocket. "Sorry about the formality. But patient-privacy regulations—"

"I understand."

"Please, come and have a seat." She hesitates, about to urge him to give her the condensed version of Erin's problem, then sighs and follows him to the back of the lab. In the corner a battered desk is covered with folders, printouts, and a computer. The geneticist slides into his seat, his fingers fly over the keyboard, then he pulls a numbered folder from a stack on his desk. "I don't know how much Mrs. Tomassi told you about her situation."

"Enough." Briley slides onto a stool. "So if you can simply tell me what I need to tell her, I'll be on my way."

The man smiles and settles the folder on his knee. "Mrs. Tomassi came to see me because she was concerned about her DNA. Apparently someone in the family suffers from a genetic illness."

"Her brother," Briley answers, content to leave the details to the doctor's imagination.

"We took the usual mouth swab from Mrs. Tomassi," Phillips says, opening the folder. "And we also took blood, in case she wanted further tests done. What we discovered was quite unusual. At first, I was convinced the lab assistant made a mistake and switched the samples with someone else. But no, as you can see, every swab and blood sample is carefully logged and each vial is labeled in the patient's presence. We even have the patient initial the vial so there are no mix-ups."

Briley glances at her watch. "What did your tests reveal?"

"Mrs. Tomassi…" He hesitates, his square jaw tensing.

Briley's impatience veers toward alarm. "Does she have some kind of genetic illness?"

The doctor shakes his head. "No, sorry. It's just so rare, I'm a little awed by the possibilities. I know of only forty cases of this condition in recorded history. I'm sure there are others, but people don't realize the truth unless they have DNA testing. Even then, the condition is unlikely to be discovered unless several swabs from various organs are analyzed and compared."

"What *is* this condition?"

"Mrs. Tomassi is a tetragametic chimera." The geneticist beams as if he's just discovered the cure for cancer.

Briley stares. "She's a *what?*"

"A chimera. The condition is extremely rare, but no one can say for sure—"

"I know, I got that part. It's rare, probably. But what is it?"

"A chimera—" the doctor lifts his chin "—is usually defined as the blending of two species. A frog, for instance, that has been injected with human DNA. Genetic engineers have been creating chimeras for years."

"Wait a minute. You're not saying that someone tampered with Erin's DNA, are you?"

"No, no, human chimeras occur naturally. When two zygotes are in the womb, sometimes they fuse together. This forms an organism with two distinct cell lines, a person with two populations of cells. One set of DNA may appear in her ovaries, another set may appear in her heart tissues."

"Is this—" Briley waves at the folder, feeling like a kindergartner trying to understand quantum physics. "Is this similar to what happens with conjoined twins?"

The doctor responds with a laconic shrug. "Similar? Consider this."

He taps on the computer keyboard and pulls up a photograph of what looks like a two-headed boy. "Seventeen-year-old David and Jonathan Violette." He points to the screen. "Two heads, two arms, two legs. There was a third nonfunctional arm, but surgeons removed it shortly after the boys' birth."

Briley stares at the image, her mind reeling. "Are they— is that—a chimera?"

"Definitely not. David and Jonathan are two separate people, two unique souls with two distinct personalities. A chimera is *one* person rising from two different embryos. Because identical twins share the same DNA, we may never know how many people were once identical twins. But tetragametic chimeras are *fraternal* twins. Fraternal twins have different DNA, they are often of different genders and different appearances—"

"I know what fraternal twins are." *And sometimes they share special languages.*

She looks away as a blush heats her face. "I'm sorry, I didn't mean to snap. It's just— I don't understand what this means for Erin Tomassi."

The doctor shrugs. "Who can say? But she needs to know. One case was uncovered when a woman gave birth to children who were not genetically related to her. Apparently her ovaries originated with her twin."

Briley shudders. "How do you explain that to your children?"

"The most difficult thing was explaining the situation to the state. As I recall, that woman's children were nearly taken away. The mother and her kids were DNA-tested when she applied for public assistance. When she didn't match her children, authorities were convinced she had kidnapped them to perpetuate a fraud. Not until she gave birth with a court representative in the room was she able to prove her claims."

Briley pinches the bridge of her nose. "Will Erin be able to have children someday?"

"Of course. But her children's DNA may not indicate that she is their mother." He taps his keyboard again. "In another case, a woman's blood work revealed the presence of two different DNA types in all her tissues. Even the hairs on her head revealed different DNA." He chuckles. "I would imagine this could cause nightmares for those of you involved in the legal system. After all, DNA is the court's current gold standard, is it not? Yet DNA can be misleading. Imagine how you would feel if the court took away the children you had conceived and carried."

Briley stares at a dusty model of the double helix on the doctor's desk. For an instant she feels a surge of adrenaline, a fleeting perception. An idea hovers at the edge of her brain, an important thought, but it will not slide into her consciousness.

She closes her eyes and moves on, considering the ramifications of the doctor's last comment. Every year convicted criminals are released from prison because they are exonerated by genetic testing that was unavailable at the time of their trials. What if one of those newly released rapists or murderers is a chimera?

She stares at the double helix as disturbing concepts shove and scramble for space in her brain. "DNA," she whispers, "may not be perfect, but it's the best we have."

"That may be true," Phillips answers, "but whatever can be used for justice can also serve injustice. A good thought to keep in mind."

Finding no answers in the dusty model, Briley shakes off her fascination and stands. "Thank you, Dr. Phillips. I'll give your information to Mrs. Tomassi."

As she rides up in the elevator, a solitary and disconnected question surfaces in her brain. Bystrowski has introduced several items as evidence in Erin's trial.

What happened to the rest of the evidence collected at the Tomassi crime scene?

Alone in a booth at the Over Easy Café, Detective Mark Malone is eating a hamburger and fries when Briley slides into the seat across from him. He stares at her, then swallows and swipes at his mouth with a paper napkin. "Hello, Counselor. Run into any bathroom muggers lately?"

His tone is teasing, but his eyes are serious and direct.

"How are you doing, Detective?" She props her arms on the table. "The only place I've been assaulted lately is in the morning papers. But you're still keeping the streets of Chicago safe for women and children, I see."

"I'm off duty, Counselor."

"So am I."

"So this is a social call?"

"Not exactly."

He shrugs and picks up his hamburger again. "How'd you find me?"

"The guys at your station. They know your routine."

He chuffs and goes in for a big bite, then chews thoughtfully, his gaze pinned on her. Finally, he swallows. "About your mugger. We circulated your description and talked to Mr. Tomassi."

"And?"

"At the time of your attack, Jason Tomassi was being interviewed on the steps of the courthouse. We have time-stamped videotape, so he isn't the guy."

She isn't sure whether to feel relieved or alarmed. "Oh."

"Anything else I can do for you, Miss Lester?"

With an effort, she pushes thoughts of her attacker aside in order to focus on the real reason she's sought out the detective. "Whatever can be used for justice can also serve injustice," she says. "I need to talk to you about the inventory your guys took from the Tomassi crime scene. I know some of it was entered into evidence at the trial, but surely that's not everything."

The detective shrugs. "Of course not. We went through the usual routine—dusted for fingerprints on the windowsills, collected hair samples, took photos of the bed, the bathroom, the body. We cataloged a drinking glass from the bathroom sink, toothbrushes, contents of the trash can."

"And in all that evidence, you didn't find anything unusual? Anything that might have pointed to an intruder?"

"What are you driving at?" His eyes narrow. "From the videotape, we know no one approached the house from the front or the rear."

"Forget about the tapes, Detective, and answer my question—did you find anything unusual in all that evidence?"

Malone rolls his eyes. "If we had, I'm sure Louis would have let me know."

"Who's Louis?"

"Our guy in the crime lab. He does DNA testing, blood-spatter analysis, gory stuff like that."

Briley sets her cell phone on the table and slides it toward the cop. "Call him, will you?"

"What for?"

"Call him for me, please? It's important."

The detective hesitates, probably wondering if he's within his rights to tell her to take a flying leap, then he picks up the cell. "He's not gonna be in the lab," he says, dialing the number. "It's nine o'clock. He's probably home watching reruns."

"Is he married?"

"Don't think so."

"Then he might be around. Just humor me and get Louis on the line."

Malone presses the phone to his ear, then the corner of his mouth quirks. "Louis? You still workin'?" He glances at Briley. "You're not gonna believe this, but I'm sitting with a defense attorney who's ready to bust a gut about something. She wants to talk to you."

He hands the phone across the table. "Knock yourself out, Counselor."

Briley closes her eyes to better concentrate. "Louis? I'm Briley Lester, calling about the Tomassi trial—"

"The politician?" His voice sounds surprisingly young.

"Yes, that's right, the politician who was murdered. Listen, do you still have evidence from the crime scene? Anything that wasn't used in the trial?"

"Sure, in the file," Louis says, a note of confusion in his voice. "Do they need something else?"

"That all depends," Briley answers. "Tell me, did you

analyze everything? Every hair, every tissue from the trash, everything the detectives brought in?"

"No need to. Once we fingerprinted the syringe, we had enough to make the case."

Briley smiles as her adrenaline level rises. "Listen, Louis, I need you to do something for me. I need DNA typing on any hair samples from that crime scene—and I need it fast." She grits her teeth, knowing she's about to ask the impossible. "Can you have something for me by tomorrow morning?"

He laughs. "You gotta get in line, lady."

"I've already been in line, and now I'm at trial. Look, I know I'm asking a lot, but I'm nearing the end of my case. I'll come down there and help if you want me to, but if I don't get those results, my client could get a death sentence. Do you understand that?"

She hears a heavy sigh, then Louis clicks his tongue. "Put Malone back on the horn."

"What?"

"Let me talk to Malone."

She offers the phone to the detective. "He wants you."

Malone holds the phone to his ear with one hand while he pinches a French fry and drags it through a pool of ketchup with the other.

"Yeah," he says, glancing up at Briley. "Yeah. She's okay." The cop hands the phone back to her.

"Well?" she asks the technician.

"I'll see what I can do," Louis says. "I might even have a couple of those hair samples already done. Anything particular you want me to look for?"

"Just anything…odd," she answers. "You want me to come down and keep you company?"

"No, don't want anyone saying you messed around with the evidence. Just let me plug in the coffeepot so I can get my second wind."

"Thanks, Louis. I'll tell your boss they don't pay you nearly enough. Detective Malone sends his love."

She snaps the phone shut and grins at the cop across the table.

"You didn't have to add that last bit." He baptizes another French fry. "Might give Louis the wrong idea."

"You need to show the lab guys a little more appreciation," she answers, sliding out of the booth. "Thanks, Detective. See you 'round the playground."

Chapter Forty-Nine

After a nearly sleepless night, at nine the next morning Briley stands in the line that leads to the courthouse security checkpoint and redials Louis's number. "Please, please pick up," she whispers, setting her briefcase on the conveyor belt.

A security guard hooks his thumbs over his waistband and shakes his head. "I'm sorry, ma'am, but you'll have to send the phone through the X-ray machine."

"But I'm on a call."

"No exceptions."

Briley steps out of the security line and watches her purse and briefcase roll down the moving belt. Finally, a man answers, his voice heavy. "Hello?"

"Louis? It's Briley Lester and I'm at the courthouse. I need to know if you found anything interesting with those hair samples from the Tomassi crime scene."

"Ms. Lester." A smile slips into that scratchy voice. "You want something *interesting?* Well, maybe you're in luck. I tested twelve samples and found three different profiles, so that means three different individuals have been in that bedroom. In fact, all three profiles were found on the victim's bed."

"Three different people? Are you sure?"

"DNA doesn't lie. The hairs looked pretty much alike— well, except the dark ones—but the other two are just a shade apart. That's why we didn't bother to test them all."

Briley catches her breath. "So this means…"

"If you were playing a hunch, my guess is that it paid off."

She turns, pressing her hand to her forehead. Time to think like a prosecutor, play the devil's advocate. "Okay. Couldn't those hairs be from the husband, the wife, and the housekeeper? The cleaning lady is on record saying that she changed the linens the day before the murder."

"Not unless the housekeeper is related to the wife. The B and C hairs belong to individuals from the same family."

"So…" Briley struggles to think through the noise and commotion in the lobby. "Those hairs could have come from the husband and his brother."

Louis chuckles. "No way. The similar samples are from females. I'd say you're talking about two sisters."

A thrill shivers along Briley's spine. "Can you bring your report to the courthouse by nine-thirty? We're in Judge Trask's courtroom on the seventh floor."

"Sure, and do you want me to lasso the moon for you, too? I'll do it, but you have to promise to have coffee with me first."

For an instant, Briley is flummoxed, then she realizes he's joking.

"Louis—" she can't stop a grin "—I'd be happy to treat you to a cup of coffee. And if you need me to vouch for your overtime—"

"I didn't stay up all night for the overtime. I figured that if you were running around at 9:00 p.m. on your client's behalf, maybe this Tomassi broad was worth a little extra effort."

Briley bites her lower lip as an unexpected lump rises in her throat. "Thanks, Louis."

"You gonna need me to testify?"

"Yes. Is that a problem?"

"Not as long as I have my coffee. And for you, I'll even do a shave."

She looks toward the security checkpoint, where Bystrowski and his associate are dropping their briefcases and belts beside the X-ray machine. "I owe you big-time, Louis. But you'd better do that shave in record time."

* * *

When Briley approaches the defense table, Erin arches a brow. "You look like the cat that swallowed the canary," she says. "Or maybe you finally got a good night's sleep."

"I got hardly any sleep, but I can't explain why," Briley says, pulling a legal pad from her briefcase, "because the judge is going to take the bench at any minute. But if all goes well, I think today we may toss Bystrowski a real surprise." She slides the tablet and a pen toward Erin, then glances at her watch, willing to let the judge take all the time he needs in chambers. Maybe he needs an extra minute to run to the restroom, slip on more comfortable shoes, or make a telephone call....

She props her chin on her hand and peers at her client, who seems subdued this morning. How will she react when she hears that she's a chimera? Briley can't imagine, but it's probably like being told you have a rare blood type. Not the sort of thing that will affect your everyday life, but something that might make a world of difference on one or two occasions.

Erin picks up the pen and begins to doodle on the legal pad. Across the aisle, Bystrowski's knees are touching and parting like the knees of a hyperactive teenage boy. Somewhere down the hall, the fourteen citizen judges have gathered in the juror assembly room, where they are exchanging small talk, sipping coffee, and waiting for the third day of the trial to begin. Behind the prosecutor, on the first row of the gallery, Antonio Tomassi and his family have aligned themselves in two rows. At the center of the group, Antonio folds his arms and stares at the empty jury box. He wears his usual somber expression, but almost anything could be going on behind that stern facade.

Briley picks up her pen and jots a list on her own legal pad. She's prioritizing the issues she wants to address when she realizes that she and Erin could be twins, arched as they are over their writing, both elbows bent at their right sides, legal pads slanted at the same angle....

Her hand freezes as an unexpected thought strikes in a barely comprehendible flash.

A moment later, a door at the front of the courtroom opens. A hand appears and taps the bailiff on the shoulder. Briley watches, holding her breath, as the bailiff accepts several sheets of paper. He glances at the first page, then walks toward Briley.

Her pulse races as she stands and accepts the faxed document. The header at the top of the first page confirms that it has come from the crime lab. A copy of Louis's report. Does this mean he's not going to show?

She winces as a cold blade of foreboding slices into her heart. Something must have happened to Louis, so he sent this fax. But though she could try to get it admitted, even a certified copy won't be admissible as evidence.

She turns, hanging one elbow over the back of her chair as she looks at William. "I need a favor." She glances toward the back of the courtroom, but there's no sign of anyone who looks like a lab technician.

William nods and silently points past Briley. She turns in time to see Judge Trask step into the courtroom. The bailiff, startled to be caught away from his post, practically shouts the traditional opening: "All rise. The Cook County Court is now in session, the Honorable Milton Trask, Judge, presiding. Be seated and come to order."

Briley drops the document to her desk as the judge surveys his courtroom. "Good morning," he says, apparently content to see that the principals have not dishonored the proceedings by being late. "Unless there is new business we should discuss, is counsel for the defense ready to proceed?"

"Your Honor." Briley stands. "The defense has new evidence."

The judge perks up. "Really."

"The state objects, Your Honor." Bystrowski stands, his tense jaw revealing his frustration. "What's the nature of this new evidence?"

Briley takes a deep breath and plunges ahead. "This evidence comes from the police lab, Your Honor. During discovery, we received an inventory of all items seized in the warrantless search of the defendant's property. We knew the state had certain evidence, but last night we discovered that not all the evidence was tested."

Trask looks at her with an expression of pained tolerance. "What evidence was untested?"

"Hair samples, Your Honor."

As a bailiff leans in to whisper something to the judge, Briley peers at the document in her hand. The second page portrays three distinct DNA profiles, revealed in graphs and notations that she doesn't understand. But she can grasp the crucial detail—the DNA of three different persons was found on Jeffrey Tomassi's deathbed. That's all she needs to establish the presence of an intruder. It's all she needs to establish reasonable doubt.

If the judge will admit the document in her hand. Or if she can stall until Louis Thomsen arrives.

She watches as the judge finishes his conversation with the bailiff, then looks out at her. "Hair samples, you said?"

"Yes, Your Honor. Early this morning, the defense received verifying documentation." She lifts the pages in her hand. "We have a witness en route, a lab technician who can testify as to the content and validity of this document."

The judge exhales in an audible sigh. "Ms. Lester, I expect you to have your witness present by the time we reconvene. This court will recess for ten minutes."

Chapter Fifty

"What's happening, Papa?"

Sofia, Antonio's youngest daughter, tugs on his arm as the order in the court dissolves into random chaos. "Why are they stopping the trial?"

"Shh, they're not stopping." He looks at the bench, where the judge is already stepping down. "They're only taking a break."

"I don't get it." On the other side of Sofia, Jason crosses his arms and glares at the back of the prosecutor's head. "What's the big deal about hair samples?"

Antonio ignores his son and stands. "Excuse me, Mr. Bystrowski."

The prosecutor turns. "Mr. Tomassi?"

Antonio studies the man charged with winning vengeance for his son. Travis Bystrowski has done a commendable job thus far, but never has his face looked so serious, so dedicated, so young.

"Is this correct?" Antonio asks, gesturing to the defense attorney. "Can she stop everything to talk about hair?"

Bystrowski nods. "It is unusual, but if she learns about evidence that she couldn't—"

"Why should we care about a few hairs?"

The prosecutor swivels toward the defense table. "I don't know, Mr. Tomassi. But we'll hear about it soon."

"Can't you force her to tell you? Aren't lawyers supposed to show their hands to each other?"

Like a father amused by the questions of a child, the

attorney replies with an indulgent smile. "In civil cases, yes, the rules for discovery are quite clear. In criminal proceedings, however, the court recognizes that full discovery is not always possible. So the law makes allowances for new developments."

"*What* developments?" Antonio resists the pulse of fury that pounds in his ear and the beat of bitter memory in his blood. "How can anything change what happened to my son? That woman killed him. We all know it's true."

"Mr. Tomassi." Bystrowski takes a side step, effectively blocking Antonio's view of the defense attorney and her client. "Sir, why don't you take your children into the hall to stretch your legs? By the time you return, we'll be ready to start up again."

Antonio glares at the young man for a moment, then allows Sofia to pull him toward the aisle. "Come, Papa." She draws him away from the lawyers who have done nothing but complicate his life for weeks. "Let's take a walk in the lobby. All this sitting is not good for you."

She's fussing over him, but for once Antonio is inclined to allow it. Sofia is only trying to prevent him from barreling through that bar and throttling the prosecutor, the defense attorney, and the judge. He wouldn't hesitate to destroy anyone who stands between him and justice for Jeffrey, and Sofia knows it.

In the aisle, Antonio draws Sofia's arm through his, then pats her hand. "So—" he gives her a wry smile "—you would rather walk in circles outside the courtroom than watch your father take on that scrawny lawyer?"

She smiles, her dark eyes dancing above the roses in her cheeks. "We can go anywhere you like. But no, I didn't want to watch you fight with the prosecutor."

"Were you afraid he would get the best of me?"

"No, Papa. I don't think any man can do that."

Antonio smiles. "No one ever will. And don't worry—no matter what happens, we will win justice for Jeffrey."

Chapter Fifty-One

Briley remains as tense as a cat throughout the recess. She sends William out into the hallway to search for anyone who looks like a sleep-starved lab technician, while she huddles at the counsel table and taps her pen on the desk. Erin pulls away, probably afraid Briley will snap if she makes an unnecessary comment.

When the judge takes the bench again, Briley glances at her watch and bites her lip. What can she do? If William was here, he'd tell her to fall back and punt, but how does that translate into real life?

"Pssst."

She turns, and nearly melts in relief when William comes toward her, followed by a young man in a rumpled blue suit. The man nods at her, then pushes dark hair from his eyes.

"Louis?"

"Yeah." He slips into the pew beside William. "We're on for coffee after this, right?"

She stares, not sure she's heard him correctly, then he gives her a teasing smile. "Just kidding."

Briley turns as the bailiff calls for order, and Judge Trask's sharp gaze pins Briley to her chair. "Is counsel for the defense ready to begin?"

"Yes, Your Honor."

"Then let's bring in the jury."

Briley skims her scribbled notes as the bailiff brings in the jury. When all fourteen have been seated, she stands. "The defense calls Louis Thomsen."

She closes her eyes as the man behind her moves through the gate and approaches the clerk. The lab tech looks like a skater and sounds like a college kid, but as long as he knows his material...

After he's been sworn in, Briley draws a deep breath and moves to the lectern. "Your name is Louis Thomsen, correct?"

"That's right."

"Where are you employed, Mr. Thomsen?"

"At the Cook County crime lab. I've worked there three years."

"What does your job at the crime lab entail?"

He shrugs. "I examine evidence, analyze blood spatter, work with DNA."

"Are you familiar with DNA typing?"

A half smile crosses the man's face. "Sure."

"Can you confirm that each human individual has a unique DNA fingerprint?"

He holds up a hand. "That's actually a bit of a misnomer. Everyone's DNA has the same chemical structure, but differences lie in the order of the base pairs. Each individual's DNA has so many millions of base pairs that every person has a different sequence—except in the case of identical twins, of course. They have identical sequences."

"So can an expert take a sample of genetic material and use it to identify the person from whom it originated?"

"Not unless we have that individual's DNA sequence on file. DNA patterns do not give every individual a unique print, but they do allow us to determine whether two genetic samples are from the same person, related persons, or nonrelated persons."

"Thank you for the explanation." Briley holds up the faxed document, then hands a copy to the prosecutor. "This report arrived from the Cook County crime lab this morning. Would you like a copy, Your Honor?" Judge Trask waves her offer away, so Briley delivers a copy to the clerk. "I ask the clerk to mark these two pages as an exhibit for identification." When the pages have been marked and entered as evidence, she holds her copy before the man in the witness stand. "Mr. Thomsen, are you familiar with this document?"

"May I see it?"

"Permission to approach the witness?" When the judge inclines his head, Briley steps forward with the lab report and hands it to Louis.

"Yes, I recognize it. I sent it."

"Thank you. Can you tell me what this document represents?"

Louis settles his elbows on the armrests of his chair. "They contain diagrams that represent DNA patterns taken from hair samples."

"How many different DNA sequences are represented here?"

"Three."

"Three unique DNA patterns, correct?"

"Yes."

"So these hair samples came from three different individuals?"

"That's right."

"Can you tell the jury where these hair samples were discovered?"

"Objection." Bystrowski stands and removes his reading glasses. "The witness had nothing to do with the gathering of this evidence."

"Objection sustained." Trask looks at Briley. "Please confine your questions to areas of the witness's direct knowledge."

Briley draws a deep breath. "Mr. Thomsen, do you recognize the term *chain of custody?*"

"I do."

"Can you define it for us?"

He nods. "Because we never know what will be needed in a trial, it's important to prove the legal integrity of all evidence. So we go to great lengths to keep an accurate written record to track the collection, possession, handling, and location of evidence taken from a crime scene. Few people are allowed to handle the items, and they are never transferred without chain-of-custody forms."

"The hair samples you tested—were they stored with the appropriate chain-of-custody forms?"

"They were."

"Did you notate on this document—" she points to the lab report in his hand "—where the samples were originally found as reported on the chain-of-custody forms?"

"I did."

"Will you please tell the jury what those forms told you."

He lifts the report and begins to read: "Sample A—dark brown hair found on bedsheet, adjacent to the victim's body. Sample B—blond hair found on suspect's pillow. Sample C—light brown hair found on bedsheet, adjacent to victim's body."

"Can you identify these hairs visually? For instance, can we assume that the dark brown hair belonged to Jeffrey Tomassi?"

"Not necessarily. Individual hairs differ in color and texture, depending on where they originate on the body. So color and length are not reliable markers. We prefer to match hair DNA with a saliva swab."

"Thank you, Mr. Thomsen. Now, can you read what you wrote at the bottom corner of the page?"

The technician reads aloud: "Analysis—these three specimens come from three different individuals, two of whom share VNTRs, indicating shared parentage."

Briley smiles. "For those of us who aren't geneticists, what does VNTR stand for?"

"Variable number of tandem repeats."

"And what does medical science tell us we can assume about two samples that share VNTRs?"

He lifts the paper in his hand. "As it says here, shared VNTRs indicate shared parentage."

"So—and you'll have to excuse me for recapping, but I

want to be sure this is clear—apparently two of these three individuals were siblings?"

"That's what the evidence indicates, yes."

"Thank you. Do you know if the defendant, Erin Tomassi, has siblings?"

"I wouldn't know."

"That's all right. Do you know if Jeffrey Tomassi has brothers or sisters?"

"I wouldn't know that, either."

Louis may not know, but the jury does. They know that Erin's only brother lives in a supervised adult home, but Jeffrey's five siblings are present. Every head in the jury box swivels toward the gallery, where Jason Tomassi and his four sisters sit with their father.

Bystrowski leaps up. "Objection, Your Honor. Counsel is leading the witness."

Briley turns to face the judge. "I'm asking about facts the witness might know. The Tomassi children are frequently in the public eye."

Judge Trask leans into his microphone. "Ms. Lester, I'm not sure where you're headed with this, but I'll give you a little latitude."

"Thank you, Your Honor." Briley takes the lab report from the witness. "Mr. Thomsen, wouldn't you agree that the DNA evidence from the Tomassi crime scene indicates three different people were present in that bedroom at some point between the housekeeper's last visit and Erin Tomassi's 911 call?"

Louis grins. "I don't know anything about the housekeeper, but I agree that when the samples were gathered, hair from three different people was found at the locations described in my report."

"And you would agree that one of those three people had to be a sibling to Erin or Jeffrey Tomassi?"

"Objection!" Bystrowski stands again. "The Tomassi children are not on trial here."

"Your Honor," Briley says, "I am simply attempting to verify a biological relationship between the people in that room."

The judge looks at the prosecutor and tugs irritably at his collar. "Objection overruled."

"Mr. Thomsen," Briley repeats, "please answer the question. Does the official report from the Cook County crime lab reveal that three different people, two of them siblings, were present in that bedroom and near Jeffrey Tomassi's deathbed?"

A sly smile plays at the corner of Louis's mouth. At the sight of it, Briley prays he doesn't reveal too much. "Yes."

She gives him a look of relief and thanks, which he acknowledges with a barely perceptible nod. "I have only a few more questions, sir. At the crime lab, do you also work with fingerprints?"

"Yes."

"You lift them from objects and identify them?"

"Very often, yes."

"Do you recall reading the police report pertaining to this case?"

Louis's brows flicker. "I don't have it memorized, but I read it."

"Would it be helpful if I produced a copy?"

Briley walks to the court clerk, hand outstretched, and waits while the woman pulls the document from the file. She waits for Bystrowski to manufacture some kind of objection, but he remains silent, doubtless aware that he has already stipulated to the accuracy of this report.

She returns to the witness stand and delivers the report to the lab technician. Without glancing behind her, she stares directly into Louis Thomsen's eyes. "Sir, from where you're sitting, can you see the defendant, Erin Tomassi?"

The man's gaze flicks away, then returns to Briley's face. "Yes."

"Is she writing on a legal pad?"

Again, the man's gaze darts away. "She is."

"Is the defendant right-handed?"

A flash of curiosity fills his eyes, and his tone is bemused when he answers. "Apparently she is."

"Would you look at the police report, sir, and read the section about fingerprints aloud. You'll find it midway down the second page, under *dactylography*."

Louis's gaze drops to the paper. "A routine dusting of the syringe revealed a partial print matching the suspect's left thumb on the plunger. Full prints matching the suspect's left index finger and thumb were discovered on the barrel."

"Interesting. Let me make sure I understand…. Does the report specify that the lab found prints from my client's *left* hand?"

"Yes."

"Thank you. Are you right-handed, Mr. Thomsen?"

"I am."

"Have you ever handled a syringe?"

"Actually, I have."

"As a right-handed technician, would you ever handle a syringe with your left hand?"

Louis grins, giving Briley a quick, admiring look before transferring his gaze to the jury. "I would not."

"Mr. Thomsen, have you seen crime-scene photos of the victim's body?"

"I have."

"Did Mr. Tomassi sleep on the left or right side of the bed?"

"The left—if you're talking about a foot-of-the-bed perspective."

"Thank you, I am. So if Mr. Tomassi slept on the left, Mrs. Tomassi must have slept on…?"

"The right."

"Objection." Bystrowski stands, glowering like a thundercloud. "Counsel is again leading the witness."

"Sustained." Trask shoots Briley a warning look.

"I'll rephrase." She turns to Louis again. "If Mrs. Tomassi

was sleeping in that bed—and she wasn't sleeping where Mr. Tomassi was sleeping—which of her arms, right or left, was closest to the edge of the bed?"

Louis's brow lowers, then he relaxes. "Her left arm...unless she was sleeping on her stomach."

Briley turns and smiles at a woman in the jury box. "What woman—with breasts—sleeps on her stomach?"

The females on the jury twitter while Bystrowski roars another objection.

"I'll withdraw the question." Briley turns back to the lab technician. "If Erin is like most women and sleeps either on her side or her back, if an intruder wanted to manipulate her hand, which would be the easiest to reach?"

"The left, I suppose."

Bystrowski objects again, but Briley steps away from the witness stand. "Withdrawn. Thank you, sir. I have no further questions for this witness, Your Honor."

A sibilant buzzing rises from the gallery as Briley walks to the defense table, but she can't tear her gaze from Bystrowski's stunned face.

Chapter Fifty-Two

Through the storm of whispers, Antonio breathes one word: *"No."* He gives the defense attorney a sidelong glance of utter disbelief and clenches his fist.

The jury may not be sharp enough to understand what that woman is doing, but he has grasped the full picture. All that business with the hair samples is an attempt to point the finger at one of his children! None of them was anywhere near Jeff's house that night, but they were all together at the fundraiser. Which can only mean that Jeffrey picked up a stray hair on his clothing and somehow transferred it to the bed linens…or someone fabricated this evidence.

That must be the answer. Someone felt sorry for Erin and recently planted those hairs down at the police department. That's why they didn't surface until today. That's why the defense attorney was able to spring new evidence on the prosecutor. That's why she went through that song and dance about the chain of custody and the police report—

That's why Antonio wasn't warned about this bombshell.

As the judge calls for order, Antonio stares at the defense attorney's pale profile. Briley Lester knew she was losing, so she must have called in a favor from someone with ties to the police department. She and Erin have grown close; hasn't everyone noticed the way she frequently pats Erin's shoulder or touches her arm? Joseph Franklin assured him this woman was inexperienced; he promised she wouldn't be tenacious.

Yet Briley Lester has one of the leading state's attorneys

on the run. Bystrowski is now huddling with his associate, nodding and jotting notes on a legal pad.

At Antonio's left, Jason's breathing has quickened. "What is she doing?" He gives the defense attorney a black look. "What is she thinking?"

"She's desperate." Antonio lowers his voice as the judge demands order. "This is a last-minute attempt to cast suspicion on someone else."

But on the off chance that the situation might spin out of control, he pulls his phone from his pocket and taps out a text message.

Chapter Fifty-Three

Briley adopts a deadpan expression as Bystrowski confers with his associate, then stands. "Your Honor," he asks, "may I request a sidebar?"

The judge gestures for both lawyers to step forward.

When Briley and Bystrowski stand at the front of the judge's bench, the prosecutor vents his frustration. "Your Honor," he says, his voice a low rumble, "the defense is required to disclose all evidence they intend to offer at trial. Reciprocal discovery requirements have not been met in this case, and the state has had no time to investigate this latest evidence. Before we commence the cross-examination of this witness, we would like to request a recess to conduct our own investigation."

Briley straightens her spine, stretching her height to better see the judge. "I beg to differ, Your Honor. The defense *did* provide the state with a list of all evidence, plus the names and addresses of all witnesses we planned to call. We intended full cooperation, and we provided it. The evidence we introduced today has been in the state's custody and available to the prosecutor. We should not be penalized because we became aware of untested evidence."

The judge strokes his chin. "Let me see if I'm understanding this correctly.... The evidence in question, the hair samples, has been in the state's possession for how long?"

Briley grips the edge of his desk. "Since the commission of the homicide, Your Honor."

"And it wasn't tested?" Trask looks at Bystrowski. "Why not?"

Not wanting blame to fall on Louis Thomsen or Detective Malone, Briley interjects an answer. "The prosecutor charged the first available suspect. They didn't test additional evidence because they thought they had their killer."

A shadow of annoyance crosses Bystrowski's face. "The difference in the samples couldn't have been apparent, Your Honor. All the samples were a visual match to either the victim or the defendant. And we never test every hair, because DNA can only be pulled from samples with an attached follicle."

The judge rubs his hand over his face, then gives Briley a wry grin. "I don't think a few hours will hurt your case, Counselor, and the prosecution apparently needs time to see what else, if anything, they might have in storage down at the police lab." He looks at Bystrowski. "I would advise you to commence your cross-examination now, Counselor. You can always recall the witness later."

Briley smothers a smile as she returns to her counsel table. The prosecutor doesn't sit, but charges toward Louis like a bull released from a rodeo chute. "Three people in that bedroom?" He shifts his gaze to the jury and adopts an expression of amazed disbelief. "Did you find three sets of fingerprints on that syringe?"

Louis shakes his head. "No."

"Did you or the police find *any* fingerprints belonging to a third person?"

"Well, yes. The third set of prints was identified as the housekeeper's."

"Could this hair belong to the housekeeper?"

"Not unless she's related to Erin or Jeffrey Tomassi."

"Is it possible that this mysterious sibling's hair could have come from a piece of clothing and dropped onto the bedsheets?"

"I suppose that's possible."

"Did the police find any other evidence of this mysterious third person?"

"Not to my knowledge—but my knowledge is hardly exhaustive. I never visited the crime scene."

Briley rests her chin on her hand, careful to maintain a neutral expression as Bystrowski searches for words. She's caught him by surprise, and that's not an easy thing to do.

"So—" Bystrowski turns to the witness again, determined to drive his point home "—in all the evidence gathered from the murder scene, you found nothing else to establish the presence of an intruder. No fingerprints, no footprints, no traces of saliva on a drinking glass. Are you really basing your theory of an intruder on one tiny hair?"

"Actually, the police collected four tiny hairs belonging to the third person," Louis says, leaning forward. "And DNA does not lie."

In a terse voice, Bystrowski announces that he's done with the witness and stalks back to his table.

A moment later the judge declares a recess and announces that the court will reconvene at nine-thirty on Thursday morning.

Ensconced in a booth at Taqueria Tayahua, a restaurant less than a mile from the courthouse, Briley lifts her soda glass. "A toast." She smiles at Kate. "To Louis the lab guy, and Dr. Phillips, who gave me what could prove to be a brilliant idea."

Kate clinks her glass against Briley's. "Don't count your chickens yet. You know Bystrowski's going to come back tomorrow and hit on the fingerprint issue again. If another person was in the room, where's the third set of fingerprints?"

"All I have to do is ask about gloves during the redirect," Briley says. "Unlocked windows and gloves. I might have the court reporter read back part of Detective Malone's testimony. I remember him saying that if there'd been an intruder, he would have left some trace of his presence. Well—" she grins "—he was right."

Kate sips from her drink, then lowers her glass. "Imagine having two different sets of DNA in your body. How weird is that?"

"I don't care if it's weird. I'm just glad we learned about it in time."

Folding her arms, Kate leans closer. "Come on, Briley, what do you think *really* happened in that bedroom? I mean, being a chimera is a lucky break for your client, but it doesn't explain anything."

"I think…" Briley hesitates, sorting through her own thoughts. "I think that parasomnia is the right—the accurate—defense."

"So you think she injected him while she was asleep."

"What else could have happened?" Briley shakes her head. "I'm only glad that unidentified hair establishes reasonable doubt. That's enough to get Erin acquitted…if the jury does the right thing."

Kate rises halfway out of her seat as someone jangles the bell above the restaurant door. "I thought Wills was coming," she says, sinking back onto the bench. "I told him we'd meet him here."

Briley shrugs. "Maybe he had to run an errand."

"Anyway," Kate continues, "that is an incredible development. I wonder how many people are chimeras and don't even know it?"

"That's not something I want to contemplate. The thought is enough to give me a headache."

The bell jangles again. A moment later, William shrugs out of his coat, hangs it on a hook, and slides into the booth next to Kate. "What's the good word?"

"The word is *celebration*." Kate gives him a welcoming smile. "All Briley has to do now is deliver her closing remarks and remind the jurors that Mrs. Walker had just changed the sheets in the master bedroom. No juror is going to pin the murder on an abused woman when the evidence proves someone else was present at the scene."

"Don't forget the fingerprints." Briley unfolds her napkin.

"I'll have to remind the jurors that someone could have manipulated Erin's hand while she was asleep. I'll mention that in my closing, too."

"But what about the Tomassis?" William looks at Briley, concern in his eyes. "What are you going to do if they pin the crime on Jason or one of the sisters?"

"They won't," Briley says. "The police will investigate. And when they do, they'll learn that the unidentified DNA doesn't match any of the Tomassis. But by that time our trial will be finished."

Kate lifts a warning finger. "What happens when they learn the siblings are Erin and her chimera?"

William's brows shoot up to his hairline. "Am I missing something?"

"You've missed a lot." Briley laughs. "Serves you right for coming in late."

"You know," Kate says, "the prosecutor has other options to explain that third DNA specimen. The hair could have come from any of the Tomassi kids and fallen off Jeffrey's clothing. The entire family was together that night."

Briley picks up her menu. "Bystrowski is probably framing that argument right now. Either that, or he's calling Louis for more information about those hair samples."

A flicker of alarm widens Kate's eyes. "What if Louis tells him the siblings in the sample are female? Won't that ruin everything?"

Briley smiles over the top of her menu. "Louis worked all night. I'm pretty sure he's home asleep and will be for the next several hours."

William looks from Kate to Briley and back to Kate. "You're speaking in code, aren't you?"

"Listen, Sherlock, and you'll catch up." Kate nudges him in the shoulder. "But we've just caught the mother of all lucky breaks."

"To be continued." William slides to the end of the bench. "Excuse me. Nature calls."

Kate watches him stand and walk toward the back of the restaurant. "I'm growing quite fond of our Wills. You have to admire a man who takes several vacation days to sit in a Cook County courtroom."

"He took *what?*"

"His vacation time. I thought you knew."

"I had no idea. I thought he had permission from the partners."

"The firm wasn't about to give him leave, so he put in for personal days. I teased him about having a crush on you, but you know William. He keeps insisting he's only trying to broaden his legal experience."

Briley stirs her drink with her straw. "Wow. Maybe I owe the man a dinner or something. Which reminds me—I meant to call the office and tell Franklin we should be finishing tomorrow, but with all that running around I did last night, I forgot to charge my cell phone. Can I borrow yours?"

Kate shakes her head. "I stopped bringing mine on the second day of the trial. The service is picking up all my calls." She pats the pockets of William's coat. "Here. Use Wills's."

Briley accepts the phone and flips it open, then glances at the screen. One name is listed under recently received calls: Antonio Tomassi.

What business would William have with *him?*

As Kate natters on about William's fine qualities, Briley struggles to make sense of her confused thoughts. Antonio Tomassi is connected to the firm. William has been a great help to Briley, but as the law librarian, his loyalties must lie with the partners. Unless...

Thoughts she dares not articulate buzz in a vicious swarm. What if Kate is wrong about William's motivation for attending the trial? What if he's not here to support Briley, but to spy for Tomassi?

The idea's crazy...isn't it?

She snaps the phone shut and hands it back to Kate. "I'll

call later," she says, trying to keep her voice light. "Too noisy in here."

Kate shrugs and drops the phone back into William's pocket. "No noisier than anywhere else in this part of town. But suit yourself."

"Briley?"

She turns at the unexpected but familiar voice. Timothy stands in the aisle, his face tanned, his eyes soft. A shock wave spreads from the epicenter of her chest, tingling her fingers and numbing her toes. "Timothy? What—? How?"

"One of the security guards at the courthouse overheard you asking for directions to this place. I took a chance you'd still be here." He gestures to the empty spot at her side. "Can I join you?"

"Sure." Briley gives Kate a bewildered look, then slides over to make room. As Timothy settles in, she tilts her head, not quite believing what she's seeing. "When did you get back from California?"

"Late last night. But I was in court this morning. And you did great."

"You were there?"

"I slipped into the back as things were starting up."

"Oh." She stares at him, her emotions roiling. "So where is Dax today?"

"At a spa, having something waxed. I didn't ask."

"Are you sure it's not the kind of spa that serves joints on the side?"

"It's the kind of spa that serves seaweed slushes. I called to make sure he'd be okay without me."

Briley falls silent as William approaches. He drops into the booth and gapes at Timothy. "Sitting at the table is kind of overfriendly for a waiter, isn't it?"

"He's not a waiter." Briley's voice comes out wavery and uncertain. "Wills, meet Timothy Shackelford. He's with me."

William's smirk fades. "Oh. Nice to meet you."

Oblivious of the change in Briley's mood, Kate flicks lint

from William's sweater. "You missed out. Briley was just saying that she owed you a home-cooked dinner."

A flush rises from the librarian's collar. "Sorry I missed that."

"Trust me, you won't hear it often." Timothy winks at Briley. "My favorite lawyer doesn't cook for just anyone."

Briley stares at the faces around the table, her emotions bobbing and spinning like a toy boat caught in a flash flood. How can William sit here and make small talk if he's betraying her? She searches for some logical reason why he might receive a call from Antonio Tomassi, but she comes up blank. Why would William betray her? Maybe for money. Or maybe the partners have asked him to be a silent link between Briley and one of their favored clients.

Ordinarily Tomassi would consult one of the partners about his business, but the partners have maintained a careful distance from this case. They've done nothing to directly involve themselves, but they've only allowed Briley to have help from a paralegal and a librarian…and with William, they've covered their tracks. If he's ever questioned about his involvement with the case, Wills could truthfully say that he attended the trial on personal time and merely provided assistance to a friend.

While Timothy and Kate study their menus, William clears his throat. "So, Briley—what's our strategy for the closing argument?"

She lowers her gaze. Are her next words about to be repeated to Antonio Tomassi or Travis Bystrowski? She can't imagine the straitlaced prosecutor being involved in an unethical situation, but one never knows what a person might do when he's under pressure. And Antonio Tomassi is capable of applying extreme pressure.

"Let's not talk business." She picks up her menu. "Let's try not to think about tomorrow morning. I think we've got this case wrapped up."

She props her chin in her hand and pretends to debate the

choice between enchiladas and empanadas. After a moment, William drops his menu to the table. "I just remembered…" He gives Kate an apologetic look. "I've got this thing I need to take care of. I'd better run."

Briley hopes he doesn't notice the frayed edges of her parting smile. "We'll see you tomorrow."

He says goodbye to the others, grabs his coat, and heads for the door. Briley peers over her shoulder and watches him take his phone out and punch in a number.

He's calling Tomassi.

Certainty settles in her bones like a bad chill. So he's calling Tomassi, so what? What does that mean?

She looks at the others. "Let me run a hypothetical situation by you," she says. "Suppose you were a rich and powerful man. Suppose you were dead set on seeing justice done when your son is killed. Let's also suppose that as the trial winds down, new evidence arrives, evidence that convinces you the defendant—the person you believe responsible for your child's death—is going to walk."

"I'll play." Timothy props his folded arms on the table. "How rich am I?"

Kate dips a chip in the salsa bowl. "Do you know something we don't know?"

"Maybe I'm just trying to cover my bases," Briley answers. She looks at Timothy. "And you're rich enough that no one ever tells you *no.*"

Timothy doesn't hesitate. "If I were that rich, I'd send henchmen to make sure the acquitted defendant didn't walk far."

"Henchmen?" Kate makes a face. "Are you talking about hired killers?"

Timothy's mouth pulls into a rueful smile. "Don't laugh, Ms. Skeptical. I've met lots of people who will do anything to be aligned with the rich and powerful."

Kate gasps. "Like…hire someone to assault a defense attorney?"

Timothy looks at Briley, his brown eyes sparking. "You were assaulted?"

"I'm fine." She holds his gaze. "Do you think Antonio Tomassi is the type to hire a henchman?"

"Yeah, I do."

"That settles it." She reaches for her purse, then groans. "Kate, are you sure you don't have your phone?"

"Positive."

"Timothy?"

"Any time, Bri." He takes his phone from his pocket and hands it over.

"Who's she calling?" Kate perks up. "What's going on?"

Ignoring her, Briley dials directory assistance, then asks for the Cook County Jail. "Make that the sheriff's office," she asks. "Or Security."

A moment later, the operator is connecting her to the sheriff's office. While the phone rings, Timothy nudges her shoulder. "You anticipating a crisis?"

She holds up her hand when a man answers and identifies himself as Deputy Mackenzie. "Please," she says, her desperation growing by the minute. "I'm calling about an inmate, Erin Tomassi. I have good reason to believe you need to take her into protective custody."

The deputy laughs. "If the woman's in jail, ma'am, she's *in* protective custody."

Briley bites her lip. The deputy might have a point, but then again... Timothy's words replay in her memory: *Lots of people will do anything to be aligned with the rich and powerful.*

"I need—" she gulps back her fear "—to speak to the sheriff."

"He's unavailable."

"Then...the head of security at the jail."

"Which division?"

"Four. Division Four."

"Just a minute, I'll put you through."

Briley waits, anxiety swelling in her chest, as recorded

music fills her ear. At her right, a waitress comes over and smiles at Timothy, then proceeds to take his order. The canned music stops. "Hello?" When no one answers, Briley looks at Kate and raises her voice. "Hel-*lo?*"

Every eye within a ten-foot radius swivels in her direction. "The line's dead." She lifts the phone to search for a signal. "I need a better connection."

"Hey, lady," a man calls from another table. "Leave the phone at home or take it outside."

Timothy looks at her, his eyes sharp and assessing. "You wanna go?"

"I do." Briley grabs her coat and scoots out of the booth, still clutching the phone. Maybe nothing is·wrong. Maybe her imagination is in overdrive and Antonio Tomassi couldn't care less about what happens to her client.

But as she strides toward the door, the frigid breath of foreboding chills her heart.

Chapter Fifty-Four

Erin's eyes fly open when a hand touches her shoulder. "Hey, Sleepin' Beauty," her cellmate says. "Somebody wants to see you."

She sits up in her bunk and sees a guard standing outside her cell. Why is he here so late in the day? She blinks to focus her blurry vision. "What's wrong?"

"You're Erin Tomassi?"

"Yes."

"You're wanted in the office. You need to come with me."

Erin runs her hands through her hair and stands, smoothing the wrinkles out of her uniform. After spending the morning in court, she came back and slept through dinner, preferring to go hungry rather than face the bullies in the cafeteria. She's tired and her limbs feel like dead weight, but if Briley's here, maybe she's brought good news. Maybe the judge has decided that the trial was a mistake and she's free to go.

She steps toward the bars and waits as the guard unlocks the door.

"Hey, handsome," her cellmate calls, "you taking me to the office, too? That place should be cleared out about now."

"Get in line." The burly man grins. "Wait your turn."

Erin steps out of the cell and extends her arms, expecting the guard to slap cuffs on her wrists. When he doesn't, she shoots him a curious glance and resists the surge of hope that springs up in her heart. Could the charges have been dismissed?

That's when she notices the short club in his right hand.

The guards don't usually bring weapons into this hallway, so why is he carrying a club?

The hair on the back of her neck rises with premonition when he slams the cell door and gestures down the hall. "After you, sweetheart."

Erin straightens her spine and walks down the hallway, keenly aware of the other inmates' taunts and curious gazes. The women in this cell block are a tough lot, having been strengthened and chiseled by bad men, bad mothers, and bad memories. During the thirteen weeks she's lived among them, she's learned to keep her mouth shut and her eyes open.

And never to turn her back on anyone.

Maybe that's why walking in front of this guard makes her nervous. His face is familiar and there are plenty of witnesses, but those spying eyes won't be able to see her once she steps through the doorway at the end of this hall.

"Go on, sweetheart," the guard says. "Open the door, it's not locked."

Erin obeys, the brass handle cold beneath her hands. They move into a stairwell, where a flight of steps leads to interview rooms on the floor above. But the guard points his snub-nosed club toward the stairs that lead to the basement.

"I thought you said—"

Without warning, he slams his stick onto her back, knocking her against the stair railing and stealing the breath from her lungs. She tries to shout, but she can barely summon enough air to breathe.

"Down." He winds his free hand into the hair at the back of her head. "We're going for a little walk."

With no choice, Erin staggers forward on legs that feel about as substantial as marshmallows. She grabs the railing and creeps downward, continually conscious of the brutal club at her back. When they finally reach the basement floor, the guard drags her forward, but she clings to the stair rail with both hands. She grips the iron rail, determined not to let go, but then the club crashes down on her fingers.

She tips her head back and releases a rattling cry that echoes in the cavern of the stairwell. Even as her scream flows over her lips, she knows no one will hear it. This place is closed off from the rest of the building, unheated and unattended. She is alone with this brute, and she has no idea what he has in mind.

Just as she never knew what Jeffrey had planned for her.

"Come on, darlin'."

His tone is oily and taunting, like Jeffrey's. She feels a strange lurch of recognition at the sound, and then another voice fills her head: *Good grief, Erin, stop it. It's time you stood up for yourself.*

"Not again."

Invigorated by pain and anger, Erin locks her arms around a vertical post, but the guard uses the club again, striking until she lets go. Then he loops an arm around her rib cage and drags her down the hallway, a limp, life-size doll. Through a haze of pain, she recognizes the door leading to the furnace room, but her tormentor keeps moving. He stops outside the entrance to the laundry.

He unlocks the door, the clink of his keys nearly drowning out the sound of her soft whimpering. As he drags her through the doorway, she tries to catch the edge of the door frame, but her battered fingers will not obey her commands. She hangs her head, gathering her strength, but the sound of a second male voice sends a wave of black terror sweeping through her.

"You sure that's the right woman?"

"What, don't ya think I can tell 'em apart? She's the one you want." The guard releases his grip, dropping Erin to the concrete floor. She pushes herself up and shoves the hair out of her eyes. Two strangers stand before her, both wearing the white shirts, white pants, and white jackets of a laundry service. A back door stands open, allowing entrance to a whistling March wind.

Shivering, she stares at the men and tries to place them

in her memory. Their faces look familiar, but they could be anyone from workers at her local grocery store to employees of her father-in-law. "Thanks," one of the men in white says. "We'll take care of things from here."

The security guard grunts, takes a back step, and hesitates. "Give Mr. T my regards, okay?"

The man on the right folds his arms. "Yeah, sure. Now, get on back before someone notices you're gone."

The guard walks away, his footsteps echoing over the concrete. The two uniformed men wait until the laundry-room door slams, then one of them kneels in front of Erin. "Seems a shame to do this to such a pretty little thing."

"We got our orders," the other one says, moving to a laundry tub. "Come on, let's get a move on. I want to get home before my fingers freeze off."

The kneeling man pulls a roll of duct tape from his jacket pocket. Erin closes her eyes, her throat tightening as Jeffrey's face plays on the back of her eyelids. "You don't think I can kill you?" he'd say, taking the duct tape from his drawer. "So easy. All I have to do is tie your arms and cover your mouth and nose with this...."

"Please," Erin rasps as the man in white unwinds a length of the sticky gray material. "No." She lifts her arms, ready to fight him off, but the second man expertly catches her wrists and holds them. Behind her, a pipe groans as water runs into a laundry tub. "You shouldn't do this," she says, resisting the urge to panic. "They'll investigate, they'll figure it out."

"I doubt it." The man binds her wrists as calmly as he might wrap a sandwich. "The sheriff's department won't want to risk the bad press. It'll be a jailhouse accident, that's all."

"But *why?*" Her voice breaks on the word. "I haven't done anything to you."

"Doesn't matter. My boss—" He shakes his square head. "The boss says you gotta go."

"Come on." Tears slip down her cheeks. "You could let me go and tell him I escaped."

"Afraid not."

"Is he paying you? I could pay you, too. I'll pay more than he's offering—"

The man chuckles. "Lady, you don't get it. There's a lot more than money involved."

"But I didn't kill his son!"

She waits, hoping, as a gleam of interest flashes in his eyes. "That's not what he says."

"He's wrong. You have to believe me, he's wrong."

"Shut up, lady." The second man releases her wrists and moves away.

Erin looks directly into the eyes of the man in front of her. "I didn't kill anyone. But if you kill me, you'll regret it. You'll always remember this moment and wish you'd done the right thing...."

"Lady, I'm gonna sleep like a baby tonight."

He can't actually mean to—

He stands, pulling her to her feet, but experience and adrenaline have prepared her for this moment. She jerks free, then turns and runs, her rubber-soled shoes slapping the concrete in sync with the pounding of her heart. She heads for the laundry door and realizes that it's locked, so she ducks behind a bank of silent industrial dryers. The low ceiling in this part of the room is webbed with ductwork, so she ducks and dodges, moving in blind panic until she runs headlong into a hot water pipe. Seeing stars, she buckles at the knees as if her bones had dissolved into ash.

"Come here, you hellcat." The square-headed man has found her; his hands close on her wrists and drag her back into the light. She kicks at empty air, vainly struggling to defend herself, then four hands fasten on her shoulders and lift her upright, then four arms press her forward into... wetness.

The slap of frigid water sharpens her thoughts to a point of startling clarity. She has been shoved headfirst into a laundry tub. The rim of the tub cuts into her stomach while the two brutes stand beside her, holding her under the bone-chilling water. In an instant woven of eternity, Erin realizes that no one is coming to save her, not husband, mother, father-in-law, or lawyer. She will never leave this jail, never again experience freedom.

Another voice echoes in her head as Lisa Marie screams, her voice ragged with fury: "Do something, you weak fool! We can't end like this!"

Grief and despair tear at Erin's heart as primal panic takes control of her body. She kicks and cries, the sound watery and muffled in her ears, but her hands are tied and her captors are as impassive as pillars. Is this how life ends? She should have learned how to resist…long before this.

Her last cry exits in a gurgle, bubbles brush past her nose, and consciousness flickers like a spent light bulb. Finally she surrenders to regret and the warm, encroaching darkness. Her pounding pulse slows, her peripheral vision narrows, and then she is floating through a tunnel, moving toward a light radiating warmth and love.

Her heart stops. Her regrets fade.

And she is not alone. As always, Lisa Marie is with her.

Chapter Fifty-Five

"What do you mean, I have to wait for a ruling?" Briley yells into the phone. "My client's life is in imminent danger. Do you know what *imminent* means?"

She glances at Timothy, whose face is tense and drawn behind the wheel. After following her to the law office, where he waited patiently while she looked up the proper procedures to type out a motion, he offered to drive her to the courthouse.

Apparently he realized she's frantic enough to be a real danger on the slick streets.

"All right," she snaps at a clerk in the Division Four superintendent's office. "I get it. I have the motion and I'm on my way to file it, but I'd appreciate it if you could send someone to check on my client. As soon as I see the judge, I'm heading over to the jail."

"Arrgh!" Briley closes Timothy's phone and drops it into the well between the front seats. "Bureaucracy! Can't anyone make exceptions in dire situations?"

His cheek curves in a smile. "Wait a minute—is this Ms. Don't-Get-Personally-Involved talking? I thought well-run cases never resulted in dire situations."

"Hush up and drive, will you?" She crosses her arms and stares out the window, reluctantly admitting that Timothy is right. Nothing about this case has unfolded as she expected, but perhaps capital cases are the exception to every rule. After all, when a client's life is at stake, how can a defense attorney help getting personally involved?

But this has become more than a case, and Erin more than a client.

"Talk to me," Timothy says, deftly handling the vehicle as they drive through a decaying neighborhood with boarded-up buildings and graffiti-splashed walls. The light rain has turned to sleet, which bounces off the windshield as they make their way through puddled potholes. He brakes as a mangy-looking pit bull darts into the street, then stops and stares at him, its muzzle quivering with the ghost of a growl. "What'd they tell you?"

Briley stares, amazed that the dog would challenge a car, until the animal backs down and trots away. "I have to file a motion for protective custody." She speaks through her nose, mimicking the clerk. "After I get in to see the judge on duty, I have to wait for a ruling. Then, assuming the ruling is favorable, I have to go down to the jail and present the ruling to the superintendent of Division Four."

"In the meantime, did you ask them to check on your client?"

"Of course, but they automatically assured me everything would be fine. The clerk said the women in Erin's cell block are locked down for the night."

"Isn't that good news? Erin's surrounded by guards, Bri. If she can't get out, it's unlikely that bad guys can get in, right?"

"I've begun to believe in the unlikely." Briley closes her eyes as a few fat flakes of snow flutter in front of the headlights. She wants to believe Timothy. She wants to blame her worries on an overactive imagination and a few unfortunate coincidences, but she can't forget William's restless manner and odd questions at lunch.

Isn't it better to err on the side of caution?

"You don't know Tomassi," she says. "I do, and I don't trust him. I'm beginning to think the man is capable of anything."

Timothy chuckles. "I've never seen this side of you, but I always knew it was there."

"What side? You're not seeing a side."

"I'm seeing the real you—a determined lawyer, devoted friend. The kind of woman who will take a few risks for someone who needs help."

"Just hurry, will you? I've a bad feeling about all this... and I can't shake it."

With the judge's ruling in hand, Briley leaps out of the car and hurries toward the entrance to Division Four. Leaving Timothy to park the car, she enters and pounds on the unattended security desk. A matronly security guard appears in a doorway and waddles forward, a steaming cup of coffee in hand. Seeing Briley, she flashes a brow. "Can I help you?"

"I have a ruling from Judge Abrams," Briley says, fumbling in her purse for her ID, "and I need to speak to the superintendent as soon as possible."

A half smile crosses the woman's face. "The super's done gone home. You can call her in the morning."

"Look." Briley waves her ID card before the guard's narrow eyes, then presses both hands flat against the counter. "I don't know if you understand the meaning of *emergency,* but that's what we have here, a genuine emergency. I need to talk to the super—so whether you have to call her, fetch her, or ship her in from Timbuktu, do it."

A warning cloud settles on the woman's features. "Now, *you* look. There ain't a thing the super can do for you tonight, and this place is locked down tight. So you can come back in the morning, Miss Lawyer."

The door behind Briley opens, admitting Timothy and a breath of freezing wind. The guard looks at him and frowns. "Let me guess—you're with Ms. Bossy here, and you want me to call my supervisor."

He slides his hands into his pockets. "I'm more of an innocent bystander. But if I step outside and discover that my rims are missing, I might want to talk to somebody."

Her brows knit in irritation. "And why are you talking to

me like that? I can't control what happens outside this place—"

"Please," Briley interrupts, ashamed to hear her voice wavering. "Let's cut the tough acts and just talk, okay? Listen, I'm worried about my client, Erin Tomassi. Will you please send someone to check on her? Or put her in solitary for the night. I have a ruling from the judge, and trust me, this ruling wasn't easy to get."

The guard shakes her head and leans forward, but before she can launch into another tirade the desk phone rings. The woman glares at the instrument, then rolls her eyes and picks it up. "Front desk."

With a frustrated groan, Briley turns to Timothy. "I don't know what else to do."

He drops his hands to her shoulders. "Are you sure Erin's in danger? After all, in a few hours she'll be back at the courthouse, sitting right next to you—"

"The trial should end tomorrow," Briley says. "And though I don't know how long the jury will deliberate, she could be free by tomorrow night. If Tomassi wants to hurt her, he'll never have it this easy again."

She glances at the security guard, who has pressed her lips into a thin line and is murmuring into the phone. Since the guard shows no sign of answering her request, Briley props her arms on the counter and prepares to wait the woman out.

The guard hangs up the phone and scribbles something on a notepad. "I've got a real emergency on my hands," she says, not looking at Briley. "So I'm not wasting any more time with you. You can just bring your papers back in the morning."

"I'm not leaving," Briley says, "until I can guarantee my client's safety."

"Then I hope you're wearing comfortable shoes, 'cause you're gonna be standing there a long time."

The guard looks toward the door as a siren whines in the night, a sound that quickens Briley's pulse.

The woman picks up a radio, says something about

opening a service gate, and steps toward the computer. Briley turns toward the door and sees the strobelike play of red-and-white lights on the low-hanging clouds. A mechanical gate opens, and an emergency vehicle crawls through the entry.

An icy finger touches the base of her spine.

"What happened?" She curls her hand into a fist. "Why did someone call an ambulance?"

"An accident." The guard turns, but when her gaze meets Briley's, a change creeps over her features, a sudden shock of realization. "The night guard found an inmate," she says, her face settling into a no-comment mask. "I can't say more until after the investigation."

"Is this inmate…?" Briley hesitates.

"Expired," the guard answers, her voice clotting with an emotion that might be guilt. "The woman they found is dead."

Chapter Fifty-Six

S now falls in slanting dotted lines as Briley peers through her car's windshield. A halogen security light casts a golden glow over the ambulance as it waits, engine rumbling, a few yards behind the fence topped with razor wire. As Timothy turns off the engine, a pair of EMTs bursts through a set of steel doors, wheeling a gurney between them.

The view is a perverse Currier & Ives print: a winter scene with no warmth, no life, no hope.

Briley grips Timothy's hand when she recognizes the slender form on the stretcher. Erin's blond hair is wet and dark, her face is covered by a mask connected to a rubber bulb one of the technicians squeezes at regular intervals. An IV line runs into one pale arm; some sort of dark binding dangles from the wrist. The pragmatic part of Briley's brain notes that the binding proves this was no accident.

She swallows the despair rising in her throat. "I'll meet the judge in chambers tomorrow morning. I don't know how to handle a case where the defendant is killed during the trial, so—"

"Hang on a minute." Timothy gestures to the stretcher. "They're still working on her. They haven't covered her face with a sheet."

Briley blinks as realization takes hold.

"I'll be back." She steps out of the car and walks up to the fence, then curls her hands into the steel mesh. "Hello?" she calls, trying to get the EMTs' attention. When one of them looks at her, she points at the stretcher and yells above the bawling wind. "I'm a lawyer and that's my client."

The technician nods, then helps his partner lift the gurney and slide it into the vehicle. He slams the doors and looks at Briley as he jogs toward the driver's door. "We got a pulse!" he shouts. "If you want to follow us to the hospital, we can tell you more there!"

Briley steps out of the way as he slams the door and puts the vehicle in gear. As the ambulance moves out of the secure enclosure, Briley stands by the gate and wonders if her client will survive this latest brutality.

"They got a pulse," Briley repeats when Timothy comes to stand beside her. "What do you think that means?"

He slips an arm around her shoulder and presses his lips to her temple. "It means there's hope. So—are you ready to go home and get some rest?"

She shifts her gaze back to the street, where the ambulance is now a blur of flashing red lights behind the falling snow. "I want to go to the hospital."

Briley shifts in the hard plastic chair as the emergency-room doors blast open. A gurney rolls past, propelled by EMTs on both sides, and for an instant Briley is convinced that she and Timothy have found themselves in an episode of *ER*.

He squeezes her hand when the trauma team pushes through another set of double doors. Except for an old woman knitting in front of the television, they are alone in the waiting room. "You want coffee, or a diet soda?" He squeezes her hand again. "I could go find a snack machine."

"I'm fine. And please…don't go."

He leans forward to look into her eyes. "Are you okay, Bri?"

She meets his gaze, ready to be honest. "No."

"But it looked like Erin was breathing. She might pull out of this—"

"Can't you see?" Her voice breaks as tears spill over her lower lashes. "I pushed too hard. I caused this. After evalu-

ating the evidence, I should have convinced her to take the
deal for manslaughter. Tomassi wouldn't be happy, but I don't
think he would have risked sending someone to kill her...."

"Do you think you should be talking about this in public?"

Briley lowers her voice to a whisper, but she can't be
silent, not now. "If I hadn't pushed for an acquittal, my
client wouldn't be fighting for her life."

Timothy drapes his arm over Briley's shoulders. "You
don't know what happened in that jail. She could have been
attacked by anyone."

"Not like that." She hiccups a sob. "The police may not
be able to prove that Tomassi was involved, but I know what
he's capable of. I know Antonio sent someone into that jail,
as surely as I know that he sent someone to threaten me."

"I'm sorry about that." He turns his face to hers, and his
eyes soften with sincerity. "I should have been here for you.
I shouldn't have gone to California—"

"Shh." She presses her finger to his lips. "You did what
you had to do. Caring for Dax is part of who you are,
Timothy...and I wouldn't change you."

His forehead drops to hers. "All the same, I can't stand
knowing that I wasn't here when you needed me."

"You're here now."

They sit in silence for a moment, then the old woman by
the TV begins to snore. Briley giggles when the woman's
knitting begins to slide from her lap, then the woman wakes
herself up, straightens in her seat, and goes right back to work.

"If Erin didn't kill him," Timothy says, "you were right
to go for an acquittal."

Briley shakes her head. "That's not how the game is
played. The law isn't about justice, it's about compromise.
It's about using an overworked system to process cases as
quickly as possible. It's about moving criminals in and out
of jail, taking bad guys off the street for a while, and
allowing citizens to feel that their wrongs have been addressed when we know we can't make things right."

Timothy's eyes rest on her, alive with speculation. "You don't really believe that."

"I do."

"You don't. The woman I saw in court this morning was determined to make her case. I swear I saw sweat trickling down that prosecutor's neck."

She lifts one shoulder in a shrug. "Bystrowski will find some way to outsmart me. Maybe I should let him."

"Stop it, Briley. I've heard enough."

She blinks, surprised by the disapproval radiating from his face.

"This isn't like you," he says, lifting his arm from her shoulder. "The Briley I know would never settle for second when she knows she can win."

"The Briley you know has never handled a murder case."

"What difference do the charges make?"

"The stakes are higher. They're the *highest*."

"All the more reason for you to fight for your client. I can't believe you're talking about giving up."

"Sometimes the struggle isn't worth the fight." She looks at him, desperate to make him understand. "Sometimes you do everything you can, you push and you pray and you beg, but the unthinkable still happens. And when you think your life can't get any worse, they come around and kick you when you're down. And they're not satisfied until they've destroyed everything that ever made you happy."

"What?" Timothy crosses his arms as concern and confusion mingle in his eyes. "You're not talking about Erin anymore, are you?"

Briley bites her lip and looks away. Years ago she swore she'd never dredge up the past and resurrect an old injustice. The shame nearly killed her once; it might suffocate her now. But Timothy has come back. If he plans to stay, he has a right to know.

"Do you remember—" she palms tears from her face "—when I told you about how my father died?"

He nods. "He was murdered by an ex-con. And you were with the cops when they found him."

"Right. What I didn't tell you was that the ex-con dropped a packet of crack cocaine near my father's body, probably when he was rifling Dad's pockets. The cops found the coke, and someone from the newspaper saw the police report. Next day there's a front-page story about how the pastor of a local church is murdered while he's hanging out with ex-cons and dealing crack. People come out of the woodwork to talk about Dad riding around with dealers, and the social worker who delivers me to my foster home asks if Dad ever tried to get me to use drugs."

"I wish I'd been there for you back then." Timothy's voice is thick and unsteady. "I'm sure there were people who stood up for your father. People who remembered all the good that he did."

"Sure, there were. But the public doesn't like to hear about the good things, and newspapers don't like to report them. Drugs and robbery make better copy. My dad had gone to that shopping center to make some convict's kids happy, and in return, that con ruined my Christmases forever. Worst of all, when the guy was tried for murder, his lawyer claimed my father was the contact for a network of dealers and ex-cons. By the time they were finished telling their stories, my father's reputation was in the toilet. Dad spent his lifetime serving others, and for what?"

A muscle quivers at Timothy's jaw. "That's why you went to law school."

She shrugs. "I knew there was nothing I could do to help Dad. My father's killer went to prison, so I was glad of that, at least. But I never forgot how it feels to be wronged and desperately want vindication…or to walk into a crowd and be stung by doubting glances. So yeah, I ended up in law school."

"And you've been defending your dad ever since."

She gives him a one-sided smile. "Ironic, isn't it? One of my professors thought I'd make a good prosecutor, but I've never wanted to punish the guilty as much as defend the innocent. Trouble is, once I started practicing, I realized that most of my clients actually committed the crimes they were accused of. That's why I assumed Erin was guilty... until something she said clicked in my mind."

"What'd she say?"

"That seeing isn't believing, believing is seeing. That sounded like something Dad would have said...and I found myself looking at the case with new eyes."

Timothy catches her hand. "Don't give up, Briley. If she pulls through, she's going to need you more than ever."

Chapter Fifty-Seven

After two hours of no news, Briley sends Timothy home to bed. A few moments later, she looks up to see one of the E.R. doctors approaching. "You're the one who came in with the prisoner?"

She stands. "I'm her lawyer. And her name is Erin Tomassi."

The doctor shrugs. "Of course. Well, she's awake and she's talking. As far as we can tell, she's suffered no permanent effects from the drowning."

"Did you say *drowning?*"

"Attempted murder, actually. One of the EMTs told me they found her beside a laundry tub. Fortunately, the water and the room were cold…and low temperatures activate the diving reflex, which causes the heart and lungs to shut down. They worked on her for thirty minutes before they got a pulse, but I don't believe she's going to suffer for it."

"Are you kidding? No brain damage?"

"None apparent. The patient is perfectly coherent, but pneumonia is always a risk. We'll want to keep her overnight to make sure she's come through without injury to her lungs or kidneys."

Briley sighs in gratitude. "Thank you."

"You're welcome." The doctor grins and backs away. "But I wouldn't be surprised to learn that your client has nine lives."

A few minutes later, a nurse allows Briley to slip past a watchful police officer and step into the cubicle where Erin is propped up on a gurney. The nurse holds a finger to her lips, acknowledging the late hour, but Briley feels as if she's moving in a timeless dimension. The clock has stopped, and she can barely remember the last time she ate.

The cubicle is quiet and warm. Erin, neatly tucked in and covered with a blanket, has a clip on one swollen finger and a machine recording her pulse and blood pressure. A pastel hospital gown has replaced the jail uniform. An IV stand holds a bag of fluid that drips into a vein on her right hand. A set of handcuffs links her wrist to a railing on the bed. Her forehead is bruised, as are her arms and hands.

Briley sits on a small stool and studies her client. No permanent effects, the doctor said. Nothing physical, perhaps, but how many nightmares will Erin experience after this?

Briley leans toward the edge of the gurney and drops her hands onto the railing. When her ring hits the metal with a soft chink, Erin stirs. Her fingers move, her eyes open, then she looks at Briley—and smiles.

"Hi."

"Hi yourself," Briley says. "How are you feeling?"

Erin's eyes widen. "She's gone."

"Who's gone?" Briley moves closer. "The person who did this to you?"

Erin shakes her head in an almost imperceptible movement. "Lisa Marie. She's gone. I can feel…emptiness. Like when you lose a tooth."

Briley remains silent, not sure how to respond. Could the doctors have been wrong about the brain damage? Is Erin delirious?

A nurse appears in the curtained opening, a determined look on her face. "Your five minutes are up," she says, her voice firm. "Our patient needs to rest."

Briley squeezes Erin's hand, then smiles a farewell to the nurse. By this time tomorrow, if all goes well, her client will be a free woman. But what price has she paid for her freedom?

Briley steps out of the cubicle, grateful for the policeman on duty. Erin is finally in protective custody. She has a vigilant nurse, a uniformed cop, and a lawyer to watch over her—but the lawyer is hungry.

She presses her hand to her midsection as her stomach reminds her that hours have passed since she ate breakfast. In search of food and coffee, she follows signs for the hospital cafeteria and finds it on the first floor. Most of the chairs are stacked on tables, but a pair of doctors in green scrubs sits in a far corner, eating sandwiches from cellophane wrappers. A custodian mops the floor near the cash register and makes small talk with the cashier.

Briley walks down the line of packaged foods and realizes she's so hungry she could eat two of everything. She didn't get to finish her lunch, and she was in such a rush to type up the motion and get it to the judge that she didn't take time for dinner.

She picks up a tuna sandwich, a package of cookies, and a fruit salad. After pouring herself a cup of coffee, she moves to the cash register, where the dark-haired woman stops talking to the custodian long enough to ring up her purchases and hand her a receipt. Briley takes her tray and walks toward the only table with an available chair. A man in a white coat is sitting alone at the neighboring table, and on second glance, he looks familiar.

"Excuse me." She stops in the aisle. "Were you treating an E.R. patient earlier tonight?"

The man's look of concern lifts the wrinkles etched into his cheeks. "Is that young woman a friend of yours?"

"She's a client...and yes, she's a friend." She gestures to the empty seat at his table. "Would you mind?"

"Make yourself at home." He lifts a brow when he sees her tray. "Better not let the nutrition police catch you eating dinner so late. Nothing heavy after seven, that's what they're always saying."

"I don't pay much attention to the nutrition police." She sits and drapes the strap of her purse over the back of the chair. "Lawyers don't have to be careful about what they eat."

"Because they can always sue their doctors." The man smiles, but his eyes are serious.

Briley tugs at her sandwich wrapper. "I don't handle malpractice suits. I'm in criminal law." She takes a big bite and leans back to savor the mingled tastes on her tongue. Hard to tell what sort of doctor her companion might be—he's wearing a blue scrub suit under his white coat, but no hat. No stethoscope around his neck. No junk food on his tray, only a coffee mug.

She swallows and tilts her head to peer at his nametag: Eric Baron, Neurology.

"Neurology?" She lifts her coffee cup. "They called you in to check Erin's brain function?"

He smiles at her. "You're a quick study."

She shrugs. "I'd say it was a no-brainer, but I imagine you hear that a lot."

"You're right on that score." His eyes soften. "The patient—she's in some kind of trouble?"

Briley pulls the plastic top off her fruit salad. "She was assaulted at the jail. Technically, she was murdered, but the EMTs revived her. And that poses an interesting question— can a man be tried for murder if his victim revives?" She shakes her head, still stunned by the night's events. "I can't believe she's okay. Apparently someone held her underwater in a tub or something. The E.R. doc said the cold preserved her brain function."

He nods. "The mammalian diving reflex. When the face is submerged, the reflex slows the heartbeat and redirects the flow of blood to the heart and brain. We've revived people who've been underwater for more than half an hour."

Briley swallows a bite of banana. "It's all so hard to believe. I mean, I just spoke to her…though what she said didn't make much sense."

"Wasn't she lucid?"

"Yes, but—" Briley hesitates, then decides to take a risk. "Are you in a hurry to rush off somewhere? Because I'd really like to talk about this, but I don't want to keep you from your family or your work."

"I'm in no hurry." The doctor taps his steaming mug for emphasis. "What's on your mind?"

She can almost see Timothy's teasing smile as she frames her thoughts. *What, you asked a perfect stranger about your client? Aren't you getting a little personally involved?*

All right. She wouldn't have done this last month, but she needs to do it now.

"Dr. Baron—" she wraps both hands around her foam cup "—have you ever heard of chimerism?"

A line appears in his forehead. "Like an animal with the DNA of another species?"

"Like a human who is two fused twins in one body. A woman with two different types of DNA."

He picks up his mug. "It's not exactly common."

"According to a geneticist, my client is a chimera. Or was. Or not. But the thing is, she had this invisible friend in her childhood. That's not so odd, right? But the friend, Lisa Marie, seemed to stick around and talk to my client in her dreams. I think—of course, I'm probably wrong—but I think Lisa Marie might be the chimera. Is that even possible?"

The doctor sips his coffee, then tilts his head. "Two twins in one body…two separate souls. I've often wondered what happened to the souls of twins in a case of fetus *in fetu*—"

"Don't forget, Doc, medical jargon isn't my first language."

"Sorry. Fetus *in fetu* occurs when one twin is absorbed by the other, but the separate body remains. I read about a recent case just the other day. Apparently a thirty-six-year-old man in India went to the hospital for a suspected tumor in his belly—the growth was huge. When surgeons opened the tumor, they discovered assorted body parts, including teeth and bones. Apparently a mutated twin had been developing inside the patient for more than thirty-six years."

A rise of nausea threatens to choke Briley, forcing her to swallow and look away from her food. "But that tumor wasn't a living person…was it?"

"It certainly wasn't alive once they cut it out. So if it had a soul…I suppose it left the body when death occurred."

She lowers her fork as her appetite shrivels. "If it had no brain, maybe it didn't have a soul. After all, the soul is our consciousness. Once you lose that—"

The doctor waves a finger. "Not so fast. Do you lose your soul when you go to sleep? Or when you lose consciousness under anesthesia?"

"All right, I spoke too soon. The soul must be part of the brain. And since my client only has one brain, she should have only one soul.…"

"Let me tell you a story." Dr. Baron lowers his mug. "Once I had a patient referred to me by oncology. By the time I was called in, the cancer that began in his lungs had invaded his brain. At the end, I knew—everyone knew—he was little more than a shell. His brain had been completely eaten up by the cancer. Scans revealed that no healthy tissue remained. He could no longer move, smile at his wife, or respond to stimuli. I checked on him on a Thursday morning and noted agonal breathing—the deep, gulping breaths that signal the beginning of death—so I told the nurse to summon his wife and children."

Briley shakes her head, suspecting what will come next. "That must have been hard for them…and for you."

"Dying isn't easy for anyone. But I knew the family would benefit, even though he wouldn't be aware of their presence. I stopped by his room later that day, thinking I'd be able to comfort the family. I found my patient smiling at his wife, patting his children's hands, and telling them all not to worry. The sound of their voices had brought him out of his coma, and from someplace he summoned the strength to tell them goodbye. Then he slipped away again and expired within the hour."

Briley stares, her heart thumping against her rib cage. "You must have been wrong about his brain."

"I wasn't. Autopsy proved what I suspected. The brain no longer existed."

"Then what—"

"The soul, my dear. His soul struggled to reach his loved ones. Did you know—" the doctor leans forward "—that the body loses approximately twenty-one grams of weight at the moment of death? It's not the weight of air in the lungs, either. Some have theorized that twenty-one grams is the weight of a soul—the invisible essence that doesn't reside in any particular organ. If your client is two individuals, one living beneath the skin of another, why shouldn't she have two souls?"

"It's impossible."

"It's inexplicable. But we doctors deal with the mysterious every week."

Maybe lawyers do, too.

"In any case—" Dr. Baron idly turns his coffee cup "—you might want to advise your client to remain quiet about her chimerism. There are doctors who would love to put her through tests to ascertain exactly where the anomaly occurs, and I doubt your client would appreciate being used as a human lab rat."

Briley lifts her hand. "What if…"

"Hmm?"

"What if one of the souls…leaves?"

For an instant, the doctor's face clouds, then it clears. "Ah. Your client died."

"But she was revived."

He considers the question, his forehead creasing, then he nods. "Maybe only one soul wanted to return. Think about it. If you had to subjugate every thought, feeling, and action to someone else, even someone as close as a twin, would you fly free if given the opportunity?"

Briley frowns. "But fly…where?"

The doctor smiles. "At this point, my dear, that's a question only faith can answer."

Briley returns to the waiting room outside the emergency unit and settles on a couch with vinyl cushions. In the chairs closer to the admissions desk, a mother frets over her crying infant, a man cleans a bloody cut on his face with a towel, and a middle-aged woman wearily holds an ice pack to her temple.

Briley takes off her coat, folds it into a bundle, and uses it for a pillow as she curls up on the couch. She ought to go home. She has to be in court tomorrow; she'll have to face Bystrowski and whatever challenge he and his associates have dreamed up. He'll be freshly polished in his suit and tie, while she might not even have the time—or the inclination—to take a shower.

What matters most is staying here for her client.

The cop keeping watch outside Erin's cubicle doesn't know her; he's merely earning his hourly pay as he barrels out his chest for the passing nurses. His gun belt is still shiny, and so burdened with gun, nightstick, and radio it's a wonder he can rise out of his chair without giving himself a hernia.

Briley closes her eyes to the guard and the waiting patients. She has things to consider.

Believing is…seeing.

She has a client who for months has proclaimed her innocence. Her client is a chimera. Her client may have had two souls.

If such a thing is possible, Briley doubts it exists in the annals of legal literature. The only situations that even come close are cases in which women have met with violence and lost their unborn babies. Illinois law considers the homicidal killing of an unborn child a criminal offense…at any stage of gestation.

Slowly her thoughts expand, joining a sliver of comprehension here, connecting with a realization there. An unborn child, an unborn twin. In a very real sense, isn't that what Lisa Marie was?

A sister of the soul. An unexpected reminder of eternity.

When the truth shines fully upon her heart, Briley realizes Timothy was right. She is her father's daughter. Though she has tried to bury her heritage beneath a mantle of detachment, her dad consistently taught her that life is about much more than the things we can see and touch. He knew that faith brought understanding. He lived to give. Now so can she.

And she will give whatever she must in order to get Erin acquitted.

The partners of Franklin, Watson, Smyth & Morton don't care about Erin, and their confidence in Briley is perfunctory, at best. They are counting on her to stick to her usual approach and remain aloof from her client. They expect a guilty verdict, and they want to please their most powerful client.

But Briley knows who killed Jeffrey Tomassi. After Erin succumbed to a drug-induced sleep, Lisa Marie took control and killed Jeffrey to protect her sister. She had protected Erin before, and if her life hadn't been cut short, she might have done it again.

At 5:00 a.m., a nurse jostles Briley's shoulder and says Erin is about to be released. The attendant police officer will escort her back to the jail to prepare for trial.

Briley pushes her bangs out of her eyes as a surge of adrenaline scatters the heavy fog of sleep. What day is it? Thursday. A court day, and she still has to prepare her closing argument and make sure her client has decent clothes for the courtroom.

She steps into the curtained cubicle, where a nurse is disconnecting the IV and the monitors from her patient. Erin dangles her legs off the gurney, then puts her feet on the floor and gently pushes the nurse's guiding hand away. "I'm fine." She glances at Briley. "I feel pretty good."

"Then why are you moving like an old woman?" Between the edges of the hospital gown, Briley glimpses a cloud of vicious bruising between her client's shoulder blades. She grimaces. "Are you sure you're up to this? I could ask the judge for a recess until you're better. I think he'd grant it, given the circumstances."

"I want to finish this," Erin says, her voice hoarse. She meets Briley's gaze. "I want to go home."

Briley nods in understanding. A thought occurred to her last night as she lay on that creaky sofa: any delay in the trial would give Bystrowski time to talk to Louis Thomsen at the crime lab. He's smart enough to ask the right questions, so he could discover that the unknown hair sample belonged not to Jeffrey's sibling, but to Erin's. The knowledge would confuse him, but if he learns the full truth they'll be back where they started, with the syringe in Erin's hand....

Briley catches Erin's wrist. "Before we go back to court, I want to hear what happened last night. Have you talked to the police?"

Erin's gaze darts toward the cop outside. "That detective came by a while ago. I told him everything."

"Malone? I missed him?"

"He said he saw you sleeping in the waiting room. I guess he wanted to let you rest."

Briley shakes her head, then looks at the nurse. "Could my client and I have a minute alone? Thanks."

When the nurse sidles out of the cubicle, Briley releases Erin's arm and sits on a stool. "You ready to tell me what happened?"

Erin shrugs. "One of the guards pulled me out of my cell, took me down to the laundry room, and left me with two guys who work for Antonio."

"How do you know that? Did you recognize them?"

"The guard mentioned it—and we talked." She turns her gaze on Briley, her blue eyes shining. "You'd have been proud of me. I tried everything I could. I didn't go down without a fight."

"Obviously." Briley looks at the bruises on Erin's arms. "Last night…do you remember me coming to see you?"

When Erin closes her eyes, Briley isn't sure if she's trying to remember or struggling to forget. "I think so."

"Do you remember what you told me?"

Her eyes fly open. "I told you Lisa Marie was gone."

"Were you… Did you realize what you were saying? What did you mean, exactly?"

Erin's gaze drifts toward the curtains. "I don't understand what happened, but you know that full feeling you get after a big meal? Suppose you've had it your entire life and then it disappears. You're glad because you don't feel stuffed anymore, but you're not so sure you want to feel empty." Her eyes catch and hold Briley's. "Lisa Marie isn't with me anymore. I don't know where she went, but I don't hear her, I don't feel her. I just feel…hollow."

Briley draws a deep breath. "I think I've found the explanation for Lisa Marie. I spoke to Dr. Phillips, the geneticist."

Erin stares, her hands trembling. "And?"

"Apparently the DNA of your blood sample didn't match the DNA of your saliva swab. The doctor said this happens when two embryos fuse together in the uterus. It's called chimerism. So your body is, in effect, a combination of two bodies. Yours and your twin sister's."

Erin remains silent, but her face seems to open as the words sink in. Briley sees bewilderment, a quick flicker of consternation, then the calm of resignation.

"I'm sorry if this is upsetting," Briley says. "The doctor says there's nothing to worry about."

"I'm glad you told me." A slow, secret smile trembles over Erin's lips, then she laughs. "I should have known. Now everything makes sense."

Briley stands to summon the nurse. "If you have any questions, I'm sure Dr. Phillips would be happy to talk to you."

Erin nods, then breaks eye contact, her gaze drifting toward the doorway. "Are you going to tell the jury about Lisa Marie?"

"Not at this trial. No one would understand, and the press would have a field day with the story." Briley turns. "For now, Lisa Marie is going to remain sheltered under attorney-client privilege."

"You know—" Erin blinks as a tear rolls down her cheek "—for the first time in my life, I feel completely alone."

"You're not alone. I'm here."

The blue eyes fill with wistfulness. "You volunteering to be my sister?"

Briley smiles. "I'll be something better...your lawyer and your friend."

Chapter Fifty-Eight

By nine-thirty, Briley and Erin are again seated behind the defense table. Erin is wearing a loose-fitting blouse and skirt Briley brought from home, and her eyes are considerably brighter than they were when the trial began.

Detective Malone has filled William's spot in the gallery. Briley told him about her suspicions regarding the librarian, so the cop sits between Kate and Timothy and occasionally glances over his shoulder to see if the law librarian has decided to sacrifice another vacation day and come to court.

Briley notices that the Tomassi family has begun to file in, but the patriarch has not yet appeared. Jason sits beside his father's usual seat, one arm draped protectively over the vacant spot.

Timothy has left Dax Lightner in the custody of his physical trainer, an amazon who wouldn't think of touching a narcotic substance. Timothy told Briley that Dax offered to come and offer moral support, but Timothy discouraged the idea. Like wolves scenting a fresh kill, reporters have crowded the gallery, their laptops and BlackBerrys ready. Even more are jammed into lobbies outside the courtroom, waiting to launch their cameras and microphones, like matadors aiming at a bull.

Briley glances at Bystrowski, who appears more subdued than usual. How much does he know about last night's assault?

"All rise." Briley straightens her spine as the deputy opens the court. "This honorable court is now in session, Judge Milton Trask presiding."

The judge takes his seat, shooting a look of concern toward Erin as the bailiff calls, "Be seated and come to order."

Before asking if the lawyers are ready to continue, the judge folds his hands and leans toward the microphone. "I understand," he says, his gaze focusing on Erin, "that the defendant suffered an assault last night. If you are unwell, Mrs. Tomassi, we could offer a recess until you are stronger."

"Your Honor." Briley stands. "We appreciate your kind consideration, but my client would like to continue. She is anxious to spare the court any further delay."

The judge nods. "Very well. Deputy, you may bring in the jury."

Briley shuffles her notes as the jury enters and files into the box, their shoes thumping in an uneven rataplan on the wooden floor. Word of the attack has not been leaked to the press, so even though members of the jury can't help but notice the fresh contusion on Erin's forehead, they have seen similar bruises before. Briley chose a long-sleeved blouse for her client, not wanting to be accused of trying to elicit sympathy by displaying the woman's battered condition.

If Erin is acquitted, let it be on the strength of sworn testimony.

As the last jury member settles in his chair, the judge looks at Briley. "Counsel for the defense, have you any more witnesses?"

Briley stands. "Your Honor, the defense rests."

The judge turns to the prosecutor. "Mr. Bystrowski, defense presented new evidence. Have you any rebuttal evidence?"

Bystrowski stands and looks at Briley, frustration flickering in his eyes. "No, Your Honor. But we'd like to call a rebuttal witness."

"Call your witness, then."

Bystrowski turns. "The state calls Jason Tomassi to the stand."

Briley gives Erin a small smile as her brother-in-law takes the witness stand. The man shifts uneasily in his chair, and his expression is far less confident today.

"Mr. Tomassi," Bystrowski says, "for the record, where were you on the evening of December 2?"

Jason clears his throat. "I attended my brother's fundraiser at the Conrad Chicago."

"What family members were with you?"

"My brother, Jeffrey, his wife, my father, and my four sisters. Some cousins, too."

"What time did the event end?"

"About ten-thirty."

"What did you do after the event?"

Jason's gaze lowers. "I, um, went to my girlfriend's apartment."

"Did you swing by your brother's home first?"

"Why would I? I'd been with him all night."

"Did any of your sisters announce their plans for after the event?"

"They took the limo to my father's house. They'd been drinking, so they didn't want to drive."

"Objection." Briley stands. "This is hearsay, Your Honor. The witness cannot know if his sisters did, in fact, go to Mr. Tomassi's home."

"Sustained."

Bystrowski looks at Briley, frustration on his face. His eyes send an unspoken message: *You want me to put all four women on the stand? I could.*

She gives him a small smile and sits down.

Bystrowski turns back to his witness. "Do you know if your sisters made it to your father's home?"

"Yes."

"How do you know?"

"I called Papa around midnight. I heard the girls laughing in the background."

"All of them?"

Jason's mouth dips in a wry grin. "Trust me. I know their laughter. All four of them were there."

"Did any of them tell you they had been to Jeffrey's house?"

"No."

"Thank you, Mr. Tomassi. The state has no more questions for this witness."

Judge Trask looks at Briley. "Any cross?"

She looks at Jason, considering the matter, then decides to remain silent. She has nothing to gain by quizzing him, and a great deal to lose by wearying the jurors. "No, Your Honor."

"Then we'll move on to closing arguments."

Briley flips to the final section of her trial notebook while the judge explains the next phase to the jury. As he stresses that they are to consider the attorneys' closing a summation, not evidence, she reviews her main points and hopes the jury is as intelligent and intuitive as she needs them to be.

Finally, the judge nods to the prosecutor. "Mr. Bystrowski."

Bystrowski steps to the lectern and unbuttons his suit coat. "Ladies and gentlemen of the jury." His voice is firm and strong, his Boy Scout face set in lines of earnestness. "We have presented a case in which the facts are simple. Erin Tomassi married an important, wealthy, and influential man. Unfortunately, this marriage suffered from domestic discord. But instead of filing for divorce, seeking a restraining order, or suggesting that they seek out marital counseling, the defendant consciously chose a course of extreme action. One night, as her husband lay sleeping in his own bed, she unwrapped a syringe, filled it with insulin, and injected her husband with a deadly dose. The massive overdose killed him before he could awaken to plead for mercy. The next morning, the defendant waited until she knew he was dead. Then she called 911 and played the role of grieving widow while paramedics attempted to resuscitate her husband. The resuscitation efforts failed, of course, because she waited far too long to call for help. Rigor mortis had already set in— because Jeffrey Tomassi had been dead at least six hours.

"Let's examine the evidence that leads us to believe these things." Bystrowski begins counting on his fingers. "You've seen and heard proof—the defendant's fingerprints on the murder weapon, videotaped evidence demonstrating no one else entered the house, sworn statements from the brother who did not visit that night, and the testimony of an experienced police detective. To paraphrase something my grandfather used to say, if it walks like a duck and quacks like a duck, you can bet that bird is a duck. The evidence proves Erin Tomassi killed her husband."

He paces before the jury box, nodding at individuals as he moves. "The defense says the defendant could not have committed the crime because she took a double dose of Ambien before going to sleep. But did they prove that claim? No. They offered no blood tests, no toxicology report, nothing but the word of an accused killer. The defense has also suggested that the defendant might have killed the victim while she was sleepwalking, but has the woman ever been treated for sleep disorders? No. Have the neighbors ever reported her walking outside in her nightgown? No.

"Finally, the defense brought in new evidence to prove a third party was present at the crime scene, even going so far as to cast aspersions on the grief-stricken Tomassi siblings. This—" he drives his clenched fist into his palm "—is a sign of desperation, ladies and gentlemen. Do not let yourselves be influenced by the eleventh-hour ploy of a defense attorney who cannot explain how Erin Tomassi's fingerprints were found on the murder weapon without incriminating her client."

Taking a deep, unsteady breath, Bystrowski steps away and locks his hands behind his back. "In a few moments the judge will instruct you about how you must deliberate and vote to conclude this trial. He will explain the law you must follow. What he will *not* tell you to do is leave your intelligence and common sense outside the deliberation room. Look at the evidence, and you'll see that the state has proven its case. Thank you."

As the prosecutor returns to his desk, Briley waits until the members of the jury are looking at her, then she stands. A quick glance over her shoulder reveals that Antonio Tomassi has slipped into the courtroom. She marvels at his chutzpah. Apparently the man is willing to risk arrest in order to see his daughter-in-law destroyed.

"Ladies and gentlemen—" Briley steps out from behind the defense table "—a moment ago, I nearly stood up to object during the prosecutor's closing argument. Perhaps I should have. I kept silent, however, because I wanted to see what Mr. Bystrowski said you had to believe in order to vote for a guilty verdict.

"The prosecutor said we offered no explanation for Erin Tomassi's fingerprints being on the weapon, but we have offered a perfectly logical explanation—whoever murdered Jeffrey Tomassi, a well-known political figure, could have easily manipulated Erin's hand and placed her prints on that syringe. An intruder acting in a hurry would not have taken the time to ascertain whether she was right- or left-handed. He or she would have simply reached for the closest arm…which would have been Erin's left. Jeffrey and Erin were not alone in the house that night…an assertion proven by DNA evidence.

"When I first took the case, I thought my work would be neat and tidy. I'd examine the evidence, I'd plan a defense, I'd do my best to give my client a fair trial. And if I lost—" she lifts her shoulders in a faint shrug "—well, in this business, you win some, you lose some. Whatever happened, I wouldn't lose sleep over it. After all, I'm a professional lawyer. I'm a defense attorney, not a miracle worker."

She strolls in front of the jury box, lightly trailing the fingers of one hand over the railing. "When I read the police reports, I began to understand why my firm assigned me to the case." She laughs. "After all, I'm only an associate at Franklin, Watson, Smyth & Morton. The lawyers who are higher up the ladder like to protect their reputations, and this case had 'loser' written all over it. No evidence of an intruder, and videotape to prove it. No one in the house but the husband and his wife. This case didn't even have a dangerous weapon, just a plastic syringe with a couple of fingerprints on it.

"The case appeared so simple, so obvious, that the crime lab guys didn't bother to test every hair found at the murder scene. They checked the doors at the house, but not the windows. They looked around the premises, but not carefully. Why bother? After all, who but the wife could have committed the crime?" She pauses, allowing her gaze to brush each man and woman in the jury box. "In the beginning, I was as ready to pin this crime on Erin Tomassi as you are. But as I began to talk to people who know her, I learned that Erin was terrified of her husband. She was intimidated by her father-in-law. This quiet woman, raised by an alcoholic mother, would rather take a beating than be disloyal to Jeffrey Tomassi."

Briley stops pacing to inhale a deep breath. "Why would she kill the man with whom she was planning to start a family? She didn't need money—Jeffrey bought her everything she needed to look like the perfect trophy wife. Frankly, she had no reason to kill her husband. She had plenty of reasons to get him to a marriage counselor, but she had no reason to murder the man she married."

She shifts her attention to the men sitting at the prosecution table. "Once the evidence revealed that Erin did not—could not—have killed Jeffrey, I began to focus on the police report. I called the crime lab and learned that they had *not* done DNA analysis on every specimen taken from the crime scene. At my request, they tested other hairs found on the bed, and we discovered that four of those hairs came from a third party. All the hairs found on Jeffrey Tomassi's deathbed belonged to either Jeffrey, Erin, or our mysterious intruder.

"You heard the lab technician—an employee of Illinois police state—declare that DNA isn't used for identification, but for differentiation. Someone else was in the room on that December night, and someone else injected Jeffrey Tomassi with insulin. Erin didn't wake, because she was deep in a drug-induced sleep. Once the fatal dose was administered, the third party retreated through an unlocked window, avoiding the security cameras and leaving Erin to take the blame. Who was the third party? I don't know, and it's not my job to lob accusations at law-abiding citizens. My job is to defend Erin Tomassi."

Her gaze sweeps over the jury, lingering on each face. "Your job, ladies and gentlemen, is to decide if Erin murdered her husband. The judge will explain your options, and he will stress this principle of law—unless the prosecution has proven *beyond all reasonable doubt* that Erin intentionally and maliciously killed her husband, you cannot find her guilty."

Briley rests her hands on the jury box railing. "Thank you for your time and attention. I have every confidence you will weigh the evidence and come to the right decision."

After Judge Trask instructs the jurors and sends them out to begin deliberations, he adjourns the court. Briley begins to pack her briefcase, but looks up when Bystrowski approaches the defense table. "I heard about what happened to your client," he says, his eyes roving over Erin's long sleeves and bruised face. "I want you to know we're pushing for a full investigation."

"I would expect no less." She slides her trial notebook into her briefcase and stands as the bailiff approaches to escort Erin to a holding cell.

Briley gently pats her client's arm. "I'll see you soon. And don't worry—I believe everything's going to work out as it should."

Erin dips her head in a grateful nod, then follows the bailiff out of the courtroom. Bystrowski watches her go. "She seems like a nice lady."

"She is."

"I'm surprised you didn't hire violins to play during your closing statement. You were pulling on every heartstring."

Briley widens her eyes in exaggerated innocence. "I only told the absolute truth. Besides—" she grins "—I'm sure you've heard worse. You should have objected if you thought I went over the line."

He snorts. "If I'd objected after you said you held your tongue, the jury would think I had bad manners."

"Can't blame them."

"Aw, come on." Grinning, he shakes his head and slides his hands into his pockets. "You have to admit you came *this close* to expressing your personal belief in your client's innocence. You know that's against the rules."

"I seem to recall saying I *didn't* believe Erin's story. I didn't say I changed my mind."

"Well, no matter what happens, it's been a pleasure. You kept me on my toes."

"That's quite a compliment." She snaps her briefcase shut. "See you when the jury comes in, Counselor. Then we'll learn if this group is smart enough to recognize the truth when they hear it."

Chapter Fifty-Nine

Kate swallows the last of her biscotti and makes a face. "So you're saying the chimera did it."

"Would make an unusual defense, wouldn't it?" Briley wraps both hands around her tall latte, grateful for its warmth. "I knew I couldn't give the jurors the entire truth. Some of them looked skeptical when I presented the Ambien defense, and *that* one has legal precedent in its favor. If they weren't going to buy the idea of a parasomnia, they'd never go for the real story. So I figured I'd let the DNA speak for itself."

Timothy shakes his head. "What will you lawyers do when the courts realize that DNA can be unreliable? They're releasing prisoners every year on the basis of old genetic evidence. What if some of those prisoners are actually guilty...and dangerous?"

"That'd be a long shot," Briley says, "because how many of those people are chimeras? We'll never know unless people are routinely tested with swabs or tissue samples from different areas of their bodies. If you're a chimera, your heart cells could have one type of DNA while your saliva swab reveals something else entirely. But nobody goes around comparing saliva swabs to heart cells."

"Or hair follicles," Kate adds.

Timothy crosses his arms. "So a rapist could have one DNA profile in his semen..."

"And another in his saliva," Briley finishes. "Yeah, I know. But chimeras can't be common. So though no system is foolproof, DNA is still the most reliable tool we have. I'm betting my case on the hope that those jurors believe DNA doesn't lie."

"I know one thing." Timothy takes her hand and gives it a squeeze. "I was amazingly proud of you this morning. You had passion, conviction—and I know the jury felt your belief in your client."

Briley rolls her eyes. "Bystrowski fussed at me about that. It's considered unethical for an attorney to state her personal belief in a case. I *did* cut that one pretty close."

"You came close to a lot of things," Kate says, grinning. "Franklin would have been white-knuckled if he'd been in the gallery."

"Which reminds me…" Briley looks out the window. "I haven't seen William since yesterday. Have you heard from him?"

"Maybe he's still on vacation." Kate lifts her cup. "He's probably lying low until your trial ends. Then he'll come back to work with a tan and tell us he's been basking on a Bahamas beach."

When her cell phone begins to play, Briley dives for her purse. She glances at the caller ID and turns to Timothy. "The jury's in."

He tightens his scarf around his neck. "That was fast."

"Too fast." Briley grabs her latte and slides off her stool. "My boss says quick verdicts favor the prosecution."

Chapter Sixty

With Briley and Bystrowski waiting at their respective tables, Judge Trask asks the bailiff to bring the jury in. The whispering murmur at the back of the gallery is silenced when a door opens and twelve responsible citizens enter the courtroom, each of them studiously avoiding Briley's gaze.

A frisson of anticipation travels up her spine. Their refusal to make eye contact may not be a good sign. If they'd voted to acquit, at least one juror ought to look her way and offer a smile. So either this is a rather businesslike bunch, or...

She refuses to consider the thought of defeat.

Judge Trask straightens in his chair. "Has the jury reached a verdict?"

"We have, Your Honor." The tall woman they have elected as a foreman stands and gives a note to the bailiff, who hands it to the judge. He glances at it and returns it to the bailiff, who returns it to the foreman.

Briley glances at Erin, who is sitting stiffly erect, her head lowered.

The judge folds his hands and looks at the foreman. "In the matter of the state versus Erin Wilson Tomassi, how do you find?"

"In the matter of the state versus Erin Wilson Tomassi," the woman reads, her trembling hands rattling the preprinted form, "we find the defendant not guilty on all counts."

Briley releases her breath in an explosive gasp as several spectators burst into noisy speculation. Beside her, Erin clasps Briley's wrist in a clawlike grip. "Does that mean...?"

The judge pounds his gavel and glares at those who would dare disrupt the proceeding. When they have quieted, he turns to the jury. "Thank you for your service, ladies and gentlemen. You are now free to talk to anyone about the case, and you are dismissed." He shifts his attention to the defense table. "Mrs. Tomassi, you have been declared not guilty, so you are free to go."

Briley looks across the aisle, where Bystrowski has stood to pack his briefcase. His smooth countenance is as unreadable as stone.

Behind the prosecutor, however, Antonio Tomassi's face has flushed to the color of a ripe tomato. He and his children have huddled together, but two men in dark suits are threading their way through the mob, gold shields dangling from their breast pockets. One of them is Detective Mark Malone.

"Antonio and Jason Tomassi?" he calls, his voice ringing above the hubbub. He reaches for the older man's arm. "We'd like you to come with us."

"Not now." Antonio Tomassi bats away the detective's hand. "I don't know what this foolishness is about, but we are grieving—"

"You're under investigation." Detective Malone calmly pulls a pair of handcuffs from his pocket and dangles them before Tomassi's eyes. "You can come talk with us peaceably, or I'll walk up to the judge over there and ask him to sign this warrant for your arrest."

"Hey, Counselor." Bystrowski stops by the defense table, distracting Briley from the scene on the other side of the courtroom. "Tomassi keeps your firm on retainer, doesn't he?"

She nods, not certain where he's headed.

The state's attorney gives her a wink and a grin. "If in a few weeks you find yourself about to defend him, maybe you should stop by our office. We're always looking for committed attorneys."

Briley is too stunned to do more than nod, but as she watches Bystrowski shoulder his way through the crowd, she realizes that she has come to a crossroads. The lawyers at Franklin, Watson, Smyth & Morton see her as dispassionate and aloof. Maybe that description fit a few months ago, but not now. And never again.

She turns to Erin and gives her a hug.

"I don't know how to thank you," Erin breathes in her ear. "You literally saved my life."

"I think—" Briley chokes on the lump in her throat. "I think you might have saved my career." She releases her client and steps back to open the swinging gate between the gallery and the front of the courtroom. Timothy waits there, and he wraps an arm around each woman's shoulder as the media mob surges toward them.

"Mrs. Tomassi!" one reporter shouts. "What is your answer to those who still believe you killed your husband?"

From the corner of her eye, Briley sees Erin shrink back. Then the woman lifts her chin and meets the reporter's accusing eyes. "I can't help what people believe," she says, her voice threaded with new steel. "But though I was a victim in that marriage, I didn't kill my husband. Clearly, someone else did."

As the listening reporters scribble on their notepads, Briley, Timothy, and Erin stride out of the courtroom.

Chapter Sixty-One

"Miss Lester."

Travis Bystrowski stands when Briley sticks her head into his small office. The cluttered space is nondescript, at best, and a great deal smaller than her old office at Franklin, Watson, Smyth & Morton. Furthermore, the air smells stale.

But that's probably due to the greasy bag of leftover something-or-other on the corner of the lawyer's desk. She lifts her gaze. "It's Briley Shackelford now." She twiddles her left hand in front of the prosecutor's face. "Been married all of two weeks."

"Congratulations, then. You want to sit, or is this a drive-by greeting?"

"I've got a few minutes." Briley drops into an empty guest chair, then looks out the window behind Bystrowski's desk. The horizon is clear and blue, a sky radiant with the promise of spring. "Nice view."

"Thanks...but something tells me you didn't come up here to check out my office."

'I came to ask about the Tomassis. What charges are they facing?"

Bystrowski swivels his chair. "We've got dear Papa T on solicitation of murder, solicitation of murder for hire, attempted murder, and aggravated battery, for starters. We've got Jason on all of the above, plus solicitation to commit battery...on you." He lifts his head like a dog scenting the breeze. "Wait—your firm isn't defending them, is it?"

She laughs. "Not hardly. I came here to drop my résumé in your boss's office. I'm done with private practice."

"Really?" The prosecutor leans back in his chair, that Boy Scout grin overtaking his face. "Hey, maybe you'll get to prosecute them. But just so you know, I was hoping to take a crack at Papa T myself."

"You can have them. If the state of Illinois will have me, I was going to ask about the DeLyles case."

His smile vanishes, wiped away by earnestness. "The drug dealer who killed the single mom and then tried to sell her kids? I don't know, Briley, that's going to be a heavy case."

"Doesn't matter. I don't want that monster hurting anyone else. If I get the job, assign me to the case. I'm up for it."

Bystrowski stares at her for a moment, then he squints in amusement. "I suppose you are. I'll put in a good word."

"Thanks." She picks up her briefcase and stands, then steps toward the door. "By the way—you might want to add another charge to the Tomassi indictment."

"What charge?"

"Involuntary manslaughter. My client survived the attack at the jail, but someone else didn't."

For a moment, Bystrowski looks confused, then his face falls. "Bummer. Was she pregnant?"

"Not quite." Briley idly runs her hand over the door frame, then raps on the wood. "On second thought, maybe you shouldn't add the charge, but I'll bet you'd be interested in the story. Sometime when you have an hour free for lunch, let me know and I'll share."

She's two steps through the doorway when Bystrowski's voice halts her in midstride. "Hey, Briley—the grass isn't greener on this side of the fence, you know. Sometimes things are downright messy over here."

She looks over her shoulder and gives him a confident smile. "I'm counting on it."

* * * * *

QUESTIONS FOR DISCUSSION

1. As you will discover if you search the Internet for information on chimeras, the central concept of this novel is quite real. Did this situation seem far-fetched as you read the story? What do you think about the human soul and where it resides?

2. Erin is an abused wife. If you were on the jury, would the history of her marriage make you more or less likely to believe she killed her husband? Would you see the abuse as a reason...or a defense?

3. Angela Hunt reports that she gained a new appreciation for lawyers while working on this book. Despite the popularity of television legal dramas, the art of examining a witness is complicated. Did your appreciation for lawyers change after reading this novel?

4. Briley is a good lawyer, but at the beginning of the story she wants to maintain a careful emotional distance from her client. What happens to convince her to begin to bridge that gap? How is she different at the end of the story?

5. Erin also changes over the course of the book. If she remarries, what sort of man do you think she will choose?

6. Why do you think Briley is attracted to Timothy Shackelford?

7. Do you think Briley will be more or less happy working in the prosecutor's office?

8. What were some of the themes in the novel? Are these themes relevant to your life? A year from now, will this story still resonate with you? Why or why not?

9. Would you say this novel is plot-driven (the plot moving the characters forward) or character-driven (the characters driving the plot)? What were the turning points for each of the major characters, and what might have happened if they had chosen the opposite path?

10. With which character—Briley or Erin—do you most identify, and why? How did their histories make them into the women they are? How will their lives influence each other's in the future?

11. Could this story have worked in another setting? Why do you think the author chose to set the novel in Chicago?

12. Have you read other novels by Angela Hunt? How does this novel echo themes in her other works? How does it differ?

References

No novelist writes alone, and I'd like to acknowledge the valuable assistance provided by the following people: police detective Mark Mynheir; attorneys Randy Singer, Jacob Radcliff, Ron Benrey, Cara Putman, James Scott Bell, Rick Acker, Jim Stamos, and Michael Garnier; forensic psychologist Dr. V. Gregory; the Cook County Sheriff's Department; and Traci Depree, Amy Wallace, Gaynel Senka, and Annette Smith. If it looks like I practically tackled every lawyer who crossed my path while I was working on this novel, it's true. An extra-special thank-you to Michael Garnier, who suffered through a rough draft and spent several hours pointing my lawyers toward solid legal ground. If Briley, Bystrowski, or Judge Trask have done anything that's not by the book, you may blame their irascible natures or my penchant for drama.

The following books were also helpful:

Black, Roy. *Black's Law: A Criminal Lawyer Reveals His Defense Strategies in Four Cliffhanger Cases.* New York, NY: Simon & Schuster, 1999.

Davis, Kevin. *Defending the Damned: Inside Chicago's Cook County Public Defender's Office.* New York, NY: Atria Books, 2007.

Geberth, Vernon J. *Practical Homicide Investigation: Tactics, Procedures, and Forensic Techniques.* Fourth Edition. New York, NY: Taylor & Francis, 2006.

Grace, Nancy, with Diane Clehane. *Objection! How High-Priced Defense Attorneys, Celebrity Defendants, and a*

24/7 Media Have Hijacked Our Criminal Justice System.
New York, NY: Hyperion, 2005.

Haddock, Deborah Bray. *Dissociative Identity Disorder
Sourcebook.* New York, NY: McGraw Hill, 2001.

Low, Peter W. *Criminal Law.* St. Paul, MN: West Publish-
ing Company, 1984.

McElhaney, James W. *McElhaney's Trial Notebook.* Third
Edition. Chicago, IL: American Bar Association, 1994.

Mullally, David S. *Order in the Court: A Writer's Guide to
the Legal System.* Cincinnati, OH: Writer's Digest
Books, 2000.

Stevens, Serita Deborah, with Anne Klarner. *Deadly Doses:
A Writer's Guide to Poisons.* Cincinnati, OH: Writer's
Digest Books, 1990.

Wilson, James Q. *Moral Judgment: Does the Abuse Excuse
Threaten Our Legal System.* New York, NY: HarperCol-
lins, 1997.

JOSEPH TELLER

A speeding sports car forces an oncoming van off the road and kills all nine of its occupants...eight of them children.

Criminal defense attorney Harrison J. Walker, or Jaywalker, is serving a three-year suspension and having trouble keeping his nose clean when a woman seduces him into representing the killer, who happens to be her husband.

Struggling with the moral issues surrounding this case, Jaywalker tries to limit the damage to his client by exposing the legal system's hypocrisy regarding drunk driving. But when he rounds a blind corner in the case, he finds a truth that could derail his defense.

DEPRAVED
INDIFFERENCE

MIRA®

Available now wherever books are sold.

www.MIRABooks.com

MJT2691

REQUEST YOUR
FREE BOOKS!

2 FREE NOVELS
FROM THE ROMANCE/SUSPENSE
COLLECTION PLUS 2 FREE GIFTS!

YES! Please send me 2 FREE novels from the Romance/Suspense Collection and my 2 FREE gifts (gifts are worth about $10). After receiving them, if I don't wish to receive any more books, I can return the shipping statement marked "cancel." If I don't cancel, I will receive 4 brand-new novels every month and be billed just $5.74 per book in the U.S. or $6.24 per book in Canada. That's a savings of at least 28% off the cover price. It's quite a bargain! Shipping and handling is just 50¢ per book.* I understand that accepting the 2 free books and gifts places me under no obligation to buy anything. I can always return a shipment and cancel at any time. Even if I never buy another book from the Reader Service, the two free books and gifts are mine to keep forever.

185 MDN EYNQ   385 MDN EYN2

Name	(PLEASE PRINT)	
Address		Apt. #
City	State/Prov.	Zip/Postal Code

Signature (if under 18, a parent or guardian must sign)

Mail to **The Reader Service:**
IN U.S.A.: P.O. Box 1867, Buffalo, NY 14240-1867
IN CANADA: P.O. Box 609, Fort Erie, Ontario L2A 5X3

Not valid to current subscribers of the Romance Collection,
the Suspense Collection or the Romance/Suspense Collection.

Want to try two free books from another line?
Call 1-800-873-8635 or visit www.morefreebooks.com.

* Terms and prices subject to change without notice. Prices do not include applicable taxes. Sales tax applicable in N.Y. Canadian residents will be charged applicable provincial taxes and GST. Offer not valid in Quebec. This offer is limited to one order per household. All orders subject to approval. Credit or debit balances in a customer's account(s) may be offset by any other outstanding balance owed by or to the customer. Please allow 4 to 6 weeks for delivery. Offer available while quantities last.

Your Privacy: Harlequin is committed to protecting your privacy. Our Privacy Policy is available online at www.eHarlequin.com or upon request from the Reader Service. From time to time we make our lists of customers available to reputable third parties who may have a product or service of interest to you. If you would prefer we not share your name and address, please check here. ☐

BOB09

ANGELA HUNT

32726 THE ELEVATOR   ___ $6.99 U.S. ___ $6.99 CAN.

(limited quantities available)

TOTAL AMOUNT $ _____
POSTAGE & HANDLING $ _____
($1.00 for 1 book, 50¢ for each additional)
APPLICABLE TAXES* $ _____
TOTAL PAYABLE $ _____

(check or money order—please do not send cash)

To order, complete this form and send it, along with a check or money order for the total above, payable to MIRA Books, to: **In the U.S.:** 3010 Walden Avenue, P.O. Box 9077, Buffalo, NY 14269-9077; **In Canada:** P.O. Box 636, Fort Erie, Ontario, L2A 5X3.

Name: _____
Address: _____ City: _____
State/Prov.: _____ Zip/Postal Code: _____
Account Number (if applicable): _____

075 CSAS

*New York residents remit applicable sales taxes.
*Canadian residents remit applicable GST and provincial taxes.

MIRA®

www.MIRABooks.com

MAH1209BL